# THE PARIS PEACEMAKERS

*By Flora Johnston*

The Paris Peacemakers
The Endeavour of Elsie Mackay

# THE PARIS PEACEMAKERS

## Flora Johnston

Allison & Busby Limited
11 Wardour Mews
London W1F 8AN
allisonandbusby.com

First published in Great Britain by Allison & Busby in 2024.
This paperback edition published by Allison & Busby in 2024.

10 9 8 7 6 5 4 3 2 1

ISBN 978-0-7490-3132-9

Typeset in 11/16 pt Adobe Garamond Pro by Allison & Busby Ltd.

By choosing this product, you help take care of the world's forests.
Learn more: www.fsc.org.

FSC
www.fsc.org
MIX
Paper | Supporting
responsible forestry
FSC® C171272

Printed and bound by
CPI Group (UK) Ltd, Croydon, CR0 4YY

*For Elizabeth and Alastair, with love.*

*There is probably no finer school for the development of courage and endurance than the Rugby football field; and consequently no finer set of men to be obtained elsewhere, in the present emergency, by the Army. It is certain that there will be a splendid answer from the players to the call of the country.*

The Scotsman, 5th August 1914

*Here we are at last in Paris and I can hardly realise it. We've landed in a place like the Ritz.*

Mildred Keith, typist at the Paris Peace Conference, 15th December 1918

*There has come upon us a great disillusionment. We thought that the great Peace Conference was travailing to the birth of Peace, and it has brough forth an abortive pandemonium. Millions who gave up their all in a frenzy of self-sacrifice during the war are asking themselves bitterly what they gave it for. What's the good? And who's to gain?*

Food for the Fed-Up, G. A. Studdert Kennedy, 1921

# Characters

* *The Rutherford family*
CORRAN, lecturer
ALEX, naval officer
JACK, student
STELLA, typist
ALISON, their mother

* ROB CAMPBELL, surgeon

ALEXANDER 'GUS' ANGUS, Scottish rugby player
MISS BINGHAM, superintendent of female staff on the British
    Empire Delegation
STANLEY BLUNT, English chaplain in Paris
SIR HENRY BROOKE, the chief, educationalist
* ARTHUR CALLAGHAN, lecturer
CONSTANCE HOSTER, owner of typing school
JOHN MACCALLUM, Scottish rugby player
DAVID LLOYD GEORGE, Prime Minister
ROLAND GORDON, Scottish rugby player
* ANNE-MARIE HARRISON, typist

\* Lady Mabel Lees, typist

\* Grace MacCallum, nurse

\* Archie Macdonald, patient

Sir William Macewen, surgeon

\* Hugh Mortimer, civil servant

\* Freddie Shepherd, member of the South African delegation

\* Lily Sheridan, typist

Frances Stevenson, private secretary to David Lloyd George

Philippe Struxiano, French rugby player

G. A. Studdert Kennedy, chaplain and poet

Charlie Usher, Scottish rugby player

Jock Wemyss, Scottish rugby player

Madame de Witt-Schlumberger, French suffragette

Poppy Wyndham, previously known as Elsie Mackay,
    actress and aviatrix

Dennis Wyndham, actor

# BEFORE

## *The Last Rugby Match*

The only tiny mercy is that none of them knew.

# 21st March 1914

Inverleith, Edinburgh

Corran pulled her scarf tightly around herself against the wind. The day had looked promising through her guesthouse windows earlier: how could she have forgotten the penetrating chill of a bright Edinburgh spring day? Now, as she hunched against the north wind that swept this bleak rugby field, she thought wistfully of the blossom-laden tree outside her college window in Cambridge.

*What on earth am I doing here?*

She looked to her left, where her youngest brother, Jack, sat beside her on the wooden bench. As usual he was sketching the scene before him.

'I don't know how you can even hold the pencil.'

He grinned at her, his eyes dancing below his untidy fringe. 'You've gone soft in the south,' he said. 'This is nothing to home.'

That was true. Home was Thurso, the harbour town perched on the exposed northern edge of mainland Scotland, where the skies were vast and the elements unforgiving. Yet that was a different sort of cold altogether from this grainy wind that picked up the dust of the setts and funnelled between the sooty Edinburgh chimneys. She had grown up with a fresh, cleansing cold, straight from the ever-moving sea. She could almost taste the salt in the air as she thought of that austere grey house where their sister, Stella, was chafing her way through her final months of school with only their mother, Alison, for company.

When the summer days stretched out at both ends, they would return, maybe even Alex too, and the house would come alive with laughter and warmth once more.

She turned her attention to the scene that Jack was sketching. Young pipers from Dr Guthrie's school entertained eager spectators who had squeezed into every space around the Inverleith playing field. The pipers came to a halt right in front of her. A pause, and a new tune: 'John Peel'. A roar rose around her from the enormous crowd, and men in white jerseys sprinted onto the pitch. They formed a line and jumped up and down, stretching and bending their legs. The tune changed again, 'Scotland the Brave' this time, and it was the turn of the men in navy blue. Corran leant forward to see between the heads in front of her, mouth suddenly dry. At first she couldn't spot him: they all looked remarkably similar, these men, tall and strong with their short haircuts. But then they formed a semi-circle and there he was. Rob.

Rugby football was his passion but she had never before seen him dressed in the navy shirt with its white thistle proudly sewn on by his own hand two years ago. *If I can stitch a wound, I can surely stitch a thistle*, he had written to her.

Rob the surgeon she knew a little; Rob the student she had known well. But Rob the Scotland rugby player? She wasn't sure who he was at all, but this weekend she might find out. She watched him take up his position with his teammates, waiting for the whistle to blow. He had told her once that these men were his greatest friends, the brothers he had never known in a sparse and solitary Edinburgh childhood.

An English player punted the leather ball down the field, beginning the game. For Corran, with little interest in sport and a head full of drifting fragments of ancient poetry, the shocking physical onslaught brought thoughts of Achaeans and Trojans, of men setting their faces to battle.

'They say this might be the biggest crowd ever at a Scotland rugger match,' said Jack, as he turned to a fresh page and began a rapid sketch of the match in progress. 'Must be twenty or twenty-five thousand here. It's quite something really, considering how poorly the Scots have been playing and the slating they've had in the papers. There are more English supporters here than I expected too.'

'I think they were all on my train north,' Corran said dryly, remembering her cramped journey up from Cambridge the day before, hemmed in by noisy English fans.

'It was grand of Rob to invite us.'

Corran couldn't quite share her little brother's enthusiasm. She had never watched a whole rugby match before, but when she had written to tell Rob she was coming north for a job interview, he had offered to set aside tickets to the Calcutta Cup match. She had agreed a little uncertainly, knowing Jack would love to come. It was good to see her little brother here in the city, where he seemed to be finding his feet at university and even growing into a man. The need to travel south from Thurso to pursue their futures had created its own independence in each of the Rutherford family.

'Oh, go on, go on!' Jack was on his feet, as was much of the crowd. But then an enormous groan resonated through the stand, and the energy slid into disappointment.

'What's happening?'

'George Will was nearly over there, but he had a foot in touch. And Pender knocked it on just before. They're doing so *well* but they have to take their chances. England won't give them this amount of field position for long.'

Corran didn't really understand a word he said, but she could see Rob running back up the pitch. Jack had told her that Rob was a forward and his main role seemed to involve crouching down in the muddy ground and pushing with Herculean effort alongside his teammates while the English tried to push in the other direction. Gaining territory inch by inch. She found she was watching Rob rather than watching the action, and so she was startled when Jack leapt to his feet once more, this time shouting and waving his sketchpad in delight.

'Did we score?'

'Didn't you see? It was Will again, an absolute peach of a pass from Turner. Now Turner will kick for points. What a player he is, I tell you, he's going to be around for many years to come.' He let out a long sigh. 'Ach, he's missed it. Never mind, this is good, this is so much better than I expected. England don't know what's hit them!'

There was certainly a lot of hitting going on. Not fighting exactly, but as man after man was slammed into the ground, Corran wondered how this could be anyone's idea of pleasure. Meanwhile the pitch, already soggy after yesterday's rain, was rapidly losing any semblance of green, and it was becoming harder to tell Scotsman from Englishman, so covered in mud were they all. Rob was one of the worst. Where now was the smart young man who had come down to visit her a few times in Cambridge?

It was easy for her mind to drift away from the match and settle on Rob's last visit. They had shared an unsatisfactory lunch in a stuffy hotel, hampered as always by the strict Cambridge University rules, which prevented Corran as a female student from even walking between classes with a man, never mind entertaining him in the college. Everything had been much more relaxed when they both lived here in Edinburgh, Rob studying medicine and Corran studying classics. But after graduating top of her class, she had won a scholarship to Cambridge to continue her studies. Her three years there were nearly complete, and she really wasn't sure how she felt about that at all.

There would be no repeat of her Edinburgh graduation, no matter how well she performed: women were not awarded qualifications at Cambridge, and were not allowed to graduate. The unfairness disturbed her, but right now the question of what she was going to do next disturbed her more. Dusty volumes containing the stories of mythical heroes, the beauty and logic and resonance of ancient languages – these had been her world for almost as long as she could remember. At the age of twelve she had told her headmaster she wanted to learn Latin and Greek. *Of course not. You are a girl, my dear, and the female brain was not designed for the classics.* Encouraged by her parents, she proved them all wrong and loved every minute of it, but now long years of studying were coming to an end. What lay ahead for a woman who had been educated in a subject that her mother's friends were quick to point out was of no use to man nor beast? The only possible answer was teaching, and so she found herself in Edinburgh, preparing to be interviewed for a lecturer's post that she wasn't sure she wanted, and wondering if this man sliding through the mud might offer a simpler future.

The battle had paused.

'Half time,' said Jack. The players huddled together in two groups, some bent double to catch their breath. 'It's a shame England scored that one before the break. We've had the best of the play, but we had the wind behind us. It will be hard going in the second half.'

An older man on Jack's other side leant in towards them. 'Aye, lad, we're missing Wattie Suddie,' he said. 'Huggan's no bad for a first cap, but these muckle English bastards widnae match Suddie's speed.'

'Why is he not playing?' Corran asked, laughing at her little brother's consternation.

'Injured, hen. Hurt his ankle agin Wales. Typical Scots luck, to lose oor best wing three quarter. I'm a Hawick man, ye ken. Watched the laddie grow up. Watched him win every sprint championship. The sooner he's back wi his brothers in airms, the better.'

'Here we go,' Jack said as the men jogged back to their positions. 'Come on, Scotland. Can we pull off another shock like two years ago?'

'What happened two years ago?'

'The English came up sure they would win easily, but our captain, John MacCallum, led from the front. It was a famous victory. That was your Rob's first cap, wasn't it? MacCallum was magnificent. He's not playing any more, but with the likes of Turner coming through we have every chance. Let's go!'

*Your Rob?*

She shrugged it aside and they turned back to the action. To Corran, the match seemed interminable. To Jack it was clearly a delight. He was in danger of crushing his sketch between his fingers with excitement, so handed the sketchpad to Corran for safekeeping. As England took control, a sense of resigned despair began to run through the Scottish crowd.

'Poulton is just too good,' Jack groaned. He had taken to addressing many of his remarks to the Hawick man, receiving a better response there than from his older sister, although he still provided her with a brief summary of events. But then, just when all seemed lost, the Scots rallied. First one man kicked for the posts – 'drop goal from Bowie' – and then another ran the length of the field. 'Will again. Terrific!' And then, not far from where they were sitting, an alarming shriek of pain rose above the general noise. Corran, Jack and those around them all leant forward. The casualty lay face down, his leg at an ugly angle. Amid the mud and the men who surrounded him, Corran couldn't see who it was. Not Rob? No, that shirt had once been white, and here was Rob now, sprinting at full speed across the field and dropping to his knees beside the injured man. The others made way for him.

It all took a terribly long time.

'Pillman. English hooker. Looks like a broken leg,' was the word being passed around the crowd. Eventually the wounded warrior was carried from the field to a round of applause. Rob accompanied him to the edge of the touchline and then jogged back.

Jack pulled out his watch. 'There can't be long to go. I just hope the referee adds on time for the injury. Come on, Scotland, one point in it. You can do this!'

There was a tension around the ground now and even Corran, who had longed for the end to come, felt herself drawn in. Her eyes were on Rob when the match ended. He was sprinting back, but as the final whistle sounded he pulled up, and she watched the hope and purpose leak from his battered, filthy body. For just a moment she could see his bleak despair and was unsettled to realise just how much this mattered to him. He bent double, hands on his knees, his face hidden from view. When he straightened up his shoulders went back, and he walked towards the nearest Englishman, hand outstretched and a congratulatory smile on his face.

The rugby was over.

Corran followed Jack down to the pitch and they waited at the edge as people milled around. Seeing them, Rob finished his conversation with another player and sauntered over. He might have been bathing in mud.

'Sorry we couldn't pull off a win for you.'

'It was close!' said Jack. 'You were terrific, Rob, and we nearly had them. We'll do it next year at Twickenham.'

'Aye.' Rob looked directly at Corran. 'Enjoy it?'

She had the uneasy sense of speaking to a stranger, plastered in the claggy ground as he was.

'It was . . . more exciting than I imagined,' she said. 'Thank you for getting the tickets. Jack, you must show Rob your sketch.'

Jack held it out along with his pencil. 'I wondered if you would sign it, actually,' he asked, suddenly bashful.

Rob rather pointlessly wiped his hands on his filthy shorts and took the pad, holding it by the edges. The sketch was a panorama of the pitch, posts at either end and action taking place.

'Jack, this is top-hole!' he said, scrawling his name across the bottom. 'I had no idea you were such a good artist. Here, I can get you some more. Gus – Gus! Charlie!'

He beckoned over two Scottish players who were standing nearby, one much taller than the other, arms around each other's shoulders.

'That's bloody good,' the smaller man said to Jack. 'Get yourself a job with the papers, son,' and he too added his name.

Then Jack's sketchpad was somehow being passed around the field, as men from both teams admired his work and added their signatures. By the time Rob brought it back it was grubby and crumpled, and he looked a bit rueful.

'Sorry, we've rather ruined it.'

But Jack's eyes were shining. He took the pad and closed the cover over, holding it tightly against his chest as if it were his passport to the future.

'Anyway,' Rob said. 'Must go. There are no baths here at Inverleith, would you believe, so we have to go back to the hotel in this state. I'll get cleaned up for dinner, and I might head round to the hospital and see how poor Cherry Pillman's doing. But we'll meet for our walk on Arthur's Seat tomorrow afternoon, Corran, as we said?' There was a slight hesitation in his eyes as he looked at her, and relief coursed through her. *There* he was, beneath the filthy layers of male strength and forcefulness: there was the intelligent and sensitive man who just might be part of her future.

'I'm looking forward to it,' she said.


The low winter sun was disappearing behind the blackened houses as they left the rugby field in March 1914, those young men from two nations, arms slung around each other, laughing, jostling and joking all the way. Splattered with mud and nursing their wounds, eager for hot baths, a slap-up dinner and a beer.

The only tiny mercy is that none of them knew.

# PART ONE
*War*

October 1918 to November 1918

# Chapter One

## London

Stella hurried down the stairs to the narrow street below. She had arranged to meet Corran in a tearoom near St Paul's Cathedral. *It's modelled on Lyons but not nearly as good*, she had written. *But it's handy for Hoster's and I don't get long for lunch.* She rather expected her older sister to be late as usual, but when she turned the corner she was pleasantly surprised to find Corran there before her. How different she looked, dressed in her smart YMCA uniform rather than her usual haphazard mix of dowdy clothes. Corran looked round, saw Stella and came towards her.

Stella felt the ground shift beneath her feet and she inhaled the thick London air, trying to steady herself. She hadn't seen Corran since those awful days last Christmas when they'd been trying to work out how to be a family together without Jack. Just a glimpse of her sister risked sending waves of horror crashing over her head. But she returned Corran's brief embrace.

'Come on inside,' said Stella, and she was glad the words

came out at a normal pitch. 'I can only stay half an hour.'

She led the way, weaving around long queues at sparse counters in the food hall and upstairs to the first-floor restaurant. A waitress dressed in black and white took their coats and hats, and led them to a table by a window that was so grimy they could barely see out.

Stella ordered for them both and then leant back, conscious of the amusement in Corran's eyes. 'What?'

'You! When did you become so grown up? London suits you.'

Stella pushed down the sense of irritation. 'I'm twenty-three, but I suppose we've hardly seen each other these past few years.' But that was skating dangerously close to the chasm of the last time they had been together. She changed the subject. 'I like London, but what about you – going to France! How did it come about?'

'Sheer luck,' Corran said, adjusting her cuffs. 'I was about to start my new job at St Hilda's when my old principal from Newcastle told me about the YMCA education scheme for the troops in France. Its purpose is to stimulate the mind and provide opportunities the men have missed out on at home. He asked if I'd like to take part and I jumped at the chance. Oxford agreed to postpone my appointment.'

'When do you leave?'

'Soon, I hope. There's been one delay after another. At the moment I'm cooped up in a hostel in Islington with a load of other women waiting to go out. There's everyone from an ex-music hall star who's off to join a Lena Ashwell party to a chaplain's wife who does rescue work – though I pity any poor soul rescued by her! She disapproves of me entirely and thinks Latin and Greek are completely unsuitable subjects for a female. Although I don't expect much call for the classics out there. I'll be teaching English and other arts subjects.'

Stella sipped her tea. 'You are lucky,' she said. 'To get to France. To see . . .' She stumbled, as Jack's shadow brushed between them.

'I know. But we'll be well behind the lines, you know, teaching base troops and men on leave.' Stella felt her sister's scrutiny and knew Corran had noticed the dark circles under her eyes that she couldn't quite conceal with powder. 'Tell me how you are, Stella. Does London live up to your hopes?'

Her hopes.

Was it even possible to fashion new hopes from the rubble of the last four years? She looked across at her sister, smart in her unfamiliar uniform. Somehow Corran had always known what she wanted and how to achieve it. Even the war hadn't stopped her. Seven years younger and trailing along in her wake, Stella knew only that the war had robbed her of every single opportunity that these years should have offered. In 1914 she had travelled down to Edinburgh University full of anticipation just as the men began to depart. None of them, men or women, would ever have believed that this nightmare could still be dragging on four years later. Her university years had come and gone, and now she was in London to learn typing and shorthand.

Anything to secure a future that would not be played out in Thurso.

Some days she was angry about all she had lost, and some

days she was determined to seize it back. But mostly she shuffled through the darkened London streets like everyone else, war-weary and a little bit hungry. She lifted the sorry-looking sandwich from her plate and took a bite.

'I'm happy in London,' she said. 'The course feels easy after my degree and the girls are fun. Mrs Hoster says there are more and more opportunities for well-trained girls to work in the big banks and offices and in government, so once the war is over I mean to find a job that will let me travel.'

Her sister replaced her cup carefully. 'I think Mother was a little disappointed that you didn't come home in the summer.'

'How could I?' Stella asked, and was immediately conscious that her defensive tone stripped away the years. 'I had just arrived in London. You know yourself how long it takes to travel home, and the expense too.' She brushed some crumbs from her fingers with her napkin as the waitress removed her plate. 'Don't you just long for proper bread again? I might come home for a short while at Christmas, although my friend Lily has invited me to her house in Ireland.'

'Please do try. Mother is on her own so much and she misses Jack. And Alex is likely still to be somewhere in the Mediterranean on his ship.'

*Jack*. Stella swallowed. They had always been two pairs: Corran and Alex, Jack and Stella.

'She's kept busy providing lodgings for the officers from Scapa naval base.'

'It's hardly the same.'

It was a well-worn argument. Thurso was home to Corran in a way it never would be again to Stella. She knew her sister couldn't bear to go more than a few months at a time without the sight of the sea and the sound of the waves crashing on the cliffs. Corran's university career provided her ideal balance – term-time immersed in academic life and long holidays back home in the north. She failed to appreciate that others might feel differently.

Stella decided to close the door on talk of family. 'Will you see Rob when you're in France?'

'That's not very likely. I don't expect it's easy for him to get away. He . . .'

She was still talking, but Stella had stopped listening. She had been vaguely aware of repeated coughing at a nearby table, but now there was some kind of disturbance, with people crowding round a young woman who had been taken unwell. Stella had lived in London long enough to react quickly. She pulled out her handkerchief and covered her face while signalling to her startled sister to do likewise. Leaving some money on the table, she grabbed their coats and hats amid a flurry of people doing the same and ushered Corran from the restaurant. Only once they were on the street outside did she lower her handkerchief.

'It's this awful flu,' she said. 'Lots of girls from Hoster's have gone down with it, and two died.'

'Well, I had heard about it, of course,' said Corran, ruffled by their abrupt exit. 'I read in *The Times* yesterday that Mr Lloyd George is so ill with it that they have rerouted the trams to avoid disturbing his rest. But it's just flu, surely.'

Stella shook her head. 'This flu is different and there's real panic in London. You need to be careful, Corran, staying in that hostel. Here, I've got mint lozenges. Lily swears they keep it away. Take some.'

'You keep them and I'll buy some for myself. But don't worry. I rarely catch anything – it's the sea air, I'm sure.' Corran glanced at her watch. 'I should go and brave my vaccinations for France. There's absolutely no way I'm using the Underground so I'll need to find a bus.'

Stella laughed. Corran might have courage enough to cross the sea to France alone, but she had always abhorred any confined space. 'Send me an address once you're settled in France,' she said. 'If only I could come with you – but no one would want me as a lecturer.'

'I'm not too sure they'll want me, but I'll take the chance!' Then Corran was gone, engulfed by the London crowds. Stella watched her go, taking with her the slightly caustic taste of home. She and Corran were bound together by so much, not least their brothers, but the orbits of their lives rarely intersected. A relationship conducted by letter could mask a great deal. She turned back towards Hoster's. It was true what she had told Corran – the typing and shorthand courses were easy enough, if not particularly interesting. She thought again about that question – *Does London live up to your hopes?* As a child Stella had dreamt of following Alex into the Royal Navy. Maybe it was the natural result of a childhood spent down on the shore, watching boats come and go and picturing the opportunities that lay over that horizon. She remembered clearly the day sixteen-year-old Alex had left for Dartmouth naval college. She had been ten and had run from the house in tears, furious not because he was leaving but because as a girl she would never be allowed to follow him. Later, Jack had found her down on the shore and brought her out of her rage, as he always could, chasing her up to the ruins of the old castle.

Jack.

There were not words enough in her head or her heart to begin to express the swirling, suffocating horror of Jack's death. Corran wanted her to spend more time at home with their mother, but Stella knew instinctively that if she returned to Thurso she would never be able to breathe again. What's more, she was pretty sure their mother understood. Even here in London she often had to steady herself against the tide of panic that crashed about her at unexpected moments. Someone with his build on the front seat of the bus; someone calling out his name in a park. Someone sitting on a bench, head bent over a pad, sketching. Oh God, sketching.

A threadbare rug littered with screwed-up balls of paper, and a keening sound she had never heard before.

Stella reached the entrance to Hoster's. There was no way she could go back to the Thurso she had shared with Jack for anything other than the shortest visit. Instead here she was, equipping herself for the kind of career that was emerging for the modern independent woman. Why, they said the Prime Minister himself even had a woman for his private secretary! She pushed open the door and climbed the steep stairs to rows of typewriters. Her generation had been cheated. The future that should have been hers, and Jack's even more, had been stripped from them when they were eighteen and nineteen, robbed by this awful war, which showed little prospect of ever being over.

Her university years had passed in a female-dominated fog of anxiety and food shortages. Somehow, amid the grief, she had to reach for something that might eventually take her away from drab little Britain to the spice-laden, warmer lands she had imagined as a child.

Hoster's was her ticket to board.

# Chapter Two

## 61 Casualty Clearing Station, France

Rob stretched out his long legs below the table in the officers' mess, rolling a cigarette between his fingers. It was unusual to be alone. He lit the cigarette, inhaled deeply, and rested his pounding head in his hands, trying to ignore the latest sounds that easily penetrated the canvas walls. Not the constant rumble of the guns – he barely noticed that. A new orderly had come down to them yesterday, just a young lad, and he'd kept glancing uneasily over his shoulder at the sound of the guns.

'Hear that noise, sir?' he asked repeatedly.

Rob ignored him. *Noise? You call that noise?* he wanted to ask, but he didn't. It wouldn't help. Pray God the lad never had to find out.

But the CCS was of necessity positioned beside a railway line, and that was where the more immediate sounds proceeded from. The shriek of brakes, the slam of doors, orders shouted, answering groans and screams of pain. Another ambulance train had arrived from the devastated wastelands near Amiens, the next load of poor buggers ripped to shreds out there, sent to him to be patched or dispatched.

The orderlies, sisters and VADs would be among them now, transferring the stumbling wounded and the stretcher cases to the reception marquee. Rob still found it strange to be working as part of a team in this small tented town that bore at least some relation to a hospital. Until just a few weeks ago he had been medical officer to his battalion, operating almost alone and following the men into battle, his aid post hastily set up wherever he could find rudimentary shelter from the shelling. He took a final gulp of tea, which was laced with whisky to steady his hands. Aye, this was a different landscape altogether, but at least with a team he could remain in the mess for another precious few minutes, smoke his cigarette and drain his tin mug before walking into the rest of this day, which would contain nothing but sewing, sawing and cutting away what was wasted, discarding what was beyond repair. Another and another and another.

By the end of the day there would be buckets of precious limbs, rotting flesh and a line of fresh corpses for the growing cemetery outside.

He jammed the cigarette in the corner of his mouth and rose slowly to his feet. God, his head hurt. Made his way along the slippery duckboards to the entrance to the tent. As ever, it was the stench that reached him first, before he even pulled aside the flap. Many of these mangled blighters had shat themselves or vomited in their terror and pain, and that was before the smell of rancid mud, burnt flesh and, worse, the putrid stink of rotting meat from those who'd lain a day or two. He inhaled one last time and dropped the cigarette to the ground, grinding it with his heel, then ducked into the tent. Sister Haines, at her efficient best, had already begun to sort them. He walked slowly among them, men huddled under blankets or filthy greatcoats, men lying out, barely moving, men rocking to and fro, men reaching out with imploring hands. Most had a label round their necks, hastily scrawled at the dressing station with name, rank and nature of injury.

He assessed them coolly. 'Resuss tent for him, Nurse.' 'Move him to pre-op.' 'Pre-op for this one.'

A young lad dressed in the grey of the German forces was coughing blood and gasping for breath, his skin tinged with blue.

Rob stopped, looked at Sister Haines. 'This is an influenza case. Are there many?'

She was flustered. 'The ones we identified were directed straight to the infection zone as you instructed, Captain. This one must have slipped through.'

'Move him.' Infection zone was stretching it, he thought – a sheet rigged up across the back of the evacuation tent, where those they couldn't help were sent to await death or the train to the base hospital, whichever came first. But the spread of this deadly influenza had been desperately rapid, particularly among the German troops it seemed, and at least his sheet made him feel he was doing something about it.

The next was a stretcher case rolled in a blanket, motionless, the sheen of death already on his thin face.

'Catastrophic abdomen injuries,' said the young orderly, reading his label.

'Evac tent. Make him as comfortable as you can.' He was about to move on. What made him stop? The smear of mud, and blood, on a cheekbone? The hair, filthy and plastered to his head? He stooped, lifted the label. 'Major Roland Gordon.'

*Oh fuck.*

He was on his haunches then, gently pulling the blanket aside to reveal blood-soaked, stinking bandages barely holding together a gaping mess. Catastrophic all right. *Fuck. Gordon.* The man groaned, but was insensible. For one unhinged moment Rob wanted to rush him straight into the operating tent, somehow pile the severed intestines and bowel back inside him, patch him up . . . but every bit of experience of the last four years told him that death was very near. His duty was to find those among the wounded who could be sewn together and tossed back to the guns once more. Harshly he turned to the orderly, the same teenage lad.

'This man's name is Roland Gordon. Make him comfortable, and stay with him till the end. Till the *end*, you hear me?' Then he stooped once more, placed his long skilful fingers gently on the clammy forehead. 'Bloody fantastic try, Gordon.'

Five hours later he was spent, poured out, empty, and his aching head rattled with machine-gun fire. But Gordon, he was told, was somehow still alive. So when the others left the ops tent to wash, to eat and drink, to rest, he followed the duckboard path round to the evacuation tent at the rear. Dusk had fallen, and though the roar of the guns continued from afar, spawning a whole new set of casualties for coming days, somewhere a blackbird sang a long song. He entered the dimly lit tent, his palms clammy and his tiredness like a cloak dragging at his shoulders. He thanked the boy who still sat there, obedient, and dismissed him. As he took his place on the flimsy camp chair the boy asked, 'How d'you know him, sir?'

'We played rugby together,' said Rob. 'For Scotland. Now bugger off and get your rations.' His voice softened. 'Thank you.'

He turned his attention to the patient. Roland's dark eyes were lucid now, and searched his face.

Rob took the thin hand in his own. 'Bloody fantastic try,' he said again.

There was recognition in the eyes; the cracked lips twitched into a half smile. Roland tried to speak, but no sound came out. Rob's fingers were on the weak pulse, and something tightened in his throat.

'Your first cap, wasn't it?' he carried on. 'Parc des Princes in '13. The one where we had to escort the ref from the field or the French crowd would have strung him up. But I still remember your sidestep, Gordon, your try.'

The hand moved weakly under his. His friend lifted two fingers. Rob swallowed, and laughed.

'Aye, right, two tries right enough. Glory days, Gordon. And what a night we had in Paris afterwards. Those French dancers, oh my.'

Roland's breathing was shallow and harsh. The cracked lips opened once more.

Rob leant close, the smell of death filling his nostrils. 'What's that?'

'Scot – land.'

And he understood. Roland didn't want to think about France, however delightful the memories might be. Here in France they had been stripped of all that life had promised on that grand Paris day in 1913. So Rob spoke instead of Scotland, of Edinburgh, of the fierce matches and cramped changing rooms they'd known at Inverleith, of a group of young men far closer than brothers who went swinging from bar to bar in Rose Street, and—

The hand quivered beneath his fingers, and then Roland's whole body jerked as he began to cough convulsively, blood projecting from his mouth across the bed. A fresh stain was spreading across his bandaged stomach and he gripped Rob's hand frantically, his eyes wide with terror as he coughed and choked and the blood continued to come, gargling up out of him. Drowning him in its scarlet fountain.

And then, at last, the eyes were empty and the thin hand was still.

The heart that pumped so fast and the lungs that filled to bursting as Roland Gordon charged up the touchline for his wonder try, they were finished. His beautiful young male body had been utterly ruined by the carnage of this vicious, endless war.

Rob sat there for a long time. Around him, nurses came and went, seeing to the patients on nearby camp beds, but no one spoke to him. The darkness had fallen completely, and the only light came now from the flickering lanterns around the tent. The other patients swore and moaned and sobbed. Still, Rob sat there. This tiredness and this pain, it wasn't a temporary thing, it was a part of him now, taking full possession of his body, blood, his bones. He lowered his pounding head onto his dead teammate's bloodstained chest, and closed his eyes. So tired.

Freddie Turner. George Will. Puss Milroy. French boys, English, Welsh and Irish boys too. Each one who died embedded him deeper into this living hell. So many of them, and now Gordon.

His team. His family.

All gone.

# Chapter Three

Dieppe

Southampton was a very long way from Thurso, but at least it was the sea. Three weeks of delay in London, all streets and no sky, had been more than enough for Corran. How her heart surged as she caught her first glimpse of the English Channel, for all that the water and sky merged into one mass of gunmetal grey on this dull October day.

They would not sail until night-time, under cover of darkness, and with a naval destroyer patrolling nearby. Her confidence was hardly improved by the clerk checking tickets, who asked for details of her next of kin 'in case the ship goes down'. But as she stepped onto the gangway leading to the steamer, her thoughts were full of Alex on his naval ship in the Mediterranean somewhere. Together they had survived shipwrecks and pirate raids all along the Thurso coastline. Tonight they would both be on the waves, and danger lurked beneath.

A short time later she stood on the deck and leant over the rail, looking into the darkness as they eased away from England. She would go inside for dinner in a minute or two, but she wanted to breathe in the cold air and listen to the surge of the waves against the creaking sides of this old steamer first. Her frozen fingers gripped the rail as she gazed down towards the black waters. She supposed there might even now be a German submarine prowling about, yet the fears that whispered most loudly were for tomorrow, not today. She felt again that familiar mix of trepidation and excitement that had accompanied every step of a career that she had never really intended to be so pioneering. What on earth had she signed up for this time? She had spent the last four years in Newcastle, teaching ever-diminishing classes the beauties of Greek and Latin, and had unexpectedly discovered that she was good at it. But now she would be teaching in a very different context. Did she really think she could communicate anything worthwhile to a roomful of uneducated, rough soldiers? Would they listen to her, or would they just laugh at her? How would they respond to being taught by a woman?

And yet, she had known from the moment the principal asked, 'How would you like to go out to France?' that there was nothing she wanted more. A flurry of letters had followed – to the War Office, seeking appointment; to Oxford, seeking a postponement; to Mother, seeking a blessing. Even to Rob, seeking nothing, but eagerly sharing her news. At this her thoughts faltered. In his reply he made no mention of her news until a postscript at the end. *Grammar for Tommy – whatever will they think of next!* She folded the letter and slipped it back into its envelope, placing it beside the scrawls of four years and firmly closing the drawer on any unreasonable doubts.

Rob. She could barely remember what he looked like,

but she could still feel his strong hand on the back of her neck as he pulled her into a long kiss in the sunlit glory of a Thurso evening in July 1914. It had been a golden week, the family at home and Rob in the guestroom. She had finished at Cambridge, achieving the highest marks in her year yet leaving with nothing to show for it. She had thought she was prepared for that injustice until it became a reality. It had been a relief to leave the narrow confines of Cambridge behind and return to Thurso to be replenished.

That week they all stood on the threshold of the future. She and Rob with their long walks on the shore, fingers loosely intertwined; Stella and Jack with their eager plans for term-time when Stella would join Jack at Edinburgh University; Alex home for a rare spell of leave. Quietly elated to have all her children home at once, their mother, Alison, took every opportunity to feed them their favourite meals and to encourage them in their dreams. Building up body and soul.

There was a bitter taste in Corran's mouth, and it was more than salt spray. The future they had imagined then was a delusion, long since tossed away on the northern breeze. Jack had been cruelly ripped from them. The last time she and Stella had been together in Thurso was Christmas 1917, just weeks after the telegram. Their mother had shrunk into herself with the loss of her son, and Stella had huddled in the corner of the sofa, dark eyes in a stunned white face. For once Corran was relieved when term started and she was able to pack up her sorrow and bring it back to her lodgings in Newcastle, where mourning was already a familiar companion. Now as she wiped the tears from her face, taking a last look down into the sinister depths before returning below deck, she whispered a line from Homer's *Odyssey*.

*'Yea, and if some god shall wreck me in the wine-dark deep, even so I will endure . . . For already have I suffered full much.'*

In the end, Corran passed the night safely in her berth in the bowels of the ship and was welcomed into her first morning in France with a quickfire volley of questions that immediately tested her French, before being released for the last leg of her journey. A train carried her through the rolling farmlands of Normandy, and how hard it was to believe in the war at all, with newly harvested fields and orchards pretty with fruit-laden trees. At Dieppe station she climbed down, took possession of her trunk, and looked around. She had been told that someone would meet the train and escort her to the school. All around her those dismounting seemed to know exactly where they were going. She noticed a tall man dressed in greatcoat and cap who was scanning the crowds and took a hopeful step towards him, but his gaze passed quickly over her, searching for someone else. As the passengers dispersed, any lingering surge of excitement stilled to a stagnant puddle. She had been travelling continuously now for more than twenty-four hours and, eyeing her trunk, knew she could not walk another step. She wanted a place to sit down, a pot of tea and above all a bathroom. She glanced across at the man, who was now making his way back along the platform, hands in his pockets. He had a YMCA badge on his cap, and might perhaps give her a lift.

'Excuse me?'

He stopped and turned. The first thing she noticed was the vivid crimson scar slashed down one side of his face. Reddish hair was visible below his cap, and his striking green eyes contrasted with that shocking scar.

'May I help you, ma'am?'

His voice told of roots in northern England, but was not the Geordie accent she knew so well. Manchester maybe.

'I'd be very grateful,' she said, suddenly conscious of just how grimy and travelworn she must look. 'I expected someone to meet me but no one has arrived. I have no idea how to get myself and my luggage to wherever I am meant to be.'

There was a light of laughter in his eyes. 'And do you know where you are meant to be?'

'I'm looking for the YMCA School of Education. You don't know where it is, do you?'

'Well, rather! As it happens I . . .' He stopped, and those green eyes narrowed. He glanced down at her trunk, and then met her eyes once more. 'Now hold on a minute. May I ask your name, ma'am?'

'Miss Rutherford,' she said a little stiffly, sensing the ground between them shifting but not sure why.

'Oh my great aunt. Someone has well and truly messed up.' He laughed aloud, and shook his head. 'Never mind, we'll sort all that at the base. Here, let me take your luggage for you. I have the car, just along here. Come along now!' He summoned a porter to carry her trunk. Corran was a little indignant at the sense he was laughing at her, but there seemed nothing to do but accompany him. He was tall but walked with an uneven gait, so that she found she had to slow her pace slightly to match his.

They reached the car and he held open the door of the rear seat for her and then climbed into the front. He himself was the driver it seemed. Seated behind him, it was difficult to engage in conversation so she contented herself with leaning back against the scuffed leather and watching as narrow streets opened up into a broad road along the seafront. On one side grand houses and hotels, and on the other a vast white shingle beach and the clearest green waters stretching out. A green she had seen just a moment before in the colour of his eyes, she thought, surprising herself. He called out comments to her once or twice, indicating this or that building, but she couldn't catch his words and was happy just to rest during this interlude before whatever awaited at her destination. Along the end of the seafront, a turn to the left, and he pulled up outside a red-gabled house, which nestled under the steep chalky overhang of the cliffs and looked out across the sea towards England. He stepped out, and came and opened her door, helping her out.

'Here we are,' he said cheerfully.

Corran stood and looked around her. As the fumes from the car dispersed she tasted the salty sea air, softer than any sea air in Scotland could ever be. It was so much more than she could have hoped for.

'It's lovely.'

'Isn't it just? Well, let's get you inside. I'll come back for your luggage but we really must find the chief and sort this out.'

'Sort what out?' she asked. 'I don't understand – I am expected, am I not? I have all the paperwork.'

'Oh, you're expected all right,' he said, trying and failing to hide his amusement. 'It's just – ah well, never mind. Here we are.' He pushed open the heavy wooden door, and led her through a cool hallway into a sitting room with broad windows overlooking that glorious sea. The walls were hung with tapestries, and the furnishings were ornately carved. 'Rather fine, isn't it?' he said. 'The artist Jacques-Émile Blanche has lent this place to us. He's in Paris for the duration. But I'll go and – ah no, here he is. Sir.'

A grey-haired, kind-looking man had entered the room, and across his face spread a similar cloud of confusion as she had seen with her as-yet-unidentified companion. She began to understand. It would not be the first time.

'You were expecting a man,' she said flatly.

It was rather funny to see them both look discomfited. The older man recovered himself first. 'My dear, how lovely to welcome you. Sit down, sit down, do. You must be wearied after the journey.'

'You've nailed it, though,' said his younger companion with a grin. He clearly thought the whole situation was the most tremendous joke.

'You see, we had a list sent out to us from England, and today we expected' – the chief consulted the piece of paper in his hand – 'Corran Rutherford, Lecturer in Greek and Latin, able to teach up to university standard in English, French and other arts subjects. We rather expected . . .'

'. . . a man,' she finished. 'It's that wretched name of mine, wished on me by my parents in some moment of sentimental madness in honour of the ferry on which they met. I'm just grateful they didn't use the Ballachulish crossing. And of course, many people still don't realise that a woman is as capable as a man of teaching classics. Don't worry. It has happened to me before.' She paused. 'I feel like Anne of Green Gables, though,' she said with a smile, not really expecting them to understand the reference to the story Stella had devoured. 'Do put my mind at ease – will you keep me, even though I'm not a boy?'

They fell over themselves to reassure her, the older one concerned, the younger one full of enthusiasm.

'We will need to make some arrangements, though,' said the senior. 'And how rude I am, Miss Rutherford. I do apologise. My name is Sir Henry Brooke, and this is Captain Callaghan. Your accommodation, you see . . . it won't do for a lady, won't do at all. We shall find you some suitable digs – Captain, see to it, would you? And then come back and escort Miss Rutherford and her luggage. Meantime, my dear, you must be tired. Is there anything I can do for you?'

Corran looked up at him. The kindness and warmth in his tone, coming as it did after her long journey and bewildering arrival, nearly undid her composure. She blinked away the threat of tears, determined not to show weakness before these men. 'I should like to find the bathroom, if I may,' she said. 'And then, perhaps, a cup of tea?'

*My dear Stella,*

*The school feels like home already. We're a strange old crowd, quite ordinary really, yet each is an expert in one field or another, and everyone is keen to share that expertise with the men who've had to give up so much in the way of education* and opportunities through these years. Now that they've got over the shock of my being a woman, the men here seem quite willing to accept me as one of themselves.

The male members of staff sleep on the top floor of the school, while the other two women and I have lodgings with French families in town. I have a simple little attic room and I love it already, with its polished floorboards and painted shutters, which open to show me the central square here in Dieppe. Every morning I rise early and hurry through the deserted streets to the school for breakfast. Meals are a hit or a miss here. We have one French cook, Henriette, and she either produces nothing to eat but Maconochie, or a table full of pheasants and butter and splendid things that one of her many nephews has brought our way. Feast or famine.

The most glorious thing about life in France is that one never quite knows what will happen next. College life at home is always so regulated, so predictable. It couldn't be more different here. The teaching itself is marvellously varied. Yesterday morning I was teaching English literature to a lorryload of troopers. Now they and I both knew that the only reason they had signed up to come was to avoid a particularly tough physical exercise parade. Many of them had read nothing since their schooldays other than the racing columns of the yellow press, but when I gave them the plot of Beowulf they lapped it up. Then in the afternoon I had a one-to-one session of Greek New Testament with the shyest young officer you can possibly imagine. He was converted by the war and has ambitions for the clergy, but he might have to learn to speak to a woman without *blushing first, poor lad. You would have laughed.*

*And the teaching is not the half of it. I've only been here a few weeks, and already I've been asked to help out in the kitchen, to play piano at a frightfully evangelistic sort of prayer meeting, and even to give marital advice while doling out mugs of tea in the canteen. Me! And it's the strangest thing, but while I would hate to do any of those things at home, here in France it's somehow different. The endless codes and rituals of proper behaviour that govern us at home, they mean nothing at all in France.*

*There are rumours of peace. We can hardly imagine that it will really happen, and have no idea what it will mean for our work if it does come. I think we will be here for a while yet. Sometime soon I believe Captain Callaghan and I will motor to a remount camp nearby and spend a week there, offering lectures to the men and to the horses too I shouldn't wonder! Camp life – it's the part of this role that daunted me most before I came out, and now I simply can't wait. The chief has warned me to wear my strongest shoes. I gather there's rather a lot of mud about. I'll let you know!*

*With much love from*
*Corran*

# Chapter Four

## Northern France

Any colour had long since leached out of the godforsaken landscape that spread out on either side of the rutted road. This sector was now firmly back under Allied control, but evidence of the enormous cost was everywhere. As the car jolted along, Rob's gaze ranged over the charred remains of buildings and the blasted stumps of trees, the tangled mess of barbed wire and the gaping oily craters containing hidden horrors in their depths. Here and there were groups of wooden crosses, hastily assembled, already sliding drunkenly into the mud.

They had passed a camp a couple of miles back but now on this stretch of road there was no sign of life. It was therefore unfortunate that the car, which had been creaking and straining for some time, chose this particular location to give a loud groan and come to a juddering halt. The driver swore. Rob leant across.

'Out of petrol?'

The driver, Bryce, was already getting out and Rob climbed out too.

'No, sir, plenty of petrol. I reckon I know what it will be. You just sit comfortable, sir, and I'll have her back on the road in a jiffy.'

'Comfortable' was not the word Rob would have chosen for this boneshaker. Glad to stretch his muscles, he twisted his back from one side to the other and then stood for a moment or two watching Bryce delve into the innards of the engine. His offer of help was rebuffed and so he turned aside and looked about him. It was strange to be alone in this emptiness: one feature of life in France was the continual press of other men. Something caught his eye a little way beyond the road, tucked behind the shattered remains of a copse. He glanced back: no sign of Bryce emerging from the engine yet. He crossed the road and made his way over a muddy expanse towards the small cemetery that lay a short distance away.

He stopped at the edge, unexpectedly moved.

Here, in this vast sweep of chaos and carnage, was a little piece of order that must have been created by the Germans before the Allies recaptured this land. The boundary of the cemetery was marked out with wooden edges. The grave markers were finely worked and carefully arranged; there was even a hint of green on the shrubs that had been planted at the end of each row. One wooden cross towered over the others. Thinking it would be a memorial to some great general, Rob approached, and found a tribute not to one man but to all the men. He walked on and soon came across a cluster of crosses all marked with English names. They were as neat and as carefully laid out as those of the Boche soldiers. The whole effect was simple, and Rob was impressed by the dignity and even beauty that the Boche had somehow managed to bring to the burial of the dead amid such carnage.

He lifted his hand to his head as if he could brush away the buzzing noise that was always there, a little quieter today perhaps, but always there. What to do with the dead. He thought about them sometimes in the night, when the buzzing became a terrible rattle, the dead who had taken possession of this landscape. Death came in so many different forms out here. Some were blown to nothingness, whatever remained of their bodies seeping into the soil. Others, whole, he had wrapped in a blanket and lowered into a trench, still others gathered up as slithery lumps of meat and offal, which were scooped into sandbags. But many had been left out there to rot, their flesh decaying as battles raged, as frontlines and trenches and no-man's-land shifted. A hand poking out of a trench wall. A foot emerging beneath a slippery duckboard.

After four years, this land they had crossed and recrossed surely consisted more of flesh and bone than of soil and vegetation.

But here the Boche had taken their dead and made something beautiful out of them. At home the families clamoured to have their boys back, without the slightest concept of what that would mean. *Here you are, Mrs Jones, I'm sure there are scraps of your Billy somewhere in this bucket of sludge.* But perhaps if this kind of order and dignity could be brought to the fallen, the people back home might find it easier to accept that they were here forever. A memorial, a place to come, even, to remember.

God, why would you ever want to remember?

All he wanted to do was to forget.

Rob turned back towards the road. Perhaps Bryce would have got her going again by now. He had welcomed today's short excursion to collect supplies, but he was anxious now to get back to the CCS and see what awaited him. And besides, this sector might be quiet now, but you could never be sure when a stray aircraft would come over and decide to shed its load. He was relieved to hear the throb of an automobile engine, but when he reached the roadside the car was still where he had left her and Bryce looked more harassed than ever. Rob turned his head. The noise he had heard, the noise of an engine, it came from beyond the brow of the hill. Another vehicle was coming – a lorry perhaps. They could hail it down and ask for help.

'What the hell's that noise, sir?'

Rob looked round sharply. Somewhere behind the constant buzzing in his ears there was indeed a new sound. A bugle? But who could be sounding a bugle out here?

As Rob and Bryce stood in the middle of the road beside their broken-down car, an extraordinary sight came into view. One large black car, followed by a second and then a third. Their headlights blazed, and Rob stiffened to realise that the soldiers on either running board of the front car were Germans. His hand went automatically to his pistol, even as he took in that one man was waving a huge white flag, while the other sounded out a long high note on his bugle.

'Fuck me, it's a bloody peace delegation,' said Bryce.

'Aye, and your tin can of a motorcar is blocking the way! Come on, man, get her moving!'

The convoy had of necessity come to a stop. Warily, Rob watched as a man in German military uniform stepped out of the first car. He advanced then stood some distance away, and Rob was reminded of many stories of cautious communication across no-man's-land.

The man indicated the car. 'Problem?'

This man was surely high ranking, but Rob saw no need to acknowledge it. Then Bryce stepped forward, his face scarlet. Addressing Rob rather than the German officer, he said, 'She's ready to go, sir, but a push would help.'

The German understood. With a sharp nod he walked back to the third vehicle in the convoy and summoned two younger soldiers, speaking rapidly in German. And then Rob was back in the car, and the driver turned the handle to get her started and leapt in beside him. German muscle heaved, and they moved forward. Rob glanced across at Bryce. His knuckles were white as he clutched the steering wheel. He was clearly spooked by the convoy trundling into life behind them, but the last thing Rob wanted was to end up in a ditch and have to repeat the whole process.

'Take it easy, Bryce, and pull to the side as soon as you can.'

His measured tone seemed to help a little, and Bryce's shoulders relaxed.

'Sorry, sir. But I can't believe it. That might be the bloody Kaiser in that car, sir.'

'I can assure you it's not.'

Rob wiped his sweating hands on his trousers and watched

as the convoy passed with a waving flag, a final toot on the bugle and – Rob was sure – a friendly salute from the German officer who had spoken to them. As their own vehicle moved forward again in its wake, Rob looked at the black cars disappearing over the horizon.

Had he really just glimpsed peace?

# Chapter Five

## London

Today of all days it was impossible to concentrate.

The clatter of typewriters, the rustle of papers, the sniffs and coughs and sighs of the other girls – usually Stella could ignore it all, particularly when, like today, she had a fiendishly complex and badly scrawled medical manuscript to type up. Yet she had no sooner memorised a sentence and placed her fingertips on the cold metal keys, than the words were gone, overtaken by the barely suppressed sense of excitement that passed from one desk to another in meaningful glances and smiles. And then there was the mysterious behaviour of Mrs Hoster. Where usually she sat at her desk at one end of the room, like a stern schoolmistress, today she had walked between the rows and summoned two or three girls to join her in her office. Right now it was the turn of Lily, whose empty desk sat alongside Stella's.

Stella sighed and looked up at the clock on the wall. 10.30 a.m. Was anything happening outside? Mrs Hoster's offices were up on the third floor – would they even hear any excitement in the street below? How awful, to endure four years of war, only to have the declaration of peace drowned out by the rattling symphony of typewriter keys. Imagine missing it! She had a vision of the Hoster's girls typing solemnly on, week after week and month after month, cloistered amid ink and filing cabinets while the world turned and turned some more, and left them behind.

She turned back to the manuscript, but no sooner had she begun to type than she heard heels clipping across the wooden floor, and Lily was beside her.

'Mrs Hoster wants to see you,' her friend said. Stella looked up. Lily's pale face was flushed unusually pink.

'Why?'

Lily shook her head. Stella got to her feet and looked round. Mrs Hoster was standing in the entrance to her office. She brushed down her skirt, smoothed her hair and made her way to the doorway at the back of the room. Mrs Hoster had retreated inside. Stella closed the door behind her and took the seat indicated.

Constance Hoster now sat behind her desk, a tall thin woman in her fifties. She lifted her steady pale gaze to Stella and smiled, a brief smile, genuine enough but contained.

'Miss Rutherford,' she said. 'You have been with us for six months, and your work is consistently of a high standard. Is it to your liking?'

'Very much,' Stella said, clasping her fingers tightly on her lap. Impenetrable medical terms aside, of course.

'And do you have particular ambitions?'

Stella hesitated. She was so full of contradictory ambitions that they often threatened to spill out of her like the contents of an untidy stocking drawer, but which ones to share with Mrs Hoster? 'In time, perhaps a position with one of the larger banks or legal firms.'

She was pleased with that. Sober and professional.

Mrs Hoster glanced down at a typewritten sheet of paper in an open file on her desk.

'Your home is in Scotland. Caithness. Some distance away. Are you likely to be needed at home?'

'Oh no!' A little less sober. She took a breath. 'I grew up in Thurso and my mother lives there, but she is happy for me to be in London. I have a sister who spends several months at home each year.'

'Scotland is a beautiful country. My brother Alfred and I spent a holiday in Peebles once.'

Stella waited politely and decided not to explain just how long it took to travel from Peebles to Thurso. She knew something of Mrs Hoster's story – they all did. Born of Jewish German parents, the brother she mentioned was a celebrated music critic. There had been a Mr Hoster once, but the marriage was not a success. Escaping matrimony, Mrs Hoster had dedicated her life to equipping young women with skills that would enable them to remain independent rather than be herded along the aisle to the altar. Shorthand, typing and translation work were her specialities. Some girls found her forbidding, for she didn't suffer fools and had no time for slackness or tardiness, but for those with ambition there was no better college and agency in London.

'As you know, we expect an armistice to be declared any day now,' Mrs Hoster said. 'I have been approached by the

Foreign Office, who require expert typists to support the drawing up of the various treaties. It will be intense, gruelling work of the utmost importance. I have considered which of my girls to recommend, and I would like with your permission to recommend you.'

'Oh, yes please,' said Stella at once. It would be her first job out of Hoster's. She pictured herself hurrying along the pavements of Whitehall with a briefcase full of interesting and vital documents. But Mrs Hoster held up one regal hand.

'Wait, please. There is more you must consider before you decide whether to accept. The treaty is to be drawn up in Paris. You will be required to cross to France within a matter of weeks, as soon as arrangements are confirmed, and are likely to remain there without leave for many months. Only girls who can make that commitment will be eligible for the role.'

*Paris. France. Jack.*

Later, she wasn't sure if she had actually answered or not, for just at that moment there came a series of bangs, loud enough to shake the window, and accompanied by the exclamations of the typists beyond the door. Stella jumped and then, as Mrs Hoster rose to her feet, followed her example.

'How unfathomable men are,' the older woman murmured as she walked towards the door. 'They welcome peace with yet more gunfire.' She placed a hand on the doorknob then paused, turning back to face Stella. 'The ceasefire has come, then. Shall I recommend you for the position, Miss Rutherford?'

Stella could only nod. As she followed Mrs Hoster out of the room to find the excited typists charging down the stairs, she had the strangest sense of unsteadiness, of everything that had been her world for the last few years shifting all at the same time. Peace. Paris! And then there was Lily, last in the room, waiting for her, holding out her hand. 'Come *on*, Stella!'

'Take your hats and coats, girls,' Mrs Hoster said, and now she was smiling. 'The others will have to come back for theirs. You may have a holiday. I shall see you back here first thing tomorrow.'

Three flights down, and a fast-flowing river of office workers was streaming through the narrows of Telegraph Street towards the crowds in Moorgate.

'To the Mansion House!' someone shouted and, unable to stop or to speak, Stella and Lily seized each other's hands and allowed themselves to be swept along amid the shouts and the flag waving, before taking their chance to jump onto a bus and climb to the top deck. The bus inched along the Strand towards Trafalgar Square. London had gone completely mad. Never had Stella seen such crowds of people, such freedom and excitement on the streets of the city. She watched it from above, laughing, and all the while ignoring the tight knot that had formed in her stomach. It was easier, amid the noise and the chaos, to allow herself to be picked up and carried along by this wave of abandoned joy. Eventually they washed up along with half of London outside Buckingham Palace. Arms linked, they forced their way through the crowds and clambered up on the wall surrounding the Victoria Memorial, giving them a view right into the quadrangle.

'Where else would you want to be on a day like this?'

said Lily, before joining in the loud chants of 'We want King George!'

Their cries were soon answered as, small and indistinct, the King, Queen and Princess Mary appeared on the balcony. Somewhere nearby a brass band was playing, the music barely distinguishable until the crowd took up some of the tunes. 'It's a Long Way to Tipperary' . . . 'Keep the Home Fires Burning' . . . 'Land of Hope and Glory' . . . and moving on to the anthems and favourite songs of each of the Allies. Every minute the crowd around Stella and Lily grew thicker, with people swarming not just around them but climbing onto the statue itself. An Australian soldier had made it to the very top, and conducted the crowds with one hand, clinging to Victory with the other. 'Advance Australia fair!' he yelled, before pretending to launch himself into the crowds below. In anticipation, those close to Stella surged and she nearly stumbled. Two hands gripped her legs to steady her, unexpectedly firm. Shocked, she looked down to see a dark-haired American soldier grinning up at her, but whatever he said was lost amid the noise.

When at last the royal family left the balcony, after a speech heard by hardly anyone, the crowd began to disperse. Stella's back was aching from the effort of remaining balanced on the wall against the heaving crowds, and she clambered down.

'I'm gasping for a cup of tea,' she said to Lily. 'Where shall we go? Anywhere open is bound to be full already.'

'It's not a cup of tea you want, it's a picnic.' It was the dark-haired American soldier, and as she turned to face him she felt again the warm imprint of his hands on her legs.

'And that's where Earl and I can oblige.'

'I can't see any picnic,' Lily said, laughing.

'That's a detail, honey. Is London not the city of street sellers? Come with us.' He walked backwards to make sure they were following, and promptly stumbled off the kerb onto the road. Laughing, the four of them linked arms and made their way into St James's Park, where the two soldiers laid their coats on the wet November grass. 'Now you girls just wait here, and we'll be back before you can say peace.'

All around them others were doing the same, though the day was raw and damp. It was a relief to sit down.

'I suppose they'll come back since they've left us their coats,' Stella said doubtfully.

'I think it may be us they'll come back for rather than the coats!' Lily laughed. 'But as long as they bring something to eat and drink, I don't mind. I'm famished.'

Stella leant back on her elbows and closed her eyes. The gnawing emptiness she'd sensed soon after the guns exploded was threatening to take over. *No. Not yet. I can't look there yet.* She opened her eyes and smiled at Lily. 'Paris! Will you go?'

'Ah, how much I would love to! It all depends on Daddy. I'll do everything I can to persuade him, but I'm afraid he'll think it's not respectable.' Her fingers were pulling up blades of grass. 'Will you?'

Stella thought of her mother, alone now in Thurso but always determined that her daughters should seize the opportunities she herself had never had.

'Yes. Mother will want me to.'

'You're so *lucky*,' Lily said, as she did perhaps ten times every week. She was wildly envious of Stella's independence in the Girls' Club, for all Stella pointed out that her shabby room scarcely compared with the grand London townhouse Lily inhabited so carelessly. From all she knew of Lily's wealthy Anglo-Irish parents, Stella could quite believe they would be reluctant to let their adored only daughter cross to France unsupervised for several months. Stella and Lily had become firm friends in their first week at Hoster's, but when they took part in any social activity, Lily's parents liked to send their chauffeur to bring her home. That would hardly be possible in France!

'What makes it worse is that Daddy's determined we will go to Ireland for Christmas this year. I so hoped you would join us. The house is awful – a hundred gloomy rooms and no heating in any of them – but if we were both there we'd have some fun regardless. Now you'll be in Paris dancing in the boulevards and I'll be counting sheep on the Irish moors.'

She looked so miserable that Stella could only laugh. 'Perhaps your father will think it's your patriotic duty. Ask him tonight – everyone is in such a mood of celebration that he's sure to say yes.' Then she straightened up. 'Are those our Americans, do you think?'

The park was thronged with people, many dressed in green American uniforms. 'The dark one was taller, surely.'

Stella couldn't really remember what the pair looked like. It had been such a fleeting encounter. But all at once the two men were before them, arms full, and she thought as she had done before how healthy and hearty most American soldiers looked. Even those who had already been to the front had not lost the sheen of the Stars and Stripes.

'Now here we are, girls,' said the smaller, broader one, handing out hot pies and buns and, rather surprisingly, bottles of milk. 'Let's drink to peace.'

It was the strangest picnic she had ever known. Earl was the stocky one, and his sole objective seemed to be to press more and more food upon the women.

Dark-haired Frank told Stella that his grandmother was from Scotland, though he didn't know where. 'Maybe I'll go visit while I'm over here,' he said. They were on leave from the front, having crossed the Atlantic with the first Americans in 1917, and they expected to be sent to Germany as part of the occupying force in a few days. 'Who knows how long that will last?' Frank asked. 'I guess we're here for a while yet, for all we've won the war.'

'We sure have,' said Earl. 'Guess you guys are glad we came in now. Li'l England and France were in a bit of a jam there.'

She caught Lily's eye. *A jam of several years' making, while you sat on your hands.*

'We hope to go to France,' said Stella to reclaim the moment. 'They're making arrangements for the peace conference now, and they need typists.'

'Hey, that's a fine opportunity,' Frank said.

She nodded. 'We're aching to see Paris.'

'I guess there's not so much to see, not with all the pretty windows boarded up and the sidewalks full of tramps. None too clean, Paris. But you girls have got lucky all the same. They say President Wilson may even come over himself. Well,

I sure hope he does; it's the beginning of a new world, and no one better to lead it than our president. You'll know about his fourteen points. This is our chance to put all these old European divisions to bed, and create a brighter future. No more war.'

Earl punched him on the shoulder, making him slosh his milk.

'Quit the campaigning, Frank. For me, all I want is a ship back across that ocean just as soon as they'll let me on it. If I can be home for next season's sowing I'll be a happy man.'

'Sure thing. I wanna go home too,' Frank said, taking out a handkerchief and mopping up the milk. 'But these girls will be part of history in the making. That's a fine thing.'

He shrugged off his friend's mockery, and Stella liked him for it. She took his words into herself, storing them up for later. There had been so little time to think about any of it, with the opportunity mentioned in the very same breath as peace was declared. But of course he was right and going to Paris was about far more than finally achieving her dream of going overseas. It was about creating a new kind of future, and that was the only thing that could possibly bring any good out of the last four years.

They finished their picnic and, increasingly stiff and cold, decided to move. Parting from their companions with good wishes, Stella and Lily made their way arm in arm back up the Mall, where singing and dancing swirled around them, a whirling carousel of elation. Stella loved it. It was growing dark now, and here and there people had set off fireworks. 'Look – they're lighting the streetlights!' Lily said. 'They haven't done that since the beginning of the war. Oh, isn't it *pretty*, all ablaze like this?'

They strolled along dreaming of Paris, and parted at Piccadilly Circus. Stella paused for a while to watch a trio of American soldiers, all dark-skinned, who had climbed Shaftesbury Memorial with their trumpets. The music they were playing was different from anything she had heard before. It seemed to mingle with the crowds, capturing their wild joy and transforming it into a stream of melody that reached right inside her, fluid and free. All around her people were dancing. *There is more*, Stella thought as she watched them. *There is more, and I want it. I want the years back that have been stolen from us.*

She walked on through the thinning crowds until she was back at the Girls' Club. She pushed open the heavy door and entered a dark, cold hallway that felt just the same as it had done every day of the past few months. No sense of celebration here! Up in her room, Stella closed the door behind her, removed her hat, coat and shoes, and lay down on the narrow bed looking up at the patch of damp on the ceiling. What a day it had been. Only now could she pause and let the impressions and emotions of these extraordinary hours pass through her mind like slides in a magic lantern show. Grasp them, order them, believe them. Her astonishment at Mrs Hoster's offer; the wild joy on the streets; the surprising encounter with the American soldiers. The war was over, and this was peace. Weary but unable to rest, she swung her legs down and walked over to her window. Pushing it up, she knelt on the hard wooden floor and leant out. She could still hear distant celebrations: fireworks popping, horns blaring, the faint sounds of music. The city was rejoicing, but here she was separate from it all, and the joy of the day ebbed away. The air on her face was cold and damp, and she realised her cheeks were wet. Here, alone in her room, conscious of all that lay behind and all that lay ahead, there was only one thing that mattered.

The war was over but Jack, her brother, the other part of her, was dead and was dead and was still dead.

The horror that was always there.

It had been a year, and she was familiar with the waves of grief that would rise up when she was least expecting them, battering and overwhelming her. She shrank from thinking of Jack, knowing the inevitable bleak destination of that train of thought, which would end in a horrible keening sound and a floor littered with paper. Yet not to think of him was to teeter on the brink of his absence as on the edge of a chasm. Today, in that split second in Mrs Hoster's office, a new reality had presented itself. For as long as the war continued, Jack's death was part of something tangible and ongoing. Now that the war was over, however foolish it sounded, his death should be over too.

But it wasn't. He was dead and was dead and was still dead.

The war was over, and Jack was still dead. The people were celebrating, and Jack was still dead. She would go to Paris, and Jack was still dead.

High above the dancing streets of London, clinging on, she lowered her head onto her arms and sank beneath the black waters of grief.

# PART TWO
## *Peace*

December 1918 to February 1919

# Chapter Six

Hôtel Majestic, Paris

Daylight slid through a gap between the floor-length wooden shutters. Stella glanced across at the other bed. Lily lay facing her, eyes closed and mouth open, snoring softly. Moving quietly, Stella lifted her winter coat from the chair where she had dropped it the previous night and pulled it on over her nightdress, then gently eased back the shutters and stepped out barefoot onto the narrow balcony. Their own balcony, high up on the top floor of this extraordinary hotel, far above the broad, tree-lined avenue Kléber. In the grey early morning light, Paris was already awake. She watched as a tramcar rattled below, and pictured the Parisian men and women inside, jolting sleepily together on their way to their workplaces. The people who hurried by down on the pavements were hunched against the cold. She leant out but couldn't quite see the Arc de Triomphe at the top of the avenue. The breathtaking sight of the white monument glowing in defiance of the dark stood out in her memory of last night's thrilling charabanc ride from station to hotel.

They had left England on the morning of the general

election. It was a historic day for many women, who for the first time walked side by side with their husbands, brothers and sons into polling stations to mark their cross. And yet this hard-won victory was only partial. Stella and Lily would not be thirty for a long time yet and so were still denied the vote that was rightfully theirs.

'So many men have been killed, particularly of our age, that they are afraid of women outnumbering them,' Stella said as they stepped down from their cab. 'As if that would be a bad thing!'

'Daddy was pacing the floor this morning. He's worried that the result in Ireland will increase demands for Irish independence. You should hear him on the subject of Countess Markievicz being allowed to stand for election from prison. A rebel *and* a woman! I swear he hardly noticed me leave, he was so busy on the telephone to his agent over there.' Lily squeezed Stella's arm. 'I skipped out as fast as I could in case he changed his mind.'

At Charing Cross, a special train awaited them. They posed for press photographers then piled on, travelling in first-class luxury to Folkestone. Stella, who had spent many uncomfortable hours on interminable train journeys from Thurso, was open-mouthed at the splendour, to Lily's amusement. The tables were turned on the rough crossing over the Channel. Stella managed to hold on to her breakfast while Lily, who had fully intended to take advantage of the opportunities presented by a steamer packed with officers returning to France, instead retired below deck with her head over a bucket. But Stella stood on deck, leaving behind a homeland that was already changing and sailing towards a conference that offered hope to the world.

By the time they were on the train to Paris, the December night had crept in. Stella spent much of the journey in the corridor looking out of the window while Lily held court in their compartment. Darkness shrouded wintry fields, but as the train travelled south, white moonlight gleamed through the clouds, revealing fleeting glimpses of a forsaken landscape. As bursts of laughter came from the compartment behind, Stella gazed in fascinated horror at ruined houses that bore witness to the carnage that had so recently taken place here. Most of the time she had no idea where she was, though a chance remark by a passing officer at one point told her they were pulling slowly through the crumbling remains of Amiens station. Stella hugged her arms tightly around herself and wondered why her fellow travellers weren't out here, every one of them, faces pressed to the glass as they absorbed the physical testament of war.

But then, many of them had known little else for the last four years.

Jack was out there in the darkness somewhere. Although she knew his grave lay further east, this ghostly moonlit otherness had been his world, a world of noise, brutality and outrage that had destroyed him long before it took his life. She pressed her palm against the glass and held it there.

Her own pale face gazed back at her, haunted, bereft.

Her face? His face?

Or a million other faces, the discarded dead in that cold darkness, rising up, drawn to the laughter and light on the passing train and crowding around it, their pleading skeletal hands outstretched, just beyond the reflections of the glass.

In France, she would not be alone.

But then came Paris, the journey in crowded charabancs through elegant streets to a hotel that lived up to its Majestic name, with more marble and gilding than Stella had ever seen in her life. She and Lily had a room to share high in the eaves, with their own narrow balcony and a private bathroom that even had hot running water. And this morning here was Paris – City of Light – spread out below her icy feet.

A knock sounded on the door and she stepped back into the warmth of the bedroom. Lily was out of bed now, her long blonde plait hanging down her back. She opened the door to find two porters dressed in the stylish hotel uniform.

'Your trunks, ma'am,' one of them said.

'You're English!'

'Yes, ma'am. From Leeds. All the staff are English. Security reasons.'

When the door closed again, Lily spun on the spot, her arms wide.

'Oh, isn't this *marvellous*! I can hardly believe we're here, Stella. We're going to have the time of our lives!' She threw open her trunk and began to unpack, humming 'I Was a Good Little Girl Till I Met You' as she tossed dresses, blouses and underclothes onto her bed.

Stella lifted the lid of her own trunk, packed with such care and anticipation in the damp and shabby little room at the club. On top was the deep blue georgette evening dress she had bought just last week in Harrods with money her mother had sent in lieu of their official clothing allowance. The first shop-bought dress she had had in over four years. She held it up and breathed in its newness. The fragrance of a promise. There was a full-length mirror on the wall and she stood in front of it, long dark hair loose about her shoulders, bare feet, evening dress pressed to her body, nightdress peeping out underneath. *Paris awaits.*

Breakfast was as English as could be, with ham and fish and eggs and porridge, yet served in the most opulent gilded dining room that was nothing but French all the way. Over the last few months Stella had become used to feeling hungry as the drab food in the club grew steadily scarcer. The Majestic really did feel like landing in someone else's life.

After breakfast there was a briefing of the clerical staff. They gathered in the lounge, a vaulted, mirrored space with flags hanging from a balcony, and stood in little groups eyeing one another. All around was activity. People queued to change money and to buy English papers, while near the doors was a growing mountain of luggage. Every now and then someone wandered through looking lost – it might be a Red Cross nurse or an officer dressed in uniform, an important-looking man in top hat and frock coat or a telegraph girl with a wire in her hand. None of them seemed to know which way to go.

'It feels like the first day of term,' whispered Stella.

And on this first day of term, a vision in tweed and pearls now stood before them. 'Good morning, ladies,' she said briskly. 'I am Miss Bingham, the superintendent of female staff with the British Empire Delegation. It's my pleasure to welcome you here, and to explain some of the procedures and rules that have been put in place for the benefit of us all.'

'She's the one Mrs Hoster told Daddy about,' Lily murmured. 'The one who made it possible.'

The only way Lily had been able to convince her father that serving on the British Empire Delegation was not only her patriotic duty but also perfectly respectable was to persuade him to meet with Mrs Hoster. Always committed to advancing the independence of her students, Constance Hoster knew what mattered to a protective father. She laid out in detail the measures that were in place to preserve the virtue of the girls, stressing in particular the fine character and discipline of Miss Bingham. Stella had imagined a stern headmistress type, but Miss Bingham reminded her more of a head girl, not so very much older than her charges but supremely confident in her own authority. She led them through to an anteroom decorated in deepest red. Here, as they sat down, she issued them all with books of meal tickets and with their individual passes, to be shown every time they entered or left either the Majestic or the Astoria, the nearby hotel where their work would take place.

'There will be a general rulebook,' Miss Bingham continued, 'but there are some matters particular to female staff to which I wish to draw your attention today. You girls are fortunate enough to be among the very first members of the delegation to arrive here in Paris. As flagbearers, it is up to you to set the standard for what follows. No girl may leave the hotel in the evening without entering her whereabouts in a register, and nor should you leave the hotel alone unless sent on official business. You may entertain guests in the public areas of the hotel but male visitors, other than a brother or a father, are not permitted

75

in bedrooms. Anyone breaching these regulations will be sent home immediately.'

Stella's mind wandered. She had heard this in every place she had lived since first moving down to the women's hostel at Edinburgh University. In her experience, those who wanted to find a way round the rules would do so. But really, there was so much potential right here in the hotel that she didn't imagine she would have to go far to find excitement. She glanced around and noticed a tall, blonde man who lingered at the entrance to the anteroom watching them. He caught her eye and winked. Miss Bingham's lecture meanwhile moved on to the people they would encounter here in the Majestic, from international statesmen to diplomats and ambassadors. They would all dine together, but asking for autographs from famous people was forbidden. They must behave with dignity and respect at all times.

Miss Bingham gave them ten minutes to return to their rooms to freshen up and collect coats, hats and gloves, before meeting back downstairs to walk to the Hôtel Astoria. As they hurried chattering from the room, Stella looked round for the young man but he had gone. Six floors was quite a hike, but another girl advised against the lift.

'It gets stuck between floors.'

Breathless, they made it back down in time. Stella tugged her new black velour hat on her head as they stepped out into the chilly Paris air. Miss Bingham led them back up to the Place de l'Étoile, with its bewildering wheel of avenues converging on the Arc de Triomphe. Round a few spokes to the head of the Champs-Élysées, which swept away before them, broad, magnificent and lined with bare trees.

'Here we are, ladies,' Miss Bingham said, with a distinct note of pride. 'This is the Hôtel Astoria, your workplace for the coming months.'

They looked up at another imposing building with a grand dome facing onto the Champs-Élysées, and elaborate carvings and balconies decorating the façade.

'Mummy and I stayed here before the war,' came one refined voice from behind them. 'It has the most marvellous orchestra in the restaurant.'

'I expect you'll find it rather changed, Miss Oliver,' Miss Bingham said crisply. 'The Astoria has served as a Japanese military hospital throughout the war. They are working hard to make it suitable for our use.'

Inside was certainly a strange mixture – the grand architecture and sweeping staircase, the bare floorboards where carpets had been rolled away, and the penetrating smell of bleach not quite masking something far more unpleasant. Miss Oliver looked horrified.

'This was the *salle à manger*,' she kept saying. 'I'm sure our suite was just along this corridor. It had the most splendid view.'

But when Miss Bingham opened a door to a large room filled with individual desks, each with a typewriter, Stella's heart soared. This was why she was here. She imagined the coldness of the keys below her fingertips and wondered what significance there might be in the words she would type here in this room with its ornate marble fireplace and its tall windows looking out onto the Champs-Élysées below.

'We will begin as soon as negotiations get underway,'

Miss Bingham said. 'President Wilson is now in Paris, and delegates are arriving every day. Once the work starts you can expect to be extremely busy, so I suggest you all take advantage of these few days to familiarise yourselves with Paris, and to make sure you have everything you need.'

Paris, just a few weeks after the end of the war. Arm in arm, Stella and Lily strolled along the Champs-Élysées in the gentler afternoon air. Tricolour flags hung from nearly every lamppost and window, with a smattering of other Allied flags here and there. The boarded-up shop fronts and gaps in the lines of trees did nothing to diminish the sheer grandeur of the broad avenue. They stopped to watch children swarm over a captured German gun as if it were a climbing frame, waving their homemade flags. A little further on a soulful young man with sallow complexion sang of France's great victory and the new world that had arrived. As they lingered, Stella looked about her. If this were London, she thought, people would hurry on, heads down. If this were London, everything would be drab and downtrodden. Here, the world was brighter, as the magnificent scale of the boulevard opened up a vast expanse of sky, illuminating life between the buildings. A woman who had paused beside her to watch the street musician was dressed in rich furs and modish grey hat, as stylish as if the war had never happened. Stella was suddenly glad of her own smart attire. When Mrs Hoster had confirmed their appointment she had passed on the welcome news that all the women would receive a £25 clothing allowance. The men, she remarked dryly, would receive £30. Stella and Lily had spent a hugely enjoyable afternoon in Oxford Street, picking out new blouses, stockings and the like and choosing an evening dress each. It was tremendous fun and a reminder of all they had missed – and Stella pushed aside her inevitable guilt at such indulgence. The Foreign Office *wanted* them to be well dressed. Here in Paris she looked at the fashionable woman and felt a wave of relief that she had discarded the shabby blue hat that had seen her through all four war years.

As they turned away, a hoarse voice called out for money. Stella glanced round. A man sat against the wall, wooden crutches lying by his side and a few centimes scattered in his cap. A grubby blanket covered the empty space where his legs had once been. She looked quickly at his face as she fumbled for some coins and realised with a shock that he was no old man, either. A young man with old eyes.

There were others too, in the shadows, at the street corners. Stella had lived in London where there were usually some wounded servicemen begging on the streets, but she had never seen as many as she did today. And then there were the children, barelegged and filthy. Women, hands outstretched, speaking in languages she couldn't understand. In this city the chic and the shattered were held together as close companions.

When they reached the Place de la Concorde, they stopped and stared. This was not a square; this was a vista. Dodging cyclists and cabs, they crossed to look at the Egyptian obelisk.

'It's all so magnificent that it's hard to believe such violence took place here during the Revolution,' Lily said. 'Cobblestones running with blood.'

'Is that so different?' asked Stella, gesturing towards the line of captured German guns in front of one of the grand hotels. Just a short time ago these had been dug into the mud on the Western Front, pounding the Allied lines. They were displayed now as trophies of victory, but Stella could only think of the destruction they had caused. *Jack.*

'Stella Rutherford!'

Startled, she looked round and Jack receded. A young man approached from the grand entrance to one of the hotels. He used an ivory-topped walking stick and carried a shiny leather briefcase in his other hand. As he came close, he tucked the briefcase under his left arm and held out a hand. She hesitated and then, even as her own hand reached out to meet his, she seemed to catch a whiff of freshly cut grass and the tang of the breweries on the air. Edinburgh in summer.

'It *is* you!' he was saying. 'What fun!'

Hugh. His name was Hugh. Hugh Mortimer, and he belonged in a lecture hall in Edinburgh's quad, or on a sunny picnic in the Meadows, but instead he was here in the bustling Place de la Concorde.

'Hugh,' she said. 'This is my friend, Miss Sheridan.'

'Lily,' said Lily at once.

'We're here with the British Empire Delegation.'

'Of course you are. I am too.' He gestured back to the building behind them, and she noticed the Stars and Stripes fluttering from its flagpole. 'I've just delivered some papers to our American friends. They're based in the Hôtel de Crillon. I take it you're in the Majestic? Fifth floor?'

'Sixth. Up in the roof.'

'Splendid.' He was speaking to them both, but his eyes were

on Lily. 'Well, I must go, but perhaps we could dine together this evening?'

Stella hesitated, but Lily didn't. 'That would be lovely,' she said. 'Shall we see you at seven in the dining room?'

'Rather!' He touched his hat and was gone. Stella watched him walk away, leaning on his cane. Infantile paralysis, if she remembered correctly, and the lasting damage to his legs had kept him out of the war. As a result Hugh had been one of the few men studying arts in her year. He had joined the civil service and so was here in Paris while his contemporaries were still scattered across the world in uniform.

Lily took Stella's arm again. 'I'm ready for a seat. The Jardin des Tuileries is just beyond these gates. Shall we find a bench? You can tell me all about the delectable Hugh.'

'He's hardly delectable and there's nothing to tell!'

'There's always something to tell,' Lily said. 'Company for dinner on our first evening. This just gets better and better.'

# Chapter Seven

## Luneray, near Dieppe

The chief caught Corran at breakfast.

'Are you sure you don't mind going down to camp in the depths of winter, Miss Rutherford? It's rather spartan.'

'I don't mind in the slightest. I'm looking forward to it.'

He smiled. 'I believe you. If anyone can do it, you can. You'll have Captain Callaghan with you too. He's been there before, so he will keep you right.'

As she climbed into the back of the car beside Captain Callaghan later that morning, she asked him about it. He nodded.

'The chief and I took a run round all the camps when we set up this whole business. Luneray is all right, a bit of a mudbath because of the horses, but the men there are splendid.'

'So you've been here since the beginning?'

'More or less.' He had leant forward to watch their driver, freckled Miss Stevens, negotiate the tricky exit from the school. Now he sat back in his seat and turned towards Corran. They had worked together for a couple of months now, but she still knew little about him. His fingers went up and briefly touched that vivid scar that contrasted so starkly with his green eyes. 'Caught a bad one on the first day of the Somme. This is what you can see, but the shell that did this smashed a few ribs and took most of one lung as well. That was my war finished. I spent a while back home recuperating, but in the end I was going mad, my wife fussing round all the time. I was a maths master in a grammar school before the war, so I applied to come out with this scheme.' He grinned. 'Best thing I ever did.'

Her eyes went involuntarily to his side as she imagined the damage that much exist beneath his uniform. Rob had helped to care for casualties after the carnage of the Somme in 1916: perhaps he had treated Captain Callaghan. Rob had finally received some leave towards the end of that long year and came to visit her in Newcastle, the weight of his experiences in France visible in his every movement. They sat amid the dying leaves in the gardens opposite her lodgings as he spoke of the way they kept coming and coming and coming, ambulance train upon ambulance train: so many casualties that he could work through the day and through the night and never hope to treat them all.

'We were warned beforehand to empty the hospitals,' he said, a bleakness in his tone that she'd never heard before. 'They knew there would be far more casualties than we could ever deal with.' And he turned his head away from her, but not before she glimpsed the desolation in his eyes.

That was the last time he told her anything meaningful about his life in France.

She glanced across at Captain Callaghan, his hand resting

on the seat beside her, his long legs cramped and bent into the space behind the seat in front. A maths master. She pictured him in a dusty black gown at the front of a class full of unruly schoolboys.

'Where did you teach?'

'A grammar school in Manchester, where I grew up. My parents scraped and saved to give me an education they couldn't afford, so I wanted to give other boys the same opportunity.' He turned to look at her properly.

'And what of you, mysterious Miss Rutherford?' he asked. 'What brought you out here? A lady classics scholar of all things!'

Corran hesitated. The car had left the town behind and they were motoring along a long straight road with tall poplar trees lining either side. She could cite the noble reasons – doing her bit, giving something back to the boys who had sacrificed so much. Probe a little deeper, and there was a layer of grief – Jack foremost of course, but so many others she had known: so many boys from Thurso and Edinburgh and Cambridge and Newcastle that she was wounded by her inability to name them all. The helplessness caused by such relentless horror certainly created an urge to *do* something. But then she remembered the bubble of excitement that had soared when the principal in Newcastle first suggested the scheme, and knew that her true motivation had little to do with either nobility or grief. In the midst of pain, in the midst of darkness, the opportunity had shimmered before her and she had seized it with eagerness – just as she had been doing ever since she was a schoolgirl.

'I wanted to come.'

His green eyes were quizzical. 'I've known clever girls before,' he said. 'Bluestockings who would have nothing to do with the likes of me. I can't imagine them out here in their best gum boots' – this with a laughing glance at her stoutly sensible shoes – 'handling a class of men like the ones we regularly meet. It's a far cry from Oxford, after all.'

'I think that's why I'm here,' she answered, surprising herself, and then clutching the hanging strap as the car jolted uncomfortably over the increasingly broken surface. 'I will go to Oxford when this is all over and teach Latin and Greek to young ladies straight out of Cheltenham Ladies' College. But somehow, after these four years . . .'

He nodded. 'We're not so different, then, you and I,' he said. 'I could have returned to teaching youngsters who play at soldiers while their mothers pray they'll never have to fight in a real war. That's what my wife expected me to do. I don't blame her, of course. But I need to be here.' He paused. 'Now that the war is over our work really begins.'

'What do you mean?'

'Rebuilding. Creating a better world. Making sure that every single man who has served out here or at home, rich or poor, has the chance of the life he deserves. They need education, skills, help to find jobs. We must equip them for that before they return to Blighty.'

Corran was silent. After the great excitement of the armistice in November, their classes had carried on pretty much as before and it was hard sometimes to picture what peace might feel like at home. A vague image of that idyllic week in July 1914 came to mind. Sunshine and laughter and family restored. The vehemence in Captain Callaghan's tone suggested something different altogether. Rebuilding. What might it mean? But he had turned towards the passing scenery.

'God knows how they will ever repair this landscape, or what will happen to all the men who died here. Before we go home I mean to go back to the battlefields. There are some chaps I want to find, though I don't know if it will be possible.'

'I would like to do that too,' she said softly.

He looked at her. 'Someone special?'

'My brother. Jack.'

'I'm sorry.'

'Thank you.' She nearly said more about Jack, but the obstruction in her throat wouldn't let her. Instead, after a pause, she said, 'My other brother, Alex, is in the navy. He was in the Mediterranean but the last we heard his ship is making for the Baltic and the conflict there. And I have a sister in Paris who is a typist with the peace conference.'

'Another independent woman!'

'What of it?' she demanded. 'We were fortunate enough to have parents who believed in education for their daughters as well as their sons.'

'Believed in it, and could afford it, surely?'

There was no mistaking the challenge in his tone.

'Well, yes.' She hesitated. 'My father was at sea. Although he himself left school at twelve he believed passionately in education. He died when I was fifteen, but left money tied up for our education. And my mother too, she wanted her daughters to have the opportunities she was denied. It means there's never been much for anything else but my brother Alex went to naval college and the rest of us to university.' She began to feel uncomfortable: this man was drawing things out of her that she would never have discussed with such a casual acquaintance at home. Yet again here in France the usual conventions were meaningless.

'You are very fortunate, Miss Rutherford,' he said abruptly. 'Oh, I'm sure you've worked hard, and your achievements are quite exceptional. It will have been much harder for you than for a man to do all that you have done. I don't doubt that for a minute. But for many women that chance simply isn't there. My sister, Cath, for instance. She was brighter than me at school, but there was only enough money for one of us to receive higher education, and naturally it came to me.'

Naturally. She had seen it time and again. Why waste money educating a young woman for a career that must end as soon as she marries? She pushed the question aside along with the deep uneasiness it caused her. Now that the war was over, Rob would eventually come home. What then?

'What happened to your sister?'

'She left school and worked in a shop for a few years, then married a man from Glasgow. They have four kiddies. Her husband was gassed at Ypres. He can barely breathe, never mind work. The two oldest boys are in the shipyards and Cath works in a munitions factory, but it's about to close. They already struggle to pay the rent. I have no idea how they will manage.'

'I'm so sorry.' She noticed that the hand resting on the leather seat was now clenched, knuckles white. His posture, languid before, was tense and angry. She was relieved to see a miniature town of huts and tents coming into view on her side of the road. Miss Stevens had slowed the car right down, for the rutted lane was barely navigable. On one side men were exercising horses in a large field.

'And here we are,' Captain Callaghan said, and his tone was easy once more. 'The men here were mostly grooms and stable hands in civvy life. Not much in the way of past education, perhaps, but don't let that put you off. They want to learn, as long as they can see that what we teach will be of use to them. Now we'll hunt down the camp commandant and find out where he can put us. Look out for the mud.'

Camp life thrilled Corran as much as anything had done to date. While the camp commandant and Captain Callaghan were fixing up a tent ready for lectures, she found the canteen: a small hut smelling of cabbage, with damp wooden walls, a counter at one side and a faint warmth coming from the stove, around which a few men were gathered. She hesitated. The men hurried to their feet, greeting her with delight, making room for her by the stove and fussing around her. Such a welcome she had never known in any drawing room or social function in ordinary life!

'You're the first woman we've seen in such a long time, miss,' one of them explained. 'A sight for sore eyes, so you are.'

She rather enjoyed the extraordinary effect of being a woman out here in France. They appreciated her for herself, it was true, but she knew that each man welcomed her too as representative of someone dear from home – a wife, a sweetheart, a sister, even a mother. And she understood that, because was she not in some way doing exactly the same thing? Spending time with these men, and in so doing imagining herself just that tiny bit closer to Jack, to Alex, to Rob.

Lectures would begin the next day, and she and Captain Callaghan spent an hour together drawing up a poster to advertise their timetable and pinned it up for all to see. Between them they would offer daily classes in English, French, arithmetic and economics, and seek to meet any specific requests that they could possibly manage.

'The more practical the better,' Captain Callaghan advised her. She spent the evening helping in the canteen and then, so tired she could barely stand, walked over to where he was lounging by the stove amid a group of men, cigarette in hand.

'I would like to sleep now,' she said. 'Can you show me where I am to go?'

'Of course,' he said politely, rising to his feet. 'See you later, chaps.' He took her arm and led her to the doorway. The black night was interrupted by glowing globes of light where lanterns hung from the various huts and tents, revealing the duckboard in between. There was a pervasive smell of horse manure and it was raining, a slow, steady drizzle that reminded her of Edinburgh. Just before they stepped out, he stopped. For the first time since she had met him, she sensed an awkwardness about him.

'There is a small chalet in the woods they use for visitors,' he said. 'It's nothing much, mind, quite basic, but I slept like a top last time I was here.'

She laughed. 'Oh, basic doesn't bother me! As long as I can wash my face and lie down, I'll be fine. Would you show me the way?'

'Well, as it happens I'm coming too. I had an orderly take our bags along earlier.'

She was relieved. The darkness outside was overwhelming, and she hadn't much fancied finding her way alone through the dense woodland that lay just beyond the fringe of the camp.

'Let's go then,' she said. 'I'm ready to drop. I just hope we don't disturb anyone, arriving at this hour.'

Still he hesitated. 'I don't think you quite understand, Miss Rutherford,' he said, and there was no mistaking his awkwardness now. 'There are no other visitors. There will only be the two of us sleeping in the chalet.'

There was a burst of raucous laughter from the hut behind.

She looked up at him, then looked quickly away. 'Surely you see that I can't do that,' she said slowly. 'Is there nowhere here on camp?'

'Not unless you want to be in barracks with the soldiers,' he said, his embarrassment now overlaid with irritation. 'I suppose I could find somewhere else to kip, but that would leave you alone in the woods and we can't do that either. And there are no other women on camp to stay with you.' He tossed his cigarette into the darkness. 'Hang it, they should have thought of this when they dreamt of sending a woman out to France!'

That decided her. She drew herself up, and moved past him into the damp darkness. 'In that case, there's no more to be said,' she said, with more assurance than she felt. 'Please show me the way.'

He paused in the shelter of the hut to light his candle, and then held it out in front of him as he led the way without another word to where the slippery duckboard came to an end and a muddy path entered the woodland. As they moved between trees, the drizzle extinguished the candle, and the darkness became as complete as if she had descended with Orpheus into the Underworld. The trees creaked and rustled and scurried with life, but she couldn't see a thing; even the shape of the man walking unevenly in front of her merged into the void beyond. She was still angry at his manner and kept her lips tightly shut. Then he stopped, and turned, and the pallor of his face showed itself, ghostlike. He reached out a hand.

'Take my hand. It's not far now.'

The path was too narrow to walk side by side, so she stumbled along behind in the mud, her fingertips touching his. She breathed in the damp air, trying to calm both her fears and her scruples. When she had first realised they were expecting a man, she had resolved not to baulk at anything that was asked of her. This should be no different.

But what would they say in Oxford?

She didn't see the chalet until he had almost led her to its wooden step, but now she stood, shivering, in a small clearing. He dropped her hand and pushed open the door. She followed him into the narrow hallway, conscious of the thick mud dripping from her boots. With no such consideration, he strode into the first room and lit the candle again, placing it on a table. In its hesitant glow she saw into a small wooden room with bare floorboards, furnished with a table and chairs, a dresser and a couple of faded armchairs by the empty fireplace. A makeshift camp bed had been laid at one side and another door, she realised thankfully, stood open to a small WC. A wooden ladder reached up through the ceiling to the floor above.

'You shall be upstairs and I shall be downstairs,' he said, his tone now rich with amusement. 'All quite respectable, you see.'

*Hardly that*, thought Corran, as she bent to untie her boots with numb fingers, but she was determined to complain no more. She disappeared into the lavatory, which was rudimentary but no worse than those she had encountered in camp, and when she came out again saw his long legs appearing back down the ladder.

'I've been up and lit your candle,' he said. 'Your bag is waiting for you. You should be quite comfortable, Miss Rutherford.'

'Thank you,' she murmured. 'Good night.' She stepped onto the bottom rung and pulled herself up, conscious of the view he must have of her stockinged feet and ankles. She hoped the room would not be too small as she really disliked confined spaces. But as she eased herself up she found a spacious bedroom that reminded her of Jack's sloping attic room in Thurso, where the walls and ceiling were covered with his drawings. In ordinary times she would have delighted in this room: the smell of wood, the unexpectedly colourful bedspread laid over the low bed, the simple china basin on the washstand. But tonight, alone at last, she was stunned and exhausted. She removed her damp outer layers, not quite bringing herself to undress, and gingerly lay down in the bed. She could hear him moving around downstairs, preparing for bed, humming softly to himself. She wondered if he had slept up here, in this bed, on the occasion he had 'slept like a top'. She wondered if the sheets had been changed. Then she rolled the bedspread around herself, closed her eyes, and did her best to sleep.

Sleep did come, eventually, and when she woke to the sound of the birds singing in the trees outside her little room, the world, as Mother always said, seemed a brighter place in the morning. Although what Mother would think could she see her now, having spent the night alone in the woods with a man, she did not quite like to imagine. Still, there was clearly nothing else for it and they were here for the week, so she would just have to make the best of it. Captain Callaghan, after all, was a respectable married man. It would make a funny story to write to Stella, although perhaps not to Rob or even Alex. She pulled herself out of bed and padded over to the small window. Her spirits lifted as she saw that the dreich weather of the previous evening had passed, and weak winter sun glinted through the trees. She turned back and straightened her clothes – tonight she might be brave enough to undress – and looked in the glass above the washstand. The face that looked back at her was even paler than usual, and her brown eyes, which she always thought too wide-set to be attractive, were heavy. She splashed icy water onto her face, and pulled her comb from her bag. Her long dark hair was tangled but she managed to bring it into some sort of order, and pinned it up once more. She would do.

They settled into a rhythm. A good number of men had signed up for classes, with Captain Callaghan's economics lectures proving particularly popular. Corran found her days passed quickly, as she moved from teaching classes to chatting with the men, and walking around the perimeter of the camp to watch the horses being exercised. Late each evening she and Captain Callaghan made their way through the woods to their little chalet, which had something of the fairy-tale cottage about it – though, as far as she could remember, little good tended to come to forest-dwellers in fairyland! As for convention, it was strange how quickly it had ceased to matter. On the first morning she had felt a touch of her former self-consciousness as they arrived along the path together, but no one looked twice at them, and she barely thought about it now.

On the fourth evening, Captain Callaghan produced two mugs. 'Quartermaster kindly gave me a bottle of cider. Will you have a drink with me before you retire?' he asked, rather as if they had been in an Edinburgh drawing room.

It was a sign of how much had shifted over these four days that Corran barely hesitated. 'I'll have a go at lighting the fire, shall I?' she suggested. They hadn't bothered with the fire until now, simply using the chalet to sleep in, but it was damp and draughty for anything other than wrapping oneself in blankets. There was a basket of kindling by the hearth. Still wearing her coat, she dropped to her knees and soon had the fire going. The sound of liquid pouring into tin mugs was homely, somehow. She scrambled up and sat in one of the worn armchairs, gratefully accepting her mug, and took a mouthful of golden cider, fresh from the Normandy orchards. Light and shadows flickered round the walls. She pulled out her cigarettes, offering one to Arthur, and lit her own. How good it was just to sit in silence, listening to the crackle of the wood and the low rustle of the wind in the trees outside, with the hoot of an owl sounding repeatedly. Who would have thought that such a short walk away was the bustle and activity of the camp where they spent their days, and then, some miles further south-east, the battlefields that had so recently been a scene of destruction. Yet here, in this moment, was contentment.

'Penny for them.'

She shook her head. 'Not worth it. I was just thinking how perfect this little place feels . . . and how awful the world outside remains, even though peace has been declared.'

'The armistice is just the beginning,' he said. 'These four years have surely put an end to the old ways, thank God, but if we're to build a better society in their place then we have to start now.'

'I suppose so.' She looked up. 'What will you do when we return home, Captain Callaghan? Go back to teaching?'

He drank deeply from his mug. 'Call me Arthur, for God's sake,' he said, reaching for the bottle and refilling both their mugs. 'After all, we're like an old married couple in our little hut here.' He laughed at her expression. 'All most respectable of course.'

Perhaps it was the cider; perhaps it was the shadowy light that meant his green eyes were half hidden from her. Perhaps it was just tiredness after another day on her feet. She inhaled her smoke, and smiled. 'Arthur.'

He leant forward and looked into the flames, and their glow reflected on his thin face. 'I don't know what I will do. It depends whether the war really is over, doesn't it?'

'Surely it won't start up again.'

'I think a great deal hinges on the terms of this peace treaty. There's so much at stake for many different countries. How do we sort it all out, and who can be trusted to do that? And what now for Germany? This is our chance to build a better world, but judging by some of the rhetoric in the newspapers, there's every possibility it could all be derailed by nationalistic fools who want revenge.'

Revenge. The peaceful, warm feeling of the cider and the woodsmoke drifted away, and a draught rattled the shutters. She set down her mug. She should go to bed. But he reached out an arm to stop her.

'Corran – I may call you Corran, mayn't I? – forgive me. I get weighed down by it all sometimes. But there must be people you long to welcome home.'

'My brother Alex.' But oh, dear God, how her heart hurt for Jack, the boy with ink-stained fingers who would never come home.

'Anyone else? In particular?'

She knew what he was asking. 'I have a – friend,' she said slowly. 'Rob. I've known him since we were at university together years ago. He's a surgeon.'

'Fiancé?'

She shook her head and took a long drink from her mug, which seemed to have been refilled without her noticing. 'Not quite. If the war hadn't happened, perhaps. But instead I began working and Rob went off to the front, and we have hardly seen each other since.' She knew there was more to say, but she could barely articulate it to herself, never mind to Captain

Callaghan – Arthur. She let the silence stretch out, filled only by the crackling of the fire and the scrabbling of something, hopefully just a mouse, in a corner somewhere.

When he finally spoke, his voice was sombre. 'My wife. Mary. We married . . . in haste, as they say. Like you, we had a friendship; we were just getting to know each other. But then the war came and there was a new urgency. I was about to leave. We knew we might not see each other again for a long time. Perhaps ever.' He lit another cigarette. 'We were intimate. You understand. Well, of course I married her. There was never any question of that. I was still at the training camp on Salisbury Plain when she wrote and told me she had lost the baby.'

This was probably the most surprising conversation she had ever had in her life.

She waited.

'Next time I was home I realised we don't even know each other. We are strangers. I know there are romantic love stories that have come out of this war, but it has made plenty of bad marriages too.' He looked across at her then, and though it was too dark to see his expression, the scar was picked out in relief against his pale skin. 'It's not just the nations that need to rebuild: we'll all be picking up the pieces of these years for a long time to come.'

And then it was the end of the week, and time to pack up her few belongings and descend her ladder for the last time. She could smile now to think of that first evening, when a lifetime of chaperones and regulations and gossip had combined to confront her with the potential ruin of her reputation. Instead, how precious this time had been. Oh, she must treat it with caution in the retelling, but she would look back fondly on those evenings she had spent at the fireside with Arthur. She had come to appreciate his quiet wisdom, his mocking humour, and above all his passionate concern for the fortunes of the men. They had not revisited the confidences exchanged over that bottle of cider, but a deep shared trust and understanding now underpinned their more commonplace conversations. She was comfortable in his company. More than that, if she cared to admit it there was an attraction between them. A glance, a smile, the briefest touch, safely exchanged in the knowledge it would never be anything more.

At her final class she encouraged the men to draft letters seeking employment. All they wanted was to be allowed home. Some were quite sure their former jobs would be open to them; others had less certainty, and the youngest among them had barely begun to work before donning khaki.

'But they'll look after us, miss,' said a young man with the dreadful teeth that were so common. 'After all we've done, how could they not? That's what my mam says.'

Her class over, she decided to take a final walk round the camp. It was a quiet, grey day, and most of the men were engaged in some duties or other. The smell of manure assailed her as she leant on a fence and watched a grey-haired man – surely too old for his uniform – slowly walking a horse round the exercise field. They made a pair – the shuffling old man and the horse so scraggy its bones were clearly visible. It was nervy and restless, and reared up with rolling eyes when a crow landed in front of it, but the man soothed it in low, calm tones. She wondered what the horse had endured to show such fear, and was unexpectedly moved by the man's gentleness.

Walking back along the treacherous duckboard, she dipped her head into the canteen but found it empty. Arthur was giving his final economics class in the adjacent lecture tent. On a whim she slipped in at the back. This was where everyone was! The benches were crammed, and people stood around the edges. The air was thick with male breath and sweat. There were far more people here than had ever come to any of her classes – even her practical lesson on letter-writing for employment. One or two men near the back turned and moved to make way for her to pass through towards the front, but she shook her head. She didn't want to disturb him, and was happy to lurk out of sight behind a tall, burly man and listen to Arthur's words.

'Make no mistake, this was an imperialist war, a war for the division of plunder, for the seizing of colonies and financial wealth. But will we allow that to be the end result? Only those who are wilfully blind can fail to see that the old capitalist society is crumbling the world over, with socialism rising in its place. It is coming, comrades, and it cannot be stopped. Now is the time to seize what is already yours by right.'

Slowly, what she was hearing began to sink in. No wonder his lectures had been popular! This was not economics – this was pure socialism, even Bolshevism, which every man in that tent knew was a forbidden subject in the army. Arthur would be sent home at once if the authorities knew, and only the fact he was not under the auspices of the army any more might prevent him being court-martialled.

'A new society,' he had said to her. 'The old ways are gone; things will be different.' And it had sounded so reasonable, and she had gone along with him, for she believed as much as he did that education for all was a noble aim. But *this* was far more than education for all. This was revolution; this was what had torn apart the empires and nations of eastern Europe, spreading murder, torture and destruction wherever it went. This was what Alex even now was fighting to defeat. The newspapers were full of it. Was that really what Arthur wanted for them in Britain?

She confronted him in the car on the way back to Dieppe. The driver who had brought the car was staying in camp for a few days, and Arthur was driving them home.

'I listened to part of your lecture.'

He didn't seem abashed, just mildly amused. 'And what did you think?'

'I see now why your economics classes were so popular! Surely it's not wise to be spreading such inflammatory ideas among the men. You'll be sent home if they hear what you're doing.'

'I don't worry about that.'

'And revolution?' she demanded. 'Does that not worry you?'

He turned towards her, heedless of the road, his eyes clear and combative. 'Not as much as it might worry you.'

'What on earth do you mean by that?'

'Look at America, look at France – they had to live through revolution to create the democracies they have today. We're entering a new world, Corran, and birth pangs are never easy. Some will march into it, and some will be dragged there kicking and screaming. But make no mistake, those who were most comfortable in the old capitalist world will find change the hardest.'

'My family has worked for everything we have!'

'That's not an argument that holds much water any more, is it? Look round our society and find me someone who hasn't worked, hasn't sacrificed, over these years. But for all that, power is *still* in the hands of those who want the old inequalities to remain, because it suits their own interests. All I'm doing is preparing these men to get what they're owed when they return. And yes, to seize it, if necessary.'

She turned away, disturbed. Perhaps his motives were good, but revolution was dangerous talk that could only lead to violence. And dear God, they had seen enough violence these four years to last them a lifetime. Was it really so wrong to long for peace to come, and life to return to normal? Not exactly how it was, of course; social conditions should be improved. But no more violence. Please.

She glanced back at him. His shoulders were tense and his white knuckles stood out as he gripped the steering wheel. The chalet in the woods had felt like a fairy tale, and perhaps she had been bewitched. Now the spell was broken. Today she could sense the molten anger simmering beneath the surface of the man beside her, and all at once she was anxious to return to Dieppe, to the everyday conversations in the school, and to the deep green sea that lapped all the way to England. White cliffs, chalky but firm, holding back the waves and waiting for all the battle-scarred men and women to return, weary but thankful, to home.

Surely that was how it would be?

# Chapter Eight

Paris

In January, their work finally began.

The pleasures of the Hôtel Majestic and Paris were all very well, but as days slipped into weeks, their typewriters remained untouched. The newspapers at home kicked up a fuss, demanding to know the reason for the delay. Who was paying for all these staff members to have an extended holiday in Paris? But today they would at last get started.

Stella and Lily dressed quickly, Lily humming 'If You Were the Only Girl in the World'. Stella looked at her reflection in the mirror and smiled. Inspired by the sight of several other women in the hotel, she had summoned the courage last week to have her long, heavy hair bobbed. She loved the result, but it was a strange sensation to get used to. She had had long hair for as long as she could remember, yanked painfully into two plaits for many years and then pinned into an uncomfortable knot on her head as a symbol of womanhood. This new style felt wonderfully fresh and freeing. Lily admired the elegant results, but refused to follow her example.

'If I had your hair I wouldn't want to either,' Stella said, with a glance at Lily's long blonde locks.

When they entered the Astoria, the unpleasant smell still lingered, but it carried with it a whiff of purpose now as they filed up the wooden stairs towards their typewriters. The atmosphere in the Astoria was very different to the colour and fun of the Majestic. Here all was determination and efficiency: doors slammed, voices barked orders, telephones rang and folders marked *TOP SECRET* passed quickly from one hand to another. Miss Bingham led them into the same long corridor as before, and Stella saw that handwritten labels had been tacked to most doors. The door to the long typing room they had seen on their first visit stood open. Miss Bingham paused on the threshold and addressed the group of expectant women.

'You will spend much of your time on this corridor, typing up the reports, minutes and correspondence of various commissions of the British delegation,' she said. 'Sometimes those of you with shorthand will also be called upon to attend sessions and take notes. I need not emphasise yet again the significant and confidential nature of your work. In many cases you will be privy to sensitive information before even the delegates and plenipotentiaries. There must be no idle chatter, no divulging of the content of your work in letters home, and certainly no speaking to newspaper men. Anyone caught breaching regulations in this way will be dismissed, and may face criminal charges. You must be alert at all times, particularly as the government has *not* chosen here in the Astoria, as in the Majestic, to replace the local French staff with people from home.' A tightening of her lips revealed what she thought of that decision. 'A lecture has been arranged for you on Thursday evening on the subject of spies. The dangers you face and the precautions you must take will be laid out to you. Attendance is compulsory.' And then she smiled, and her face softened. 'But now, let me allocate you to your rooms. Let's see . . .'

Miss Bingham looked down at her clipboard, and Stella and Lily found themselves in Typing Room 3 along with two others: dark-haired Anne-Marie Harrison, whom they had not met before, and a tall, languid woman who had introduced herself at the tepid New Year's Eve dance as Lady Mabel Lees. Their office had once been a single bedroom, and only just had room for four chairs and folding desks, each with a typewriter. A world map was pinned on one wall, and against the opposite wall stood a stained washbasin with ornate mirror above. They hung their coats on a coat stand in the corner and Stella walked towards the one tall window. With a thrill she saw that it looked towards the Arc de Triomphe. Miss Bingham appeared in the open doorway, this time bearing a pile of documents, which she placed in a tray.

'You may begin with these,' she said. 'When you have completed a document, place it in this other tray to be collected by the couriers. You will work on the material provided here unless any senior member of the delegation requires you for a different purpose. You will never remove any paper from this room without permission. Lunch will be back at the Majestic at 12.30 p.m. Make a start, girls, your work has begun!'

Stella took the top document from the pile and sat

down at her typewriter, her fingers trembling slightly as she inserted a sheet of typing paper into the machine. It was an Underwood, rather than the Remington she had been familiar with at Hoster's, so would take a little getting used to. She grinned across at Lily. How absolutely marvellous it all was. She remembered Frank the American soldier on Peace Day, and his conviction that they would do something really worthwhile here. Well, a month had passed, but as her fingers tentatively found their place on the keys, she was ready to type her way into a new Europe, a new world, where nations would come together to fashion everlasting peace.

She skimmed the document before her. Mrs Hoster had taught her always to read each page in full before beginning, identifying anything that might disrupt her flow as she typed – an unfamiliar word, a doubtful spelling. It all seemed straightforward enough. It contained the minutes of a meeting of members of the British delegation, which urged that, for strategic and security reasons, the island of Cyprus must remain a British possession. Stella glanced up at the map on the wall and focused in on the Mediterranean, then began to type. She knew where Cyprus was, of course, and had a vague idea that Britain had become involved there some time last century as a peacemaker between the Turks and the Russians. She had not, however, realised how important the island was, guarding as it did the Suez Canal and the major trade route to British India. The paper set out unequivocally the strategic importance of Cyprus to British interests and the need for stable government in this turbulent area. It was so much more interesting than medical terms!

Nevertheless, for a while she could have been back in

Hoster's, working to the rattling machine-gun fire of typewriter keys. It was Mabel who first broke the spell. Pushing back her chair, she sighed and reached into her handbag.

'Dear Lord, I never imagined this would be so dull! Time for a cig break.'

Stella had just finished her first document, so carefully removed it from the typewriter and carried it over to the tray before pulling out one of her own cigarettes.

'Mine was rather interesting.'

'Oh, it's not the *content*,' Mabel said. 'It's the endless monotony, tip tip tip, tap tap tap, tip tip tip. I could be typing the latest John Buchan thriller and still be bored. Really, I do hope we get to see a bit of the action. I must have a word with old Bing, get myself into one of those sessions at the Quai d'Orsay.'

Stella said nothing. Of course, she too hoped at some point to attend the actual conference sessions but really, what had Mabel expected? She looked across at the taller woman standing at the window with her cigarette in its diamond-encrusted holder, and reflected that she was exactly the sort of aristocratic type who rarely lasted long at Hoster's. Mabel had sat down beside them at the New Year's Eve dance in the Majestic, which had promised much and delivered little. Rumours of men from the British Embassy joining them had turned out to be unfounded, much to their disappointment. As the Majestic filled up it became clear that women far outnumbered men.

'It's more like a convent than a conference at the moment,' was Lily's grumble, as her hope of meeting suitors away from the disapproving gaze of her father began to disappear.

Still, Lily never lacked for dance partners, and Stella had been sitting alone when Mabel joined her, just as a line of waiters brought in trays of food and placed them at one end of the glittering room.

'I do wish the food here were a little less British, don't you?' Mabel said, looking with distaste at the sandwiches and sausage rolls. 'Surely a French chef or two wouldn't hurt – after all, the French are our allies; they will hardly spy on us! The meals are atrocious.'

Stella looked at her in surprise. She had never before eaten as well as this last month at the Majestic! To think of this evening's dinner – five courses, beginning with hors d'oeuvres and ending with ices – and to compare it with the grim food she had eaten at the club in London was laughable. Even at home food was on the plain side. *There are starving children who would be grateful for what you have* – that was her mother's voice.

*Yes, and those starving children are not so very far away.* She thought of the thin and ragged groups she had seen in the streets of Paris, and even more so of the disturbing stories beginning to emerge from Germany about the effects of the Allied blockade. She mentioned this to Mabel, who brushed her aside with a disdainful hand.

'Squeeze Germany until the pips squeak. They caused this war so they must pay.' Then her tone changed. 'Freddie darling! Dance with me, won't you? Let's liven this place up a little.'

Stella looked up and saw the blonde man she had noticed on that first morning. He led Mabel onto the dance floor with a wink and a smile in her direction. She had seen him around the Majestic, always in the thick of conversation. He really was very attractive, and she resolved to find out more about him. But just then Lily whirled over and dropped into a seat, laughing. Hugh followed behind. This had evidently been the pianist's grand finale. An officer in uniform emerged from behind the screen of palm trees, and stood wiping his forehead with a handkerchief and demanding a stiff drink. The energy slid out of the evening as the minutes ticked by towards midnight. Stella felt tired, but it wasn't possible to slip off to bed on this night of all nights. From the time when she and Jack had been considered old enough to stay up, Hogmanay had been the most special night of the year. She could hardly bear to think of her home with the fire blazing, and the sitting room overflowing with family and friends, and music and singing and the first foot arriving after midnight. But those days were long gone. Hogmanay 1914 had arrived with a mingling of horror and hope. Each successive New Year had come and gone with deeper loss and the grim disbelief that the living nightmare had not yet ended.

Sitting now at her typewriter, Stella recalled the moment the lights had gone out in the ballroom, cutting across the chatter and producing gasps and screams. Two waiters had walked in, carrying a huge flaming punch bowl between them. They placed it on a table that had been brought into the middle of the room, and everyone gathered round.

The fluttering and the flirting and the dresses and the dances were gone, ethereal wisps consumed by the fierce flames that blazed from the punch bowl.

In the grand foyer outside, a clock began to chime, its note deep and sonorous. Stella curled her fingers tightly into her palms. The circle of men and women stood in silence as its chimes sounded out for the end of 1918: the end of bloodshed and fighting, grief and heartache. The end of war.

Twelve chimes. Twelve months.

Last Hogmanay had been a tidal wave of horror.

This New Year she could scarcely believe she had lived through a whole year that had not contained Jack in any tiny part.

The final note died away and the lights slowly flickered into life again. As the waiters handed out glasses of warm punch, she looked around. Lily, Hugh. Miss Bingham. Lady Mabel. Other pale faces she hardly knew, each one surely with his or her own ghosts for company. She watched as the present tussled with the past for supremacy. When the glasses clinked, when the toasts were declaimed – the King, the peace, the future – something had changed. The frivolity was strained. They joined hands all in a big circle, Hugh on her right and Lily on her left, and sang 'Auld Lang Syne' – and Stella's heart nearly broke to hear something at once so familiar and so alien. Where were the warm cadences of home?

Where was Jack?

That had been the dawning of the new year, but now in this room she could make her own contribution to the new world. She lifted her next document, and as she did so, the door opened. She looked up. 'Hugh!'

'Here you are!' he said, looking across the room at Lily. She was leaning over her typewriter in concentration, and ignored him as her fingers flew over the keys. Only when she had completed the page did she lift her head, tucking a stray strand of long blonde hair behind her ear as she did so. 'Isn't this thrilling?'

Hugh leant against the doorframe. 'It's chaotic upstairs. Grand to get started properly, though. Our office is on the floor above this one, but you have to pick your way through boxes and maps to find it. I'm looking for Miss Bingham – any idea where I would find her?'

'Next door, I think,' Stella said. 'That's the main typing room.'

'Thank you. I need a couple of scribes for meetings this afternoon.'

Mabel was facing the mirror, and hadn't turned when Hugh entered. Still looking at his reflection, she said, 'God, ask for me, won't you? You would do me such a favour.'

Stella caught Lily's eye and tried not to laugh.

Hugh loosened his tie slightly. 'I don't imagine that's my decision,' he said slightly stiffly, then turned back to Lily. 'I must go, but I may see you back at the Majestic for lunch.'

'Almost certainly.'

Stella watched Hugh lean on his cane as he walked away, then turned her attention to her work once more.

Mabel picked up another document and paused by Lily's desk. '*Someone* has an admirer.'

Lily coloured slightly. 'Nonsense,' she said. 'Stella and Hugh were at university together. He was speaking to all of us.'

Stella agreed as she inserted a fresh sheet of paper, but she reflected that Mabel was absolutely right. Hugh's enthusiasm for Lily was second only to his enthusiasm for President Wilson and his fourteen points, upon which he expounded at the slightest opportunity. Despite his claim to have no influence, she would be surprised if Lily didn't find herself taking minutes, if not at this afternoon's meeting then some time fairly soon. Stella suppressed a smile, fairly sure that Lily's sights were set far higher than a junior member of the delegation. Would that be what it took to sit in on discussions – an admirer? If so, she might be waiting a long time! Her hand went up unconsciously to her bare neck. She loved her new hairstyle but she sensed amusement and even judgement in some glances cast her way. Jack would have laughed, she was sure of it, but he would have supported her too. But then, as always happened, thoughts of Jack led to thoughts of the last time she had seen him. She closed her eyes as she fought for control, then opened them again to scan the sheet in front of her.

This document concerned the ongoing war in Russia, its invasion of neighbouring countries including Estonia and Ukraine, and the exclusion of the Bolshevik government from participation in the conference. Russia, where the brother she hadn't seen in such a long time was even now sailing into more danger. For a moment the ongoing relentlessness of it all threatened to overwhelm her. She took a breath, and focused her attention on the document. A list of key Russian exiles living in the area of Paris now known as little Russia: she would have to take care with the spellings. She glanced out of the window. This city really had become the centre of the world.

The rest of the morning sped by, and soon it was time to return to the Majestic for lunch. They hunched against the sharp winter wind as they hurried the short distance between the two hotels. It was a relief to show their security passes and step into the warmth of the grand foyer of the Majestic. Stella and Anne-Marie slipped off to the cloakroom while the others wandered into the dining room for lunch. They reached the cloakroom at the same time as an older woman, and stood aside to allow her to enter ahead of them. The woman smiled and uttered a quick '*Merci*', but even as Stella wondered where she had seen her before, Anne-Marie gasped. Stella gave her a curious glance but Anne-Marie, her face pink, shook her head.

The high-ceilinged dining room was a lively place at lunchtime, with chatter bouncing off the walls and laughter slipping through the palm trees. Stella looked around to find her friends, and waved across at Hugh, who was seated with some of his own colleagues. After a month of living together, she recognised many members of the delegation now, but there were always other people around the hotel too – a smattering of army and navy personnel of the various Allied nations; journalists with their notebooks, anxious for a story; campaigners trying to press their particular cause earnestly over a bowl of soup. She walked slowly through, picking up snatches of conversation from the different tables, as everything from the rising price of toothpaste to the borders of Romania mingled into some rich, meaty aroma. The new world was being created right here, right now, in this dining room. And she was part of it.

As the waiter pulled out her chair, she noticed the woman from the cloakroom sitting with a group of older ladies at a nearby table. They didn't look like typists and they couldn't be delegates.

She leant across to Anne-Marie. 'You recognised that lady, didn't you?'

'That's Marguerite de Witt-Schlumberger,' Anne-Marie said at once. 'She's an absolute beacon in the French women's suffrage movement, rather like our Millicent Fawcett. The others are probably from the French Union for Women's Suffrage.'

'How do you know?' Lily asked.

'My mother is French. She disapproves but I think they're marvellous.'

'I didn't know you were half-French!'

'*Mais oui!*' Anne-Marie laughed. 'I'm sure that's why I was employed, because I certainly can't type as quickly as the rest of you! I was in awe this morning. I'm bilingual, though, so I imagine I'll be needed for translation duties at some point.' She glanced across at the other table again. 'I wonder what they're doing here? I'm sure there's more to it than a cup of tea.'

Stella had followed her gaze and so when the grey-haired woman in the plaid dress sensed their scrutiny and lifted her head, their eyes met. There was a directness in the older woman's gaze that was startling, and then she smiled at their table and gave a definite nod.

'Did you see that?' Anne-Marie hissed, pushing back her chair. 'She noticed us. I'm going to speak to her.' She was away for some time.

Back at their own table, the typists discussed various

entertainments being planned in the hotel – amateur dramatics and a concert, with a call for contributions.

'I'd much rather dance,' said Lily. 'I love the new dances, and the dance lessons we're having are a scream, aren't they? I wonder when the next dance will be.'

'I believe there's to be one on Saturday. I—' Stella stopped as Anne-Marie returned, her face flushed with excitement. 'Well?'

'I was right. They are French representatives of the International Women's Suffrage Alliance, and they're calling for the vital role played by women over the last four years to be acknowledged. There's a salon on Thursday evening, and they've invited us all to attend. Do come along.'

'A salon?' Mabel laughed. 'Too dull for words. Things are really poor if I can't find a better option for Thursday than that!'

Lily also shook her head. 'My French isn't nearly good enough,' she said. 'Yours isn't too bad, Stella. You go, and you can tell me about it afterwards.'

'Please come, Stella,' Anne-Marie begged. 'I don't want to go alone.'

'My French isn't great either.'

'I'll translate for you. Come on, we can't say no to Madame de Witt-Schlumberger. You might as well refuse the King.'

Three days later, Stella and Anne-Marie stepped out arm in arm into the darkness of a Paris evening. Miss Bingham had given permission, asking them to be sure to tell her all about it. It had begun snowing earlier that day, and the pavements were white and slippery underfoot, while snowflakes continued to dance in the streetlamps.

'The salon is in an apartment she has rented,' said Anne-Marie. 'Many diplomats and visitors have taken apartments in Paris, which has made the city's housing crisis even worse.'

'Where does she usually live?'

'In Alsace. Her family remained when the Germans took over. They refused to abandon the workers in their factories there. I did hear that she sent each of her sons to live with relatives when they reached sixteen to avoid them being conscripted into the German army.'

'I suppose I've seen the war from a British perspective, really,' Stella admitted. 'One doesn't think much about what it was like for the French.'

'It was dreadful,' Anne-Marie said simply. 'One in four young men killed, and then there are the industries destroyed, the mines flooded, the villages and farms and crops that are laid to waste. I have no idea how this land will ever recover.' She stopped. 'But here we are.'

The women paused and looked up at the apartment block, ornately carved in creamy stone. Lights blazed from tall windows on the first floor. Anne-Marie pushed the door and they entered a communal hallway, with a staircase curving its way around a central lift.

'It's the first floor. Let's take the stairs,' she whispered. With arms linked, they climbed the steps and arrived at a door that stood slightly ajar. There was the muffled sound of conversation and laughter.

'Should we just go in?'

Anne-Marie shook her head, and rapped on the door.

Almost immediately a young maid appeared.

'*Entrez, par ici,*' she said, taking their damp coats and ushering them along a hallway with gleaming polished floor, and into a crowded room on the left – the room from which light had shone into the street below.

Tight rows of chairs faced the tall windows, where Madame de Witt-Schlumberger and a couple of others sat facing their audience. All the seats were taken. Stella and Anne-Marie squeezed into the space between the final row of chairs and the wall, where a few other women already stood. The atmosphere in the room was warm and thick, as the intense heat from the stove accentuated the mingled scents of perfume and sweat. Madame de Witt-Schlumberger rose to her feet.

'*Bonsoir, mes amies,*' she began.

At first Stella tried to listen, but as she had suspected her French was not nearly good enough. Fairly soon she decided there was no point in concentrating when Anne-Marie could fill her in later. Instead, she looked around the room. The shutters remained open and she could see the snow falling more thickly now, with some flakes sliding down the tall windows and creating a little white trough on the sill. She noticed a grand piano in one corner, but most other furniture had been pushed back against the walls to make space for rows of chairs. As for Madame de Witt-Schlumberger, she spoke for a long time, giving Stella ample opportunity to observe her. She had a long, serious face and used her hands expressively to illustrate her point. The audience mostly listened in respectful silence, but there were occasional murmurs of agreement or indignation, and once a ripple of laughter. No men were present, but there were women of all ages and, judging by the voices, of many different nationalities.

No longer paying attention to the stream of French words, Stella was caught by surprise when Madame de Witt-Schlumberger sat down. After a round of applause, another woman rose to her feet. She read from a piece of paper, and was followed by a longer spell of applause. It seemed appropriate to join in.

Stella turned to Anne-Marie. 'Is it finished?'

Anne-Marie's cheeks were flushed and her eyes sparkling. 'Wasn't she *splendid*?'

The buzz of chatter rose around them and the woman on their left moved out of the row.

'We should go,' Stella said. 'We mustn't miss curfew.'

Some women lingered chatting in the room, but most were leaving. This was not a social occasion and the business was at an end. The girl who had let them in distributed coats and hats in the polished hallway. As Stella and Anne-Marie waited their turn, Madame de Witt-Schlumberger herself turned back from bidding someone else farewell. About to pass them, she stopped.

'Ah. My friends from the Majestic. You are members of the British delegation, yes? *Très bien*. That may yet be useful. Did you find the evening informative?'

Her blue eyes were piercing and Stella felt herself blush. 'I didn't quite – that is—' She turned to Anne-Marie for help.

Her friend beamed, a huge smile. 'Oh, it was wonderful! My friend Stella has little French but I will share your plans with her.'

Their hostess nodded and moved away. As she did so she said something in French to Anne-Marie, who glanced at Stella, laughed and replied. They wrapped up warmly and descended the stairs out into the Paris night. The snow had stopped falling and everywhere was shrouded in a soft, thick whiteness. It reflected its eerie light around them, while the black branches of trees were delicately decorated with a frosting of white.

'It's beautiful.'

As they walked beneath glowing streetlamps, Anne-Marie explained the purpose of the meeting. 'Her campaign is for women to be fully part of the discussions and decision-making of the treaties. She says it's a disgrace that women, without whom the war would never have been won, are now excluded from the peacemaking. She fears that without involvement of women, the peacemakers will concentrate on the wrong areas.'

'What sort of areas?'

'Oh, so many! She fears the delegates will get caught up in the same old struggles over territory and power and revenge, when we have a unique chance to improve the welfare and safety of all peoples. Women's issues are already being ignored, despite the dreadful impact of war crimes like rape, torture and slavery on women in particular. And then many countries still exclude women from participating in their political process. Madame has written to President Wilson to ask for a meeting, and for representation of women on all the committees. He's the obvious person – he has such influence and authority, and speaks often of a new world. Someone read out the text of her letter and I really don't see how he can fail to be moved by it. It's marvellous.'

They paused to cross Avenue Kléber and approached the Hôtel Majestic. Yellow light streamed from tall windows onto the snowy pavement, and some young American soldiers were throwing snowballs at each other on the street outside. Stella and Anne-Marie dodged them and showed their passes to the doorman. As they entered, Stella unwound her thick woollen scarf from her neck and Anne-Marie laughed.

'That reminds me. As we left, Madame said she was sure you would be a good supporter of our cause.'

'Why on earth? She has never met me before.'

'Because of your hair.'

Stella's hand went quickly to the sharp, smooth line of her bob, exposed now by the removal of her scarf. 'My *hair*? But that's ridiculous. It's just a hairstyle. I wanted something quick in the mornings. It doesn't mean – well, it doesn't mean a thing.'

'It's never just a hairstyle, Stella. Your hair told Madame all she needed to know about you. You must tell me where you had it done. I'm determined to have mine cut too, although my mother will weep.'

Stella was silent, and utterly bemused. They collected their room keys from reception. The sound of a piano and muted laughter and chatter drifted over, but Stella was tired. Her mind whirled with impressions of the evening and with all that Anne-Marie had told her, and tomorrow she must get up and go back to the Astoria for another full day's typing.

'I think I'll go to bed.'

'Thank you for coming,' Anne-Marie said as she slipped off her coat. 'It will be quite something to say we were present at the meeting that led to women being included in the peace conference.'

As Stella climbed the stairs, she wondered. Anne-Marie seemed quite sure, inspired by her French heroine, but would President Wilson really listen?

What if he didn't?

# Chapter Nine

## Near Arras

There was just enough moonlight to light his way along the rutted, broken track. One foot after the other and watch those ankles. He wasn't drunk, exactly, but that wine was powerful, as well as bloody good. Rob clasped the final bottle against his chest. How Gus had managed to find an untouched cellar after four years of war was anyone's guess, but he always was a lucky wee blighter.

In the distance, across the fields, he could see the glow of the miniature city of tents and huts that made up the hospital. He had been moved up the line from the clearing station to a bigger camp not far from Arras. Still the casualties came his way, wave upon wave upon wave of men broken by their time in the trenches: broken in body, broken in mind. With rotting corpses and body parts seeping into water supplies, the cases of disease were increasing, and meantime there wasn't a day went past without another poor bugger blown up by one of the unexploded shells carpeting the ground. More and more, though, it was influenza that confronted him. This terrifying Spanish flu swept through the camps, attacking already weakened men with an effectiveness far beyond anything the enemy had managed. By the time they reached him they were usually vomiting blood and turning blue, and there was little he could do.

The war might be over for now, but this battle had a long way left to run.

A half-broken wall ran alongside the lane here, and he paused for a moment to lean against it. He took his knife from his pocket and eased the cork from the bottle. Another mouthful slid down his throat, just to see him home. And a little more, to make sure the wine wouldn't slosh out of the bottle as he walked. Spending the evening with Gus, his teammate, dear God it had been wonderful, but it was also like ripping open a wound as you tore off the bandage, exposing all that festered below.

They had begun their evening in the remains of a bar in Arras, but the whores were insistent and that wasn't what either of them wanted this evening. So Gus took him back to his lodging in the ground floor of what had once been a grand townhouse, and they drank fine French wine straight from the bottles and laughed too loudly about their schooldays through a fog of cigarette smoke. Swapping memories of lessons and masters and dinners and beatings, and most of all of playing rugby together. At first they'd been fresh-faced youngsters who followed the First XV boys round like eager puppies, hero-worshipping the likes of Sandy Morrison and Puss Milroy. The years passed and they became grandees of the First XV themselves, and those days were surely the best days: on top of the school, on top of the world, winning every match they played and striding arm in arm down Morningside Road, exchanging knowledge of which pubs would serve them. They went their separate ways but Gus was soon invited to play for Scotland, and Rob a few years later. The ultimate honour. Watsonian boys made up the core of that pre-war Scotland rugby team, with wee Jimmy Pearson and Tommy Bowie alongside them too.

Sandy. Killed at Loos in 1915.

Puss. Blown apart on the Somme in 1916.

And Jimmy, Gus's closest friend and centre partner, shot by a sniper near Ypres while fetching water, of all things.

'You'd think he could have fucking dodged it, Jimmy dancing feet,' Gus said, swigging his wine. Then he banged down his bottle, reached across and grabbed Rob's arm with a ferocity that recalled his fearless commitment as a player. 'We're fucking going to play for Scotland again, Rob. God knows how we cobble a team together, but it's the only thing that's kept me going these last months. You've come through and so have I, and we are going to pull on the thistle again and we are going to pick up a rugby ball, and we are going to smash them all off the bloody park.'

Then he put his head down on his arms and wept.

The lights of the camp were closer now, and Rob's pace slowed. He was going nowhere near the mess with a bottle as fine as this, and he wasn't ready to sleep yet either. The clouds had cleared completely and the sky was scattered with stars, a million pinpricks of light that had tenaciously kept shining down on four years of hellish darkness below. He took another long drink. No flashes rent the sky; no crash of guns shuddered through his feet, but still the explosions sounded in his head.

Gus had wanted to speak about the future. Rob wasn't yet sure he believed in a future. He thought back to that crazy day when he'd watched the German peace convoy pass through France. They had declared an armistice a few days later, but it seemed to Rob that the peace conference was every bit as likely to grind to a halt as the convoy itself had been, scuppered by a clapped-out old machine. The politicians used fine words, speaking of a League of Nations that would put an end to power struggles and to war – and at the very same time more soldiers were sent to bolster the troops in eastern Europe, where fighting still raged. This blessed silence on the Western Front was likely no more than a pause.

The men meanwhile just wanted to go home. He wondered about that. Home. He'd hardly had a moment to think about it since the guns fell silent, but Gus had asked him tonight, 'Will you go back to Edinburgh? Marry your sweetheart?'

The question rang its pounding echo in his head. What did he want? What didn't he want? That might be easier to answer. There was no place at all in his frightened glimpse into the future for the surgeon he had once been, setting the collarbones and extracting the appendixes of the good people of Edinburgh, and not only because his hands still shook now the guns had fallen silent. Whenever he tried to imagine operating in such a safe and clean environment, he was instead knee deep in poisoned water at the foot of the shell hole that served as his aid post. An incessant kaleidoscope of images was burnt on his retinas. Peterson's startled, ragdoll body flying through the air towards him. The major crouched behind the latrines. The Irish lad screaming as Rob sliced away the thin tendon by which his foot dangled impossibly from his leg. The terrified eyes of the Boche prisoners he'd ordered to act as stretcher bearers, carrying the wounded back through their own relentless fire.

Where could he turn after such horror?

Over these past months he'd grown ever more frustrated by his own feeble efforts, knowing all the time that he was leaving men with scars and disfigurements that would blight the rest of their lives. He had sat with lads whose faces had been ripped to shreds and who wished they were dead, and others who had lost limbs simply because there was no way of getting them to the treatment that would have saved them. He had longed for the skill, the time and the equipment to help them properly. Perhaps there was somewhere at home he could do so.

*Will you go back to Edinburgh? Marry your sweetheart?*

Corran. Such a long time since he had seen her. The bottle was nearly empty; he might as well just finish it off, leaning on the rubble and looking up at the stars. She was like no other woman he had ever met. He pictured her, tall, with her hair drawn off her face and her steady gaze, which was so direct, so incisive. He loved her intelligence and her quiet determination: look at all she had achieved, none of it easy. She had such an insatiable thirst for knowledge that she had questioned him about the intricacies of his medical exams, really wanting to understand. The only time he had seen her disinterested had been when he took her to that rugger match, and that was hardly surprising. A man's game.

They'd been friends for years but it was during the week he spent in her family home on the north coast that he made up his mind to marry her. It was shortly after midsummer, and the clear light stretched each day into the hours that should be night-time. He felt as if he were suspended, with Corran, in some golden, unending, captivating paradise. On his last evening with her they stayed out late in the garden overlooking the shimmering sea. Below them on the shore they could see her young brother and sister. Corran was pensive, drinking in the beauty of the evening, and telling him stories of the north. In the morning he would leave for a hotel twenty miles away where he was booked in for a few days of fishing and shooting. It had seemed a good idea when he organised the trip, but now he really didn't want to go. The youngsters were picking their way over the rocks; they would be back soon. The midnight sun glinted on her hair as they kissed. He very nearly asked her at that moment but he thought he should buy a ring and do it properly. Only then war was on the horizon, and it seemed better to wait. It would all be over by Christmas.

As a surgeon, he would probably have enlisted anyway, but here in the broken darkness his skin was clammy as he remembered the fervour and madness of those early weeks. The whole Watsonian rugby team and most of the Scottish team joined up within days of the declaration of war. *Play the game . . . do your duty . . . serve your country . . . just the kind of tough, disciplined lads we need.* The language of rugby and the language of war merged, and they might have been making plans for an upcoming tournament. The comradeship that had carried them through exhilarating wins and devastating losses had, in August 1914, marched them as one to the recruiting station.

Or almost as one.

Only John MacCallum, Rob's hero, hard as nails, stood out. How they scorned him for it.

Perhaps only John had understood.

It hadn't been over by Christmas and now here he was, four and a half years later, still in France. Unmarried. The wine was long finished. Rob lobbed the bottle into the field to land among far more deadly debris and then ducked backwards, hands covering his head, just in case. Gus wanted to talk about the future. Corran was the only part of a future he had once envisaged that was still waiting for him. Although they had only seen each other a couple of times during the war – and last time he had been convalescing and not much good for anything – she had written to him faithfully with news of her doings in Newcastle and Thurso. Now, rather unexpectedly, she was here in France. He must find a way to meet her.

But as for rugby?

That was much harder to imagine.

# Chapter Ten

## Paris

Now that the conference had started in earnest, the typists worked long hours. They had only one half-day off a week, but would each have a couple of days' leave on a rota over the next few months. As yet, the four women in Stella's typing room had not been called for any other duties and sat at their machines day after day as the air grew more stale and the pile of documents to be typed grew ever higher. Little hard blisters had formed on the tips of Stella's fingers and increasingly she worked mechanically, without taking in the import of what she was typing. And then, when they had rushed back to the Majestic with barely time to change for dinner, there was generally some entertainment or other in the evenings. Last night had been a concert, and tonight's dinner would be followed by a dance. They were surrounded by a discordant symphony: the clatter of typewriter keys, the ringing of the reception bell, a march bashed out on the piano or the latest hesitation waltz, and always, always, the chatter of a hundred voices.

It almost drowned out Jack's voice, but she could hear him nevertheless.

At least the standard of the dances had improved since the unimpressive affair at Hogmanay. Stella and Lily had become used to seeing famous people around the hotel, and stifled their giggles at the sight of Sir Henry Wilson and Marshal Foch practising the sailor's hornpipe together.

'Doesn't Foch seem ordinary, though?' Lily said. 'He's so small and insignificant looking.'

Small, insignificant and powerful. It was true. As they passed these men in the corridors and at dinner, it was hard to believe that so many lives had been extinguished over the last four years on the orders of such unimposing, elderly individuals. And the future still rested on their shoulders. Stella shivered and took a sip of her gin just as a new party entered the room and took seats in a corner nearby: the British prime minister, David Lloyd George, and his secretary, Frances Stevenson, trailed by his teenage daughter, Megan. They had a private apartment just round the corner on rue Nitot, and often joined the delegation in the evenings. Stella watched as tall, dashing General Smuts from South Africa crossed the floor and with a little bow extended his hand to Megan Lloyd George, who blushed but got to her feet with all the awkwardness of her sixteen years, and allowed herself to be led around the dance floor. The Prime Minister himself did not dance, but contented himself with watching his daughter and exchanging remarks with the many delegates who pressed near him like moths around a gas lamp.

Stella turned her attention to Miss Stevenson, whom she found far more interesting. She sat beside the Prime Minister, simply dressed in soft green, with her hair curling back from her face and a tiny smile on her lips. It had been a surprising move for Mr Lloyd George to employ a woman rather than a man as his private secretary, even in wartime. To Stella, Frances Stevenson was a fine example of the opportunities that now existed for well-trained professional women. Perhaps when the conference was over she could get a similar position as a private secretary: not to the Prime Minister, of course, but to some important diplomat or businessman. They would travel together in luxury across the world and meet interesting people.

Her dreams were disturbed by Mabel sitting down beside her. She had noticed Stella's gaze. 'They say she's far more than his secretary, you know,' she said. 'Must be rather uncomfortable for the daughter, don't you think?'

Stella felt her cheeks flush. 'Surely not.'

'You watch them. It's the little glances they give each other – see, even there, see the way he's resting his fingers against hers. She's his mistress, you mark my words. And otherwise, why is his wife not in Paris? Even the new Mrs Wilson is here.'

Stella wanted to protest, but Mabel had already moved into conversation with someone else. She looked at Miss Stevenson again. Was it true? Was she naïve and foolish to hope to gain such a position using her brain alone? Would any man who employed her as his secretary also expect to take her to his bed? But then she thought of Mrs Hoster, and her determination to equip her girls for a career that would enable their independence. Stella refused to believe it. Whether or not Frances Stevenson was the Prime Minister's mistress, she herself would strive for a professional life based on talent alone.

Stella turned to watch the dancing. Lily was floating round the room in the arms of the handsome man she had noticed on that first day. She now knew him as Freddie Shepherd, a member of the South African delegation, often in the company of General Smuts. Hugh watched them rather glumly, fiddling with his cuff.

Stella smiled across at him in sympathy. 'It's rather fun to see all these bigwigs here among us, isn't it?'

Hugh didn't smile. Barely shifting his eyes from Lily and her partner, he said, 'Damn sight more life about some of them here than in the discussions at the Quai d'Orsay.'

'At least you attend some of the sessions. We sit at our machines, typing up report after report, and it's easy to forget that what we're doing is really quite important.'

Hugh nodded and took a gulp of his whisky. 'I fear that's a danger with this whole affair. We're so bogged down in the minutiae that we lose sight of the bigger goal. Wouldn't it be dreadful if this opportunity were squandered, after everything that's gone before.'

Stella nearly told him about Madame de Witt-Schlumberger, and her conviction that the peacemakers had already squandered a huge opportunity by excluding women, but something stopped her. She and Lily had gone up to Hugh's office in the Astoria a few days before. It wasn't large, and there were three men sharing it, all of them working at desks piled high with maps and files and books. She had peered over Hugh's shoulder as he explained that he was preparing a report for the Commission on Fiume. And perhaps it was because of her encounter with Madame de

Witt-Schlumberger, but as she looked around that cramped room she couldn't help but recall that she had finished above Hugh in every single class at university. So how was it that she was at the peace conference to type up documents, while he was doing research and sitting in on meetings? Sitting beside him now and watching him swirl his whisky around his glass as he waited in vain for Lily to notice him, she wondered why on earth she had never considered it before. She liked Hugh well enough, but he had the more interesting role here simply because he was a man, rather than because he was more intelligent or experienced or better equipped than she was. It felt like a moment of revelation about something she had always known and accepted and never once questioned.

Well, she was questioning it now.

Hugh was speaking, and she hadn't really been listening. Something more to do with President Wilson and his League of Nations. They all knew that this ambitious covenant was the American president's answer to the world's troubles, but there was growing unease that he was more committed to the league than to negotiating peace with Germany. Meanwhile people continued to die in war-torn eastern Europe, and to starve in blockaded Germany. The soldiers were agitating to be demobilised, but that couldn't happen until there was a genuine stable peace. With each day of rising unrest in Germany, the Allies became more determined to maintain their armies to enforce whatever terms they chose to impose. What had seemed simple in November was anything but.

'Wilson's going to the battlefields this weekend,' Hugh said. 'The French are furious that he hasn't gone sooner, but maybe when he really sees the devastation it will make a difference.'

The whistle of a chill wind stirred about her. She clasped her hands tightly.

'I wish I could go.'

Hugh shook his head. 'It's not allowed. I know a fellow who tried, but you need the right sort of pass. There's a company preparing to run excursions, I believe, for tourists from England, but the cost is enormous.'

Excursions. Tourists.

Jack huddled in the corner, a keening sound, and a floor littered with screwed-up balls of paper.

Her mouth was dry. She looked around at the light and the laughter. How in the world could they all carry on like this? The dignitaries, the delegates, the lowly typists like herself, whirling and dancing and laughing, negotiating and briefing, as if the grief and the chaos and the blood and the violence were nothing at all. Unsteadily, she rose to her feet. Hugh looked at her in surprise.

'I say, are you all right?'

'Just need a breath of air.' She made her way around the edge of the room, almost brushing against Lloyd George's knee as she avoided a spinning couple, and hurried towards the arched doorway onto avenue Kléber. As she moved towards it, she had the strangest fancy that she might step through, leaving behind the music and glittering mirrors, and find herself on a blasted landscape riddled with shell-holes, mud and corpses, a landscape where Jack lay rotting while she revelled in frivolous luxury. She pictured the Majestic, lifted by some giant hand and thrown down on the ravaged battlefields to the east.

She was almost disappointed that it wasn't the case.

Instead, the Paris lamplight glowed softly over a perfectly civilised winter scene. Stella breathed in deeply and fumbled in her bag for a cigarette. Behind her came another burst of warmth and laughter as the hotel door opened. Her lighter failed to work.

'Allow me.'

Freddie Shepherd leant close to her with his own lighter and she caught a scent of woody soap. She tried to control her breathing and let the panic recede.

'You're shivering,' he said. 'No wonder, it's cold out here and you've no jacket. Here, take mine.' He shrugged out of his jacket and laid it gently over her shoulders. As he did so she noticed that one hand was encased in a black glove of some silky material, and guessed that some kind of war wound was hidden under there. Another deep breath.

'I'm sorry,' she said. 'I just came out for some air. Foolish to come without a coat.' Then she looked up. 'But you were on your way somewhere. Please – take your jacket. I'm quite all right. I'll have this cig and go back inside.'

But he had lit up for himself now and leant back against the wall. 'Take your time. I'm in no hurry, Miss . . . ?'

'Rutherford,' she said. 'Stella Rutherford. I'm a friend of Lily's.'

'Ah yes, the fragrant Lily! We had a lovely dance together, but her surly Scotch suitor has claimed her once more. My name is Freddie Shepherd. I've wanted to meet you, Miss Rutherford.'

His voice was smooth. She couldn't make out the colour of his eyes in the soft lamplight, but she could sense the warmth that shone from them. The fear and tension of the evening eased in his company.

'You're here with General Smuts and the South Africans, aren't you?'

'That's right. And you are one of the typing girls.'

'I am.'

'Splendid! As I told your friend Lily, you girls really are the beating heart of the delegation. People might believe that power lies in the Quai d'Orsay, but really, it's the ladies of the typing pool who keep this show on the road. The secrets you could tell are worth a pretty penny, I'm sure.'

She laughed, finished her cigarette and slipped his jacket from her shoulders. 'Here – take this back, and thank you so much. I really am all right now. I'll go back inside and you can carry on to wherever you were going.'

'Oh, as to that, I scarcely remember. I'm sure it was unimportant. Will you return to the dance, Miss Rutherford?'

'Yes – for a little while at least. Lily will wonder where I am.'

He held out his good hand towards her and she felt something unexpected shift within her. 'In that case,' he said, 'I'd much rather dance with you. Would that be all right, do you think?'

# Chapter Eleven

## Dieppe

The breeze whipped up the white tips of the waves, stinging Corran's cheeks with salty spray and pulling long strands of hair loose below her hat. She welcomed its bite. She came down to the shore most days when she had a break in teaching. She had been in Dieppe for three months now, and savoured the rhythms of this new life. She remembered being apprehensive about her ability to cope with classes of soldiers. She needn't have worried. Lorryloads of men sent in from outlying camps, demobbed soldiers passing through Dieppe on their way back to England – she loved every one of them and they almost without fail treated her with courtesy and respect. If anyone unwisely tried to have some fun at her expense, she could be sure his fellows would soon jump on him.

Less engaging but satisfying in its own way was the task of 'instruction by correspondence', where she sent teaching materials out to camps across France and even occupied Germany, and received assignments to mark by post.

Rumours constantly circulated that the education scheme

was about to be closed down and the staff dispatched to England, but week after week went by and they were still here. It was a life that felt all the more precious because they knew it couldn't last for long. They were a close team and managed well enough for fun. There was often a dance at one of the hotels when the officers were in town, saying their farewells to French soil with determined abandon. Corran attended some of these but her preference was for the entertainments that the staff at the school devised among themselves. At her insistence they had held a Burns Supper, which had been a real success, even if haggis was impossible to come by and had to be replaced with some unidentifiable French sausage. But her fellow tutors had entered into the traditions surrounding the meal with enthusiasm, and she had laughed until she cried at their chief's anglicised rendering of the 'Address to a Haggis'.

Corran thought of Stella's letters from Paris, describing the luxurious Hôtel Majestic, the dances and concerts and dinners that the British Empire Delegation enjoyed. Here in Dieppe the school was cold and draughty, there was never enough fuel, the meals were as hit or miss as they had ever been – but not for anything would she have swapped with her little sister. She was teaching, and that was all that mattered.

Corran breathed deeply, tasting the sea air, and watched a fishing boat struggle against the waves as it approached the harbour, trailed by shrieking gulls. Then she turned back along the promenade towards the cliffs, the sea on her right and on her left a line of grand hotels, reminders of the town's pre-war life as a luxury bathing resort. The hotels had mostly been commandeered by the Allied armies or the Red Cross but soon, she supposed, tourists would begin to return. In Dieppe, the scars of war were rarely physical and so it would perhaps be easier here, on the surface at least, to rebuild some sort of normality. She thought again of the letter she had received from Rob in that morning's post: his unexpected invitation and her own reaction to that. Was she really so afraid to face the reality that Jack, Rob and the others had experienced? Or was she afraid of something else entirely?

She arrived back at the school and pushed open the heavy wooden door, stepping into the sitting room overlooking the sea. No lamps were lit and the grate was cold. She crossed the room to light a lamp and then gasped as someone rose to his feet from a high-backed armchair.

'Arthur! You startled me! What on earth are you doing sitting in the cold and the dark like this?'

'I'm sorry I frightened you,' he said. 'Is it cold? I hadn't noticed.'

'Sit down, do,' she said, looking at him more closely. He held a newspaper in one hand and his face was ashen. 'Is something wrong? Have you had bad news?'

'Not exactly. Not in the way you mean. But the news is bad, yes.'

She glanced again at the newspaper in his hand and then made a decision. 'Well, let's get a cup of tea and you can tell me. I'm frozen. Do you know if the coal's been delivered? Good. Why don't you build up the fire and I'll run down and make us a pot of tea.' Not waiting to see if he agreed, she hurried down the stairs to the kitchen, where she made some tea and begged a couple of slices of bread from Henriette. They could toast them at the sitting-room fire. As she waited for the water to boil, she wondered what could possibly lie behind Arthur's distress. They had rarely been alone together since Luneray, and sometimes she wondered if he was avoiding her. She loaded up her tea tray and realised she was quietly content that the fates had drawn them together today.

Back in the sitting room, Arthur had lit the fire and now stood at the window.

Corran sat down and picked up the newspaper he had laid on a table. After a moment she looked up. 'I'd heard about the strikes and riots in Glasgow,' she said. 'It says here they were caused by terrorists.'

Arthur turned, and his scar stood out even more starkly against his pallor.

'My sister, Cath, sent me that newspaper with her letter. If the demonstrators are terrorists, Corran, then my sister is one – and her eldest boy along with her. They were there.'

'They were *there*? In George Square? When the fighting happened?'

He nodded and came forward to take his tea, sitting down on the sofa opposite her. The cup rattled in its saucer and she thought he might break the delicate china, so tightly was he clutching it.

'Cath and young Arthur were there. Named for our dad, like me. Young Arthur works in the docks. They weren't looking for trouble; they were there to hear the Lord Provost's response to their proposals.'

'What proposals?'

'Nothing unreasonable.' He spoke with a hard edge

to his tone. 'The main one is a forty-hour working week. Back home, conditions are as bad as I feared and worse, Corran. Cath writes of endless lines of men with no work, of overcrowded tenements, no money, no hope. If those who do have work could move onto a shorter working week there would be jobs for more men. It's a fair enough suggestion, surely. And how did our government respond? They set the police on them with batons, and called in the army as back-up. Young Arthur was hurt, although not as badly as some.'

'I suppose the authorities are scared of revolution,' she said, thinking back to Arthur's lecture. She knelt down before the fireplace and held out the bread on a toasting fork.

'Munro calls them Bolshevists. That's not true, but if the authorities carry on this way they will have every reason to be scared.' He laid down his teacup and balled his fists. 'And we're stuck here! I need to get home, Corran.'

'You were the one who told me how useful our work here is!'

'And it was. It still is, in a way, but our time here is winding down and meanwhile there are people back home who need my help.' He took a slice of toast. 'Those men and women in George Square – just a couple of months ago some of them were in the trenches risking their lives for a government that has already turned against them. Or they were working themselves into an early grave producing the munitions and heavy weaponry that won us the war. Where's the thanks? A baton charge?'

'How is your sister?'

'Angry. Distraught. Hungry.' He took a bite of toast. 'I send her what I can, but I have to send money home to Mary too. Though God knows what she does with it.'

Her own toast was ready now. As she eased herself back up onto the sofa, he said, 'Whatever we fought the war for, it surely wasn't this.'

They sat in silence for a while. It was everywhere, this creeping sense of fear that, after everything they had been through and all they had lost, the world might not be so very much better after all. She heard it from the men in huts and in classes, and she sensed it in her letters from both Alex and Stella, although neither was free to write without censorship. And then there was the other letter she had received. She hadn't meant to tell Arthur about it, but found herself saying, 'I had a letter this morning too. From Rob.'

His green gaze held hers steadily. 'Everything all right?'

'He has a few days' leave. He wants me to come to Arras and meet him.'

'Arras? But that's in the battle zone. It's impossible.'

'That's what I thought. But he has managed to get the right passes. I've to write to my sister in Paris and see if she can arrange some leave. We'll go to Arras and meet Rob, and he'll take us to Jack's grave. He's buried not far from there.'

'When?'

'Next month.'

'But that's splendid, Corran,' Arthur said. 'It's almost impossible to travel into the battle zone. You must be relieved that you'll see your brother's grave before we're sent back home.'

'Yes. It will mean a lot to Mother too.'

Those green eyes were still watching her. 'But . . . ?'

Corran looked into the flames. If anyone would understand, it might just be Arthur. She turned back to face him. 'If I tell you what I'm really thinking, you'll think me terribly selfish.'

'Try me.'

A piece of coal shifted in the grate, emitting sparks. Corran took a deep breath. 'I haven't seen Rob since he was sent home while wounded in 1917, and that was just a brief visit to his convalescent home in Oxfordshire. Before the war I thought I would marry him, but I've only seen him a handful of times since. In the meantime I've discovered teaching. I can't imagine giving that up, but Rob has been through a *war*. How can I even begin to think of choosing my work over him?' She looked down at her cup of tea. 'I told you I was selfish.'

'Selfish?' Arthur asked. 'I don't know about that. But I do know you're a bloody good teacher. One of the best.'

She looked at him then, and quickly looked away, laying down her cup. 'Thank you.'

Arthur checked his watch. 'I must go and prepare for my next class. Thank you for listening, Corran. And I really am glad you will get to go to Arras along with your sister. You'll want to do right by your brother, whatever else happens.'

She nodded and watched him go, his words stirring a memory in her mind. Her bag of papers still lay where she had placed it when she returned from her walk. She rummaged inside until she found the slip she could use to order up books, and scribbled a request.

*When all else fails, there's always Sophocles.*

# Chapter Twelve

## Paris

Stella was alone in their room. Lily was across at the Astoria but Stella had a free morning, and had sat down to reply to Corran's latest letter. She began easily enough, writing about the wintry weather and the beauty of the snowy trees on the Champs-Élysées, and remarking on her long hours while avoiding any direct reference to the actual content of her work. She described dances and concerts, knowing Corran would skim over these, and spoke of her encounter with Madame de Witt-Schlumberger, which would interest her sister far more. She wrote of the latest developments: the disappointing response of President Wilson to the delegation of women who had attended his flat, and their reluctant decision to establish a parallel women's conference instead. They would prepare submissions on matters that they believed so passionately should be part of the Central Powers' discussions, and would continue to lobby the main conference. If there was anything they knew as women, it was that determination, persistence and creative thinking could achieve significant results. So there was plenty for Stella to write about. But now she sat with her pen hovering over the official British Empire Delegation writing paper as she reread that little postscript hastily scribbled onto the end of Corran's letter.

*Rob has secured passes for us to come to Arras. He'll meet us there and take us to find Jack. Only it must be that particular week. I do hope you can come, Stella. Please try to get leave.*

Find Jack.

A blot of ink dropped slowly onto the paper. She watched it, mesmerised, as it spread across the page.

Bleeding.

She laid down the pen. Her sister's words were so simple, in her familiar, sharp, scratchy handwriting . . . but now the letters blurred and the meaning was indecipherable.

Corran had loved Jack too, of course she had, and yet Stella could not make her pen form the words, not even to her sister. Especially not to her sister, who still held in her memory the Jack who had left Thurso with a cheerful wave. The Jack whom Stella now found it so hard to summon, never mind commit to the page. Hugh and Lily, yes. Madame de Witt-Schlumberger, yes. The snow on the chestnut trees, yes.

Jack, no.

Perhaps if she saw the place where he lay, the keening sound would be silent. But she feared it might just be louder than ever.

Impatient with herself, Stella got to her feet. She had an

Edith Wharton novel to exchange in the library in the basement and the letter could wait until later. As she scrubbed the ink from her fingers, a knock sounded at the door. A bellboy held out a note to her. The unfamiliar writing was clear and bold.

*Dear Miss Rutherford,*

*I believe this is your free morning, as it is mine. Would you do me the pleasure of joining me in the salon for morning tea?*

*Yours ever, Freddie S.*

She thanked the boy and turned back into the room, stepping out onto her balcony for a moment. The cold wind that stung her cheeks felt good, and she leant on the railing, gripping Freddie's note. Five minutes ago she had been sinking under the weight of her grief, and now a thrill of something that felt very like excitement ran through her. How could she hold those two things together? Was it a betrayal of Jack to want so desperately to seize back the years that the war had stolen from her?

She thought back to the evening of the dance a couple of weeks ago when Freddie had been so tender and kind outside, and then had whirled her round the room in a wonderful few moments of laughter and freedom. They hadn't spent much time together since, but earlier this week a cinema had been set up in the Majestic and they had chatted when the picture ended. Perhaps that had prompted him to think of her again.

She stepped back into the room and checked her reflection.

If these few months since the armistice had taught her anything, it was that the war would never really be over for any of them who had lived through it. It would be part of her always, just as she feared that keening sound would chill her soul forever. But she was still here, and so was Freddie. It was something to build on.

Down in the salon, she looked around. There he was, seated at a small table, frowning over a newspaper spread before him. He looked up, and her heart quickened as a warm smile lit his suntanned face. He rose to his feet.

'I wasn't sure you would come.'

He pulled out a chair for her and then sat back down, summoning the waiter to order some tea. 'I'm so pleased you were able to join me,' he said. 'What did you think of the film the other night? Rather fun to have our own cinema, wasn't it?'

'It was marvellous, and the pianist did awfully well,' she said. 'Isn't the actress Poppy Wyndham splendid? She's Scottish, you know.'

'Actually, her husband and I—' Freddie cut off as a commotion broke out across in the adjacent foyer, drowning out the general hotel hubbub. Voices were raised, there was a short scream and someone shouted, while nearby a door banged.

'What the devil?' He jumped to his feet. Stella was close behind him as they hurried into the gleaming foyer. A telephone rang shrilly, unanswered, and there were people everywhere. Freddie caught the arm of one uniformed porter. 'What's happening?'

'It's Clemenceau, sir. He's been shot.'

'Here?' gasped Stella, looking round in alarm.

'No, outside his flat, ma'am.'

'Is he dead?'

The man shrugged. 'Some say yes, some say no. No one knows, sir.'

'He was hit several times. Doesn't look good,' said another man nearby.

'What happened to the assassin?' Freddie demanded.

'He's been arrested. Bloody Hun spy.'

'Or a Russian Bolshevist.'

Stella looked around. As the news spread through the hotel, people spilt into the foyer from the restaurants and upper floors, anxious to hear what had happened – yet the words ricocheting around the gleaming marble foyer were no more than rumour and speculation. She grasped after her scattered thoughts. How could an act of violence so extreme as the assassination of the French prime minister have intruded on their world of reports, diplomacy and evening entertainments? Yet even as she wondered, there came a recoil to the sharp ring of the bullet in her mind.

This brutality of man to man was the reason they were all here, after all.

She looked round for Freddie. There he was, leaning across the reception desk and speaking urgently into the telephone. He slammed down the receiver and turned, quickly scanning the crowded foyer, a strange sort of eagerness in his expression.

Then he saw her and moved through the chaos towards her. 'Are you all right, Miss Rutherford?'

'I'm fine. It's just – rather horrible isn't it?'

'Horrible, yes,' he said, still with that feverish undercurrent. 'And what this will mean for the peace process I can't imagine, what with Wilson currently halfway across the Atlantic on a visit to the States and Lloyd George back in Britain to sort out those blasted rioters.' He glanced at his wristwatch. 'Listen, if you don't mind, I must seek out General Smuts. I'm terribly sorry to run out on you like this. I wonder – if the events of today allow, would you perhaps have dinner with me this evening?'

Dinner? She almost laughed. It summed up the surreal nature of life in the Majestic, that within the space of a few moments she would hear of the murder of a world leader and be invited to dinner with one of the most handsome men she had ever met. She nodded.

'Shall I meet you here?'

He flashed a smile then, the same warm, disarming smile he had given her when she approached his table earlier.

'Please do, but I was thinking Maxim's rather than the Majestic. I'll make the reservation. I'll see you at seven, Miss Rutherford.' He bowed his head slightly, then hurried to the main door and was gone.


Clemenceau was not dead.

By the time Stella joined her colleagues at the Astoria that afternoon, more news had filtered through. The French prime minister was sitting up and talking.

'It's a miracle,' said Hugh, who had come downstairs to join them. 'They say the bullet is lodged too deep in his lung to be removed. And it was a Frenchman who carried out the attack! Clemenceau is ashamed a Frenchman could shoot so badly. Six out of seven shots missed him.'

'Why ever did a Frenchman shoot him?' asked Lily.

'He was one of those anarchists, apparently. The man was nearly lynched by the crowd. He'll hang now.'

Lily shivered. 'It's horrible to think there are people out there who hate what we're doing so much that they're ready to kill us.'

'I hardly think they'll come for you, Lily!' drawled Mabel.

'Oh, I know. But we see them all at dinner, don't we? Coming and going so freely. Lloyd George, Foch, Massey, Smuts. What if someone comes to the hotel and starts shooting? It could happen.'

'They'll be on high alert after today,' Anne-Marie said.

Lily's reference to General Smuts reminded Stella of her news. 'Remember that chap from the dance, Lil, the South African one?'

'Freddie?' Lily asked eagerly. Hugh, standing beside her desk, made a tiny movement.

'That's the one. I met him this morning. I was with him when the news about Clemenceau reached the Majestic. He's taking me to Maxim's for dinner tonight, actually.'

'What?'

'You're a dark horse!'

'Maxim's? I say!'

Stella ignored them all, and turned to face Hugh. She had noticed his tension, and thought her statement would probably bring some relief.

'Do you know him, Hugh?'

Hugh hesitated. 'I haven't had much to do with him. A

little, in relation to the initial reports on the German colonies in Africa. He's close to Smuts.' He glanced at Lily and then back to Stella. 'He's very suave, of course.'

'But?' Stella prompted.

Hugh shook his head. 'I really don't know him well at all. Anyway, I must get back to work. There's a bit of turmoil upstairs too, you know, over the death of poor old Mark Sykes. Did you hear about that? He went down with Spanish flu and was dead a few days later. Every time we think we're clear of it someone else goes down. I don't know what this will mean for British interests in Palestine. What a dreadful week this has been.'

Freddie was waiting for her in the foyer. As he kissed her cheek, Stella felt again that intoxicating sense of having stepped right into someone else's life.

'Stella. I may call you Stella, mayn't I?'

'Of course.' She noticed one or two glances cast towards them and lifted her head a little. The Majestic was an absolute rumour hothouse: no doubt she and Freddie would provide a topic for gossip at dinner this evening. 'I must just sign out. We have such tiresome rules and regulations.'

'Security.'

'Oh, not security! This is Miss Bingham's regime. To preserve our virtue, you see.' Then she blushed. Heavens! What would he think she meant by that? To cover her confusion, she hurried over to the reception desk and entered her details in Miss Bingham's register. By the time she returned she had composed herself, and took his arm to leave the hotel.

They cut through to the Champs-Élysées and walked down towards the Place de la Concorde. Stella remembered strolling here with Lily on their first day in Paris. Everything had been new, and they had so little idea of what to expect. The work had been slow to start, but now her head simply birled with place names and government representatives, protocols and proposals. Paris was bursting at the seams with groups seeking representation from Albania to Syria, Palestine to Mesopotamia. There were anarchists, Bolshevists, Quakers, Zionists, pacifists. The women led by Madame de Witt-Schlumberger were not the only group to set up their own alternative conference in response to being excluded: the Grand Hotel was the location for the Pan-African Congress, which was said to be the brainchild of an African-American woman, Ida Gibbs. Whenever Stella lifted her head far enough above her typewriter to consider it all, she found all these people and their wildly different ideas stimulating and intriguing. As they learnt the steps for this new age, they were dancing through history in the making.

Until today.

Today, with the shooting of Georges Clemenceau, the streets of Paris felt sinister. She walked down the Champs-Élysées and glanced uneasily from left to right at the people who had chosen to come out into the Paris evening. Why were they here? What nationality were they? Where did their sympathies lie?

Freddie had told her that Clemenceau would recover. 'The street outside his house is carpeted with flowers,' he said. 'The French people are scandalised. Old Clem is their war hero.'

They arrived in the Place de la Concorde, busy with people despite the darkness, and turned to the left. Stella had never been to the famous Maxim's restaurant, although she and Lily had peered in from outside.

'This should make a change from the hopelessly British fare in the Majestic,' he said as they approached.

The assault on her senses as she entered the restaurant was bewildering. The Majestic was grand, but it was a grandeur she understood, albeit from afar. Here was something completely unfamiliar. She didn't know where to look first – the ornate ceiling; the beautiful colours radiating from the stained glass; the sweeping curves on the glowing lamps and mirrors. The air was rich with the creamy scent of hot garlic, and piano music flowed as smoothly as the finest wine.

'Rather splendid, isn't it,' Freddie murmured, as their coats were whisked away and they were led to their table.

Splendid it most certainly was. Somehow she pulled her gaze away from the décor and turned her attention to the menu.

'The choice is still more limited than it would have been before the war,' Freddie said.

'You call this limited? I think I've forgotten how to choose.'

'Let me help you. Do you like fish? I'd recommend the Normandy sole then. The sauce is exquisite.'

'A good choice,' she said. 'I grew up on the north coast of Scotland, and there's nothing like fish fresh from the sea.'

'And how did you come to be involved in the conference?' he asked. As she told him about Hoster's, the waiter brought a carafe of white wine and poured some out for them. She noticed Freddie sliding his glass from beside his gloved right hand to his left. He caught her glance and lifted the injured hand. 'Mangled in '15,' he said laconically. 'I lost a few fingers.'

'Loos?' she guessed.

'Oh no. In South West Africa. You likely don't know much about it; most Brits don't remember the fighting that took place in Africa. Botha and Smuts led us as we drove the Germans out. Our place – my family's farm – lies on the veldt just across the border from South West Africa.' He paused. 'I lost my fingers and the use of this hand,' he said. 'Pieter, my brother, was not so lucky. We buried him at Gibeon.'

The brightly coloured lights suddenly seemed harsh. 'I'm sorry.'

Freddie nodded, and raised his glass towards her. She took a sip. Much of the wine she had drunk in France had been sharp, but this was light and slid down her throat very easily.

'That was the end of my war,' he continued. 'I came to Oxford for my studies and to see the old country. Then I found work with the diplomatic service, and General Smuts invited me to join the delegation.' He took another drink. 'I know Jan rather well. He's an old friend of my mother's family, and a fine man.'

'I've not seen much of him, but he seems more approachable than many of the plenipotentiaries.'

There was a distinct glow of hero worship in Freddie's blue eyes. 'There are no airs and graces about Jan at all. He's a proud South African and he's determined that the dominions will be properly consulted in this peace process. We've given too much in blood to be excluded from the creation of the new world by those who controlled the old. South West Africa is rightfully ours.'

Stella hesitated. 'I thought Germany's former colonies were to be run by the League of Nations? Leading eventually to self-determination?'

Freddie laughed as the waiter brought their food. He waited until they were alone again.

'Self-determination? Stella, have you ever been to Africa? No, I thought not. Well, let me tell you, it's a ridiculous notion. The natives have had years of harsh treatment by the Germans, and are no more able to rule themselves than an infant could take care of its own needs. This is the time for white South Africans – Afrikaans and English alike, and I'm a child of both – to bring civilisation and enlightenment. Tell me . . .' And he leant forward, the flickering candle reflected in his startling blue eyes. 'Have you heard any talk of self-determination for *India* in your British discussions? Or Egypt, or Cyprus? And what of Ireland? Has Lloyd George recognised the Irish parliament yet? Seems to me the British Empire is less keen on self-determination when it comes to her own territories.'

Stella thought of Lily and her father with their Irish estate. Surely they would say Ireland was different. And as for the other places he mentioned – 'There's a good deal of unrest in Egypt,' she said, remembering recent newspaper reports.

'Which will only be made worse by deluded liberals spouting nonsense about self-determination and stoking the flames of every nationalist rebel! Did you hear about the lad who works in the kitchens at the Ritz and who actually tried to get himself a hearing at the conference? Ho Chi Minh, his name is, and he wants some obscure part of French Indochina he calls Vietnam to be an independent country. He was laughed back to his pots and pans, of course. Firm and fair government, that's what's needed for the good of the world.' He poured some more wine. 'What do Wilson and his cronies know of the veldt and its endless skies? What do they know of the culture of those of us who live there?' He drained his glass and brushed his golden hair away from his face. 'I'm sorry, Stella, that was a bit of a speech. But Piet died for our piece of land. I can't return to my parents until I can tell them he didn't die in vain.'

She heard the tremor in his voice. Taking a deep breath, her heart thudding, she said, 'My brother died too. Jack.'

His good hand reached out and covered hers then, and his blue eyes were no longer hard and angry but filled with the pain of shared loss.

'It's terrible to be the one left behind, isn't it?'

She stared at the tablecloth, fighting back tears. When she could trust her voice, she said, 'I have the chance to visit his grave next month. Near Arras.'

Freddie nodded slowly. 'A big thing. Will you go?'

'I must.'

'That's good. One day I'll go back to where Piet lies. But there is a great deal to achieve here first.' Then he smiled, and she wondered irrelevantly how he kept his teeth so white. She and Lily often laughed about how much healthier and stronger the colonial men were. Was it breeding? Was it diet? Or just the contrast between their vast sunny landscapes and Britain's narrow, grimy industrial streets? She turned her attention back to what he was saying. 'Let's talk about something more cheerful. Tell me about your life here. You work in the Astoria, don't you? You girls must have some fun.'

'Not as much as you might think. Miss Bingham is in charge, and her sole mission in life is to make sure we have as little fun as possible. The entertainments in the Majestic are just about acceptable, but anyone who ventures beyond is in Severe Moral Danger. We're here in Paris, City of Light, and sometimes it feels as if all we see is the route between the Majestic and the Astoria!' She gestured round the restaurant. 'This is the greatest excitement I've had since coming out here.'

'We must change that!' Freddie's eyes sparkled. 'Will you let me introduce you to the Paris you may not have encountered, Stella?'

'Such as?'

'Oh, nothing too racy. We'll leave the cabaret until later in your education! But have you been to the Opéra Garnier yet? No? That's a must, let me see what I can do about tickets. And there are some wonderful cafés in Montparnasse.' He paused. 'And your work? Do you focus on one particular area? The German treaty, I imagine.'

'A good deal of that, but we type whatever comes our way.' She finished her glass and this time placed her hand over the top to prevent him refilling it. 'Minutes of meetings, preparatory reports, submissions. We can be dealing with the Balkans one minute and Asia the next. We all aspire to attend the actual sessions, but I haven't had the chance yet.'

'Still, it must give you a good overview of what's going on. I'm sure you know far more than I do. Much of the time my colleagues and I are left kicking our heels, waiting for them to establish mandates for the colonies. We expected to come for a few weeks and here we are, two months later, and a lasting settlement seems further away than ever. You haven't seen anything this week relating to South West Africa, I suppose?'

She shook her head. He leant forward, blue eyes fervent, and she was reminded of the eagerness she'd sensed in him when the news came through about Clemenceau. 'If a conference like this is to be a success, Stella, the flow of information is crucial. Understanding who needs to know what when – that's an art form, and one I'm really rather good at. The established channels are as clogged up as the sewers of Paris, but once you know how to circumvent them, everything becomes much more fragrant. It can be very rewarding too.'

She didn't really understand what he was saying. 'Rewarding?'

'The advancement of peace is its own reward, of course, for the sake of Pieter and Jack and all our brothers. But there are also those who value the smooth running of this conference, and offer incentives accordingly.' Then he smiled, and reached out to take her hand. 'I'd love to show you more of the Paris you want to see, Stella. May I?'

She felt as if the conversation had run out of control, somehow, but there was no mistaking the warmth in his gaze and the tingle of her skin under his touch. And he too had lost a brother. She smiled. 'I'd like that.'

# Chapter Thirteen

### Near Arras

'At ease and take a seat, Captain,' said Major Farrell.

Rob's arm dropped from his salute. He sat, and declined a cigar from the outstretched box. He waited while the major lit his own, wondering all the while what this summons could be about. Farrell wasn't in a hurry. 'You're a rugby man, Campbell,' he said idly.

'Yes, sir.'

'Hmm. Played a bit myself when I was younger, until I buggered my knee.' Smoke from his cigar, strong and sickly, mingled with the damp smell of the hut. Through the grimy window Rob could see Leonard still working on the ambulance. He rubbed his hands surreptitiously on his trousers, trying to wipe off the black grease, and hoped the major would get on with it. Leonard couldn't do the job alone. But Major Farrell had slid into one of his long reminiscences, something to do with an Oxford rugger match and an upstart Kiwi winger. Rob made interested noises and wondered how to move the conversation on. But then—

'I was in the crowd at Twickenham in '13 when we beat the Jocks, you know. Did you play that match, Captain?'

'I did.' *For Pete's sake, please stop droning on about rugby and tell me what this is all about.*

'Hardly a classic.'

'Three nil to England, I believe, sir.'

'That's right. The Jocks had beaten us the year before up in Edinburgh, and our boys were damned sure it wouldn't happen on home turf.'

Rob shifted in his seat and clasped his hands tightly to keep them still. This was not a conversation he wanted to have. But still the major continued, and despite himself Rob could not shut out the images from his mind. That victory over their oldest rivals at Inverleith in 1912 had been his first cap, and what a way to start. Scotland's hard-as-nails captain and best ever player, John MacCallum, hoisted high on his teammates' shoulders in triumph, tears mingling with mud and sweat, for he'd known that was his last match.

How things changed.

They missed MacCallum when they went down to Twickenham the next year for a turgid affair that was, as the major said, 'hardly a classic'. And then they were back at Inverleith in '14, with Corran and young Jack in the stands. The final match before the world went mad. Rob became aware that the major had stopped speaking and was looking at him, waiting for an answer. He searched for the major's last words.

'You leave on Saturday.'

'Leave, sir?'

'Didn't think you were listening, Campbell.' The major got to his feet and pushed a piece of paper across the desk. 'Read this while I pour us both a celebratory whisky.'

Celebratory?

Rob scanned the typewritten letter. It was headed *Inter-Services and Dominion Forces Championship* and informed Major Farrell that Captain Robert Campbell, Scotland internationalist, was invited to play for the mother country and should be released to return to Great Britain immediately to begin training. Rob read it carefully. The thin typewritten sheet trembled in his hand, and the pounding in his head was all too familiar. He laid down the letter and accepted the drink, swallowing a mouthful quickly. 'I'm not sure I understand, sir.'

'Well, it seems bloody clear to me. Some wiz has come up with a splendid notion, that we lift morale and give the lads something to focus on while they wait to be demobbed. Squash any disturbing unrest before it takes hold. The dominion boys are all still here and you know what a show they can put on – I hear the Kiwis kept training right through the war. His Majesty supports the idea and will present a cup to the winning team. The home nations will play as one team, the mother country. We've lost so many boys that we might struggle to pull together individual teams and besides, it celebrates our united allied victory and the spirit that won us the war. Some fellow in London has the job of identifying former internationalists who made it through, and he's tracked you down, Campbell. It's a real honour for you, and for your regiment.'

Rob listened to this speech in silence. When the major finished speaking, he drained his glass and laid it carefully on the desk in front of him. 'I'm grateful, sir, but I won't be taking up the opportunity.'

The major jerked. 'Eh, what?'

'I would prefer to stay here, sir.'

'Prefer? I'm not sure it's about what you prefer, Captain.' The major poured some more whisky into both glasses. 'They'll feed you, you know, to build you up for the team. Extra rations. Less mud. And it's not as if there are so very many patients left here for you. We'll close down anyway in a month or two.'

'Nevertheless, sir.'

The major leant forward then, and it seemed to Rob that he looked at him properly for the first time. 'Now, why in the world would you prefer to stay in this shithole rather than return to England, I wonder? What's on your mind, Captain?'

Rob hesitated. Not for the world would he begin to share his reasons with his superior: he wasn't even entirely sure he understood them himself. But he knew there was no way he could take part in this grotesque folly. He prevaricated. 'You signed a leave form and some travel passes for me, sir, just the other week.'

'Did I? Did I? This supersedes that, of course.'

'Yes, sir. Thank you, sir. But you see, the passes are for . . . a friend of mine. A woman. Her brother was killed at Arras and I have promised to take her to his grave. It means a great deal to her. I'd like to honour the promise, sir.'

'Since when was serving your country about what you might like, Captain?'

Rob breathed slowly, tried to ignore the pounding, and looked into the cold eyes of the major. 'Sir, I was under the impression the rugby call up was an invitation rather than an order.'

The major stared at him for a moment, then reached out, picked up the letter and ripped it in two. 'Very well, Captain. Have it your own way. There are plenty boys would jump at the opportunity, you know. Never mind all the poor sods who don't have the choice any more. Maybe you should think about them, eh?'

All at once the neat whisky was harsh in his stomach and forced its way back up his gullet as acid. He swallowed. 'Sir.'

*As if I ever think about anything else.*

The major shook his head. 'I'm disappointed in you, Captain. Dismissed.'

That was only the start of it. Next came a letter from Charlie Usher – Charlie, who had spent most of the war in a German POW camp, his long limbs and restless energy straining against corrugated iron and barbed wire. Freed at last, Charlie couldn't wait to pick up a ball and run with it.

*We need you, Rob. Don't let us down.*

He and Charlie had gained their first caps together, ribbing the nerves out of each other on the way to that 1912 match against England. You never lost the bond forged by sharing such a significant moment. Charlie had got off to a flyer, scoring the winning try. Captain John MacCallum had bought them both drinks in the North British that legendary evening. 'Well played, lads,' he'd said, and Rob had had to grip the sticky wood of the bar to be sure any of this was real. But Charlie was a career soldier, already serving with the Gordon Highlanders, and so was one of the first to see real action when the world imploded in 1914. He found himself a prisoner behind enemy lines before the rest of them had even made it out of training camp. Rob could only imagine the frustration he must have felt. The Hun had done well to keep Charlie out of the action.

And now Charlie was free, and in England, and had thrown himself into this deluded scheme to hold an international rugby tournament with all his trademark energy and enthusiasm. He had, if his letter to Rob was to be believed, spent much of his time as a POW organising fitness drills and competitive sports for his fellow prisoners, and was more than ready to transfer these activities to the restless troops awaiting demob. Anything to prevent revolution. Rob stuffed Charlie's letter in his pocket and made his way between the huts towards the mess. The duckboard paths were quiet now, and the wards nearly empty. The major was right about one thing: they would be closing down as soon as the final casualties were evacuated to the larger hospitals up on the north coast, and then across the sea to England. The buses commandeered to serve as ambulances had already returned to the city streets, and soon the huts would be demolished, the tents packed away. Maybe grass would even grow here again, one day. Rob leant on a fence and looked out across the rutted track leading back towards Arras, listening to the stillness. It felt not peaceful but abandoned. Desolate. The ravages of war were not gone: they were just gone from here. He thought of all the men he had encountered at this and other field hospitals, clearing stations and aid posts. He hadn't the slightest idea how many men he had spoken to, touched, operated on. Night after night he saw their faces in his sleep, and even now he could hear their screams in the silence.

Where were they now? Returned to England – and to what? The shattered bodies, shattered nerves, shattered faces could not be tidied away along with the huts, the beds, the medicine stores. So many had passed under his hands, and yet there were a few who haunted him particularly. He didn't know their names. The dark-haired boy with most of his face missing: Rob often wondered whether his attempt to clean, close and cover the wound had done more harm than good, yet surely the lad would have died of infection before reaching Blighty otherwise. The major crouched behind the latrines, hands over his head, screaming the names of his men over and over. *Officers don't suffer from shellshock.* And the ginger-haired Irishman who had cursed him with all kinds of Gaelic fates when he discovered what Rob had sawn away. The foot had had to go, but could he have saved the rest?

Ruined men, returned to their homeland. It seemed to Rob, not having crossed the Channel since 1917, that when he did return it would be to a land overflowing with casualties. The streets and cities and country lanes of England and Wales and Scotland and Ireland must be so filled with broken bodies and broken minds that there couldn't possibly be room for anyone else.

And that was before you started on all the ones he'd let die, who now lay two to a grave in the wasteland of wooden crosses behind the hospital.

Did they really think a game of rugby could fix any of it?

A plan was forming in his mind to continue to treat the men whose battle was far from over. He'd heard there was good work in neurasthenia taking place in Edinburgh, but although it interested him that was not his area. He was a surgeon – he thought he might even once have been a good one – and surely he could use his surgical skills to undo some of the damage he feared he had inflicted when working under fire. And so this week he had written to Sir William Macewen of the Princess Louise Hospital near Glasgow. Hopefully he would hear back soon. Meanwhile he would help with the final weeks of closing up and then he would take the leave he was due and meet up with Corran and her sister.

He thought again of the proposed rugby tournament. Why did it repulse him so much? *Play the game. Discipline and duty. Team spirit, honour and pride. Your country needs you. Don't let us down.* Those words had caught them up in such a fervour in 1914, and carried them off to a hellhole that bore not the slightest relation to the rugby field. Now he heard the echo of those days in the major's suggestion and in Charlie's letter. And he wasn't having any of it.

*No, no, no.*

# Chapter Fourteen

### Paris

Somehow, now that Stella had opened the door to new experiences, they came striding in. In the typing room the others were anxious to hear every detail of her evening with Freddie. She obliged, though she kept to herself the way his hands had gently pulled her close to him outside the hotel, and the kiss goodnight that had lingered far longer than she expected. But Mabel latched on to Freddie's reference to the delights of Paris.

'I spent a month here with my older brother in the autumn of 1913,' she said, inserting a sheet of paper in her machine but not beginning to type. 'You should have seen Paris then, girls. Everyone who was doing anything new or exciting was here. A friend took us along to one of Gertrude Stein's Saturday evenings. You know about her, surely? She's an American writer who has lived in Paris for years and she collects the most extraordinary pictures. Her walls were simply covered with paintings unlike anything I'd ever seen before. Pablo Picasso was there, you know, that strange experimental artist. But they have all been scattered by the war. Last I heard, Miss Stein was working with refugees in Alsace.'

Stella felt a quick, hot stab of pain. Jack would have loved this talk of art and artists. To protect herself, she said, 'If our work can make a lasting peace, maybe the artists will return. And the fun too.'

'Oh, there's fun already if you know where to look,' Mabel said. 'I'm going to a party tomorrow evening as it happens. Elizabeth Asquith invited me. I can bring you girls along if you like. Meet me in the foyer after dinner.'

Anne-Marie cried off and Stella was inclined to do the same, but Lily was insistent.

'You had your evening at Maxim's, but what about me?' In the end Stella gave in and next evening Mabel led them to a house on the left bank of the Seine. They found themselves in a crowded, glittering room, lit by what seemed to be hundreds of wax candles, the atmosphere hot and heavy with perfume. Mabel ushered them in and introduced them to the elegant French count who was hosting the evening and then, typically, disappeared.

Stella and Lily stood at the side, each clutching a glass of champagne, and watched the guests. Across the room they could see Mabel talking with Elizabeth Asquith, the vivacious young daughter of the former Prime Minister. They recognised her from breathless *Daily Mail* reports of her recent engagement to a Romanian prince more than twenty years her senior. Conversation flowed around the room in several languages, and although there were some faces they recognised, there was no one they particularly wanted to speak to. It was everything Stella had feared and more.

'Let's drink this and go somewhere more interesting,' she murmured. But then, just as they prepared to leave, a tall man with a prominent moustache positioned himself in front of them. Stella had seen him in the Majestic and knew he was a member of the British delegation. Something to do with the organisation of it all, she thought vaguely. He had a bottle of champagne in one hand and a glass in the other.

'Leaving so soon, ladies?'

'We've somewhere else to go,' Lily lied.

'You've time for another drink, surely? Here.' And before they could protest he had emptied the bottle into their glasses. He leant forward, almost across Lily, placing one hand on the wall so that they were effectively blocked in by his large girth. Stella took a tiny step back but he was still far too close, the smell of his hair oil and his sour breath assailing her.

'There we are. I've seen you in the Majestic of course, fluttering alongside all the other butterflies. Such pretty girls. It was a grand notion, don't you think, to take special care when we selected the girls for secretarial roles. Only pretty types need apply.'

Lily trod on her foot so painfully at this point that she nearly spilt her champagne. The man carried on, his voice loud and strident.

'I took a look round the typing pool in Whitehall to begin with. Far too many maiden aunts in dowdy cardigans who wouldn't do at all. We all want negotiations to go *smoothly*, after all. The peace of the world is at stake. A touch of lipstick and a pretty pair of ankles will go a long way to improve the mood of the delegates.' He ran his tongue along his lips below his bristling moustache. There was a sheen of sweat on his forehead.

Stella, who had wanted to giggle at first, found herself feeling slightly sick.

'We were chosen on merit,' she said, keeping her tone as even as possible. 'We wouldn't be much use for our roles otherwise.'

The hideous man winked. 'If you say so, my dear. Oh, I'm sure you can *type*.'

'I have a degree!'

But Lily was shushing her and pulling her by the arm. 'Stella, shut up. Excuse me, sir, but we really do have to be somewhere else.' Still outraged, Stella found her glass removed from her hand, her coat thrust into her arms, and she was bundled down the stairs by Lily. They spilt out onto the dark Paris street.

'What an *odious* man!'

'I know, but you can't upset him. I've an idea he's someone quite important. You might be sent home.' Then Lily laughed. 'Wasn't he ridiculous? Lecherous oaf. We'll have to make sure we don't bump into him in the Majestic later on.'

Stella didn't find the situation in the least bit amusing.

'It's slanderous! As if we would be chosen on the basis of our looks.'

'Oh, as for that, it's true enough,' said Lily carelessly. 'Listen, I don't want to go back yet. Shall we walk on a bit further? I've always meant to explore Saint-Germain and it's just along here. It might be quite fun at night.'

But Stella stopped walking and turned to face her. 'What do you mean it's true enough?'

'What? Oh yes, someone else told me that. Mabel, I think. Prettiness was top of the selection criteria. And if you look around the Majestic you can see it's true. There isn't an ugly face or a fat girl among us. The men who were planning all this knew they would be leaving their wives behind for months on end. They wanted some pretty girls on hand.'

'That's horrible.'

Lily shrugged. 'Horrible for the plain ones who didn't get to come, perhaps. But *we* are here.' She linked an arm through Stella's. 'Come on, Stella, don't let it bother you. You know the way the world works.'

Stella let herself be led along the wide boulevard Saint-Germain, but she felt as though the man's leering eyes still watched her and the degrading things he had said clung to her clothes. Lily stopped outside a café on the corner.

'You're still upset,' she said. 'Come on. Let's go in here and have some supper.'

There were tables and wicker chairs on the street outside but they decided it was too cold and pushed open the door to the Café de Flore. The rich red interior was busy and vibrant. A waiter led them to a seat by the window and they ordered some wine and patisseries. Stella looked around. A man sat alone, covering sheets of paper with writing, while another table nearby was crowded with a group of young men and women all speaking over one another in French. There was a wonderful freedom about it, so different from the oppressive atmosphere of the party. She sipped the warm wine and felt the tension in her neck and shoulders ease.

Lily was watching her. 'You mustn't let it bother you, Stella. I thought your plan was to get secretarial work that will take you overseas? You're likely to have to put up with all sorts of unpleasant men.'

'Yes, but *is* that what I want? I'm not sure any more. The work I do, the work you do, a girl who left school at sixteen and did a typing course could do it.'

'Pretty much what I did. Only without the school bit.'

Stella stopped and stared. Lily, like many wealthy girls, had been educated at home by a governess who taught only those subjects that were considered useful for a life of marriage and leisure. Stella felt a stirring of gratitude for her visionary parents – her father an adventurer with a horizon as wide as the seas he sailed, and her mother determined to give her daughters the opportunities that had been denied to her, whatever the cost to herself.

She reached for her original train of thought. 'When I first met Mabel I thought she was arrogant, always bored with typing. Now I realise she was right. I've had the same education as many of the men here, but for what? All we're allowed to do is type up reports while Hugh and the others get the interesting work.'

'That's why Daddy wouldn't let me go to university,' said Lily. 'He says education just makes women discontented for their role in life. I only persuaded him to send me to Hoster's because he thought it would keep me out of trouble.'

Stella's journey of learning had been mapped when firstborn Corran began to show her academic prowess. Both parents had encouraged and supported their eldest daughter towards higher education, and by the time Stella came along the path was well worn. True, Corran strode along with her books tucked under her arm and her gown sweeping aside all doubters, while Stella, when her turn came, rather shuffled in her sister's wake. Still, she had earned her degree, and now she wanted her rightful reward.

Lily, who had come to Paris to have fun, laughed at her.

'Forget it for tonight, Stella. Look at that man over there, the handsome one with the long hair. He's *writing*! Do you think he's a poet? I'm going over. Watch me.'

Stella watched as Lily wandered across the café and struck up a conversation, but she couldn't brush her cares off as easily as her friend wanted. She wasn't here because she had pretty ankles, and she would prove that to them all. The League of Nations was whispered to be the next big opportunity. If she worked hard and efficiently, would that be enough to get her noticed for a position? Her worst fear was that when the conference came to an end her only option would be to return to Thurso. She just couldn't do it.

Lily came back. 'He *is* a poet, but he's American so I don't know if he can be a good one. The Americans don't strike me as a particularly poetic race.'

'That's nonsense. What about Emily Dickinson?'

Lily shrugged. 'Anyway,' she said, making a face as she sipped her wine, 'it's tremendous fun, but I wouldn't want to live this way forever.'

'What will you do when we're finished?'

'Get married, I suppose. Make a home.'

Stella thought she detected a slight flush on Lily's creamy

cheeks. 'Get married to – anyone in particular?'

Lily's dark eyes twinkled but that flush was quite definitely there.

'That's the question, isn't it? But what about you? Surely you want to marry one day?'

Did she? She had hardly had a chance to meet any men over the last four years. She thought of Freddie last night, of the tender wistfulness with which he had spoken of the broad landscapes of the veldt and his farm in southern Africa. As if she read her mind, Lily said, 'You want to travel. Maybe with Freddie you could do both.'

'We've only been out together once,' Stella protested. 'You're getting ahead of yourself.'

'Still, you never know. We said this would be the perfect place to meet interesting men. Maybe you've met your future husband in Freddie!'

'And maybe I haven't!' She watched a glamorous couple climb out of a taxi in the darkened street outside. 'At university there were never enough men at a dance or a social event because they were away fighting. At some point we stopped saying we would wait until the boys came back. They aren't coming back, and there will never be enough men to go round. This war will be with our generation always.'

'Your sister's fiancé came through, didn't he?'

She nodded. 'Rob. He's the one who has arranged for us to go to Jack's grave. I'm glad for Corran. They've had a long wait, but they can start planning their future.'

The future – but the tangled briars of the past stretched out and held them all so tightly. She and Lily finished their drinks, paid the waiter and stood up. Lily blew a kiss to the writer but he didn't respond.

'Lost in his creative genius,' she murmured, and they were laughing as they left the café.

# PART THREE
*Battles*

March to May 1919

# Chapter Fifteen

Amiens

Corran boarded the train at Dieppe station in the smothering darkness of an early morning.

Her mood was sombre – she was, after all, on her way to her brother's grave – and yet she couldn't quite suppress a secret surge of exhilaration. Travelling at last! She had been in France for nearly six months, yet had only left Dieppe on a few excursions to outlying camps. Every time she had enquired about visiting Paris or travelling along the coast, she had been told firmly that she had the wrong colour of papers, and a woman couldn't possibly travel alone anyway. Her time in the seaside town was fast drawing to a close: how could she bear to return to Britain with such limited experience of France? Here today, thanks to Rob's pass, she would at last see something more.

She was first to arrive in the compartment and gladly took a window seat, where she sat gripping her overnight bag on her knee and watched with surreptitious interest as her bleary-eyed fellow travellers arrived. There were soldiers returning from leave, a little subdued, and a red-faced padre. No other women, but one man in civilian clothes. Polite greetings were exchanged and then Corran turned her face to the window. Darkness stared back at her and challenged her confidence. She wouldn't think twice about travelling alone at home, having done so since her teens, but in France?

She had never known such a slow train. When it finally creaked into motion, it crawled between the fields at walking pace. There was nothing to see and yet she sat with her gaze fixed on the window, waiting for the first glimmer of daylight to spread across the landscape. Slowly the grey world emerged into view: flat, unremarkable and, as yet, unscarred.

At Abbeville the line came alongside the River Somme and she looked in awe at the slow, sluggish waters, which were tranquil here, but had been stained vivid scarlet further upstream. Trees lay hewn beside the banks, and as she travelled south the life seeped out of the landscape. The man in civvies got up and left the compartment. A moment later she was astonished to see him on the bank, walking quickly. He bent, lifted something and then swung himself back up on board the slow-moving train.

'An empty shell case. For my boy,' he said briefly as he rejoined them.

For the past couple of miles, Corran had been conscious of the padre's eyes on her, and knew he couldn't contain himself much longer. The other man's re-entrance broke the silence and provided his opening.

'Travelling alone, miss?'

'Just with ghosts,' she replied quietly.

'Humph. Ridiculous fancy. What brings a young lady like you to France anyway?'

'I'm a lecturer with the YMCA education scheme. We provide instruction for the soldiers.'

He ran his tongue over his lip. 'No men available, eh? Is that the best they can do, find some provincial schoolmistresses to teach our lads? Didn't they consider the temptations of the flesh? Sorry state of affairs.'

Corran felt herself colouring. 'The men are courteous at all times. As for my credentials, I teach Latin and Greek at Oxford University.'

'Which college?' he demanded.

'St Hilda's.'

He shook his head, his disapproval obvious. 'Precisely what's wrong with our world,' he declared, sweeping out one arm as though in the pulpit. He almost looked ready to get to his feet. 'Why anyone would think it a good idea to teach the classics of all subjects to our young ladies I will never fathom. Sowing the seeds of discontent, and of infertility too I believe. It's not natural, not natural at all. With such forces of evil at work, does anyone wonder that we had a war?'

Corran's mouth was dry and her hands were trembling. She had heard it all before, but the endless casual prejudice never became any easier to stomach.

'I think you'll find it was men, rather than women, who caused the war,' she said, keeping her tone as even as possible. 'There's no good reason whatsoever to deprive girls of the classics. And as for my work here in France, I have the utmost respect for the men I teach, who have treated me with nothing but kindness.'

The padre stared at her, open-mouthed, perhaps unused to having his monologues challenged. Then he muttered something, which she hoped wasn't 'harlot', and pulled out his newspaper, disappearing behind it. Corran glanced round the compartment. The man in civvies had turned to the window, quite deliberately ignoring the conversation, but one young soldier winked across at her and gave a silent round of applause. Despite herself, she grinned.

That was the end of conversation. The soldiers mostly slept for the rest of the journey. As for the civilian, he sat with his fingers locked together so tightly that the knuckles were white and his gaze rarely shifted from the scene outside. They each had their war story. What was his?

She pulled her book from her bag, not sure whether or not she wanted the padre to notice she was reading the Sophocles she had ordered up from the stores. It wasn't the first time she had considered that her family, like that of Oedipus, consisted of two sons and two daughters, but the prospect of visiting Jack's grave had stirred in her a desire to reread *Antigone*, that story of a grief-stricken young woman determined to see her brother properly buried and mourned. Not that Jack, thank God, lay unburied, but what kind of grave was his, here in this desolate landscape? She opened her book, but found her thoughts too full of the days ahead to allow her to concentrate. She would meet Stella in Amiens, where they would find a hotel, before carrying on tomorrow to Arras, and Rob. She had last seen Stella in London, when the war still struggled on. They hadn't imagined that their next meeting would be in France but Stella had always wanted to travel. Corran's heart ached for her little sister in her desolation without Jack. Perhaps Paris would go some way towards restoring her.

As for Rob, she had last seen him in a mansion house in the Oxfordshire countryside, recovering from an infected wound in his leg and screwing up his eyes against awful headaches. Corran had taken the train south from Newcastle and walked three miles through the rain along a country lane to visit him. She remembered the long, polished floor, the room smelling of carbolic, the men at various stages of recuperation. She remembered most of all how cold his hands were when she gripped them before leaving, knowing she would quite likely never see him again.

But he had come through.

It was late afternoon by the time the train finally rumbled into Amiens. Stiff and weary, Corran followed the line of passengers out onto the platform. The atmosphere on the train had been torpid, but the station at Amiens bustled with activity. French and British soldiers crowded the platforms, pushing and hurrying, their loud shouts mingling with the screech of the brakes and piercing whistle. Corran paused and looked around. She couldn't see Stella anywhere, so followed a stream of servicemen towards an exit marked *FOR ENGLISH ARMY ONLY*. The officer on the gate looked at her curiously, one woman amid a crowd of men, but after scrutinising her permit he let her through. Out in the street she looked around. There was Stella, perched on a broken-down wall, looking far more trim and fresh after the journey than Corran felt.

Their embrace was tight: evocative not only of months

of parting but of difficult days ahead. Then Corran held her sister at arm's length. Where was the teenager who charged up and down the staircase of her memories?

'Take off your hat,' she said, and then, 'I like it.'

Stella laughed and touched her short hair. 'I'm used to it now. For the first few weeks it felt wrong and I kept trying to sort my hair pins. How was your journey?'

'Perfectly fine, despite an obnoxious padre. Did you have much trouble?'

'No, although most people I encountered were astounded at a woman travelling alone into the war zone. But we'll have to change our plans. I had a long chat with a lovely officer who says we mustn't on any account go to any of the hotels. Those that are open are already overcrowded with French refugees who've returned and found their homes destroyed, and anywhere that will take us is likely to be the kind of place we couldn't possibly go, if you understand my meaning.'

Corran stared at her. 'Then where are we to sleep?'

'There's a ladies' hostel run by the YMCA just five minutes' walk from here. He suggested we try there,' said Stella with a grimace. 'I know it doesn't sound very exciting, but if hotels are out of the question then we don't have much choice.'

'I'll sleep anywhere that will give us a bed and the use of a bathroom,' said Corran. 'And if it's near the station then so much the better. We've another early start ahead of us tomorrow.' They set off in the direction that Stella's friendly officer had suggested. The streets were every bit as muddy as any camp Corran had visited, and signs of the terrible bombardment the residents of Amiens had endured were everywhere. But the hostel still stood, its YMCA sign nailed above a peeling wooden door. It took vigorous knocking to rouse anyone, but at last a grey-haired English woman came to the door. Her expression was not welcoming and her response even less so. There was no room in the hostel, and nowhere they could sleep, not even on the floor. They had better return to the station and sleep in the waiting room. Had they really imagined there would be beds to spare up the line for those who were merely sightseeing?

The uncompromising way in which she closed the door emphasised her words, and Corran and Stella were left looking at each other. Corran felt a stirring of unease, but her sister's eyes were stormy.

'Sightseeing!' Stella said. 'How dare she?'

'I suppose it's the station then,' said Corran with some reluctance. 'We can use our bags as pillows and I think we'll be safe enough with so many people about. At least we brought our own food.'

Stella wasn't listening. Without warning, she darted across the road. Startled, Corran watched as her sister hurried up to a military policeman on the opposite side of the muddy street. Her hands gestured firstly towards the ladies' hostel and then towards the station. A moment later she was back, smiling widely.

'There's an officers' leave club in the middle of town: badly shelled, but it takes VADs so will likely take us. He told me how to get there.'

For the second time that afternoon, Corran wondered at this sophisticated version of her little sister. They picked their way along the Grande rue, avoiding more than one large shell hole in the road. Past the heavily sandbagged cathedral, through one winding street after another, and at last found themselves outside a gloomy building. It was late afternoon now, and Corran reflected that this really must be their last try. It was this or the station.

'Looks more like a prison than a club,' she murmured to Stella. They were standing in a courtyard that was ankle-deep in mud, surrounded on three sides by stark walls and tiny, high windows. 'This can't possibly be it. How in the world do we get in?'

Stella pointed. 'Up there, do you think?'

A rickety-looking stair led up to a door in the wall – the only door they could see. They waded through the mud, noticing recent motor tracks, and climbed the steps to repeat the weary process of seeking a room. But at last their luck had turned. The English orderly who answered the door was delighted to see them, and steered them to the lady who ran the place. Miss Armitage turned out to be tall, gracious and thoughtful.

'I can't offer you anything to eat other than tea, bread and jam,' she said. 'And we've had no light or running water since the shelling.'

'We've brought food with us,' Corran said, thinking gratefully of the chocolate, sandwiches and eggs that her landlady had pressed on her so many hours before. 'We just need somewhere to sleep. Even the floor would do.'

'And you're going up the line tomorrow?'

'Yes.' Corran hesitated. 'We're meeting an army friend who will take us to our brother's grave.' She was aware of Stella's involuntary movement beside her.

'I understand,' Miss Armitage said gently. 'Come, I'll take you to your rooms. I believe there may be a couple with doors on.'

With doors on? As Miss Armitage led them up several flights of stairs into a large loft area, Corran understood.

'This was once a warehouse,' their host said. A row of small rooms opened off a makeshift sitting area. Most of the rooms had been created by tacking sackcloth to beams, but at the end were four wooden doors. Miss Armitage opened one of these. It would be the smallest room Corran had ever slept in, and the most welcome. She stood in the doorway looking at a bed with a couple of army blankets and a pillow, a stand with enamel basin and candlestick, and even a tiny mirror high up on the wall.

'This is heaven,' she said, laying down her bag, as Miss Armitage led Stella through to the next room.

A few minutes later the door opened, and Stella came in. 'No sheets!'

Corran laughed. 'A bit different from your luxurious hotel.' As she spoke there was a tap at the door, and the English orderly who had welcomed them stood there, a tin can of steaming hot water in his hands. 'Some water for you ladies in case you'd like to wash,' he said shyly.

'Better service than the Majestic any day!' said Stella. 'Thank you so much. Could I please have some next door too? It will all feel better after a good wash!' She slipped out again and Corran was left alone. To wash in warm water was luxury, and then came the challenge of sorting her hair. The tiny square mirror was high on the wall, positioned for someone a foot taller than she was, and even by kneeling on the bed she couldn't get a glimpse of herself. Eventually she gave up and combed and pinned her hair by feel.

'Stella has the better of this one anyway,' she murmured to herself.

Mindful of Miss Armitage's warning, she rummaged in her bag for food before opening her door. Stella hadn't emerged yet, so Corran wandered along into the sitting room. Here to her delight a map of the area was pinned on the wall: the very first she had seen in France, as the shops were forbidden from selling maps of the war zone. Excitement wrestled with dread as she identified Arras and Vimy, and pointed them out to Stella when she appeared. Together they examined the ground they would cover tomorrow, the ground Jack had fought over. Stella's lips were set tight and her dark eyes were almost black. Corran touched her gently on the arm and felt her tension.

'Shall we go and have some tea?'

In the dining room they laid out their sandwiches and a tin of condensed milk for the tea, and were glad to see plentiful bread and jam, while a teapot sat steaming on the table. After a long, weary day of travelling, simple food had rarely tasted so good. There were a few officers scattered around the room. As soon as they sat down, Corran asked, 'Have you heard from Alex lately?'

Stella shook her head.

'Nor have I,' Corran said, her hand not quite steady as she poured the tea. 'I know it's probably just taking longer to get through, but still—'

She felt the warmth of her sister's hand briefly covering her own. There was no room for platitudes, not after all they had been through. *Already have I suffered full much.* Corran pushed aside the fear that never left her and changed the subject, asking Stella about the conference.

'You never say much in your letters.'

'We're not permitted,' she replied. 'I'm glad of these few days away, to tell you the truth. I simply love Paris: everything is so grand, so spacious, so extravagant. And we get to see important delegates and work on reports that will shape the treaties. But there's an uneasy atmosphere for all that.'

'In what way?'

'We arrived with such optimism, but it's hard to hold on to amid the long hours of work. We are all dead tired, and there's a growing fear of an opportunity being missed.'

'What opportunity?'

'To make a better world. The longer things go on in this unsatisfactory way, the more obvious it is that each of the powers – large and small – has its own set of demands, and there's no way to fit them together. France wants Germany destroyed, to protect her borders against future attack. Britain wants control of the seas and her colonies. It's the same old thing, each nation looking out for its own interests rather than working together for the good of the world. Other voices are excluded. My friend Freddie says—'

'Who's Freddie?' Corran asked, and was interested to see the slight flush.

'As I said, a friend. He's with the South African delegation.'

'And?'

'He's taken me out a few times, that's all. It's very early days.'

Corran raised her eyebrows but Stella said nothing more. But then, was she likely to confide in a sister she had seen so rarely over these last few years? Their relationship was the strangest mixture of deep familiarity and distance. Corran drained her cup.

'Shall we take a walk outside before night? It's not quite dark. Let's have a look at the cathedral. There won't be time tomorrow.'

Stella agreed. They finished their rather unusual but welcome meal and collected their coats, then set out into the narrow side streets of Amiens, trying to find their way back to the Grande rue. Some shops stood open, selling coffee and tiny cakes, embroidered handkerchiefs and other souvenirs, as if the town were filled with tourists rather than soldiers and refugees. The light was fading as they approached the cathedral.

'It's said to be a Gothic masterpiece,' Corran said as they paused and looked up. 'But you wouldn't know, would you?'

The façade of the cathedral was hidden beneath layers of sandbags and scaffolding, which had protected it from the fate of the ruined buildings all around. They entered the cool, dimly lit space. A brilliant blaze of colour came from two rows of tricolour flags defiantly lining the aisle to the altar. Several women knelt before the altar, dressed in black, muttering in prayer and weeping. Corran felt Stella shiver beside her. As they turned, they noticed that the inner walls too were lined with sandbags.

'Paris is like this,' Stella said. 'All the stained glass has been removed from the churches, and there are sandbags everywhere.'

'We must come back, some time, when things are normal.'

The moment the words had left her mouth, she regretted them. The silence between them stretched back to 1914 and as far ahead as anyone could imagine.

Nothing would ever be normal again.

# Chapter Sixteen

## To Arras

Another day began in darkness. As they entered the station waiting room, Corran clasped Stella's arm.

'Thank goodness for Miss Armitage,' she murmured. 'Sleeping here would have been appalling.' Every available surface – benches, table, floor – was covered with sleeping soldiers, mostly dressed in the blue of the French poilus, and the air was heavy with male sweat and damp clothing. They hurried out onto the platform where their train stood. It too was crowded even at this hour, but as they squeezed their way along the corridor in the dark, they eventually came to a compartment that might have some space. 'Is there room for two in here?'

'By Jove, yes,' came the reply, and a flickering lantern was raised. A couple of officers sat at one side, while the rest of the space was filled with enough kit to supply a whole regiment. The men at once started moving their possessions and made space for Corran and Stella. 'Here, sit here, won't you? But what in the world brings you on board a train here of all places?'

'We're meeting a friend at Arras.'

'We're on this train all the way to Arras and beyond, to Valenciennes,' said the older one. 'We'll show you what's what.' He was about her own age and in the dim shadowy light of the lantern he appeared thin and weary, with a threadbare look to him. Many of the officers she met in Dieppe were boisterous and apparently carefree, enjoying a final fling before going home. This man, she guessed, was returning to his regiment after a time of leave. His war, like Alex's, was not yet over. She turned her attention to his comrade. Goodness, was this boy even old enough to serve in the army?

Of course he was.

Jack had been a teenager too when he left.

The train began to roll through countryside that was as dark as the carriages themselves. With nothing to be seen outside, they spoke quietly about their time in France and the world they had left behind. The older man had come through all four years. At home he was a pharmacist. The lad, as Corran suspected, had joined up last year, the minute he turned eighteen. His life experience consisted of school and war. Nothing else. There was something strange about sharing your life story with near strangers when you could barely see their expressions across the carriage, but Corran had become used to unexpected conversations in France.

Stella, meanwhile, barely said a word.

Eventually the train gave a jolt and began to slow.

'We're coming into Albert,' said the older officer. Corran stood up and leant out of the window, and after a moment Stella joined her. The grey light that was now creeping across the sky revealed a town more shattered than anything Corran had seen before, or could even begin to imagine. The damaged buildings of Amiens were nothing to this. Of the station itself, nothing remained.

They stood in silence and watched, and then one of the officers spoke softly behind them.

'The cathedral – see? The virgin has fallen. She fell shortly before the armistice.'

The once grand cathedral was nothing but a gaunt shell. Corran had heard the story of the statue of the Virgin and Child on top of the tower. It had been damaged in 1915 and leant at an impossible angle through the next three years, becoming a talisman to the troops of both sides who fought in her shadow, before finally being obliterated in the devastating battle of spring 1918. The virgin had fallen, taking with her all that was good and pure and holy. As the train passed on through the shattered town, nothing struck Corran so much as the stillness. But what else could there be? There was no one left.

'That's the road to Bapaume,' said their guide, pointing to a long white road curving away from the railway line. 'Topping road, that.'

Albert – Bapaume – names from the newspaper reports she had devoured over the breakfast table in her Newcastle lodgings each morning. And now she was here, where the echo of the guns still reverberated. The next stretch of the journey was something that Corran would never forget. It was impossible to imagine what this wasteland had looked like before the war, as they travelled slowly through ravaged, abandoned fields of death. The streaky light of dawn revealed the blackened, disfigured remains of what had once been trees.

'That's Thiepval Wood, you know,' said the older officer, who had come to stand close behind her. 'Thiepval Wood at dawn. The hour when the boys stood to.'

Thiepval Wood at dawn: the first day of the Somme. The day Arthur received his injuries. She saw the shadowy figures of those she had known, saw their slow walk into machine-gun fire and, unable to bear it, returned to her seat and buried her head in her hands. *Dear God, I thought I knew*. But Stella remained where she was, motionless, knuckles white as she gripped the edge of the open window. Dry-eyed, her gaze never once shifted from the scenes of horror through which they passed.

They reached Arras in that same state of stunned silence. Saying a subdued farewell to their companions, the sisters climbed down onto the platform of what was called Arras station – although there was little left that looked anything like station buildings. Corran looked round for Rob, feeling a tightening in her stomach that was nothing to do with the devastation around them. There he was. She remembered again the walk along the wooded lane from his convalescent home in September 1917, wondering if she would ever see him again. She lifted a hesitant hand in greeting and he straightened up, strode towards them, and took her in his arms.

'Corran. At last,' he said, holding her fast and kissing her on the lips.

The gear shift from the desolation of the journey to Rob's

vigorous welcome was more than she could cope with and despite herself she flinched.

He released her and turned to Stella. 'And Stella. My oh my. Four years is a long time. You were just out of school when last we met.'

'These four years have been an eternity,' said Stella in the small voice she had used all morning. Rob turned his hands upwards in a gesture of contrition.

'I'm sorry. This is a terribly hard day for you both. But I can't begin to tell you how good it is to see you. A little piece of home – *here*.' He waved his hand around the ruined station. 'Now, we go this way.' He led them across the railway lines – 'Don't worry, there won't be another train for ages' – and they clambered over piles of rubble and through a broken section of wall, out into what had once been a street beyond.

'Is it far?'

'Duisans is five miles or so outside Arras. I nabbed a car so we don't need to look for a lift from a lorry, which helps. I've left the car on the edge of town because the roads here are so torn up. But look here – shall we eat first or do you want to go straight there?'

'Straight there,' said Stella.

Rob nodded and led the way. At first Corran thought the town was empty and abandoned as they passed along narrow streets with the fronts of the houses all torn away, but gradually she became aware of people moving in the shattered homes. 'Do people really live here?'

'The French are returning,' he said. 'They are making the most of what remains. And there are still troops billeted here too.'

They turned a corner, and Corran found herself in what had once been a grand square: a vast space now strewn with rubble and surrounded by burnt-out buildings.

'Don't walk too close to the buildings,' Rob warned. 'More bits crumble and fall all the time.' They picked their way across the square and he led them to the edge of the town.

The sun had forced its way through the blanket of morning cloud and Corran felt its faint warmth as she climbed into the car beside Rob. As he moved into gear and pulled away, she found herself inconveniently thinking of her drive back from Luneray beside Arthur. She pushed the thought aside and glanced at him. She had been taken aback by the exuberance of his welcome and the apparent normality of his tone but now, as she looked more closely, she could see deep shadows under his eyes. His hands gripped the steering wheel more tightly than she might have expected too. As they drove on, the ruined buildings fell away and the landscape opened up: empty, scarred and littered with debris, but somehow gentler than the devastated town.

'The cemetery is just along here,' he said quietly as he drew up at the roadside. 'There were several casualty clearing stations – temporary hospitals behind the lines, you know – in this area. That always means there's a fair-sized cemetery nearby.'

Corran took Stella's icy hand as they walked towards the cemetery, and thought again of Antigone. Jack's sisters would do what was right by him; they would come to his graveside; they would mourn him. She had not been sure what to expect: there had been groups of crosses planted in twos and threes near the railway line, and perhaps Jack was buried somewhere like that. But no: this was a proper cemetery. Weak rays of low sun spilt across the ground ahead of them. A muddy track led to a rough fence, and then continued on between tightly packed rows of wooden crosses on either side. The crosses were not all of one kind; most were simple and plain while others were more intricate. The ground sloped upwards, and the forest of crosses – for this, surely, was more forest-like than the blasted remnants of Thiepval – stretched as far as the horizon.

'This way,' said Rob, leading them along the path. The weight of what was to come now felt almost too heavy to bear. Corran tried to distract herself by reading names scratched on wood as they passed, but soon gave up as they became a blur. Most were dated April 1917. Jack had come through the carnage of that spring only to die in a minor trench raid in the stark chill of winter. Then Rob branched off, walking between the rows on what was now just thick, sticky yellow mud. He stopped before a group of three identical crosses, simple but a little larger than some. 'Here,' he said, his tone brittle. 'The other two are the men who died with your brother.' He stepped back to make way.

*IN MEMORY OF CAPTAIN J. RUTHERFORD*
*SEAFORTH HIGHLANDERS*
*KILLED IN ACTION 8.11.17*

One hand still gripping Stella's fingers, Corran reached out and rested the other on the rough wood. The morning light was soft and gentle and the sky curved above them, empty and vast. Jack might not have the sea, but she was glad that he lay somewhere so open, so limitless. Huge skies were his Caithness birthright. Already she was framing reassuring sentences for Mother: *Jack's grave was dignified and orderly, and in a peaceful place*. If only she had a camera. If only Jack were here, he would have sketched the place. They had never yet gone on a family picnic without Jack pulling out pencil and paper and capturing the scene. It was an absurd thought, yet somehow she took comfort from picturing her brother sketching his own grave.

And then she heard a slight sound beside her and Stella pulled free of her grip and dropped to her knees. Shockingly, her sister was on all fours, her palms pressed down on the ground covering his grave. A noise came out of her, a long, loud howl interrupted by great ragged gasps for breath. Every instinct in Corran wanted to reach forward, to drag her sister to her feet, to shush that terrible noise. *For all our grief we will hide our sorrows in our hearts, for weeping will not avail us.* Homer's words, but so very British. What good would it do to give way? Couldn't Stella see for herself those vast skies, and draw from them the comfort that Corran had drawn? But as she looked down at her sister's shuddering, huddled form, she crouched down and placed a hand gently on her shoulder, saying nothing.

And as she sat there, confronted by Stella's raw grief, her own sorrow flowed inexorably into tears. Tears for Jack, and tears too for Alex, still out there, still in danger.

The sisters sat for a long time on the thick mud that oozed

196

above whatever was left of their brother. Rob had moved away to walk slowly among the crosses, looking at their inscriptions. He had his back to them. Corran felt the sobs running through Stella's body begin to slow, and her breathing became steadier. The face she turned towards Corran was tear-stained and streaked with dirt – the child Stella – but her voice was steady and authoritative.

'Please give me a minute on my own.'

Corran hugged her quickly then released her and moved away. She watched from a distance as Stella struggled to her feet and fumbled in her coat, then bent and with her bare fingers scooped out the mud at the foot of Jack's cross. There she buried something. She straightened up again and placed a hand on the wood, just as Corran had done, before turning away. Rob by this time stood beside Corran on the central path, his arm around her shoulders. Stella walked up to them. Her shoes, skirt and coat dripped with yellow mud: mud that also covered her hands and was smeared across her face and hair. 'I'm ready,' she said.

# Chapter Seventeen

## Vimy Ridge

Stella followed Corran and Rob down the path back to the car.

*There is so much Corran doesn't know.*

She glanced down at her coat. She was covered in sticky mud, which had already begun to harden into a kind of yellow plaster-of-Paris covering. Plaster of Arras. At some point she would have to clean up, but a deep weariness had set right into her bones, and it was hard to care. She knew they had several hours before the return train to Amiens, but had paid little attention to Corran and Rob's plans. For her, today had only ever been about Jack.

She watched the two of them walking ahead of her. Rob had his arm around Corran, and she leant against him. It would be good to have Rob as a brother-in-law. She thought about Freddie. He had lost a brother too and she knew that was partly why she was drawn to him. He sometimes joined Stella and Lily in the evenings, pulling up a chair and talking about the childhood he and Pieter had shared together in the vast open veldt, always eventually leading the conversation round to their work. But Freddie belonged in the sparkling world of the Hôtel Majestic. Whatever would he think if he could see her now, coated in mud?

She rather wished he could.

Corran and Rob stood by the car. Although Corran was not filthy from head to toe quite in the way that Stella was, her skirt and coat were smeared from where she had crouched beside her sister. Even Rob's trousers were splattered with mud.

'We should find somewhere to wash,' Corran said as Stella approached.

'We'll go back to Arras,' Rob said. 'I know a small café that has reopened. They won't have running water, but the owner will give you a basin to wash in. We can have something to eat and then I propose we drive out to Vimy. The views from the ridge are extraordinary.' He broke off and shook his head, rubbing at his forehead. Stella thought there was something almost bewildered in his tone as he said, 'Listen to me. You must think I'm cracked – rabbiting on about glorious views! But it really is a damned mystery, don't you think? How can there still be glorious views in such an accursed spot? How can the sun keep shining after all we've done?'

Corran sat up front beside Rob, and Stella was glad to slide into the back seat. Between the emotional storm and the early start, she was exhausted, and her head ached. Perhaps she could just wait in this café that Rob had mentioned until the others returned from Vimy. She closed her eyes as the car jolted its way back to the edge of Arras.

Rob led them to a small street just off the Grand'Place. They were becoming used to empty buildings and piles of rubble, but as they crossed the square Stella heard the unexpected sound of music. A gramophone? She recognised the song as 'Roses of Picardy', one of the melodies that Lily constantly sang in their room. But where on earth could it be coming from? And then her eye was drawn to one of those buildings whose front had been ripped away. On the first floor, heedless of the broken world around them, an elderly man and woman were dancing. Her arms were around his neck while he cradled her close to him and they swayed, slowly, gently, in time to the music. Behind them, Stella could see a room with rich crimson wallpaper, a bed and the table on which the gramophone stood. Amid the remnants of their lives, or perhaps of someone else's life, they danced. It was one of the most beautiful and extraordinary things she had ever seen. She stood, captivated, until Corran plucked her sleeve.

'The café's just here.'

There were five or six tables in a building that had more or less survived. Two were occupied by men in British uniform. The elderly owner rushed forward, welcoming Rob, and then turned to the two women. His eyes widened at the state of them. Then, with a stream of French that she could not follow, he ushered them through a curtain into a dark room crowded with furniture. A teenage girl was there, and the man issued a few abrupt commands. Before long the girl had placed a large bowl of water on the table. They couldn't do much about their clothes, but Stella scrubbed the mud away from her hands and face before thanking the sulky-looking girl and returning to the café.

The café owner poured some coffee and they brought out

their own supplies to make a simple meal. All the while, Stella could feel the tension easing. Nothing would ever change the horror of the past few years and what had been done to Jack, but in burying the box she had tried what little she could to restore something of his true self, and perhaps to quieten the sounds that ripped through her own dreams. She sipped the bitter coffee and felt its warmth slide through her body, reaching into her numbness. By the time the meal was finished, she decided to join them this afternoon after all. There was more to understand.

The road to Vimy took them through yet more devastated areas that had once been villages. It was shocking how quickly that felt commonplace. They passed between fields of huts where soldiers waved to them, and they laughed at signs for Balmoral Camp, thinking of home. The horizon opened up, just as it had done at Duisans. The vast expanse was littered with debris – stretches of barbed wire, heaps of sandbags and piles of camouflage. But somehow in the afternoon sunlight it felt less oppressive and less real than the devastation they had seen from the railway line – almost like viewing a piece of the past in a museum. Rob parked up on the verge. 'Here's as good as anywhere,' he said.

Some men in uniform watched them. Rob walked over and spoke with one of them before beckoning the sisters to join him. 'They're Royal Engineers clearing the battlefield,' he said. 'Making it safe. Take care where you put your feet and what you touch; there are any number of unexploded shells around. It's the most common cause of injuries that we deal with in the hospital now. But these chaps have told me where we may go. I can show you a dugout along here. It was a Boche one originally – far better than anything we created.'

Up here on the ridge, the sweep of the sky brought a grandeur to the abandoned battlefield. Rob had borrowed a candle from the Royal Engineer. He lit it now and held it out, showing the way down some slippery steps. Another layer of mud for their already caked shoes. Stella stepped carefully down behind the two of them and into a cavernlike, dark space, lit only by the candle, which trembled in Rob's unsteady hand, sending shadows leaping around the walls. The air was damp and fetid. She could make out two narrow bunks against one wall, and as her eyes adjusted she was startled by the grey army coats abandoned on them. A crate serving as a table had a tin plate and mug on it, and a newspaper cartoon and a drawing of a naked woman were pinned to the wall above. Rob placed the candle on the crate and sat down on one of the bunks.

'This is a fine dugout,' he said. 'I'd have given a great deal for a place like this under fire.'

'Did you sleep in one of these?' Stella asked. Corran had remained at the foot of the stairs where some dim light filtered in, her arms hugging her chest tightly.

'There wasn't much sleeping involved,' Rob said, and he brushed his hand across his eyes with a strange gesture as though knocking away an annoying insect. 'Night was often when both sides had a go at each other. You'd be pretty glad of a shelter like this then.'

Stella realised she knew very little of Rob's war. She had vaguely pictured him walking through a tented hospital, treating injured soldiers. 'I thought you were in a hospital,' she said. 'Not on the front line.'

That gesture again, and in the shadowy light of the candle Rob's face, brown with exposure to the open air, looked gaunt. 'I spent two years as MO to a battalion. I was with them in the trenches as well as behind the lines. We'd set up an aid post wherever we could. A dugout like this would be the best we could wish for. Often I used a shell hole or a ruined building we were holding. We needed to be close to the men, you see, to treat their injuries as soon as possible.'

'Under fire,' she said softly.

'Under fire.'

'You saw it all.'

'Yes.'

'Like Jack.'

Rob looked up and their eyes met. She could almost hear the explosions that had rocked this little hiding place, feel the ground shake. Smell the raw fear. Up above was a world where they said the war had ended. Here in the damp darkness of the dugout, this man's haunted expression said otherwise.

'Like Jack,' he agreed, and Stella felt her skin prickle with goosebumps. Their gaze held.

There was a movement and they both turned in time to see Corran's feet disappear up the muddy steps. Stella had temporarily forgotten how much her sister hated being underground. Rob jumped to his feet and hurried after her. Stella took a final look round, reluctant to leave. This was the closest she had come, since that last night with Jack, to the reality she needed to understand.

Up above the light at first was dazzling. Rob had his arms round Corran.

'I'm sorry,' she said shakily. 'It was too dark in there. I'm not good in small spaces.'

Stella took a deep breath of the March air. Although fresher that the dugout, it still carried an insistent tinge of something damp and rotten. She looked around. On the horizon was a big white cross.

'The memorial to the Canadians,' said Rob.

'The Canadian prime minister, Robert Borden, is at the Majestic.'

'Are there many from the Dominions?'

'Oh yes. They are determined to have their say. My friend Freddie from South Africa says their losses must be rewarded in the final settlement.'

'Quite right. Vimy Ridge is soaked in Canadian blood.'

They stood for a moment or two longer, thoughtful in the soft breeze, before Corran suggested they should return to Arras for their train. On their way back towards the road, they passed a party of Chinese labourers heading in the opposite direction with spades in hand. Stella had noticed one or two similar parties by the railway line and watched them curiously as she climbed into the car.

'Thank you, Rob,' Corran said from the front seat. 'The papers say people at home are clamouring to come and see, to find their loved ones.'

'People at home have no idea,' Rob said shortly as the car spluttered into life.

'What do you mean?' Stella asked.

He turned his head so that he took them both in. 'You are lucky, girls,' he said. 'Losing Jack is dreadful, but at least you have a grave. That's because Jack died in a clearing station. I think people at home believe this is how it is – cemeteries, neat rows of graves. They have no idea that most of the men are still out there.'

'Where?' Corran asked. But Stella was remembering.

'Those Chinese,' she said. 'Digging. They're digging up the dead, aren't they?'

Rob gave a quick nod. 'I was careful where I brought you,' he said. 'I know this sector is fairly well cleared, and that's why I checked with the RE chap. There are places where you'd still come across the very worst of war. Corpses. Bits of corpses. Rats, gorging themselves. You really don't want to see that.'

Corran shuddered. 'No, we don't.' But in the back, Stella turned round and strained as hard as she could to see the Chinese labourers. The worst of war, the very worst of war.

Jack hadn't left her the luxury of closing her eyes.

They returned to Amiens exhausted and with their mud-caked skirts and boots weighing them down. In the officers' leave club, it was a relief to rid themselves of their outer layers and to scrub the grime from their skin as best they could. Stella began to think with longing of the hot running water in the private bathroom that awaited her in the Majestic the following day, and the laundry service that would take her filthy clothes, albeit they would charge extra. She wouldn't have missed this experience for the world, but it would be good to be clean again, and to sleep in welcome comfort between crisp, clean sheets rather than scratchy army blankets.

They were too tired after their meal to go out and explore Amiens again, so found themselves a corner of the gloomy sitting room, pulling two wicker chairs close together beside a guttering candle. Stella was in her stocking soles. She pulled her feet up on the seat and hugged her knees. Corran wandered over to the map and retraced their travels with her finger. Stella watched her and wondered when they had last spent so much time together, just the two of them. Tomorrow morning Corran would board a train for Dieppe while Stella would return to Paris. It would be many months before they would meet again.

'How much longer will you be in Dieppe?'

'Not long at all.' Corran left the map and took a seat beside her sister. 'Our work is winding up and the army will take over the education scheme. My post in Oxford has been held for me so I will take that up.'

'Until Rob comes home.'

There was a pause. When Corran spoke, Stella had the feeling it wasn't what she had originally intended to say.

'I'll go to Thurso if I can and help Mother sort the house. You know she has decided to leave.'

'She told me in her last letter. She's quite right. There's no longer as much demand for lodgings for officers, and she shouldn't be alone. Not now. It's good she can stay with Aunt Maggie in Aberdeen.'

Corran shook her head. 'I'm not sure. Won't she miss Thurso? I can't imagine not going back. And what about Alex?'

'Alex hasn't spent more than a few weeks at a time in that

house since he was sixteen. Once you marry Rob, you'll have your own home somewhere else, and I won't ever live in Thurso again. It's far better for Mother to have company, and will make it much easier for us to visit her.'

Stella could see Corran was unconvinced. She had always been the one with the strongest pull northwards. But their mother, always decisive, was quite clear that it was time to move on. 'There's every chance I won't be back in our old house at all,' Stella said. 'This is the only leave I'll get until the German treaty is signed, and we still don't know when that will be.'

'And then?'

'There will be further treaties, and there's talk of work on reparations. Or there might be opportunities with the League of Nations.'

'And would you want that?'

Stella thought of the Chinese labourers digging up the rotting corpses of boys who had deserved a future. 'More than ever,' she said. 'This must never happen again. I thought the peace conference was the answer, but too many countries are still focused on their own interests. We need an international body that exists to prevent the utter waste of war. That's what the League of Nations is about.'

Corran nodded and then yawned. 'We've an early start in the morning and I'm no good for anything but bed – even bed without sheets! Coming?'

Stella nodded, and picked up the candle to light their way through the loft. Bed without sheets, but at least with a door.

'Good night.'

# Chapter Eighteen

Paris

Stella stepped into the glittering foyer of the Majestic, her head held high and her skirt stiff with yellow mud. She collected her key, rather enjoying the startled glances she received. She wondered if Lily would be in their room. Now that she was back, her body yearned more than ever for that hot bath and a nap between clean white sheets.

She braved the lift for once, too weary to face the stairs, and inserted her key in the lock. Opened the door, walked in and stopped.

The woman standing at the dressing table, busy scooping lotions and lipsticks into a bag, was not Lily.

Stella's first thought was that someone had claimed her bed during her three-day absence. 'I say, this is my room.'

The woman turned to face her, and Stella's tired brain tried to catch up. She had seen this small, slim woman with immaculately coiffed hair and pale face before somewhere. In a London mansion house, at the foot of a grand staircase, her hand outstretched in gracious welcome. This was no member of the delegation; this was Lily's mother.

'Oh, I'm so sorry,' Stella began. 'I—' And then she stopped again.

Lily's mother's eyes were red-rimmed and tears had made tracks through her make-up.

Something was shifting, something was horribly wrong, and yet, drained by three days of uncomfortable travel, little sleep and heightened emotion, Stella's thoughts simply wouldn't join up with her words. Lily's mother returned in silence to her daughter's possessions.

A knock on the door. Stella sprang to open it and was hugely relieved to see Hugh. 'Hugh! What's going on?'

'I heard you were back,' Hugh said. His face too was strained and pale and he was breathless, as if he had hurried up the stairs. Lady Sheridan ignored them both.

'Where's Lily?'

'Lily's very ill, Stella. She's in hospital. Flu.'

'No! But she was fine – I've only been gone three days! Is she going to be all right?'

'I don't know.' Hugh stood in the centre of the room like a bewildered, lost child. 'I don't know.'

Stella looked at Lily's mother. 'Lady Sheridan?' she asked pleadingly.

At last the woman turned, and Stella realised she was doing all she could to hold herself together.

'They sent for us yesterday morning and we took the air service from London. It's military, of course, but Clive knows someone. They didn't think she would see evening but she has rallied a little.' She moved over to the wardrobe and added a few items to the bag. 'I must get back to her.' Hugh opened the door and she hurried out without acknowledging him. He closed it slowly and sat down on the edge of Lily's bed. Stella sat opposite him.

'Tell me.'

'She had a cold for a day or two – but we've all had so many colds in this place that I doubt she thought anything of it. She went to work as usual; it must have been the morning you left. She became feverish and collapsed over at the Astoria. They brought her to the sick bay here but she was so ill, they thought she would die.' He looked up at her, his eyes dark with fear. 'Her parents came and insisted on her being moved to hospital.'

'Have you seen her?'

Hugh shook his head. 'No one will let me. It's too contagious. Mabel and Anne-Marie are in quarantine because they helped her when she took ill.'

Stella sat for a moment, trying to collect her thoughts. Lily – so full of life and flirtation and fun – dying? Was that even possible? And then her mind pulled her back through the last couple of days, to Jack's grave and to the ravaged landscape surrounding it. There was no longer any horror that was not possible.

Hugh lifted his head. 'If Lily comes through, I'll ask her to marry me,' he said. 'I can't think why I didn't do it before. Only I thought we had time.'

Stella nodded and reached out a hand to clasp Hugh's. Her nails, she could see, were still encrusted with yellow mud. He noticed too and looked at her more fully, taking in her clothes this time.

'How did you get on?' he asked her.

She paused. 'It was – like nothing you could imagine,' she said. 'Here in Paris it's easy to forget. The treaties are what matters, almost as if the fighting and the killing have disappeared. Out there – you can't ever forget.' She pulled her hand back. 'Hugh – I must change out of these clothes and send them down to the laundry. And I'm simply longing for a hot bath. Besides . . .' She hesitated. 'Now that Lily's mother has gone, I don't suppose you should really be here.'

He got to his feet. 'No. Of course. I wanted to tell you myself, that's all. I was hanging about downstairs but I must have missed you. I'll get back to work, although I can't concentrate at all. I can't think of anything other than Lily.'

'It's hopeful, surely, if she has come through the worst of it.'

'Perhaps,' he said, one hand on the door handle. 'I'll see you at dinner, Stella.'

He was gone and at last she was alone in her room. She had longed for this space, this peace, to pore over all she had experienced over the last few days, but now her thoughts were full of fear. Lily, with her laughter and her singing and her flirting. This dreadful flu sounded so innocuous, but it had swept in as soon as the armies stopped killing each other, and left a trail just as deadly in its wake. She stepped out of her filthy skirt and let it drop to the floor. Poor Hugh. How he loved her. Would Lily survive? If she did, would she love him back?

Yet by the time she reached the bathroom and let the steaming hot water rise about her tired body, it was not Hugh

211

she thought of, or even Lily. It was not Corran and it was not Rob.

It was Jack.

Lily did survive, but she never returned to work. Once she was strong enough, her parents whisked her off to Biarritz to recuperate. Stella visited her in hospital before she left. Lily was so thin, pale and fragile that it was hard not to gather her into her arms, but physical contact was not advised. So Stella stood at a distance from the bed and strained to hear as Lily whispered about the letter she had received from Hugh.

'He wants to marry me, and I want it too,' she said, glancing towards the open door. 'I always did, really. But he'll wait until I'm stronger before he speaks to Daddy. My parents wouldn't contemplate it just now. He'll come to Biarritz when he next has leave, and we can tell them then.'

'I'm pleased for you,' said Stella. And she was. But as she walked away from the hospital and back through the Paris streets to the Majestic, she felt again the familiar, empty ache of loss. She and Lily had come here together, and although she had formed other friendships, these were superficial by comparison. Now some other girl would be allocated Lily's bed, and she would have to share with a stranger.

She was so very tired of losing those she loved.

Work, however, left her little time for despair. She had returned to find the Astoria in a panic over spies.

'We're leaking like a sieve,' Mabel told her cheerfully. 'Bingham's beside herself. There have been reports in German newspapers that can only have come from the inside. Two girls from the accounts section were sent home in disgrace but they're just scapegoats if you ask me. No one really believes they knew anything worth passing on.'

Meanwhile the pile of papers in the in-tray in their depleted typing room grew ever higher, and now dealt with a bewildering range of territories. Stella had travelled to Paris imagining that the conference would all be about Germany, and discovered that the Great Powers were slicing up the whole world like a pie to be shared between themselves. She had no sooner finished typing up a report on the case for a plebiscite to determine the fate of Germans living in Danzig, than she would move on to angry Italian insistence that the secret treaty with Britain and France that had lured them into the war should be honoured in the final settlement. She searched her atlas to identify Shantung, a key demand of the Japanese delegation, and then skimmed a report suggesting that the newly discovered oil in the Mosul region of Mesopotamia could be the fuel of the future, making that land highly prized. The Ottoman Empire had collapsed, and Britain and France scrambled to seize hold of its Arabian territories, while the Arabs argued in vain for their own independence. Self-determination, it seemed, was only for the select few. Stella paused, thinking of the evening before, when she had been intrigued to watch the glamorous Lawrence of Arabia drifting through the Majestic alongside Arab leader Emir Faisal, both dressed in flowing white robes. They had dined with a tall thin woman who smoked incessantly, and who was later identified to her as Gertrude Bell, the only woman taking part in the peace conference in her own right.

Meanwhile Anne-Marie, who continued to visit Marguerite de Witt-Schlumberger in her apartment, told her that the Inter-Allied Women's Conference had presented resolutions to the League of Nations Commission.

'We should have been part of the conference proper, of course,' she said, balancing on the windowsill in their room in the Astoria, 'but it's still an immense achievement that has never happened before. Thanks to our efforts, women will participate fully in the League of Nations, as staff and as delegates, and the league will consider issues like outlawing the sale of women and children, and will work to prevent the exclusion of women from political life. All because we didn't go away when they told us to. This idea that women's issues are domestic issues while men deal with the serious stuff – that can't hold water after the last four years.'

The rattle of typewriter keys, the lines of closely scribbled notes, the maps and charts and diagrams: they swam across Stella's mind as she lay in bed craving sleep. It was as much a relief as a thrill, therefore, when she was at last summoned to take minutes of the sessions in the salons of the Quai d'Orsay. The first time this happened she was so excited to witness the treaty negotiations in person that she hurried across the magnificent Pont Alexandre III and barely paused to take in the fresh loveliness of the April sunshine sparkling on the waters of the Seine. She and Lily had strolled this way during their explorations of Paris, standing outside the creamy stone building that looked more like a palace than a government ministry office. Today she pushed her way through the crowds surrounding the gates and nearly stumbled over a beggar woman who thrust herself right into her path, hands outstretched. Righting herself, she hurried up the steps to the west door.

Inside, she barely had time to notice the grandeur before Miss Bingham strode towards her.

'Miss Rutherford. This way.' Stella followed up a wide staircase, pausing briefly to admire the elaborate tapestry on the middle landing but not wanting to be left behind. Another grand hallway led to several doors. One stood open and Stella could hear deep laughter and conversation coming from within, but Miss Bingham opened another door. 'In here. The session starts in ten minutes – the delegates will be through shortly. This is your desk here' – indicating a folding table and uncomfortable-looking chair set against a wall. 'Prepare,' she said with a nod, and was gone, closing the door behind her.

Alone, Stella looked around the marbled and mirrored splendour. More French magnificence. Two long tables ran the length of the room, set out with blotting pads and inkwells, and with a gilt chair at each place. A series of maps lay along the centre of the tables. At one end was the most ostentatious, intricately carved mantelpiece she had ever seen. Tall windows ran along the opposite wall, hung with heavy scarlet curtains. Her feet sank into the carpet as she crossed to look down on the garden below. Arcs of water shot upwards from the fountains, sparkling in the Paris sunlight.

She heard their voices out in the hallway before she saw them, and by the time the dark-suited men filed into the room, Stella was seated at her desk, pen at the ready and shorthand pad open. Feeling like an intruder, she hardly dared breathe, but not one of them glanced her way. She might not have been there. She watched as they took their seats, and mentally crossed them off. There was Lloyd George with his shock of white hair, and there was tall, thin Balfour. There was Clemenceau, remarkably recovered from his assassination attempt, seated alongside Poincaré, the French prime minister. At the other end was Woodrow Wilson, dressed formally in frock coat despite the warm weather. She had never seen him in the Majestic so looked at him curiously: the man whose fourteen points, supposedly the foundation of peace, had quickly been watered down while he himself turned his energies towards the League of Nations. He leant forward, fingertips pressed together and a frown on his face. He resembled an old-fashioned preacher. He raised his eyes and saw her watching him; she blushed and looked away quickly. There were more junior aides there too whom she recognised from the hotel, and a friend of Hugh's flashed her a smile. She picked up her pen, and realised her fingers were trembling. This was a different order altogether from typing up reports. This was history in the making, and she was its designated witness.

And then it became one of the longest days of her life.

She very quickly discovered that instead of insightful debate and deeply considered decision-making, she was here to witness procedural wrangling and unintelligible pontificating. In the morning session they discussed the Balkans. Stella knew from reports she had typed up that they had been discussing the Balkans for weeks. No one had really expected the Habsburg Empire to collapse quite so dramatically at the end of the war, and now these men wanted to superimpose a new map onto a mix of nationalities, religions and cultures that spread over at least seven countries. A difficult task when the shape of Russia – not invited to the conference – remained completely outside their control. Alex was somewhere on the Baltic Sea with the navy right now, trying to defeat the Bolsheviks. How would today's discussions affect him? She swallowed. He was a shadowy figure, the older brother she hadn't seen for years.

*This cruel war robs us of those we love in a thousand different ways.*

A new name was thrown around – Yugoslavia – and that sounded interesting, but instead of any grand proposals, today's discussions consisted of an interminable debate about the relationship between one particular border and one particular railway line. The room was already hot and airless, and tempers grew fractured. By the afternoon the air was thick with cigar smoke and the heat soared. They closed the heavy red curtains to shut out the sun and light blazed instead from chandeliers. Where in the morning the delegates had been quarrelsome, by this afternoon they had grown weary. Stella looked around. Only the Italian prime minister remained animated. President Wilson, she was sure, was asleep. Little wonder – these were old men, and old men like to nap in the afternoons. How she longed to be back in their little typing room at the Astoria, where at least they could open a window and lean out for a cigarette, watching the bright colours, life and laughter of the Champs-Élysées below.

And then came a knock at the door. There had been interruptions on various occasions – some junior clerk or other sent in with a note – and Stella was relieved to have anything break up the monotony. She looked up and took a quick breath as, lithe and confident, Freddie Shepherd entered the room. He murmured an apology and walked up behind Mr Balfour, placing a folded piece of paper onto the table in front of him, before turning to leave the room. She watched him notice her, his eyes widening, and a smile lit up his face. His youth and vigour rippled through the musty air, and he brushed so close to her desk that her papers shifted. She glanced up at him and he whispered, 'Meet me outside.'

She heard the door close behind him and struggled to gather her scattered thoughts, to grasp the last few sentences of discussion from the thick air. Mercifully the session was drawing to a close, and the delegates would retire to the banqueting hall for tea and macaroons. Miss Bingham stood in the doorway.

'Thank you, Miss Rutherford. You may return to the Astoria and type up your notes. Today's final session is a closed session. No minutes.'

*No minutes, as they carve up the world.*

Stella gathered her papers together and left the room, then paused. *Meet me outside.* Outside the room? Outside the building? She lingered for a moment then descended the grand stairs, enjoying the feel of her hand gliding down the polished banister. The entrance hallway was busy with groups of people, yet somehow her eyes found him immediately. He stood near the doorway, laughing, one hand resting on another man's shoulder. He saw her and said something to his colleague. By the time she had reached the door, he was waiting for her.

He leant forward and kissed her cheek. 'I'm so glad you finished early. Are you walking back to the Majestic?'

'No, the Astoria,' she said. 'I've still to type up my notes.'

'May I walk with you? I have something to ask you.'

She felt her heart beat quickly. After long, turgid hours in the company of those white-haired, pompous men, Freddie's youthful good looks and energy were exhilarating.

'Yes, of course,' she said as they emerged into the brightness of the Paris afternoon. 'It's such a relief to breathe fresh air again.'

'Isn't it awful?' Freddie said with sympathy. 'My afternoon wasn't bad, a meeting with Smuts and a few others, but I've sat in on a couple of the main sessions – when they've been dealing with our business in southern Africa, you know – and they really are exasperating. All these plenipotentiaries making a noise about things they can't possibly understand.'

'If people at home knew what's really going on . . .'

'Why do you think they're so keen to keep the newspapermen out?'

They stayed on the left bank of the river until the Pont de l'Alma. Stella glanced at him. Over the last few weeks her long hours had left little time for socialising. Meaningful conversation at the Majestic was useless as someone always interrupted, dragging Freddie off to be part of some fervent discussion. Now, as they strolled together along the riverbank, she remembered how much she enjoyed his company.

'You said you had something to ask me.'

'Indeed I do.' He slipped his good hand inside his jacket pocket and pulled out an envelope. 'I promised you tickets for the Opéra Garnier. *Castor and Pollux* a week on Saturday. Will you join me?'

Amid the fog of negotiations, the horror of the battlefields and the dark shadow of Lily's illness, Freddie's presence sparkled like a Kimberley diamond.

'I'd love to!' she said. He slipped his arm around her waist and pulled her in towards him ever so slightly. She felt the strength and the hardness of his body and remembered how good it had felt when he kissed her. He kept his arm lightly around her as they walked on up the avenue that had recently been renamed after King George V, before turning onto the Champs-Élysées near the Astoria.

He told her of his afternoon. 'Jan – General Smuts – has been called in to help with this Japanese situation.'

Stella only had the sketchiest knowledge of the Japanese situation, but thought of the report she had typed up on the Shantung Province. 'They want Shantung.'

'They do,' said Freddie. 'It looks as if they'll get it too, though that's a devastating blow for the Chinese and makes a mockery of all Wilson's high-minded principles.'

'Then why on earth?'

'Because Wilson will give them anything they want to prevent their racial equality clause being included in the League of Nations wording.'

'What would the clause say?'

'They want foreign settlers to be treated equally and not discriminated against on the basis of race or religion. It's unthinkable, of course. Wilson knows how afraid his voters back home on the west coast are of the "yellow peril" getting hold of the Pacific Islands and using them as a stepping stone. Meanwhile the Japs are upset because they joined in with the Allies in the war, but feel they're still treated as second-class citizens by the west.'

'They have a point, surely.'

'Do you really think so?' Freddie asked. 'The Aussies are beside themselves. Hughes says it would threaten the very idea of a white Australia. He's right, of course. I know that from home. To say that all races are equal, that yellow and brown and black people are just the same as white people, is dangerous nonsense.'

'In what way dangerous?'

'Have you seen what's happening in Egypt? Or in India? Nationalist uprisings everywhere. We've all had enough of war. It's the role and responsibility of white people to bring harmony and order to the lives of backward races. This conference is about establishing a lasting peace that will be good for everyone, not stoking the flames of rebels and fanatics.'

Freddie was not saying anything particularly unusual, but Stella felt a stirring of something discordant deep within. She pushed her unease aside as they reached the Astoria. Freddie took her hand and smiled his warm, winsome smile, his vivid blue eyes looking into hers.

'Here already! What a shame.' He looked up at the hotel. 'It's a splendid building, though last time I was here I did think it smelt a bit off. Which is your window?'

Stella pointed. 'We have a wonderful view of the Arc de Triomphe.'

'I'd love to see,' he said. 'Could I?'

'I don't see why not.' She led him in, greeting the French doorman. They climbed the stairs to the typing room, where Mabel and Anne-Marie were both at work and more than happy to take a break. Freddie made straight for the open window and leant out. Then he turned around and smiled at them, sunlight glinting on his golden hair.

'So, this is your hidey-hole! What fun you must have.'

'A lot less than you imagine,' Stella said, moving over to her typewriter and laying down her papers. 'But I must get these notes typed up before dinner. I'm afraid you'll have to go now.'

'Don't mind me,' he said gaily, wandering around and casually lifting a sheet of paper from their in-tray.

Anne-Marie looked up. 'You should leave,' she said. 'We're not supposed to have visitors in the typing rooms and Stella's right, we have a lot of work to get through.' Her tone, if not quite unfriendly, was firm and Freddie held up his hands.

'I'm going, I'm going! Stella will escort me from the premises.'

With a glance at the work awaiting her, Stella sighed. 'Can't you go yourself? No, I suppose it's better if I show you out. Come on then.'

As they descended the stairs, Freddie said, 'You hear things before anyone else, you girls. Meanwhile I hang around, waiting for them to make decisions that could have been made weeks ago.' He stopped and took her hand again. 'You do remember what I said before, Stella? About how people like you can actually help this conference run more smoothly, just by ensuring the right people have the right information?'

'I can't talk about my work.'

'Not to outsiders. Of course not,' he said, as they continued on downstairs. 'But after all, you and I both serve the British Empire Delegation. It's no different from me telling you about the Japanese situation out there. It's natural to discuss these things among ourselves. You can't tell me anything that I wouldn't hear sooner or later. The problem is it's so often later. You know how it is here: documents get buried in piles and take weeks to see the light of day. In the meantime all sorts of decisions are made that can't be unmade. You are in a position to help prevent that. All you would need to do is keep a list of the papers you type up and the main points from sessions like today, and pass it to me. I would do the rest.'

They reached the bottom of the stairs. The hall was empty but they could hear the voice of the doorman, who had stepped outside to open a cab door.

Freddie pulled Stella into an unexpectedly lingering kiss. 'It's so important we make time for pleasure amid all this work,' he murmured. 'I'm glad I got those opera tickets. Plenty more where those came from.' Then he released her quickly as the voices and footsteps drew closer. Stella turned, her lips burning and her cheeks no less so. There in the hallway stood Miss Bingham, her steely blue eyes boring into the couple at the foot of the stairs. Freddie touched his hat in acknowledgement and strode briskly through the door.

'Why was Mr Shepherd here?'

'Delivering something upstairs,' Stella said quickly. 'I was just seeing him out.'

Miss Bingham's chilly gaze held hers for an uncomfortably long time. The friendly efficiency of just an hour earlier was gone, replaced by barely contained hostility.

'Indeed. I must speak to all the typing girls. Go upstairs, please, and ask your colleagues to gather in Typing Room One.'

The two girls from accounts who had been sent home were fresh in Stella's mind as she fled upstairs, heart racing. Was she about to be dismissed? She entered their room to a silence that screamed that Mabel and Anne-Marie had been discussing her, but she ignored that for now. 'Miss Bingham wants to see us all next door.'

The message passed along and typists piled out into the corridor, whispering and wondering. They crammed into the largest typing room and waited. Miss Bingham closed the door. She looked at them for a moment, her movements tight and her lips pressed together in a thin line. Stella curled her fingers tightly into her palms and breathed in the nervous tension that filled the room.

'I must inform you that there has been another breach of confidence within the last twenty-four hours, one that may have serious consequences for the conference. The matter is even as we speak being discussed at the highest levels.'

Each word was sour, coated with displeasure. As Stella awaited the interrogation that must surely come, she tried to push down the rising tide of guilt. She had done nothing, not a thing, but Freddie's words on the stairs echoed in her mind. Who else had heard him?

'The authorities are of a mind that this leak has most likely come from among ourselves.' Miss Bingham paused, and something shifted in her stance. 'I might add that they have not one shred of evidence for this allegation. I have told them that you are honourable women, every last one of you. It's all too easy for them to cast the blame in this direction, speaking of idle chatter. I have suggested they should pay more attention to what is said amid the cigar smoke of the bar in the evenings, but that is somehow regarded as *diplomacy* rather than gossip.'

As a ripple of stunned approval ran round the room, Stella realised she had underestimated Miss Bingham. She had not brought them here to harangue them but to warn them that, as ever, the women would be first to be blamed. Her fury was not directed at the typists but at the authorities who casually threw such damaging allegations around. She spoke about additional security measures and dismissed them.

'Please don't let me down, girls.'

Stella returned to her desk, still marvelling at Miss Bingham's words. Her sheaf of papers lay untouched beside her typewriter. She would be lucky to finish in time for dinner tonight. She inserted a sheet of typing paper.

'You and Freddie look cosy,' said Mabel.

'We finished at Quai d'Orsay at the same time. He walked me back.'

She sensed rather than saw the glance between them.

'He's rather a dish,' Anne-Marie admitted. 'But you should be careful, Stella.'

'Don't worry, I won't let him break my heart.'

'That's good, of course, but it's not entirely what I mean. Freddie always likes to be in the know, doesn't he? At the centre of things. I wouldn't like him to be—' She stopped.

'To be what? Using me?'

'Well – yes.'

For a moment Stella said nothing. Something of the fog

of that stifling room at the Quai d'Orsay had seeped into her brain and she could do with the fresh breeze of Caithness to bring clarity. She rose and walked to the window, still open, and hung out, looking down on the Champs-Élysées. Her shifting thoughts moved into focus and she turned to face them.

'I like Freddie. He's fun, he's charming and he knows all the best places. I'm not in love with him. I'm also not about to give him any of the information he wants. But why *shouldn't* I have some fun? Why shouldn't we all have some fun? These last years have been utter hell. If the price of Freddie showing me a good time is stringing him along a little bit, so be it. I'm sick to the back teeth of being *careful*.'

Mabel leant back, laughed and clapped her hands. 'Splendid! Anne-Marie and I were afraid for you but it seems we shouldn't have worried. Freddie Shepherd had better look out.'

Stella smiled back, but Anne-Marie shook her head. 'I don't like it,' she said. 'Not after what Miss Bingham said through there. You know the women are always first to be blamed. You're playing a dangerous game, Stella.'

By the time she finished work, with the prospect of another session at the Quai d'Orsay ahead of her tomorrow, the day had taken its toll. Strangely, it was not so much the encounter with Miss Bingham that bothered her as everything that had gone before. Her head ached and she just wanted to rest.

'Are you sure?' Anne-Marie asked. 'Mr Malcolm – Mr Balfour's private secretary, you know – will perform his comic poems tonight. It should be a scream.'

Stella shook her head and headed for the sixth floor and

her sanctuary, which miraculously remained just that as the powers-that-be had failed to notice Lily's spare bed. Closing the door, she sat down in front of her mirror. There were shadows under her eyes, and her elegant bob looked lank. She watched her own eyes fill with tears. Having a room to herself might be a luxury, but oh how she missed Lily – missed her simple friendship, her constant singing, her ceaseless flow of gossip about people in the hotel, and more than anything her sense of fun. Lily would have laughed her out of her misery, but without her presence Stella felt herself sinking beneath the growing sense of exhaustion and despair that had spread inexorably throughout the Majestic. Hugh didn't help. He lurched from wild idealism to bleak cynicism in the course of one conversation. Only yesterday, a little tight after dinner, he had told her of troubling rumours out of Amritsar in the Punjab, where his brother worked for the bank. The whispers were of a massacre by British troops.

'Wouldn't surprise me,' Hugh said, knocking back his whisky. 'Last time James was home he told some awful stories, like the day an Englishwoman was harassed in the street by a group of Indian youths. She wasn't badly hurt, but she was shaken up. And do you know what the colonel in charge did? Instead of trying to identify the culprits, he set an officer at either end of that street and every single Indian man who needed to pass along there during the whole of the next week was made to crawl the length on his hands and knees on pain of being flogged.'

The dreadful scene had recurred in Stella's dreams last night. Now she stepped onto her balcony and leant over the iron balustrade. The evening air was soft and warm, a gentle breeze drifting up from the south, a world away from the bitter northerlies that had hustled Jack and her along their childhood beach. As she stood high above Avenue Kléber, looking down on people moving in and out of the pools of golden light that spilt onto the street from the hotel, she felt herself to be looking down on the thoughts and ideas that had swirled around in the febrile atmosphere of the Majestic for months. She had come out here with high hopes of making a better world. What had changed?

There was the evening in Marguerite de Witt-Schlumberger's apartment, surrounded by new ideas and a fresh way of doing things. Those women were passionately committed to dismantling and rebuilding the edifice of international diplomacy. Take the session she had endured that afternoon: how different would that have been if the room had not just been full of the same old men, but had included those intelligent, committed women too?

The problem, Stella was finding, with looking at things from a different point of view was that once you had considered *one* alternative scenario – what if the world was not being reshaped by a roomful of men – *other* scenarios presented themselves.

What if the world was not being reshaped by a roomful of white men?

There were so many nations represented here in Paris, yet she knew that the real decisions were still taken by the Council of Four: Britain, America, France and Italy.

She thought of Hugh's stories; she thought of Freddie and his bewitching blue eyes. Despite Anne-Marie's concern, it was

228

not Freddie's clandestine activities that troubled her but the things he had said as they walked back from the Quai d'Orsay together. Was the racial equality clause really so different from the demands of the Inter-Allied Women? Surely both were attempts to build a fairer way of living into the foundations of this new world. Yet just as the women had been forced to set up their own parallel conference, the Pan-African Congress was meeting across Paris in the Grand Hotel with no real influence while Africa was parcelled out around the table right here.

Yet Freddie's views, she knew, were commonplace. They were shared by much of the British Empire Delegation, so why did she feel uneasy?

Perhaps it had something to do with her seafaring family. First her father and then her brother had travelled the globe, and she would have done so too given half a chance. Her father's tales of adventure in far-off lands may have been exaggerated to cause his children's eyes to grow wide with wonder, but they were spiced with a wholesale respect for different cultures, which Stella had absorbed with her alphabet. What's more, that same innate sense of fairness that had led him, against the norm, to champion his daughters' education would, she suspected, be in sympathy with Japanese expectations to be rewarded for taking up arms. What long-term harm might it do if the Western powers betrayed Japan now? And if the Japanese were bought off with Shantung, the Chinese would also find the treachery hard to forgive.

Layer upon layer of misinformation, prejudice and hypocrisy.

And their hopes had been so high.

She gazed down on the Paris streets below and thought about Alex. She would like to share her thoughts with him, but any such letter would be heavily censored. She might even be removed from the delegation for her radical views.

Her head ached, but her thoughts were crystallising. Something at the core of her had reacted against Freddie's views, however widely held they might be. She had long been convinced that the world would be a better place if women as well as men were involved in running it. Now, for the first time, she was confronted by the idea that other nations might have an important role in diplomacy too.

After all, thinking of the last four or five years, and of Hugh's despair swirling in his whisky glass, could anyone do a worse job than those who had recently been in charge?

# Chapter Nineteen

Erskine, Scotland

Sir William had offered to collect him from Bishopton station but Rob chose to walk. It was further than he anticipated. Now, as he reached the stone gates and realised that a long tree-lined driveway still stretched out ahead of him, he almost regretted that decision. Almost, but not quite.

He laid down his bag in order to rest for a moment or two. It had rained overnight here, but now the air was still, warm and laden with the fragrance of a thousand trees and flowers spreading out around him. He breathed in slowly, as if the pure air might somehow cleanse all that had been foul inside him for the last five years. He had been back in Scotland for less than a fortnight, and felt like a stranger in a landscape that had once been his own. Some things had changed and caught him unawares: a new shop where he expected a pub; an old oak tree blown down by the wind; a whole tenement block demolished with an ostentatious modern house rising in its place. Yet it was the pieces of his old life that had remained the same that bewildered him most. Surely nothing could be untouched. Everything within him shrieked out in protest at a country that carried on oblivious to the hellish destruction that had become his entire world.

He spent a week in the gloomy rooms of his Edinburgh childhood home. A week was enough. His father was proud of him. His father loved him. His father was relieved he had come through relatively unscathed. But they no longer fitted together with any sort of ease. The old man was set in his ways and had a housekeeper to care for his needs. Rob sat opposite him in the silent drawing room of an evening with a glass of whisky and a book, and found he couldn't breathe.

The easy camaraderie of the mess tugged at his sleeve.

But it was only ever going to be a temporary visit to the old man. Edinburgh held nothing for him now. He had spent these past few months of uneasy peace dealing with diminishing cases and seeing to the logistics of closing down the hospital, and had put his plans in place. The war might have ended, but its catastrophic consequences had just moved location. And so now he found himself at the end of the long driveway of a grand and secluded estate on the banks of the River Clyde. A couple of years ago, thanks to the generosity of some Glasgow dignitaries, this mansion house had been transformed into the Princess Louise Scottish Hospital for Limbless Sailors and Soldiers. He had corresponded from France with its founder, the brilliant pioneering surgeon Sir William Macewen, and had agreed to come and work here for a month in the first instance, with the hope that he would stay for as long as he was needed.

Rob picked up his bag again, heaving it over his shoulder, and began the walk up the drive. High in the trees all around him he could hear the twittering song of tiny birds. Somehow it was all still here. The sweet warmth of a May morning; the lush green of early summer; the heavy scent of wet grass. Just two weeks ago he had looked out for the last time on the wasted terrain of northern France as they juddered towards the coast, and had found it hard to believe that any other world really existed. Now, that other world surrounded him.

There had been times in the darkness of dugout or tent, as the guns pounded outside, that Rob endured long sleepless hours by imagining himself walking in the Scottish countryside. Step by step by step. Cullen, say, on the north-east coast, where he had spent holidays as a boy. He became again that child leaving the house, closing the door, running over tufted grass to stand as close to the cliff edge as he dared. He watched gulls and cormorants and razorbills soaring above and beneath him. Then he took the rough path down to the beach, clutching long grasses here and there to steady himself, and emerged onto that vast expanse of golden sand stretching to the ocean beyond. He took off his shoes and crossed the wet sand until the sea trickled icily over his small white feet. Watched gannets dive for fish and, if he was really lucky, spotted a dolphin further out among the waves. And then he turned and sprinted across the sand, heading for the distinctive Three Kings rocks. Maybe later a game of golf on the course above. He lived every hole. Every stroke, even the duff ones.

All this as the shells thundered down.

Now, as he placed one foot in front of the other and the trees arched over his head, he told himself – *it's real this time. It's real.*

It was the same on the train over from Edinburgh. He looked out for a while at a landscape that was both familiar and alien, but somehow the views created a sense of dissatisfaction within him, and soon he picked up the copy of *The Scotsman* he had bought at Waverley. Turning the page, he read about May Day riots in Paris, and wondered how Corran's wee sister was faring amid it all. Stella, no longer a schoolgirl. The German delegates had arrived in Paris, he read, but were still awaiting the terms of the treaty. It was marvellous work that Stella was involved in, but the next few weeks would reveal how much it had actually achieved. He pictured her, bereft and smeared with mud at Jack's grave. Stella's life would be marked forever by the death of her beloved brother. He saw Jack too, a lad brimful of boyish enthusiasm at that Calcutta Cup match in Edinburgh, Corran by his side.

Corran.

She was on British soil now too, he knew. In her last letter from France, she had described the closing down of the education scheme and her mixed feelings on leaving the freedoms and friendships of Dieppe for college life in Oxford. A postcard had awaited him at his father's address, a brief message to tell him she was now settled into St Hilda's College until the end of term, when she would travel north to Thurso to begin sorting the house.

*Hope to see you soon.*

He had slipped the postcard into his bag on a whim. Hope to see you – when? Where? When they had met in France, neither of them had been sure what they would be doing just a few weeks ahead. Now, if this position at the hospital worked out, the future might at last become more settled. They had waited a long, long time to make plans.

He reached the top of the drive and found himself looking onto the side of the house, which had a grand portico entrance. He paused again, placing his suitcase on the ground, and breathed slowly. A terrace overlooked the River Clyde at the front of the house, and here he could see two nurses pushing wheelchairs, their patients wrapped in blankets. Rob slipped a hand inside his jacket pocket and pulled out a couple of pills, which he swallowed dry, and then picked up his bag once more and stepped forward.

Fifteen minutes later, he sat in the cluttered study of one of the greatest surgeons of the age. Sir William Macewen was in his seventies but held himself as erect as a man twenty years younger. His white hair was thinning slightly, and sharp blue eyes looked out of a narrow face dominated by a bristling moustache. Now that he was here, Rob felt unexpectedly nervous. Macewen, he knew, had trained under Lister, and was famed for groundbreaking work in bone grafts and in brain surgery. And from what he could gather, this edifice around them largely owed its existence to the great man's endeavours. But Sir William was asking about his time in France.

'You were out from the off?'

'Pretty much,' said Rob. The utter insanity of those early days. The bravado and swagger of the rush to join up – the *great game*. The heartbreaking folly of it all. He glanced at the man across the desk. Did people at home still think it was a badge of honour?

But Sir William wasn't interested in Rob's honour. He leant forward, chin on his hand, his blue eyes keen.

'I want you to tell me what it was like out there,' he said. 'The hospitals. The dressing stations. The procedures. The facilities. All of it. From the perspective of the surgeon, you understand, rather than the patient or the nurse. I have plenty of those here already.'

The request was so vast, his words hopelessly inadequate. 'All of it?'

'Yes. What was the chain of command – where did you fit in? Were you equipped for the work you were required to do?'

'It was a war.' He cleared his throat. 'It was very different to a normal hospital.'

'Go on.'

'I'm not sure what you want to know, sir.'

'Tell me about your own experiences. Where were you based?'

'At first I was sent to one of the big hospitals on the north coast. We took serious cases, patched up those we could, and either returned them to the front line or sent them on to Blighty. It was makeshift, of course – a crumbling French château with tents in the grounds and stretcher cases laid out on the grass when there had been a big push – but yes, we had trained staff and we had fairly good equipment, even if some of it was antiquated.'

'And then?'

*And then.* 'And then I moved up the line. Became attached as MO to a regiment.'

'Your choice?' Sir William asked, watching him closely.

'My *request*. Nothing in war is choice. But after many months my request was granted.'

'And why did you want to go?' Sir William demanded. 'To be part of things, eh? To see the action?'

Rob stared at him. Surely this brilliant surgeon couldn't be as much of a bloody fool as he made out. He remembered the constant stream of overflowing ambulance trains arriving at the base hospital, many of their passengers already far beyond help, and the frustration he and other young medics felt as they realised that most resources and the best-trained staff were stuck a day or two's journey behind the lines. It became their ambition to get nearer the fighting, not out of bravado or glory-hunting but because anyone with an ounce of sense could see that men were dying simply because it took them too long to reach proper medical help.

The top brass realised it a couple of years too late.

'After that,' he said, ignoring the question and keeping his voice as even as possible, 'I was sometimes based at a casualty clearing station just behind the lines, and when our men were in the trenches I set up an aid post wherever I could.'

'Such as?'

His hands were trembling, and, however much he swallowed, his voice remained hoarse. 'Such as a dug-out if we were lucky. On an attack we'd go along just behind the boys. One time—' He faltered. Sir William reached for the whisky decanter on his left and poured some into a glass, pushing it across the desk. Rob took it and sipped. He had long since learnt to drink spirits at all times of day.

'Go on.'

'One time we were holding a village – not a village really, more a heap of dust and ruins. Our reinforcements hadn't shown up. I was with some of our lads holed up in the church. There was a room – a sort of vestry, I suppose. I used that. We worked anywhere we could.'

*Dust, and the screaming sound of shells, and his orderly sobbing, and lad after lad being bundled through the door to him. Flesh stripped from bone and limbs hanging off. Such a sense of fucking helplessness.*

There was silence in the room. Rob rested his pounding head in his hands. Sir William rose to his feet and walked to the window behind his desk. With his back to Rob, he said, 'It's only by understanding just what went on out there that we can begin to rectify the goddamned mess we've been left with here.'

Rob felt his weariness shot through with a flash of anger. *Goddamned mess* you're *left with? Try holding your hands steady enough to close a gaping wound in that crumbling church vestry while the ground shakes with explosions. Try persuading the stretcher bearers, weeping with terror, to run beneath the fire and get a casualty to the treatment he desperately needs. Try moving through the carnage of a clearing station after an attack, working out which men have received their tetanus injections and which have been missed.*

*Try weeping through the night because they were at your mercy and you failed them.*

Sir William turned to face him. 'Far more men came back from this conflict missing at least one limb than after any previous war. Amputation is mutilation. It should *always* be

238

the last resort of the surgeon, the absolute last resort. I'm not convinced that was the case on the battlefields of France.'

And the Irishman, cursing him to high heaven when he found his leg was gone. But Rob would like to see Sir William make the right decision every time when a hundred fiery hammers were beating their way out of his skull.

'With respect, sir, there is a world of difference between decisions made under fire and decisions made in an operating theatre.'

'And did you get those decisions right?'

'In an ideal world we'd have sent them somewhere better equipped to deal with their injuries. But often they wouldn't have survived the journey. We had to do the best we could and weigh the risks. So yes, amputations took place where another outcome might have been possible in a well-equipped hospital, if that's what you're asking. But lives were saved. I don't call that a wrong decision.'

'Makes little difference to the man left without a limb.'

'Better than being dead, surely.'

Sir William nodded slowly. 'Better than being dead. But now we have to help those men to live. That's why we're here. I know you're wondering right now if you should have come, but you are the man we need. Come, let me show you round.'

Rob had anticipated a visit to wards or an operating theatre but instead they returned outside.

'We opened in October '16,' Sir William said as they walked through the maze of long corridors to the reception hall and stairs leading down to the front door. 'By then hospitals everywhere were overwhelmed and I could see that amputations had become a particular problem. Well, Mason, how's that knee coming along?' He stopped and exchanged a few words with a young lad who was navigating the stairs on crutches, before picking up his flow where he had left off. 'The stump is tender and swollen at first. It needs weeks or even months of healing before it can tolerate an artificial limb. Men were sent home from hospital after amputation with no aftercare – no support for body or soul. Here, we accommodate them for those long difficult months. We build up their remaining muscles, teach them to adapt to the shock of life without the limb and prepare them for the fitting of the replacement.' He led Rob out through the grand portico onto the forecourt and round a corner. 'Grand to see you out here, Hillary, just grand. And then there was the problem of obtaining sufficient supply of good-quality artificial limbs. Everyone tried to tell me we would have to import them. Utter poppycock.'

They had reached the entrance to a long low courtyard building. Sir William paused, his hand on the handle.

'We are on the banks of the River *Clyde*, for heaven's sake! The workshop of the world. If Glasgow shipbuilders can design and build HMS *Hood*, they can surely manufacture a few wooden legs! Thankfully Harold Yarrow agreed with me, and where he led the way others have followed. Come and see our workshop.'

He pushed the door open and Rob followed him in. There was a powerful smell of sawdust and varnish. Ahead of him he saw a row of workbenches with two or three men clustered round each one. Shelving along one wall held a remarkable collection of wooden limbs, each labelled. Sir William and Rob moved to the first bench, where two men and a teenage boy, all dressed in long aprons, paused in their work.

'Carry on, men, carry on. This is Captain Campbell, a surgeon who has come to join us. I'm introducing him to the splendid work you shipyard men do for us.' He stepped forward, closer to the nearest man. 'May I?' He took the polished wooden arm in his hands, holding it as reverently as a priceless antique. 'See here, the clever jointing of thumb and fingers. And this section will be padded to protect the stump. Each limb is carefully designed for the individual needs of the man concerned. It's no compensation, of course' – and the edge to his tone reminded Rob of his 'mutilation' comments – 'but the work of these fine gentlemen will enable Private MacDonald, in this case, to live a very satisfying life.'

Rob glanced round the shipyard workers at the bench. On the left was a lad, skinny and young, with bad skin. Too young to have served, and thank God he wouldn't now need to.

'Tell me about your work.'

'I dinna work on the limbs, sir. No yet. I fetch and carry, do the wee jobs.'

'Young Arthur's a bright lad,' said the oldest man at the bench. 'No long joined us but he learns fast.'

'Well done, well done,' said Sir William. 'Back to work then, men. Thank you for your time.' He turned away, striding through the workshop towards another door. Rob looked back at the little groups of men and was assailed by an unexpected but powerful memory of faces gathered round a steaming billycan in the flickering shadows of the evening. The boy was watching him, his green eyes sharp and intelligent. Rob nodded a quick farewell and followed Sir William from the room.

The first thing he noticed in the next workshop was that these men all wore the hospital uniform of bright blue shirts and scarlet ties. Patients, then. Some fitted with their new limbs, some without. Sir William moved along the benches, speaking to each one, introducing Rob or admiring their work.

'This is the woodcarving workshop,' he said. 'We also have basket making, boot making, French polishing. Outside you'll find beekeeping, and opportunities for men to work in the market garden.' He took a step back and opened his arms expansively. 'This is the heart of what we do, Captain Campbell. Not the operating theatre. Not even the limb-making. This. It's our aim that every man who is able to leave here will do so trained up in skills he can carry into this next phase of his life. Those few whose injuries keep them with us longer term will find useful work they can do here too. Look at this fine sailing yacht; why, you would be hard pushed to find—'

The door opened and he broke off. A tall woman dressed in a nurse's long white apron and cap stood before them.

'I'm sorry to interrupt, Sir William,' she said in a soft west-coast voice. She moved closer and spoke in an undertone. 'Matron would like to speak to you urgently concerning Lieutenant Lamont.'

Sir William's white brows drew together. 'Indeed,' was all he said at first. Then he turned towards Rob. 'Captain Campbell, I must leave you for now. This case has proven to be a particularly tricky one. Nurse, perhaps you could finish my tour? Take Captain Campbell through the house, if you please; show him our facilities and introduce him to the men.' He hurried away, and as soon as he had left the room, a low hum of chatter broke out among the men. Rob wanted to linger and speak with them, but the nurse who had been instructed to take him to the house was already through the doorway. He followed.

Outside in the warm May air, they both paused. 'I'm grateful to you, but you are probably busy with other things,' he said. 'I don't want to take up your time.'

She inclined her head. 'Matron said the new surgeon had arrived today. I guess that's you?'

'It is.' He held out his hand. 'Captain Rob Campbell.'

He thought he saw a glimmer of something unexpected pass across her face as she took his hand. She was tall for a woman, nearly as tall as him, with dark eyes and a glimpse of dark hair peeking out from under her nurse's cap.

'Nurse MacCallum,' she said. 'I'll show you the house, shall I?'

She led him along a long gallery, which served as the recreation room, with books and magazines, billiard tables and a dartboard among the entertainments on view, and introduced him to patients in their blue and scarlet as they went.

'Sir William's next ambition is to build a whole recreation block,' she said. 'Most hospitals don't prioritise entertainment. In the place I was before I came here, they thought themselves lucky to get local schoolchildren in to sing a few songs. But when men recuperate here for months, with long hours to fill and the need to regain some dignity and self-belief after all they've been through, boredom is destructive.' She gave him a strange look then, similar to the one he'd seen on her face when he introduced himself. 'We get them out in the fresh air as much as possible. Bowls, golf, outdoor sports. You might be able to help with that while you're here, Captain Campbell.'

It was lightly said, but the undertone was serrated. 'I would be glad to,' he said warily.

She nodded. 'Having a former Scotland rugby footballer here will be good for morale, I'm sure.'

Surprised and slightly embarrassed, he held out his hands with a little laugh. 'It's a long time since I've played any rugby.' He paused and looked at her, still unable to fully decipher the strange expression on her face. 'How did you know?'

'Oh, Sir William told us all. He's thrilled. A surgeon *and* international rugby player who's served at the front. You're his perfect recruit, don't you know?' There was no mistaking the scorn in her tone, but why would a woman he had never met speak with such naked hostility? 'I must go. You'll find your own way from here, won't you?'

'Nurse—' He stopped. What name had she given? She watched him closely, a cold little smile on her lips. She shook her head.

'You really don't know, do you? It's true Sir William told us, but I knew who you were anyway.'

Far too late, something stirred at the back of his mind. Those dark eyes. The way she held her head. MacCallum.

'You must be John's sister,' he said at last.

# Chapter Twenty

Paris

It was raining when Stella stepped out of the cab with Freddie and tugged down the silky green fringe of her borrowed frock, which was much shorter than anything she had ever worn before. The Place de l'Opéra was busy with glamorous couples in evening dress. She paused and looked up at the façade of the Opéra Garnier, magnificent even under this evening's heavy skies. Freddie led her up the steps to the entrance, steering her quickly past beggars who approached them with outstretched hands.

Inside they came to a sweeping staircase, ornately carved and surrounded by pillars, statues and alcoves. The rain outside had made the marble steps treacherous, and Stella gripped Freddie's arm. How mortifying it would be to lose her footing and slip down these stairs, especially wearing Mabel's revealing outfit! She made it safely to the top and looked around the milling crowd of theatregoers. The colours of the women's evening gowns dazzled against the cool white marble. Stella touched her dress again. When she had tried it on in her room, the sensuously clinging emerald costume had seemed gaudy, but here in this palace of fashion she was immensely glad that Mabel had pressed it upon her. On her next day off she would visit Galeries Lafayette and find out if she could possibly afford a new evening dress in the latest style. Her blue georgette, which had seemed so modish in London, might be all right for the unremittingly British social life of the Majestic, but tonight she wanted to feel Parisian.

She waited for Freddie, who had stopped to greet a fellow member of the delegation. She watched as he moved through the crowd, a smile here, a touch there. Always at the heart of things, charming everyone. *You're playing a dangerous game*, Anne-Marie had said. Perhaps, but she'd rather be in the game than out of it.

Freddie came up to her at last and they entered the horseshoe-shaped auditorium. Stella caught her breath. She had visited the new Usher Hall in Edinburgh and thought it grand, but it paled into insignificance alongside the lavish splendour of this rich red and gold amphitheatre. Their seats were in a raised area, with at least four tiers encircling the space above them. As they sat down, her eyes were drawn upwards to the painted ceiling with its massive chandelier.

'Have you read the novel *The Phantom of the Opera*?' she asked Freddie. 'It's set here.'

He shook his head. 'You can tell me the story afterwards,' he said, laying a hand on her slim wrist. Her skin tingled at the feel of his fingers on her bare arm and she breathed out slowly, telling herself to relax. She had just lived through the busiest week she had yet known in Paris. The Germans had finally arrived and all leave was cancelled in the rush to finalise the treaty terms. What a relief just to sit down without typescript swimming before her eyes.

She took Mabel's mother-of-pearl opera glasses from her bag and scanned slowly round, watching elegant audience members find their seats amid a buzz of chatter and anticipation, and looking for faces she recognised from the Majestic or the Quai d'Orsay. A fresh murmur ran around the audience. Freddie gestured to the presidential box.

'Look, there. It's Paderewski, isn't it?'

Stella adjusted the opera glasses to scrutinise the wild-haired Polish pianist and composer turned prime minister, who had laid his career aside in pursuit of an independent Poland.

'I have a marvellous gramophone recording of Paderewski playing Chopin back home in Thurso,' she said. Paderewski waved to the rapturous crowd and she shifted her gaze to the tall, dark woman beside him. Helena Paderewska was a tireless social campaigner who had founded the Polish version of the Red Cross during the war. Stella thought of the questions of national identity that had been tossed back and forward over the past months as the conference sought to determine the borders of the newly reborn Poland. Would Paderewski be happy with the outcome? Would anyone? What about the Germans?

What about the Germans. It was all anyone could talk about at the Majestic, and Freddie was clearly thinking along the same lines as they looked up at the Polish prime minister.

'I saw Jan Smuts earlier,' he said. 'He's worried the Germans might not accept our terms.'

'The document isn't even ready yet. Miss Bingham warned us we'll be typing through the night tomorrow.' Common knowledge, and safe enough to share.

'After so many months, how the blazes can it be such a scramble at the end?'

She slipped the opera glasses back into her bag. 'I don't know. The focus seems to have moved from getting the right treaty to just getting something down on paper to hand over to the Germans. But let's hope we're wrong.' The lights in the auditorium dimmed, and she sat back in her seat. 'Tonight I just want to forget about it all.'

That was easier said than done. *Castor and Pollux* was new to Stella, a revival of an older opera by French composer Rameau. Rediscovering French culture was fashionable as no one really had the stomach for the German musicians like Beethoven and Wagner, who had been so popular before the war. The music soared into the space perfectly designed for it. She tried to give herself over to the unfolding performance, and to push aside for a while the unease that churned within her.

When the interval came, Freddie took her hand. 'You haven't seen the grand foyer yet,' he said. 'Come, let's get a drink.' He led her through to a long gallery, which was so extravagantly gilded that she just shook her head in bewilderment. A richly painted ceiling arched above them, and the whole space sparkled with the light of row upon row of chandeliers. They lifted glasses of champagne from the tray of a passing waiter. 'Enjoying yourself?'

'The performance is marvellous.'

'But?'

Stella gestured around. 'Does it never seem – a bit much to you? Maybe it's because of where I come from. We don't really go in for displays of wealth and luxury at home. But it's more than that. It's—' She stopped, not quite able to articulate her feelings.

'It's that you don't believe you deserve to enjoy yourself when your brother is dead, and the world is still in chaos.'

As Freddie expressed so perfectly what she felt, she was horrified to feel tears forming. He took her arm and tenderly guided her towards a quieter space by a window. Rain streamed down the glass, distorting the lights of night-time Paris beyond.

'I'm sorry.'

'Don't be. I understand – you know I do. But you should fight those feelings, Stella. It's not what Piet or Jack would want. We have to live for them, and live to the full.' His hand came up and stroked her hair, resting on the back of her neck. She shivered.

'It's been such a difficult week. I can't bear to think they might have died for nothing.'

She saw her own grief reflected back at her in his blue eyes. 'We won't let that happen,' he said and then pulled her close and kissed her. 'I promise you, we won't.'

When the performance ended and the rapturous applause and curtain calls finally died away, Stella and Freddie collected their coats and made their way back out to the Place de l'Opéra to look for a cab. The rain had stopped but its freshness lingered, almost masking the usual dubious Paris aromas. Freddie paused.

'We could go back to the Majestic, of course,' he said.

'But we don't have to. In the interests of living life to the full, shall we go on to a club? I know just the place over at Montparnasse.'

His good hand held hers lightly, and his right arm, the damaged one, rested on her waist. She thought about that: thought about the fighting that had robbed him of the use of his hand and, far worse, of his brother. The pain she had seen in his eyes was genuine, however duplicitous other parts of his behaviour might be. She thought about Jack, and a grimy rug littered with screwed-up balls of paper. She thought of Lily, dancing through Paris one day and barely clinging to life the next. So much had been stolen from them, but they were still here.

She said yes.

The club was not at all what she had expected. After the glamorous brilliance of the Palais Garnier, her throat constricted as they descended into an underground cavern whose darkness was illuminated by strings of coloured bulbs tacked along the walls. She needn't care about her dress: no one could see what she was wearing anyway! At one end of the room was a small empty stage. Freddie led her through the thick, smoky atmosphere to a zinc-topped table at the edge of the dance floor. A solitary couple drifted round, undeterred by the lack of music and wrapped only in each another, their bodies entwined with an intimacy that was strangely compelling. Stella remembered the old couple dancing to 'Roses of Picardy' amid the ruins of Arras. Clinging on amid the chaos.

Freddie broke the spell, snapping his fingers for a waiter, who soon returned with two cocktails. He clinked glasses.

'It will liven up when the band returns,' he said, a light of anticipation in his eyes.

The small room was hot and airless with a strange sweet scent. Freddie had slung his jacket over the back of the chair and his good arm rested on the table beside her while the other was on his leg, almost out of sight.

'Look, there's that awful buffoon from the third floor.'

Stella looked across and recognised with a shock the tall, sweaty man who had told her she was only here because of her pretty ankles. She told Freddie about the conversation. He immediately bent down under the table and she gasped aloud as she felt his cool, firm grip on her ankle. He came up again, hair dishevelled, eyes laughing.

'Splendid ankles, I'm pleased to report!' he said. Then he gently reached out and touched her face. 'You really are far more attractive than you realise, Stella. And I have wanted to do this properly all evening.' He leant forward and kissed her, slowly, gently, on the mouth.

Taken by surprise, Stella had no idea how to respond. He had kissed her before, but nothing like this. His tongue lightly probed her mouth, and she felt his hand on her leg. His fingers slid up under the beaded fringe, and she felt a strange, new sensation moving within her as she responded to his kiss. His hand slid further up to the top of her stockings, and just as she wondered if he intended to undress her right here in front of everyone, a loud clatter came from the stage. They moved apart. Stella tugged her dress back down, and

Freddie slipped his arm around her shoulders and pulled her close to him.

'Later,' he whispered. He released her and lifted his glass to his mouth.

Her heart pounding, Stella drank her cocktail quickly. She liked Freddie, and she was sure that he liked her too, whatever murky motives might have been there at the beginning. This evening he hadn't tried to find out anything about her work, and the shared loss of Jack and Piet was not a burden but a magnetic force pulling them closer. But still, she hadn't expected him to kiss her so passionately in such a public place. Last week Miss Bingham had caught a couple in the Majestic in a state of undress, and had given them the choice of announcing their engagement or going home. But looking around, more than half the people here were wrapped around one another. Women sat on men's knees and one man had a girl on each side fondling him. This must be how people behaved in nightclubs. She should have asked Mabel.

She turned her attention to the stage, where the band was warming up.

'Now you'll see something,' Freddie said. 'Ragtime. Some people are calling it jazz.'

She remembered the trumpeters she had seen playing in Piccadilly Circus on peace night. The man seated at the piano said something that she couldn't quite make out. '"Tiger Rag",' said Freddie. 'Come on!'

And then they were on the dance floor with people crowding around them, and the music filled that small space, swinging them round with its rhythm and energy. She was aware of

Freddie's hands on her body, but this was dancing unlike any she had known. Not the careful steps they practised at the Majestic; not the gay abandon of the Highland reel; this was a surging, swinging, sensual movement.

'I don't know the steps.' Stella laughed as he steered her round.

'Don't worry. It's instinct. Just go with the rhythm.'

And he was right, and she was in his arms, and her body was moving with his in a way it had never moved before, light and free. When the music ended she was breathless with laughter. As they returned to their table, the band moved on to a slower number, and something liquid filled the space.

'The Americans brought this music over with them when they joined the war,' Freddie said. 'Ragtime bands are sweeping the London scene, and have been playing for the troops here too. Just what we all need after the last few years, a bit of fun.' He stood up. 'None of those lazy blighters seem to have noticed we need another drink. I'll chase them up. You sit tight.'

Alone, Stella leant back and watched those still dancing. Freddie was right, this music was full of energy and optimism and fun – but there was something more soulful there too, something that reached into the place where her deepest hurt waited. It seemed to express perfectly the tension she felt so often these days between pleasure and pain, and as she looked around she decided she was not alone. In the shadows, a man in the uniform of a colonel sat weeping, his table littered with empty glasses. Those who laughed, laughed too loudly; those who danced did so with a frenzy that was surely only this side of fun.

Freddie returned with two more cocktails, accompanied by an older man who barely acknowledged Stella before entering into a long diatribe connected to the mandates for the colonies. She could only catch part of their conversation above the music, and turned her attention back to the room as she sipped her drink. A movement at the door caught her eye. A tall, fair man had entered with a dark-haired woman dressed in shimmering, sensuous silver at his side. Stella sensed the atmosphere in the club change, as the energy that had swept through the room was redirected towards the newcomers. It was, she thought, a practised move by the couple, pausing in the doorway as if to adjust to the dim lighting, but all the time aware of the impression they made.

She knew she had seen the woman before, but where? Just as she made the connection, Freddie astonished her by getting to his feet, excusing himself from the old bore and crossing the room to grasp the male newcomer by the hand. She sat at the table, frozen in disbelief, as he led glamorous screen couple Dennis and Poppy Wyndham over to join them.

*I might need more to drink.*

That, at least, was not a problem: unasked, a waiter immediately set a bottle of champagne and four glasses on their table.

'I had no idea you were in Paris,' Freddie was saying. 'Come and meet Stella. She's one of the typists at the Peace Conference. These girls are the ones in the know. Stella, meet Dennis and Poppy Wyndham.'

Fortified by cocktails and champagne, Stella learnt that the two South African men had become friends on a long sea voyage from Cape Town to Southampton. And Poppy was from Scotland, like Stella. As the film star exclaimed over the coincidence, Stella tried to gather her scattered self-possession. She enjoyed spotting important dignitaries in the hotel, but this was a different sort of fame all together. The last time she had seen Poppy Wyndham had been on screen in the basement of the Majestic where she had starred in the film they watched. Most of what Stella knew about her came from newspapers, which had eagerly reported every detail of the scandalous elopement of Poppy and Dennis Wyndham. She wasn't Poppy Wyndham then, but Miss Elsie Mackay, the cossetted daughter of wealthy shipping magnate Lord Inchcape. She had defied her father to run off with the wounded soldier who was now her husband, and forged a career as glamorous cinema actress Poppy Wyndham. And now, unbelievably, she was sitting across from Stella and smiling at her.

'You work at the Peace Conference? I say! How thrilling!'

Her smile was warm, and put Stella a little more at ease.

'It's not always thrilling,' she admitted. 'Some of it's quite tedious. But it does feel a grand thing to be involved in, and we have some good times at the Majestic. Dances and the like.' Then she winced. As if this sophisticated society star would be in the least bit interested in the tea dances and amateur dramatics they got up among the delegation!

But Poppy leant forward, dark eyes glowing in her creamy face. 'I do envy you. You're doing something worthwhile. Are there many women taking part?'

'Oh yes.' Then Stella hesitated – and perhaps it was the music that still throbbed through her with that strange mix of joy and pain or maybe it was the cocktails and champagne, but in a burst of honesty, she said, 'But really the women get the menial tasks and the men do all the interesting work.'

'As ever, darling.' Poppy pulled out a gold cigarette box and offered one to Stella. Leaning forward to light it, she said, 'The women have set up their own congress, I believe?'

Stella tried not to reveal her surprise that an actress would know much about politics.

'Yes. Miss Pankhurst and Madame de Witt-Schlumberger and others wanted to participate in the Peace Conference but the men wouldn't have them. They are now planning their own meeting for peace in Zurich.'

'How exciting!' She glanced across at her husband. 'I wonder if we could go on to Zurich? Is anyone flying there, I wonder?' Then she laughed. 'No, I think not. We have to be back in the studio in London by Tuesday.'

'Flying?' asked Stella. 'Did you fly here?'

'Of course. Civilian flying's not really allowed but a chap we know from the Royal Air Force was coming anyway. It's tremendously exciting and so much faster than the dreary old train. Have you been up yet?'

Stella shook her head.

'Oh, you must. I went up for the first time last year, when I worked as a driver for some of the pilots. It's like no other feeling in the world. I'm quite addicted now, and I'm determined to learn to fly for myself. Come out to the aerodrome at Versailles on Monday and I'll find someone to give us a quick spin before Dennis and I head home.'

'I'm afraid I have to work on Monday.'

'Of course you do. Well, never mind. Another time.' Poppy reached out for the champagne bottle and refilled their glasses. The men were deep in conversation, but Stella saw that Freddie kept glancing towards Poppy. 'Don't you miss Scotland terribly?' the film star asked. 'There are days I simply *ache* to stand on the cliffs and feel the fresh breeze of home whipping up from the sea. London is so awfully filthy. Even the rain feels dirty.'

For all she professed not to want to return to Scotland, Stella found that phrase *the fresh breeze of home* unexpectedly moving. She too had grown up with cliffs and the sea. But with their mother moving away, would she ever be back in Caithness again? Where was home anyway?

'I grew up in Thurso,' she said. 'It takes a long time to get there. I won't be able to go until my work here is finished.'

'Unless you fly!' Poppy laughed. 'I've never been as far north as Thurso. My family home is Glenapp Castle in the south-west – about as far from Thurso as you could get and still be in Scotland. Although my father and I aren't exactly on the best of terms at the moment so it may be some time before I can return.' Her lovely dark eyes clouded momentarily and then, as she lifted her head, the grave expression vanished with the speed of a mother wiping a muddy smear from her child's face. It was a useful reminder that this woman was a polished actress. Poppy leant towards Dennis. 'I thought we came here to dance, darling?'

Dennis drained his glass and took Poppy by the hand, leading her onto the dance floor. Freddie looked across at Stella. 'Shall we dance too?'

She saw how his gaze followed the glamorous Poppy onto

the dance floor and thought how clumsy her own steps would look by comparison. She could feel energy draining out of her and her head had started to spin. There was the prospect of an all-night shift tomorrow too. She shook her head.

'I'm tired, Freddie, and I've a busy day tomorrow. I think I'd like to go back to the hotel.'

Wondering about that 'later'.

Reluctantly, Freddie turned his attention back to her.

'Of course,' he said, but his disappointment was evident. He helped her on with her coat and steered her towards the door, watching Poppy all the time. As they passed the film stars swinging gracefully across the dance floor, he said, 'Isn't she splendid?' and Stella suppressed a smile. No doubt most of the men in the nightclub were a little bit in love with Poppy Wyndham.

Out in the balmy darkness of boulevard Montparnasse, Freddie hailed a taxi. He helped her in and then stepped back.

'You'll be all right now, won't you? There's something I want to see Dennis about before I come back to the hotel. You don't mind?'

So there would be no later. He was as fickle as a summer's morning in Scotland. She found she didn't mind nearly as much as she should. Tiredness had taken such a grip of her that all she wanted now was to return to her bed. Leaning back in the cab, she watched the Paris streets go by. She had never been out as late as this and was surprised to find how many people were still about. Well-dressed couples wandered along the boulevards; whole families huddled under blankets. Young women shivered on street corners, stepping out to approach a lone soldier, while raucous groups of men in uniform – often American – jostled with one another and laughed loudly. How unsettling this city was, with its glittering nightclubs surrounded by the desperate poverty of broken soldiers and refugees.

As she neared the hotel, wondering if she would have to slip in the service entrance, she found herself thinking not of Freddie but of Poppy Wyndham. She might be a glamorous actress playing a part, but there had been an honesty in her sadness as she spoke of looking out to sea from the cliffs near Glenapp. It was a sadness that had found an unexpected echo in Stella's heart. She had told Corran that she was happy to let their old home go but now, for the first time, she wondered if that was really true.

After Paris – what then?

# Chapter Twenty-One

Erskine, Scotland

Rob didn't see Nurse MacCallum again for quite a while. His days were busy, full of new routines and procedures, and he spent as much time as possible getting to know the men who had landed in the Princess Louise. There were patients here at all stages of recovery. Some had just arrived from other hospitals, their stumps angry and inflamed and their faces white with fear, while others had been here for many months and were learning to accomplish daily tasks with their newly fitted arms or legs. Some wanted to talk to him about their experiences: that strange feeling when your toes still gave you grief on a foot that was blown off two years ago; the sense of achievement at managing a new task like tying a tie or shaving; the fear of re-entering the outside world. Others refused to discuss anything to do with their injuries, past, present or future, but would happily engage in a game of chess or billiards. Some knew about his past as a rugby player and wanted to talk about that, which he found as hard as ever but tried to accept.

No one mentioned John MacCallum.

He looked closely at all the nurses he passed in the corridors, the wards and consulting rooms, but there was no one with the tall stature of Nurse MacCallum. She must be avoiding him. Fair enough, she had made her displeasure clear, and on balance he would probably prefer to avoid her too. And yet his mind was full of questions. His days might be busy but his nights were as restless as ever, and now John had come to join the insubstantial parade of people from his past who haunted his dreams.

One evening he was alone on a bench on the terrace, smoking a cigarette and watching the river below, when he became aware of footsteps behind him. He turned his head and there was Nurse MacCallum, standing silently beside his bench. An avenging angel? He got to his feet at once.

'May I join you?'

'Please do.'

They sat at either end of the bench, the space between them a tangible thing. She refused a cigarette and leant forward, elbows on her knees and chin in her hands, looking out towards the opposite riverbank. The wind rustled lightly in the trees and voices came from the direction of the house, but all else was quiet. Rob finished his own cigarette and dropped the end on the ground. He had to say something. Anything.

'One of the greatest pleasures of returning to Scotland is the long summer evenings. I had no idea how much I had missed them.'

'It's even more beautiful in Argyll. The light is softer there, somehow.'

'My fiancée comes from Thurso. I stayed with her one summer. It barely got dark at all.'

That conversation exhausted, the silence returned. Yet she had chosen to join him.

'I haven't seen you recently,' he said.

'I took some leave.' Her voice was steady, yet the tension in her body transmitted to him along the bench. 'I went to see John. To tell him you'd turned up.'

A tight band surrounded his chest. 'How is he?'

'Recovering.'

'Has he been ill?'

She looked at him then, a flash of scorn in her eyes. 'What do you imagine?'

'I try not to imagine,' he said, surprising himself by being honest. 'There's enough horror without it.'

She nodded. She was a nurse: she knew all about horror. 'Anyway,' she said. 'John seems to think a lot of you. So I said I would speak to you.'

Rob could feel the hammers starting up inside his skull. He lit another cigarette, hands trembling, but what he really wanted was a drink. 'Your brother was my hero,' he said quietly.

'Was?'

'Yes. When I started out. He was ahead of me in medical school, ahead of me in the Scotland team. He was the finest player ever to play for Scotland, and everything I wanted to be. My first match was his last, and I count myself lucky to have played with him as my captain even once.'

She picked at a loose thread on her cuff. 'John has never stopped being a hero.'

Rob inhaled slowly, remembering. By the time war broke out, John had already been away from Edinburgh for a couple of years, working as a medical officer in Argyll somewhere. He wasn't with them during those fevered days in August 1914, when the Scotland players swung their way through the streets of Edinburgh, brothers in arms on the rugby field against the English and the battlefield against the Germans. Play the game with rugby values. Invincible, an unbreakable bond.

The first he knew of something not being right was an evening with Gus and Jimmy Pearson in the bar at Myreside, the Watsonian rugby pavilion. Their enthusiasm for the war grew with each beer they sank, and they basked in the plaudits of the old boys at the next table, who lamented being too old to join up themselves. Rob shrugged it off when someone mentioned 'that shirker MacCallum'. Utter nonsense. John MacCallum, the hardest and most fearless man he'd ever played alongside, a shirker? Malicious gossip. Poor John likely wasn't free to sign up, his medical work making him essential. Rob thanked his lucky stars that his own role as a junior surgeon held no such responsibility, and he could swap Edinburgh for France as soon as the authorities permitted.

And then he went to France, and the world and everything he thought he knew about it began to fracture and disintegrate.

News reached him surprisingly often about his rugby teammates and opponents. The first Scottish player to die was Ronnie Simson, someone he hardly knew, but when just a few days later he heard that Jimmy Huggan had been killed, he felt as if someone had slammed him to the ground in a crushing tackle. Like him, Jimmy had studied medicine at Edinburgh. That last Calcutta Cup match at Inverleith had been his first cap. He'd scored a try.

March: Jimmy's first international.

September: dead.

And yet still he understood nothing. It would be over by Christmas. Rob thought ahead to next season. It would hurt to line up without Simson and Huggan, but they would honour their two fallen teammates, ensure their names lived on. They had played the game right nobly.

How little he had known even then.

Five years later, and silent rugby grounds up and down the country were no longer playing fields but were graveyards of shadowy corpses. Among them were some of his greatest heroes – Puss Milroy, Bedell-Sivright – and closest friends – Jimmy Pearson and Wattie Suddie. Even now bile rose in his throat as he thought about brilliant Wattie – real name Walter Sutherland – the Hawick flyer who made it all the way through only to be killed in October 1918. Five weeks later the guns fell silent.

It was beyond comprehension. All these young men he'd played alongside and played against, lives extinguished one after another after another. Rugby was over forever. It had been blasted into fragments by the power of the guns.

Sometime in the midst of all that grief and horror he'd heard further rumours of the choice that Scottish captain and hero John MacCallum had made. He pushed them aside. There were many tangled trails of thought that you couldn't afford to start down in France, not if you wanted to remain sane.

But now the war was over, though its consequences were not. Somehow he was still alive, and so was John MacCallum. John's sister sat beside him in the soft evening light, her body rigid and her fingers clasped so tightly that her knuckles were white. That tangled pathway was still there. Was he brave enough to step onto it?

'Tell me what happened to John, Nurse MacCallum.'

'My name's Grace,' she said. A pause, and then a question. 'What was he like to play with?'

Rob watched a chaffinch that had jumped onto the balustrade in front of them, emboldened by their stillness.

'He wasn't one for big speeches; he led by example,' he said at last. 'By the time I came along his reputation did the speaking for him. He was Scotland's most capped player, the forward who could just as easily play at three-quarters. He'd scored a legendary try against the All Blacks. It was an honour just to share a changing room with him. "Harder, boys." That was his phrase. Your brother was the toughest and bravest player I ever played alongside or against.'

'That sounds like John. He didn't say much, but when he spoke you listened. Even as a boy he had a deep faith and deep principles, but if there was ever the slightest chance of those being mistaken for weakness he would soon put the other fellow right. I adored him.'

'My first game for Scotland was his last,' said Rob. 'That unforgettable win against England. I wish he'd stayed around but he was working in Argyll by then, wasn't he?'

'That's right.' Grace shrugged off the stillness that had clung to her and got to her feet. 'Can we walk? I'd find it easier.'

They set off together along the terrace and round the side of the house. At the back, looking out over grassy slopes and woodland, was another wide sitting area where several groups of patients were enjoying the warm evening. Not wanting to engage in conversation, Rob and Grace turned away from the house and walked among trees and rhododendrons, slowly looping back towards the river.

'John has always been a pacifist, so when war broke out there was no question of him going. You could no sooner imagine John killing someone than you could imagine Mary Slessor smothering the African children she cared for. No one questioned it; he was doing such valuable work.' She stopped beside a particularly large rhododendron and reached out, gently pulling the scarlet flower towards her. 'Isn't that glorious?' She released it and moved on. 'When conscription came in, John could easily have had an exemption. He was fighting the battle against tuberculosis – much more useful than fighting other men, don't you think? Saving lives, not taking them. But as the utter foolishness and evil of the war became more obvious, he felt he had to stand against it. He was too honourable not to speak out.'

Rob's mouth was dry. He said nothing.

'They called him a coward. My brother, my dear courageous brother. But if he'd been a coward, if he had only wanted to save his own skin, he could so easily have pled essential occupation and been allowed to continue his work. Instead, he told them what he thought and he paid the price.'

'What happened to him?

'Apart from being despised, you mean? He was sent to prison with hard labour. Prison. Scotland's most capped international player, treated as a criminal. But John never once tried to use his status as Scotland captain, as rugby hero, to gain an advantage. As for his teammates and the Scottish union, they turned their backs on him. The authorities sent him to Broxburn to make fertiliser from animal carcasses.' She laughed without humour. 'They made a mistake there. As a doctor, John was horrified at the dangerous conditions these men were forced to work in, so he kicked up a fuss. They didn't like that, so they sent him back to prison and left him in solitary confinement this time. They were determined to break him.' Her voice cracked and she stopped, looked across at Rob. 'You should see him now,' she whispered. 'He's like a scarecrow.'

They found themselves back at the terrace and walked to the edge, leaning over the balustrade and looking down at the River Clyde beneath them. It carried all the detritus of Glasgow towards the Atlantic, flowing faster than the sluggish Somme. For the first time that evening, Rob felt a coolness against his skin.

'The rugby world didn't speak up for him but others did,' Grace said. 'Questions were asked in parliament about him. Lord Parmoor pointed out how much John could be doing for his country, with all his training and medical expertise, and instead he was locked up in solitary confinement. But it didn't make any difference. No one could bear to hear a different voice.'

Rob looked down on the river with the sensation of teetering on the edge of a great void. His mind flashed to an evening at the base hospital in 1914, when he and a young Canadian doctor had drunk far more than was good for them.

'How can they expect us to do this?' the Canadian, whose name he couldn't even remember, had demanded. 'Being a doctor is a calling to heal, to restore life. But we treat these men so they can go back to the front to kill or be killed.'

The Canadian doctor had soon moved on and Rob had been glad. Even then he had grasped that the only way to get through what was demanded of them was to focus on the task in hand and refuse to consider the bigger picture. Private Hamilton's trench foot. Captain Mallory's burns. There was no moral dilemma involved in treating those. But the moment he let himself consider what it all might be for, he risked lighting a fuse beneath the whole bloody thing, and the only person who would be buried under the weight of the blast would be himself.

Each month that passed and each teammate who died led him deeper into a place from which there was no possibility of retreat.

But now he stood on the banks of the River Clyde beside a woman who held up her brother's principles so brightly that they threatened to expose everything he had pushed into the shadows all these past years. If John were right, what did that make him? If more of them had stood out, how different might it have been?

He couldn't do it. It was too late. He owed too much to the fallen. He took a step backwards, lifting a hand as though to fend off that light. 'I'm sorry,' he said, and turned on his heel, unable to face what he might see in her uncompromising gaze.

Another sleepless night, but that was not unusual. Next day the habits of the past five years came to the fore. *Focus on the men who need you today.* As long as he didn't come across Grace MacCallum, he would be all right. There was a new chap in

Ward Two. Archie Macdonald had been on board HMS *Princess Royal* when she was hit during the Battle of Jutland in 1916. He was a young man with a West Highland accent and a wry turn of phrase. 'Lost my old legs in the princess's battleship, got my new ones in her hospital,' he was fond of saying. He'd left on two wooden legs a few months ago, but had returned to sort out some trouble he was having with an infected stump. Rob introduced himself and examined Archie. Some embedded shrapnel had been missed during earlier operations. Surgery was required, and the lad had been through so much already. He explained what lay ahead, checked with the nurse what Archie had taken for the pain, and gave the boy an encouraging pat on the shoulder before turning away.

'Doc?'

Rob turned back.

The boy's face was flushed. 'Could I please have your signature?'

It wasn't an unusual request now that word had gone round about his rugby exploits. Rob felt in his pocket for a piece of paper, but Archie leant awkwardly towards his bedside cabinet.

'On here would do just fine, Doc. If you would.'

He held out a folded newspaper. As Rob took it, the boy said, 'I'm surprised you didn't play in the tournament. You're every bit as good as the men they chose.'

Rob glanced curiously at the newspaper. It was folded open at a report headed *NEW ZEALAND TAKES KING'S CUP*. The match had taken place last month, while he was still in France. This must have been the climax to the tournament that the major and Charlie Usher had wanted him to join.

'The mother country lost,' Archie said from the bed, 'but there's no shame in that. I heard the All Blacks kept training together right through the war, whereas ours was a team cobbled together from all our nations. And we don't have the best of our men back yet. Men like yourself.'

*The best of our men.*

*The best of our men are never coming back, son.*

But there was an eagerness in the boy's voice that he couldn't ignore, and anything that distracted him from the pain was a good thing.

'Keen on rugby, are you?' he asked, as he scrawled his name at the top of the page and handed it back to him.

'Oh yes. I played at school in Glasgow, and at the university. I hoped—' He stopped, closed his eyes briefly, and then looked down at the newspaper report. 'Usher,' he said. 'He's a tremendous captain, isn't he? Did you play with him?'

'Aye. Charlie and I won our first caps together.'

Young Archie's eyes were shining again. 'Really? What was he like to play with? Terrific, I imagine. And Cherry Pillman from England was playing too. I was in the crowd the day he broke his leg at the Calcutta Cup match in 1914. D'you remember?'

'I do.' Knee-deep in mud, running his hands urgently over the damaged bone before summoning help to get the casualty moved to hospital. No guns, though.

'This match was just a warm-up, really,' Archie went on. 'I'm glad there were a few Scottish players in the team. When will the internationals start up again? Have you been told?'

'I'm not sure they will,' he said. 'I'm not sure they can.'

'Oh, but that's all wrong! They have to.'

Rob shook his head. Where could he begin to find the words to tell this enthusiastic young man how impossible it would be to field a team when its members had been ripped to pieces. Aye, and if John MacCallum were right, he himself was complicit in their destruction. But then the lad looked at him across the newspaper, a youthful face aged by trauma and loss.

'Captain Campbell,' he said, and though he spoke with deference, there was a strange authority in his tone. 'You still have your legs and I still have my eyes. I want to see you play for Scotland one day soon. Sir.'

# Chapter Twenty-Two

## Aberdeen

Alison Rutherford slipped a comforting hand through her daughter's arm. 'I knew it would be harder for you than for the others,' she said. 'But Maggie and I have always rubbed along well together and it's time to move on.'

Corran said nothing. Her mother was quite clearly happier here, so why did she feel so uneasy? Perhaps it had something to do with the fact she had been in France when Mother had moved down to Aberdeen with nothing but two suitcases, leaving the rest of her life behind in Thurso. Now Corran had returned to Scotland, and the world had shifted so far she was struggling to find her bearings.

She stepped aside quickly as two small boys came charging past them and slid to a stop on the gravel path, narrowly avoiding plunging into the pond. Corran and her mother watched as the boys launched their model boat with whoops of excitement, then set off chasing after it.

Memories rippled over the dark surface of the artificial lake.

'Boys and water,' Alison said quietly.

Duthie Park was busy with families out enjoying a June Saturday morning. Corran had arrived in Aberdeen from Oxford two days earlier. Tomorrow she would continue on her journey north to Thurso, where she had promised to make a start on sorting the contents of the house. Even as she longed for the north, she dreaded what awaited her. The two women strolled on around the park until they found themselves facing a tall column with a statue of a Greek goddess carved from Aberdeen granite on top. Corran looked up.

'That's Hygeia with her snake: goddess of health, looking down with approval on all the citizens of Aberdeen who have come out for some fresh air. There's a statue rather like this in a park near me in Oxford.'

Alison sat down on a nearby bench and Corran joined her. 'How are you finding Oxford? It's quite a change after Dieppe.'

'Everyone has been very welcoming. Although it's new to me, it's a world I know well. I'm sure I'll get along fine. But I do miss France.' She hesitated. 'Our work out there was somehow more straightforward. More . . . elemental.'

Alison's keen gaze held hers and Corran was reminded of her mother's unsettling ability to see beneath the surface. 'You can be very proud of the work you did in France. And I imagine you made some lasting friendships?'

'Perhaps.' Corran shrugged off the gentle query and returned to the earlier conversation. 'Won't you miss Thurso, though?'

Alison looked out over the park. 'Of course I will. But

there's nothing left there for me except memories, and I carry those with me wherever I am. I always told you young ones to go after all that life might have for you. I'm just listening to my own advice, that's all. I'd rather not live out the rest of my life alone.'

'We wouldn't let that happen.'

'Perhaps not. But the last thing you and Rob need at the start of your married life is Granny in residence. Stella is seeing the world at last, and I can hardly stow away on Alex's ship! I won't have any of you curtailing your lives to keep me company. Aberdeen is the best solution for now. I have a notion to travel too, when the time is right.'

The sun was bright but the air was cool, and Corran shivered. Everyone was so sure. Everyone but her. She thought again about how their mother had pushed and cajoled them to take advantage of every opportunity. It seemed poor recompense somehow that her children had scattered, while her friends in Thurso had grandchildren living nearby. But Alison hadn't wanted it any other way.

They had been still for long enough in that sharp air. 'It's a bit chilly; shall we take a look at the palm house?' Corran suggested.

They made their way to the great glasshouse and pushed open the door to be engulfed in fragrant, steamy air. Strolling between exotic species, Alison took great interest in the labels, checking their different origins.

'This one's from China. Now that would be a fascinating country to explore, don't you think?'

Corran followed on behind, watching her mother dart

from side to side as she marvelled at the array of colour and fragrance. For herself, she was thinking more about roots. Each breath she took of this humid air made her long more than ever for the fresh northern breeze.

Tomorrow she would travel to Caithness. Whatever else lay ahead, for her it would always be home.

# PART FOUR
*Treaty*

Late May to July 1919

# Chapter Twenty-Three

Paris

All Paris held its breath.

The Germans had finally received the treaty terms – controversially refusing to stand as the sheaf of papers was handed over in the Trianon Palace Hotel – and now there was nothing to do but wait.

'Anyone with half an ounce of common sense would have invited them into the negotiations before now,' Stella said as she and Hugh ate breakfast together in the Majestic.

'Indeed. We thought we were drawing up draft terms to be shared with the Germans for their response. A starting point, like when you buy something in the market – you start low because you expect to haggle. We were told just to get something down on paper, and then somewhere along the line that became the accepted treaty. Take it or leave it. It very much looks to me as if they will choose to leave it.'

The typists in the Astoria had worked all hours to get the treaty finalised, sustained by late-night deliveries of lemonade and biscuits. Now at last the mad scramble was over. Hugh and

Stella discovered over their bacon and eggs that they both had the day off.

'It looks like being a scorcher of a day too,' said Hugh. 'Let's get out of Paris.'

Stella was more than willing. The last few weeks had been gruelling, and tempers in both the Astoria and the Majestic were frayed. It would be good to escape for a while and enjoy the warmth of a summer's day away from the stifling heat of the city streets.

They decided to collect a picnic from the hotel and take the train to Saint-Cloud, and from there on to Versailles.

'I know several girls who have done it and made a really good day of it.' The ongoing strikes made the trains a bit unpredictable, but enough workers had returned to provide some sort of service. Stella sat in the stuffy carriage and felt a surge of pleasure as she watched the crowded backstreets of Paris slip by. A whole day away from the conference, a whole day away from the steamy hothouse of demands and orders, rumours and intrigue that the Majestic had become. Travelling with Hugh, who was so completely in love with Lily, was comfortable; there was none of the caution she felt when she spent time with Freddie. But the train was crowded and airless, and it was with relief that they reached the little platform.

Here in the Parc de Saint-Cloud, they were high above the city. The warm summer breeze was soft and sweet, and made her realise just how fetid the Paris air had become as the temperature climbed.

'Let's eat something here before we go on to Versailles,'

she suggested. 'It's early but it will set us up for the day.' They wandered along the terraces of the former château until they found a grassy spot with a glorious view over the city. They stood side by side, pointing out various landmarks and trying to work out if they could see the Majestic. 'I believe the Germans shelled Paris from here in 1870,' Stella said. 'Then the château was destroyed by French fire. It does make one wonder if there can ever be peace.'

They sat on the fragrant grass and unwrapped their sandwiches. 'It's good to get away, even for a day. I hadn't realised how *grimy* I've been feeling. The last few weeks have been rather awful, haven't they?'

'We'll be allowed to apply for leave soon.'

'Will you go to Biarritz?'

'Yes, as long as they are still there. Lily is much better now.' Hugh crumbled some bread and then looked at her, frowning. 'I just hope she still wants . . . you know, me . . . when she's well again.'

'Oh Hugh! Of course she does. Her letters are full of you.'

'Are they?' He sounded so eager, and so young.

'Yes. Not that I'm going to tell you what she says.'

His shoulders relaxed and he smiled at her. 'What about you, Stella? Will you go home?'

That word again. She thought of Poppy – *the fresh breeze of home* – and of Corran's reluctance to let their Thurso house go. And what did she have – the London Girls' Club? It was hardly a home. She looked out over the city spread below them. Even now men were scurrying to and fro down there with attaché cases and reports, trying to prepare for every eventuality. Stella's future, and all their futures, were somehow bundled up in those documents.

'It all rather depends, doesn't it?' she said. 'Whether or not the Germans sign. What will happen if they don't? Some people think they will turn Bolshevist and take up arms again, with the Russians on their side.'

'And who knows what the Italians will do? They've already walked out of the negotiations once over our refusal to honour the secret treaty.'

The peace they had longed for was almost within grasp, but the fear of failure and renewed fighting stalked the corridors of the Majestic. And Alex was still out there. The stakes were so high. Stella gave a shiver.

'Let's not think about it today.' As she folded up the sandwich paper and wiped her fingers on the grass, she became aware of a movement on the terrace behind them. A child – small and scrawny – watched them from behind a statue. As she looked, he slid out and began to move towards them, low to the ground like a cowering dog. He came closer and held out his hands in supplication, staying just out of reach. Hungry. Poor child. There were so many hungry people all around them, and in the Majestic their meals remained lavish and plentiful. Meanwhile in Germany the children were not just hungry; they were starving, and it was thanks to the Allied blockade. But the politicians wouldn't lift the blockade while the threat of renewed conflict remained. She put her hand in her rucksack and pulled out an apple, holding it out. The boy snatched it and bolted.

'Better get out of here,' said Hugh in an amused tone. 'Once they hear there's free food we'll have half the local urchins on our trail.'

She followed his example and clambered to her feet, brushing grass from her skirt. 'We should be on our way anyway if we want time to explore Versailles.'

By the time they reached the little town of Versailles, south-west of Paris, it was after midday and the streets were quiet. 'All the sensible people have gone out of the sun.'

'Let's find a shady café then and have a cold drink. Then we'll feel more like walking round the palace gardens.'

The huge courtyard of the palace sprawled before them but they carried on past in search of a café. At first they were unsuccessful, passing houses and hotels that looked grander than they wanted. Then Stella stopped.

'I wonder what this can be?'

Near the palace walls and positioned at the head of a broad street was a mansion house with windows rising over several floors. A high picket fence surrounded it, and French policemen guarded the gates. Stella asked one what the building was. He spat on the ground before answering. This was the Hôtel des Réservoirs, and the German delegation was in residence.

'Can you hear any music?' Hugh laughed. 'Apparently they play gramophone records day and night in order to stop our people listening in to their discussions.'

Stella looked up. Many of the shutters were closed, but she glimpsed a shadowy movement at one of the upper windows. The defeated enemy. She turned away, but as they continued down the broad road in search of their café, she remained conscious of the tall building behind them, of malevolent German eyes watching them.

At last they found a shady café terrace where they sat beneath trees and drank lemonade with just one tarte au citron to share. Prices in Paris were now going up by the day and their salaries barely covered essentials. As they chatted, Hugh was full of enthusiasm for a story he'd read in the newspaper about two British airmen rescued from an unsuccessful attempt to fly the Atlantic. It reminded Stella of Poppy and her passion for flying, and she told Hugh about their encounter.

'I don't suppose I'll ever see her again, but I would like to somehow,' she said, as they paid their bill and rose to leave.

They stepped out onto the pavement just behind an elderly French woman dressed from head to toe in the dusty black that many wore despite the heat. Bent, she walked unsteadily, lurching from side to side. Drunk. Even as they moved to go round her, there was a loud noise from the road and a crowded motor car came tearing along. The woman staggered and fell into the road, right into the path of the vehicle. Stella cried out and sprang forward but a young man coming in the other direction was ahead of her. He threw himself in front of the car and pushed the woman towards the pavement. The car – barely slowing – hooted its horn as it missed them by a hair's breadth. Stella looked after it angrily and saw it was carrying British officers.

'Beasts!' she cried. 'You could at least stop to help!' But the car was gone and she turned back to the group on the pavement. Hugh and the young man between them had pulled the old woman to a chair at the café. She muttered to herself in words Stella couldn't make out.

'She is weak from hunger,' said the young man in French. 'Can we have some water please? And perhaps some bread?'

Stella spoke to a waitress and then turned back to the woman. '*Vous sentez-vous mieux?*'

'I do not think she is French,' the young man said, switching to fluent English. 'I think she is refugee, perhaps from Hungary. There are very many here in Paris from different countries.' He gently eased the headscarf back from the woman's face, and it was with a visceral sense of shock that Stella realised the thin, sunken face did not belong to an old crone, as she had assumed. The woman's beautiful dark eyes gave her away and as Stella watched they filled with tears, which overflowed and ran silently down the hollow cheeks. The waiter brought bread and water and the woman accepted them. She drank the water, but broke off only a tiny piece of the bread to chew. The rest she slipped inside her shawl, and her dark eyes met Stella's with a mixture of fear and defiance.

'She must have children,' Stella said quietly, remembering the urchin in the park who had snatched her apple. 'She will give it to them. Here.' And she spoke to the waitress once more, fishing some coins from her purse. The waitress returned with some cheese and a pastry, which Stella laid before the woman. 'Take this,' she said, in English now, as it seemed to make no difference.

The woman snatched the food and concealed it from view beneath layers of clothing. With an abrupt movement she pushed the chair back and stood up, still unsteady. She leant forward, gripping the table, and Stella saw with horror that three fingers were missing from her left hand. The space where they should be was raw, inflamed and weeping with yellow pus. But even as Stella exclaimed and reached out, the woman pulled her mutilated hand away and stepped quickly backwards. A torrent of speech came out: Stella couldn't understand a word but the force of anger was unmistakeable. Then she wrapped her good arm protectively around the hidden food and hurried away, leaving Hugh, Stella and the young Frenchman rather stunned.

'Well!' said Hugh. 'It's not as if we just saved her life or anything!'

'Did you see her poor hand? That must be what's wrong with her. It's infected. She's feverish. She needs a doctor.'

'She will have had rings on those fingers,' said the Frenchman quietly.

'Oh, how horrible! Who—?'

He shrugged. 'It is war. French, English, Russian, German. Who knows? Perhaps another woman whose babies are starving.'

Surely not the English. Surely not a woman. Stella knew these thoughts were naïve, and swallowed them down with her nausea. Instead she looked more closely at the man who had come to the rescue. He was probably in his twenties, with dark hair and olive skin, and was remarkably handsome. He wore civilian clothes, so wasn't a soldier. The waitress arrived and asked if they would like anything else, but Stella was desperately hoping she had left enough money in her purse for the return train fare. She shook her head and got to her feet, followed by the men.

'I must go,' the newcomer said.

'That was all rather shocking. We are on our way to the palace for a stroll in the gardens. Won't you join us?'

The man hesitated for a moment, and then he smiled. 'Thank you, I will. A walk in the gardens will be – pleasant.'

His voice was soft, and although his English was fluent, his accent was strong and, Stella thought, somewhat unfamiliar. Perhaps he came from the south rather than Paris.

'My name is Mortimer and this is Miss Rutherford,' Hugh said. 'We're with the British delegation. The conference, you know.'

There was a hint of laughter in the man's tone as he said, 'I know. You are easy to spot, you English.'

'Scottish, actually.'

He was interested at that. 'Really? From Scotland? I had a Scotch schoolmaster when I was a boy. From Dumfries. I always hoped to visit him.'

'Surely you could, now the war is over?'

He shook his head. 'I have not told you my name,' he said in his soft voice. 'My name is Wenger. Nikolai Wenger. I, too, am part of a delegation, you see. The German delegation.'

Once, when they were children, Jack had fired a football at full power straight into her stomach, knocking all the air from her lungs. That was exactly how Stella felt now. The handsome, quiet hero was not French but German. Not an ally but the enemy. They stopped walking and he faced them, eyebrows raised and a soft smile lurking at the corners of his mouth.

'You speak pretty good French,' Hugh said. He sounded suspicious, as if he thought the man wanted to trick them. But who would pretend to be German?

'That's why I am here. I am a translator – I speak French and German equally. English, not quite so well.' He looked between them and acknowledged their doubt. 'Those of us who grew up in Alsace have a complicated history. But I am German. I fought for my country in the war.' He said this without emotion but with clarity, leaving no room for error.

They reached the entrance to the gardens and stood, uncertain.

'Might as well go in,' Hugh said, and disappeared through the gate. Stella and Nikolai remained. He touched his hat as though making to leave.

'Do come in, won't you? Just for a while. It would be—' She stopped, unsure what words to use, but suddenly not wanting this young German to walk away. Not yet. He nodded politely, as though he was only coming to oblige her, and they both followed Hugh through the gate and into a broad, tree-lined avenue. For a while they wandered along woodland paths. She asked him about his Scottish schoolmaster, and told him a little about Thurso. All the time she was conscious of her heart thudding. When she hadn't known he was German she had thought him brave and compassionate. But he was the enemy. He had stood on the opposite side of the trenches and fired at Jack.

Soon they came out from the trees into the formal gardens, where a sweeping vista led up to the splendour of the palace itself, and down to a vast ornamental lake. A few other visitors strolled around, but most people Stella could see were busy preparing the gardens for the grand occasion to come. Clemenceau had insisted that the treaty must be signed here at Versailles, where fifty years earlier Germany had humiliated France. The gardens had been neglected during the war, and even pressed into service to grow vegetables. Now hedges were carefully manicured while borders were replanted with flowers, and workmen undid the protective sacking on some of the statues.

The sun was hot, and they sat on a marble bench to rest and watch for a while. Nikolai removed his hat and wiped his brow with his handkerchief.

'I have not walked here before,' he said. 'My colleagues and I stroll some days among the beautiful magnolias and crab-apple trees in an area of the Trianon Park that is fenced off for us. We are rather like animals in the zoo, don't you think? I'm sure the Parisians would throw us apples and nuts if the fence were not too high. But since we received the terms of the so-called peace, we have had little heart for sightseeing.'

Stella glanced at Hugh. Neither of them had been present when the terms were handed over, but the Majestic that night had seethed with indignation at the failure of the count who received the treaty to stand while he made his angry speech.

'Were you at the session when they handed over the peace terms?' she asked.

'I was.' He took out a cigarette and lit it. 'We will not sign, of course. It would be a catastrophe.'

Hugh turned his head sharply. 'Why?'

'Have you read this abominable treaty? Then you must understand. Germany alone is stripped of her nationhood; Germany alone is required to disarm. Our people in disputed territories are denied the right of self-determination, which was fundamental to President Wilson's fourteen points, the basis on which we laid down arms.' The hand that held his cigarette shook. 'The theft of our assets and outrageous demands for reparations will cripple our economy, and leave my country prey to every fanatic, Bolshevik or nationalist who wishes to stir up our people. We do not deny that those who held power in Germany in 1914 bear some responsibility for the war, but so too do the leaders of other nations. This is not a peace treaty: it is revenge. We will never sign.'

He had not raised his voice, but he spoke with quiet passion. Stella clasped her hands tightly and thought of the other night in the Majestic when she had heard the English economist John Maynard Keynes making almost exactly the same points. And had the Inter-Allied Women's Conference not already denounced the proposed treaty as likely to lead to more war? Yet she knew there were others who believed that its firm terms were exactly what was needed to secure a lasting peace.

'You don't really have much choice, do you?' Hugh asked. 'After all, you lost the war.'

Nikolai dropped his cigarette end on the ground and crushed it under his foot.

'We prepare counter-proposals. Perhaps President Wilson, at least, may see sense. We shall discover if he really is a man of integrity. If not – we go home.'

'And then?'

He got to his feet. 'Let us pray that good sense prevails, because it seems to me that what you currently call peace is war by another name.' He touched his hat and bowed his head. 'I thank you for your company. *Auf Wiedersehen.*'

They watched him depart and then stood up, stunned into silence, and headed in the opposite direction.

'Rum fellow,' Hugh said eventually.

Stella felt as if Nikolai had just spoken aloud every fear that churned within her. 'He's right, though, isn't he?'

'I don't know,' said Hugh, and there was a weariness in his tone. They had wandered through between hedges into another part of the garden that had not yet received its makeover. 'We can only hope there will be some negotiation over the next week or two because otherwise we are in a very sticky position. So many of our troops have been demobbed already. Others are fully committed to the fighting in the Baltic and Afghanistan.'

Stella stood looking at a circular fountain, once beautiful but now brown, slimy and filled with leaves. The surrounding borders were overgrown with weeds.

'If war breaks out again our work has failed, but I'm not going back to Britain,' she said with sudden certainty. 'I can't bear just to sit at home and wait for news again. There has to be something more I can do, and I'm going to find it.'

# Chapter Twenty-Four

Erskine

Sitting alone on the hard wooden bench on the platform at Bishopton station, his old kitbag by his side, Rob found it hard to believe that more than six weeks had passed since he stepped off the train here on a balmy May morning. Today a persistent thin drizzle hid the landscape from view and clung to his raincoat, not quite wet enough to drive him into the dismal waiting room but dreich nevertheless. He had begged a seat on the coal lorry to get here. He remembered how, when he first arrived, he had refused the offer of a lift and walked all the way to the hospital. Since that time a weariness had wormed its way into his bones and he had no more inclination to walk all that distance than to ask one of the amputees to do likewise. And so here he was in the deserted station a good hour before he needed to be. He pulled his crumpled almanac from his pocket.

North or south?

The tiny numbers on the timetable danced before his eyes and made no sense. Rob shoved it back in his pocket and pulled out his cigarettes, lighting one with trembling fingers.

The shaking had worsened. That was partly what had drawn Sir William's attention: that, and his irrational outburst at dinner the other evening. He was still ashamed of his behaviour. He wouldn't have minded the Welsh lad's incessant questions about his rugby days nearly as much if he hadn't been so horribly conscious of Grace MacCallum sitting just across the table, her dark eyes pools of reproach. Or so it seemed to him. But when he brought his hand down sharply on the table and barked at Davies to give it a rest, he became aware of Sir William watching him quizzically. He wasn't really surprised to be invited to take a turn round the grounds after dinner.

Here on the platform, a few people had gathered and he could hear the distant rumble of an approaching train. Rob didn't move. The grind of brakes, the screech of the whistle, the slamming of doors and a loud burst of steam. Laughter, chatter, a flurry of movement, and the train pulled away. Still he sat, unmoved by the curious glances of the stationmaster. North or south? He would sit here until he had made up his mind.

Sir William had waited for him on the terrace, looking out over the vegetable plots towards the river and hills beyond. Rob wanted nothing more than to thrust his hands into his pockets, but childhood training prevented him. Useless, anyway. The first thing his superior did when he turned was to hold out a cigarette, his sharp blue eyes missing nothing.

'How are the headaches?'

'Much the same.'

'Which means?'

Rob breathed the smoke down into his lungs and decided to be honest.

'Fairly bad. But I'm used to them. I have pills.'

Sir William gestured towards his hands. 'And the trembling? I don't remember noticing that when you first joined us.'

'It's happened before – when I was out there – but it seemed to improve. It's – a little worse again now.' He bit his lip. *Not much future for a surgeon who can't hold his hands steady.*

'Sleeping much?'

'Not much.'

Sir William nodded. 'Let's walk,' he said and turned, leading the way around the side of the house towards the gardens behind. Some patients were out on the gravel area, enjoying a last breath of evening air. Sir William waved a greeting but led Rob past formal borders and into the lush seclusion of the bushes. He paused beneath a magnificent cedar tree. Its thick dark mass of intertwined trunks spread upwards, supporting vast green branches and dwarfing all other trees around it. Sir William rested a hand on the mighty bark and turned to face Rob.

'This is what I think. Hear me out and then tell me afterwards if you disagree. I believe you are experiencing the effects of long-term concussion and nerve damage caused by shellfire, but I also think you are suffering from sheer exhaustion. How much leave have you actually had? Very little, I'm sure. You came here more or less straight from France, yes? Now I know a little of what you experienced out there, Captain Campbell, because you have told me yourself, but also because of what I can see with my own eyes. You spent years holding everything together under pressure for the sake of your men. That's the doctor's lot in wartime, is it not – to operate in the midst of a firefight; to bring calm and comfort to men who are beside themselves with pain and fear. To be the strong one. And you did it well, Captain Campbell, you did it very well.'

*Long-term concussion and nerve damage.* At first that was all Rob could hear, confirming his own bleak diagnosis. Gradually the rest of Sir William's gently spoken words began to penetrate.

'With the human body there must always be a reaction eventually. After intense physical and mental strain, you have come here' – he waved his arm around the leafy mansion grounds – 'and relaxed. That is when reaction is most likely to set in. We see it with patients time and again, but it's not unusual to see it among staff too. And so, I want you to take a holiday. Go and visit friends; find yourself a woman; go in search of the sun. I don't care what you do, but I want you to take at least a month. Then come back here and we'll see what's what.'

Rob looked up at the spreading branches. 'And my work, sir?'

'Your work can wait. This hospital has much to offer, but at this point in your recovery it's not the best place for you. How can it be, when at every corner there's a reminder of the carnage of war?' Sir William stepped forward and placed a hand on his shoulder. 'You're a good surgeon, Captain Campbell, but you'll be a better one if you do as I say. Now, is there somewhere you can go?'

Rob thought of the two letters lying in his room and nodded his head. One from Corran, who was in Thurso sorting out the house, and one from Gus, whom he had last seen on that drunken night in Arras. Gus was in Paris on liaison – *the lightest of duties and the swishest of digs. I've been invited to these games the Yanks are so keen on. Come and stay and we'll go to them together.*

And so he packed his bag and said his farewells, shaking hands with Grace MacCallum with the usual hot flush of humiliation. Clambered down from the coal lorry outside the station, brushing soot from his trousers.

'At least a month,' Sir William had said. By the time the next train rumbled into the station, he knew what he would do. He would go and stay with Gus, but first he must see Corran, who was his greatest hope of leaving the war behind.

North and then south.

# Chapter Twenty-Five

## Thurso

Corran pulled back her faded bedroom curtains and looked out at the early morning sunshine sparkling on the Pentland Firth. Thank goodness the sun had returned for Midsummer's Day, after a spell of grey, dismal weather when Caithness hid her beauty behind a stubborn veil of mist. Today she would take Rob to Orkney. Today might also be the day when the veil that hung between them would be tugged away, and they could speak openly about the future at last.

She wasn't sure if that filled her with hope or with fear.

It meant an early start, but she didn't mind that. She always woke early in the north in summer. Downstairs to the chilly kitchen where she filled the kettle and placed it on the stove to heat. After a week she was becoming accustomed to being alone in her childhood home, which had felt so very strange for the first day or two. When she had been small this room had been the preserve of the cook. After her father died there was far less money and Mother did more for herself, but there was generally a girl in to help. Since her late teens, Corran had lived in one academic institution after another, in which meals of varying quality appeared without any input on her part. Hurrying footsteps, coughs and female laughter had been the constant backdrop to her days. To live alone was a new experience, and to cater for herself an untried novelty.

*At least I can scramble eggs.*

Rob had checked into the Pentland Hotel yesterday. Perhaps that was ridiculous with a whole empty house at their disposal, but she knew the quiet streets of Thurso would hum with scandal if she had a man to stay. She remembered the comforting honesty of her week with Arthur in their fairy-tale woodland cottage, and wondered if his wife, Mary, had been waiting to welcome him home. They had all scattered in different directions when the education scheme closed. She had written to tell Arthur her new address, but had heard nothing back as yet.

She rinsed her plate under the spluttering tap then moved through the house, pulling back curtains and opening windows. The empty rooms sulked at her, mournful in their loneliness. Perhaps it *was* better to give up the house and let another family live here. New children with new games and songs and dreams. But what in the world would she do with her holidays? How could she endure the confines of college life without this expansive homeland awaiting her return?

She had gathered together all the provisions she thought they might need for the day and now she picked up her warmest sweater. The sun might be shining but she knew from experience just how chilly the Pentland Firth would be even on the brightest day. Was Rob a good sailor? Yet another thing she didn't know about him, for all they had been friends for so many years. She had been shocked at the sight of him when he stepped off the train yesterday. True, no one looked good at the end of that ordeal of a journey, but his face was pale and drawn, his eyes dark with shadows, and his hands shook uncontrollably. He appeared to be in a far worse state than when they met in Arras in March, although she had expected the opposite to be true.

Or could it be that his brokenness had not stood out amid the horror of the battlefields in the way it did here in clean, untouched Caithness?

He had wired from Glasgow to tell her he was coming. When he arrived he explained that he intended to visit a rugby teammate in Paris but wanted to see her first. 'Take up your offer of midsummer in the north.' She wasn't sure she had quite offered that, but never mind. Anything important remained unsaid between them as they took tea and scones in the gloomy hotel lounge but surely today, amid the invigorating sea air and the Orkney landscapes she had loved since childhood, she would be brave enough to find words to define their future.

Rob was waiting for her outside the hotel and she was pleased to see that he too wore a thick jumper and even had a woolly scarf round his neck.

'Were you able to rouse someone for breakfast?' she asked.

'Not only that. They gave me a picnic lunch too.'

'You must have charmed them!' He would still be able to do that, she thought, even as she felt a tug of compassion at the sight of his thin face. He looked better after a night's rest, but fragile. So very fragile. 'We should get on our way,' she said. 'It's a fair walk to Scrabster Harbour, though it couldn't be more beautiful. It's not too far for you, is it?'

'Not at all. I can feel the air up here making a difference already.'

She led the way through the grey streets, and soon they left the little town behind and walked along the coast road, white sea foaming at the foot of the cliffs to their right.

'We're fortunate with the weather,' she said. 'It's been dismal up here ever since I arrived last week. I wouldn't suggest this crossing for a minute if it were anything but a still day. We need to know we can get home again!'

'It looks perfectly calm to me.'

'Yes, but this is the Pentland Firth. The currents of the Atlantic Ocean and the North Sea meet right out there, and create one of the most treacherous stretches of water in the world. I've seen hardened sailors turn green on the steamer taking them to their ships in Scapa. But don't worry. Today should be uneventful.'

The little steamship *St Ola* was waiting in Scrabster Harbour when they arrived. Rob glanced down.

'Is she not a bit small?'

'Small but sturdy. This is a ship with personality.' A lightness entered into her as they descended the path to the harbour. This little boat had taken her family across the firth so many times. How good it was to be on her again! How good it was to set sail on the sea, to leave behind even for one day the cares that had mounted up so persistently over these months. They had all thought their troubles were over on that momentous armistice day in November, but how false that hope had turned out to be. The news from the conference was grave: no one knew whether the Germans would sign or not. The Bolshevik threat increased every day. She worried constantly about Alex, whose ship was still caught up in the conflict in the Baltic. The papers claimed that the Baltic would be the location for any renewed fighting, and the British had already sent over an airship. Coming home to this empty house had filled her with dark grief for Jack. She couldn't bear to think of losing Alex too.

Yesterday she had climbed the stairs to the boys' wood-panelled bedrooms, crammed with the useless clutter of a vanished family life that would never return. She had sat on Jack's floor to sort through his possessions, tears streaming down her face as she pulled out one memory after another. The sloping walls and ceiling were covered with his sketches, a vast collage of his life and acquaintances, and she carefully unpinned each one and slipped them into a writing case. But she left Alex's door firmly closed. It was a superstition, she knew, but she couldn't help herself. If she began to empty his room, he would never come home.

The steamer pitched a little, but the skies remained clear and the views were superb. Rob pulled a pair of field glasses from his bag and she pointed towards the cliffs of Hoy.

'We sail past these all the way. With your glasses you should spot all sorts of seabirds. We'll see the Old Man of Hoy – he's magnificent – and the waterfall at St John's Head. It's been known to spout upwards when the wind is strong enough.'

Rob said little during the crossing, but she watched the

sharp wind sting colour into his cheeks. As they sailed nearer to Orkney, she noticed other passengers pointing to something and followed their gaze. There in the distance were the dark ships of Her Majesty's Fleet, speeding out of the channel between Flotta and South Ronaldsay.

'That's a sight that always thrills me,' she said. 'Oh, if only Alex were based on one of the destroyers here rather than in the Baltic.'

Rob lifted his glasses to his eyes. 'It must have looked just this way when they left for the Battle of Jutland,' he said, then let the glasses dangle by their strap around his neck and gripped the rail, his knuckles white. 'One of the Scotland boys, Cecil Abercrombie, was on board the *Defence* when she was blown up at Jutland. He was a good chap. We ribbed him silly when his penalty came off the post in France in 1913.'

Corran glanced at him. These rugby men had been brothers to him, and that's a lot of brothers to lose. Like Achilles mourning Patroclus, wrapped in a black cloud of grief. She touched his hand in sympathy and he put his arm around her shoulders, pulling her close. It felt warm and comforting and for a moment they stood like that, watching the great naval ships disappear in the other direction, memories and fears following in their wake. But she couldn't allow herself to lean on Rob. Corran twisted away.

'Look – over there. That gannet's about to dive – see! Splendid!'

They sailed alongside red and yellow sandstone cliffs, pointing out seabirds to each other and marvelling at the sheer majesty of the rockface and the gravity-defying strength of the

Old Man of Hoy sea stack, standing proud of the cliffs as the sea surged about its base. Eventually the mouth of the channel opened up, and the little ship carried them into sheltered waters and the pier at Stromness.

'A cup of tea to warm us up, I think,' said Corran. 'And then I have a surprise for you.'

They drank their tea in a tiny café in a narrow street before Corran led Rob up a steep, flagstone-paved hill to a cottage. Curtains were drawn in the windows and the paint on the door was peeling.

'Doesn't look as if anyone's in.'

Corran didn't approach the door but instead led him round the back into an overgrown garden with a shed. She tugged at the door and it creaked open. 'Bicycles!' she said, a note of triumph in her voice.

Rob stepped into the darkness. The shed was musty and cobwebby, but Corran had already wheeled out one of the bicycles stored there. He followed her example and leant the heavy bicycle against the wall. Corran disappeared back into the shed and emerged with a pump in one hand and an oil can in the other.

'They'll need some air in the tyres and some oil on the chain, but should be fine to use after that. They belong to my friend Jean.' She saw Rob look at the abandoned house and said, more quietly, 'Jean is nursing in the south. Her brother was killed at Loos and her parents both died of influenza. But I know she would be happy for us to borrow these today.'

Rob nodded and she watched as his trembling hands gently brushed the cobwebs from the frame of the dead boy's bicycle. She felt again the overwhelming sadness of sorting through Jack's possessions yesterday. All over the country there were houses like this, filled with the ephemera of hundreds of thousands of lives that had unexpectedly ceased to exist. Clothes and footballs, bicycles and egg collections, razors and comics and diaries and gramophone records. So much of it: surely far too much for the nation's attics or rubbish heaps or junk shops to absorb. Where would it all go?

She shook off the gloom and turned her attention to Jean's machine. Soon they were ready and Corran wheeled it through the gate and onto the road. 'We only have a short time. Stromness is lovely but I want to show you the views when you get further out. Bicycles make that much easier.' She pulled herself up, tucking her skirt out of the way as best she could, and began to pedal.

'We used bicycles a lot at the front.' Rob's voice came from behind her, as they both wobbled a little before establishing a rhythm. 'It was a good way of getting around – or it would have been if the roads weren't so churned up.'

Corran took a deep breath of clean, cold air, even as his words brought to mind the hellish scene she had travelled through on the train in France. Their generation would live with it for ever; the war could never be simply a memory. It was a more visceral part of them than that.

Dear God, it simply mustn't start up again.

She pedalled steadily and soon they left the final houses of Stromness behind. The way was gentle and reasonably flat so they made good ground between the fields. After a while Corran turned off. 'We'll go this way. There's a lovely spot for a picnic near Orphir, high up, where you can see right over Scapa Flow. Then I can show you the round church before we make our way back.'

The sun was high in the sky now and there was barely a cloud. The scent of whin filled the air, and wild flowers danced in the breeze. It was easier here to push down the dread and breathe in the light. War and threat of war felt far away. But of course, that was an illusion. They reached their picnic spot, surrounded by the expanse of sea and sky, and the dark ships of the surrendered German fleet lay far below, anchored in the bay while the delegates in Paris wrangled over their future.

Rob gave a long whistle. 'That's rather impressive, isn't it? I knew they were here, of course, but somehow I hadn't envisaged so many ships. There have to be more than fifty here!'

'More like seventy, I believe,' Corran said. 'And that's without the British fleet that we saw heading off on exercise this morning.'

They stood watching the scene for a moment or two, holding their bicycles, then Rob laid his down and dropped down beside it. He stretched out on the grass with a groan and closed his eyes. Corran looked down at him, concerned. 'I'm so sorry,' she said. 'I forgot you haven't been well.'

'I haven't been ill exactly,' he said, opening his eyes again and grinning up at her. 'And that was a topping ride. I haven't experienced something so – restorative – for a very long time. But I'm ready for some lunch.'

Corran remained on the headland. This beauty never failed to move her: the vast expanse of blue sky, the sunlight gleaming on the waters below, the sheltered bay and the islands surrounding it stretching out as far as she could see. Today was midsummer and there was nowhere better to be.

'I only wish we could stay until evening,' she said. 'I believe some old pagan rituals still take place at midsummer in Orkney.'

She could tell Rob was not really listening. He had delved into his haversack and was now unwrapping his picnic.

'Want to share?'

Corran came to sit beside him, pulling out her own lunch. 'You would do poorly out of that exchange. I've a couple of corned beef sandwiches and an apple. There was no food in the house when I came north, and I've bought the bare minimum until I work out how long to stay here. I'm not much of a cook – I've never had to do for myself before.'

Rob broke his meat pie in two and handed her a piece. 'No – take it, do,' he said, licking gravy from his fingers. 'I've plenty. So how long will you stay?'

Corran paused, pie halfway to her mouth. 'I really don't know. Mother has moved to Aberdeen to live with her sister and it's by far the best thing for her. Stella won't be back either. She was never keen on coming home to Thurso, even before Jack died. And Alex – who knows? It makes no sense to keep this house on now that we are all scattered – but I will find it very hard to give it up.' She took a bite of the pie. 'I've always spent my holidays at home in Thurso. I'm not sure what I'll do without it.'

Rob took a drink from his flask. He was looking out to sea.

'Do you remember when I came to visit that other time?' he asked. 'Before the war.'

Corran felt the hairs on her arms prickle. She had spoken

without thinking, intoxicated by the taste of the sea in the air and the sense of freedom that this place always brought her. But here it was. The conversation she knew they must have.

'Of course.'

He turned then and faced her. There was more colour in his cheeks but such sadness in his grey eyes. 'We were at the beginning of something, weren't we, Corran? Only then the war came, and everything since has been so dreadful that there has been no time to think about the future. There has been no future.'

She waited.

'Now – I still find it hard to think about the future, to be honest. I'm not sure what kind of surgeon I will be if I can't do something about my hands.' The strain in his voice was almost too much for her to bear. He reached out and took her hand. 'The memory of those days we shared up here kept me going through it all, Corran. Shall we try again? See if we can find a future? You know, as we're both still here. We came through.'

Was this a marriage proposal? She wasn't sure. The breeze whipped over the headland and pulled her hair loose. She gently removed her hand from Rob's in order to pin it up again. 'Rob. I can't ever marry you.'

She hadn't meant to sound so blunt.

He closed his eyes. For a moment he said nothing and then, when he opened them again and looked at her, the pain in his face told her it had been a real proposal and he had thought she would say yes. 'Is there someone else?'

'No – no! But we can't just go back five years. I'm not the same person now and nor are you. Everything has changed.' She spoke quickly, terrified that if she paused she would lose her nerve. 'Rob, if I married anyone it would be you. It would be you. You're clever and you're kind and you have been through so much.'

'So marry me than,' he said with a shaky laugh.

She shook her head. 'You're not hearing me. I won't marry you and I won't marry anyone. Today has been marvellous and I love spending time with you, my dear friend, but it will never be more than that. It's important that you know that.'

'Look, I know we've hardly seen each other these five years. But there's no rush. You said it yourself, we enjoy being together. I'm happy to wait. We've both been through so much and yes, we've changed. Maybe we should just get to know each other again and see where it takes us.'

She tried not to look at his trembling hands, knowing how easily she could waver. 'No, Rob. Or only if you accept that I will never marry anyone. Not even you.'

'But – why not?'

She gazed out over Scapa Flow, and the brilliant light sparkling on the water, reflecting off the German ships. 'Because I would have to give up my work, and I just can't do that.'

It sounded even more selfish spoken aloud than it did in her head.

To her surprise, Rob laughed. 'Is that all? I don't mind you working, Corran. Haven't I always been interested in your career? I know how hard you've worked and I'm proud of all you've achieved. We could sort it out.'

She shook her head. 'The principal would never allow me to stay on as a married woman.'

'Then we'll find one who will!' He seemed relieved that the difficulty was so trivial, and convinced he could fix it. 'In Edinburgh, for example. You're known in the classics department: they might take you on despite being married. Or what if you were to offer private tutoring? No one could stop you doing that and you could do it from anywhere.'

'But that's not what I want to do, Rob.' Carefully.

'Not just now, perhaps, but I'm sure you could make a damned good career out of it. Why, you could even combine it with bringing up children! And you know I would support you all the way.'

She could feel tears of frustration pricking her eyes and scrambled to her feet. She absolutely mustn't cry. She walked back to the edge of the headland and stood looking over the bay, her arms hugging herself tightly. It had always been this way. Always. It was exhausting. *The female brain is not designed to cope with Latin and Greek . . . These women's residences are full of moral dangers . . . Whatever will your husband think . . . Too much studying affects fertility, you know . . . You could even combine it with bringing up children.* She heard him move. He came up behind her but didn't touch her.

'Please, Corran.' The break in his voice stripped away more of her resolution, leaving everything raw. 'Can't we find a way? I promise to do all I can to support your career. Maybe we – we wouldn't even need to have children, if—'

The tears blurred her vision. She turned to face him, her back to the sea. 'It's no use, Rob. Oh, I feel a complete cad, because you've been away for five years having the most awful time while I-I have spent the war teaching, and it turns out I love that. It's who I was born to be. And whatever you say, there is just no way of combining that with marriage.'

He reached up and rubbed his forehead. 'Your letters kept me going when I was in France.'

'I'm glad.'

'Perhaps—' He stopped. He was looking beyond her. 'Blimey,' he said in a completely different tone.

Bewildered, she turned and followed his pointing finger. At first she could see nothing out of the ordinary: just the shining waters of the bay, the dark shapes of the German fleet and some small boats moving among them. But then she looked more closely where he indicated.

'That ship's in trouble. Look, they're evacuating into the lifeboats. There's been an accident. I must try to help.'

'Rob, we're miles away, there's nothing you can do. But you're right, it does rather look as if she's going down, doesn't it? I wonder what can have happened? How dreadful for them. I hope everyone gets off all right.'

He didn't answer but instead went back to dig in his haversack, soon returning with the field glasses he had used on the crossing. He lifted them, scanned for a moment and then drew in his breath with a long whistling sound.

'By Jove!'

'What is it?'

He handed her the glasses. 'Take a look. Every single ship down there has raised the German Ensign. And while that dreadnought is first to go, I'm fairly sure several others are beginning to list too. Corran, the Germans are sinking their own ships!'

They stood and watched in near disbelief. Within a very short time the truth of Rob's unlikely statement was borne out. This was no accident. The first ship they had noticed listing was already gone from view, capsized and sunk within just a few minutes. Dreadnoughts and cruisers disappeared into the waves over the next hour while the German sailors clambered into little boats and rowed frantically away from the danger of being sucked under in the wake of the mighty battleships. Even from their vantage point high above the bay, Corran and Rob could hear noise drifting upwards: groans and creaks and repeated explosions, and distant shouts and screams. The waters seethed as iron, fiery coal and saltwater combined, sending up clouds of steam and creating a deadly maelstrom, for all the world as if the ancient sea monster Charybdis had surfaced here in the sheltered Orkney waters.

'I can't believe they've done this to themselves,' Rob said. 'It's bloody dangerous. Men will die down there today. We *must* go and help. Stop them.'

'You know how long we took to get here,' Corran said. 'There isn't a thing we can do.' Sick fear churned within her. 'This is an act of war. They've decided not to sign the treaty and they're afraid the British will seize their ships to use against them. Germany is preparing to fight again.'

'It could be that,' Rob said. 'But it could equally be a last act of defiance. If they can't keep their navy, they're damned sure we're not going to have it either. If you look at it that way, there's something quite admirable about it.'

'Admirable? It's treachery!'

Rob raised his glasses again and then pointed towards the far end of the bay. 'The Grand Fleet is returning. They must have been summoned. It's no coincidence of course that the Huns waited until our ships were out on exercise.'

Utter carnage. Soon the only sign that this bay had been filled with enemy ships at anchor was a hull or a funnel protruding above the waves. Rob and Corran were not alone in finding the spectacle a compelling view. In fields and outside isolated houses, men and women had downed tools to watch, while even the nearby kirkyard wall was lined with mourners dressed in black, the funeral they were attending abandoned.

'We should go,' Corran said eventually. 'We've still to cycle back and we must be in time for the crossing.' They wheeled their bicycles back to the path. 'I wonder what they'll say about it in Stromness.'


The little town of Stromness was in uproar. It emerged that a party of around two hundred local schoolchildren had been taken on a boat trip to see the German fleet that morning. They had been sailing around the mighty battleships when the scuttling began, and no one quite knew what had happened to them. Meantime there were reports of gunfire and casualties.

'Our men opened fire,' said one old man, shaking his head. 'It's a bad business. A bad business.'

Rob and Corran made their way down to the pier and joined the anxious crowd awaiting the return of the *Flying Kestrel* with her cargo of excited children soon to be scooped up by frightened parents. Eventually they boarded the *St Ola*, where all the chatter among the passengers was about the scuttling of the German fleet. Corran reflected that it seemed a long time since Rob had proposed to her on the headland. They had both become completely caught up in the drama of Scapa Flow and not one word of a personal nature had passed between them since. Had he really taken in what she had said? But then, glancing across at her from his place at the side of the boat, he said, 'I'll take a train south tomorrow. I can cross to Calais or Le Havre, and then go on to Paris. Visit Gus.'

The cold sea air wrapped itself around her. 'Will you come in and say goodbye?'

'If you would like me to.'

'I would.' Her voice sounded small.

'Very well.' He nodded, and then turned and addressed a remark about the scuttling to the man on his right. Corran pulled her coat tighter and tried her best to feel glad.

In the end he had very little time the next morning, and their farewell was rushed. She tried to ask if he was fine but he kept the conversation firmly focused on the journey ahead of him. She picked up a leather writing case that she had laid on the table. 'Do you think you could give this to Stella in the Hôtel Majestic when you're in Paris? It belonged to Jack and I think she'd like to have it.'

'Of course.' He bent down to his kitbag, tucked the case inside and then hoisted it up onto his shoulder. He held out his right hand. 'Well, I must catch that train. Goodbye, Corran. Thank you for the trip to Orkney. I won't forget that in a hurry!'

*Why? Because you watched the German fleet sink, or because the woman you proposed to turned you down?* She shook his hand and stood in the doorway, watching as he disappeared along the road towards the station.

Corran closed the door and walked through to the kitchen to make herself a cup of tea. The house was silent once again, a mausoleum of memories. Her china cup rattled in its saucer as she carried it through to the sitting room. Mother always liked this china service. She must find out whether she wanted it sent down to Aberdeen. Suddenly the enormity of dealing with the house and the utter loneliness of doing so alone threatened to overwhelm her and she had to fight a desperate urge to run after Rob, to call him back and ask him to help her with it all. But that formal handshake had felt very final. She had turned him down; now she must let him go.

It was the only thing she could have done.

She had known it at some level for several years, but there had been no way of confronting it, not while Rob remained at the front. She should feel relieved that the matter was finally settled, but instead she felt utterly bereft. The newspapers were already full of the problem of 'surplus women', and she had just turned down her one and only chance of marriage. There were not enough men to go round, and there would be many spinsters in her generation. Oh, she knew she had chosen correctly. The domestic sphere was not for her; she could never be happy unless her mind was stimulated. What's more, the spirit of independence she had had to foster to complete her studies and build her career would not take easily to being yoked to another. But even as her mind told her she had made the right choice, that same spirit rebelled. She didn't *want* to be lonely! Why did she even have to make this choice? Career or marriage. Rob didn't have to choose between being a surgeon and finding a wife, building a family home. Why should she? True, he had suggested she could have both, but even his solutions were full of compromise. *Her* compromise. A different university. Private tuition. Combine it with bringing up children.

Compromises a man would never be asked to make.

# Chapter Twenty-Six

Paris

The champagne flowed liberally in the Majestic that evening. Just before dinner, the crash of guns sounded again in central Paris. Even as they flinched, white-faced, and ducked to avoid torpedo-fast memories reverberating off the walls, a messenger came sprinting into the foyer.

'*Les Allemands ont accepté de signer!*'

The German delegation had returned to Berlin with the degrading treaty terms, and their entire government had resigned rather than accept them. It seemed inevitable that Europe's destructive blaze would be rekindled and spread out to engulf the world once more. But now the new German government had agreed to sign.

Maybe the war really was over.

Stella sat with her friends and watched Freddie, deep in conversation across the room with his hero, Jan Smuts. She knew that Smuts deplored the terms of the treaty, although Hugh remarked dryly that his desire for compromise with Germany did not include releasing his grip on their former colonies in South West Africa. Smuts shook his head and gestured as Freddie leant back against the wall, listening to him. Perhaps he sensed her watching him; at any rate, he turned his head slightly and caught her eye. He smiled and tilted his champagne glass towards her, then said something to Smuts. Soon he crossed the room.

Mabel, Anne-Marie and Stella exchanged glances as he joined them. He invited Stella onto the dance floor and she followed him into a sedate waltz. How different from the raw energy of that night in the club! Freddie had asked her out a few times since then but she had always found a reason to decline. She wondered when he would leave Paris. *What will you do next?* was the main topic of conversation in the Majestic. Some couldn't wait to go home; others dreaded the return to the mundane. And in shadowy moments in quiet corners, couples tried to work out if relationships formed in this hothouse were strong enough to survive the cold blast of reality.

Freddie's mind was on a more immediate matter. As they rejoined the group at the side, he asked, 'Have you been out to the games?'

The games! As if negotiating world peace wasn't enough, Paris was concurrently hosting a major international sporting tournament. The Inter-Allied Games were the brainchild of the American army, and were intended to foster the good relationships and healthy rivalry that had grown up between the Allied nations as they fought in a common cause. Or so they said. There were billboards advertising the games all over Paris and civilians could obtain tickets from a booth in the hotel foyer. Men in uniform didn't need a ticket for entry.

'Mabel and Anne-Marie went to the opening ceremony yesterday, but I was working and couldn't go. My day off is tomorrow.'

'The opening ceremony was a celebration of peace,' Anne-Marie said. 'Unfortunately, Wilson and Clemenceau had to call off because they were busy planning their invasion of Germany.'

'Which has surely been avoided tonight, thank God,' said Freddie, raising his glass. 'I plan to get a ticket for tomorrow's games. Would anyone like to join me?'

He addressed his question to them all but his eyes were on Stella. Mabel and Anne-Marie both pleaded work.

'It's not for me,' Hugh said brusquely. 'I can't abide this American obsession with pretending the state of the world can be sorted with some hearty college games.'

'I'm not sure hand-grenade throwing ever made an appearance in college games.'

Stella looked up. 'They surely haven't included hand-grenade throwing as a *sport*?'

'Oh yes,' said Freddie. 'Anyone who was in the trenches knows there was great debate about the most effective approach. The Yanks say the baseball throw is the best action to use: now they want to prove it. But that's not all. I heard that bayonet thrusting was only ruled out as an event because they couldn't agree how best to judge it.'

'Bloody tasteless,' said Hugh.

Freddie laughed. 'Lighten up, old man. I was there today and it was all perfectly conventional, if a bit of a crush.' He shifted position, stretching out his legs, so that his left one pressed up against Stella's. 'And the Pershing Stadium is marvellous.

Whatever you think of the Americans, they've made a damn fine job of that place while the French labourers were on strike, and then gifting it to the French people.' He got to his feet. 'That's settled then. I'll get us a couple of tickets. It should be fun.'

Next morning, Stella pulled on her summer hat and left her room, descending the stairs to meet Freddie. She was looking forward to the day. Unlike Hugh, she had enjoyed both watching and playing sport at school and at university, and had really been quite good at tennis. A day out at the games would fit well with the general sense of relief and celebration. The Germans were expected to return to Paris tomorrow and the treaty should be signed at the Palace of Versailles – the final triumphant French gesture – on Saturday. Only a select few would witness the historic event inside the Hall of Mirrors, but charabancs had been arranged to take them all out to the magnificent gardens to share in the occasion. The climax to these long months was finally approaching, and it didn't do to dwell on the currents of unease that tugged ominously beneath the surface.

And then there was Freddie.

That too seemed settled after weeks and months of uncertainty. Stella knew that Freddie – foolish, grieving and addicted to intrigue – had initially befriended her in a futile effort to pump her for information about the peace process. She had chosen to go along with his games, reasoning that the Paris he could show her was far more interesting than the entertainment on offer in the Majestic. Somewhere along the way she was fairly sure his attraction to her had grown in its own right. Nevertheless, when he bundled her into the taxi and hurried back to gaze at Poppy Wyndham, he closed the cab door on her lingering dreams – and she found she didn't mind at all. And so she joined him in the foyer, looking forward to a day of harmless flirting. Now that the treaty was finalised, there was little for Freddie to find out anyway.

He stepped towards her, holding out his hand. 'Simply stunning. That blue frock matches your eyes perfectly. Come, we take the *métro* from Étoile to Porte de Vincennes.'

She loved the feel of an early summer morning in Paris, as warm air caressed her and hinted at more intense heat to come. They walked a short distance to the ornate ticket building, and descended the curved stairway to a cool cavern beneath the Paris streets.

'It's strange down here to think of all that activity going on above us,' Stella said. 'My sister won't use the Underground in London – she hates it – but I rather love it. It reminds me of the games Jack and I used to play in the caves at home, pretending to be smugglers.'

Freddie shrugged. 'It's a means of getting around,' he said, taking her elbow and guiding her through the crowd. 'I prefer open skies myself, but this is by far the quickest way to reach the stadium.'

Many of their fellow travellers were clearly heading for the same destination, as the train emptied out at Porte de Vincennes. From there they climbed onto a crowded tram, which took them to Pershing Stadium. Freddie handed her a white ticket.

'We're in the general terracing – the *tribune populaire*,'

he said. 'The *tribune d'honneur* is the grandstand, but it's invitation only.' They followed the directions of a friendly French military policeman and were soon seated on hard wooden benches, overlooking the vast oval field with its cinder running track around the edge, and 'invitation only' grandstand at one end. The flags of the Allied nations fluttered around the stadium. 'There was a bit of a panic when they realised no one knew the flag designs for some of the new nations taking part,' Freddie told her. 'The flags for Hejaz and Czechoslovakia had to be made up specially.'

Men in all varieties of uniform predominated in the crowd, but Stella could see civilians and women and children too. Freddie read out various events from the programme while she sat back, glorying in the sense of celebration. The noise levels and heat increased rapidly as the benches around them filled up. A military band was performing down on the field but she could scarcely make it out. When the action finally began, she hardly knew what to watch. Somehow, she hadn't realised that different sports would take place at the same time. There was a boxing ring set up in one corner, but the figures dancing around each other were so tiny as to seem comically unreal. It made her feel like one of Corran's Greek gods, looking down on the puny efforts of the Olympian athletes. Or a general, perhaps, far removed from the brutal consequences of the fighting he had unleashed. Unsettled by that thought, she turned her attention to the track events, which she found far more interesting. Or at least, they would have been interesting if the Americans hadn't won every race in sight. Athlete after athlete, strong and healthy in his white vest with the red letters

*US* emblazoned on his chest, surged far ahead of his rivals.

'There don't seem to be many British,' she said.

'The British are only taking part in the rowing and golf, I believe. There are no South Africans either, and not many Aussies or Kiwis.'

'Why not?'

'Who knows? It's a Yankee and continental affair, mainly. I suppose many of our men have already returned home. Now that the peace is to be signed, the demob process will speed up. They've staged this just in time.' He gazed out across the playing field. 'I expect to leave soon myself.'

'Back to South Africa?'

'I need to go to London first for a few weeks. Tie up some loose ends. But then – yes. I'll get a passage to Cape Town as soon as I can. With Piet gone, the farm is my responsibility now, and I'm ready to feel that soil beneath my feet once more.' He turned to face her again. 'What about you, Stella? What will you do?'

She had thought of little else these last couple of weeks. 'I intend to stay in Paris,' she said slowly. 'Miss Bingham has mentioned one or two possibilities – there's a place on the reparations committee, settling the amount Germany must pay, and a few girls are needed to accompany the commission to Danzig. But I have a hankering to find out more about opportunities with the League of Nations.'

'I'm interested in their future work too,' Freddie said. 'As you know, the League of Nations holds the mandate under which we will govern South West Africa. No one yet knows quite what that will look like.' He reached out a hand and took hers. 'I will be glad to return, of course. I haven't seen my parents for more than three years. But I will miss you, Stella. You must keep in touch, tell me what you're doing.'

She remembered how her skin used to tingle when he touched her. This time, she gently removed her hand and smiled at him.

'Of course. But I won't write to you about my work, Freddie, even if I join the League of Nations.'

He opened his mouth as if to deny the thought, then laughed. 'Fair enough. You can't blame me for trying. You never did tell me anything worthwhile though, did you?'

'Of course not.'

'And I swear that's not the reason I want to keep in touch with you. We've had some fun, haven't we?'

She nodded, looking away as a loud cheer signified the end of a race. But then in a different tone, he said, 'Of course, everything will change if the Germans don't sign the treaty.'

'They arrive in Paris tomorrow. Surely they will sign now.'

'I don't believe anyone really knows. Some people think it's all a stunt and once everyone has gathered, they will refuse to sign and lodge a protest.'

Stella remembered the young German she and Hugh had met at Versailles, and his quiet conviction that his country could never sign. But surely that danger had now passed. It was just Freddie being Freddie. She couldn't bear to let insidious fear cast a shadow over this glorious day.

'Nonsense,' she said, turning her attention back to the action. Every American success was cheered, but every plucky challenger was supported even more loudly. Without really meaning to, she found herself joining in. She knew that only those who had seen active service were permitted to take part. It was hard to believe that these men who now put every ounce of their effort into running, jumping or throwing had just a few months ago been pushed to the very limits of human endurance, living with the constant threat of danger and death. And what about the spectators roaring their encouragement? What had their war experience been? *We have lived through hell, but we are trying to crawl back out.*

After a couple of hours, Freddie suggested they find one of the YMCA refreshment huts. They squeezed their way along the bench and descended the concrete stairs to join a queue for lemonade and buns. The sun blazed down on them here and the queue moved slowly. Stella could feel sweat trickling down her back and between her breasts, and her underclothes were sticking to her. Eventually they reached the front and were served by a middle-aged Welsh woman who somehow still managed to keep her broad smile. Collecting their purchases, they turned away from the hut and came face to face with two men who stepped aside to let them pass.

Stella stopped.

He was thinner than when she had seen him in March: thinner, and older, and more tired. He stood amid the heaving crowd, and the thick hot air carried the raw stench of poisoned earth. As she felt the breath being squeezed from her lungs, she met his gaze, and stood in flickering candlelight in an airless dugout. She swayed.

She felt Freddie's arm firm around her waist and he

steered her to the edge of the crowd and pushed her down, while the sounds of the games swirled around her head. She found herself seated on a concrete step, head between her knees. Someone crouched in front of her and took her hands. Gingerly she raised her head and found herself looking directly into the eyes of Rob, whom she had last seen in the wastelands of Arras.

'Keep your head down and take deep breaths.'

She obeyed and gradually felt a steadiness return. Freddie was there too and pushed a lemonade bottle into her hands. She must have dropped hers. She drank gratefully.

'I'm so sorry,' she managed to say. 'It was the heat.'

Rob's grey eyes held hers. 'Better now?'

'Yes. I think so.' She took another deep breath. 'Freddie, this is Rob Campbell. He's engaged to my sister. Rob, this is Freddie Shepherd.'

The two men shook hands. Stella sat on the step drinking lemonade and trying to steady herself, and heard their voices floating somewhere nearby. Bizarrely they were talking about football.

'The Czech manager's a Scotsman. Johnny Madden. Played for Celtic and Scotland before moving out there to coach Prague.'

'They were pretty successful before the war, weren't they? I rather fancy their chances against this Yankee team.'

Stella used the railing to pull herself up and they both turned to look at her, almost as if they had forgotten she was there. Rob touched his hat.

'You've more colour in your cheeks now. I must find Gus.

Enjoy your afternoon. Stella, may I call on you soon? I have something to give you from Corran.'

She nodded and watched him go, then followed Freddie back to their seats, her legs still a little shaky. The unsteady feeling continued during the afternoon, as the crowd roared the footballers representing the new nation of Czechoslovakia and their Scots manager to an eight-two victory over the USA. The light in the stadium gradually changed as ominous dark clouds gathered on the horizon. By the time the football match ended, a few drops of rain had begun to fall and it seemed wise to return to the hotel. Stella was relieved, feeling more drained by her faint than she cared to admit.

As they hurried, heads bowed, towards the *métro*, she replayed the experience in her head. It was a few months now since she had felt those waves of panic rise up and restrict her breathing. She had begun to hope that seeing Jack's grave and burying the box had helped. Yet when Rob had appeared out of nowhere today, he had somehow transported her from the sweltering heat of the stadium to a dark hole where she stood dripping with yellow mud, and peered through a door half ajar to the horror Jack had been forced to endure.

She looked about her, trying to root herself back in the reality of this place and this time. And this person – Freddie – who caught her hand and ran with her from Étoile station through the rain that now was torrential, bouncing off the pavements, and drenching them to the skin. Rivers of water streamed down the road. A loud burst of thunder exploded right above them, and the lightning lit up avenue Kléber just as they reached the hotel entrance and tumbled in, breathless and laughing. Freddie caught hold of her. His blonde hair was plastered to his head and drips of water streamed down his face. Stella removed her sodden hat and shook out her wet hair, aware all the while that her dress now clung to her, revealing every contour of her body. His eyes were on her. She slipped out of his grasp. 'I must get out of this dress.'

Freddie laughed. 'Ever the innocent.' He took out a handkerchief and rubbed his face dry. 'Shall I see you at dinner?'

She wanted nothing more than to get warm and dry, but dinner was a long time off. 'That would be lovely,' she said.

In the end, Stella didn't appear at dinner. She had no sooner changed and towel-dried her hair than a message was sent up to the room telling her she had a visitor. A little irritated, she checked her reflection in the mirror and then descended the staircase to see who wanted her. At the edge of the lounge, seated at a small table with a glass of whisky in front of him, was Rob. She hadn't expected him to come round so soon. He got to his feet. 'You look much better, I must say. Drink?'

She wasn't really warm right through even now. 'I'd love a cup of tea.' As she sat down, she was aware of his grey eyes observing her.

'What happened earlier, Stella?'

The heat and the crowds had been her excuse to Freddie, but Rob had seen her prostrate above her brother's corpse.

'I'm not sure,' she said. 'It happens sometimes. Everything is quite normal and then something reminds me of Jack.' She stopped. That didn't sound right. 'I don't mean remembering with my *mind*, but more as if I can sense him, smell him, feel him. Then I can't breathe. It doesn't happen as often as it used to, but when I saw you unexpectedly it took me back to – that day – and everything went swimmy.' She paused then looked across at her doctor-nearly-brother-in-law. 'Am I going mad, Rob?'

Rob didn't laugh off her concerns, or rush to reassure. He rubbed his temples and then leant forward, chin on hands, which were not quite still. She could see a pulse beating hard below his skin.

'I think we've barely begun to understand what this war has done not just to our bodies but to our nerves and our minds. It's not my field, but there are people doing really good work on shellshock and neurosis.'

'I can't possibly have shellshock,' she protested.

'No,' he agreed. 'Like I say, it's not my field.' His hand rubbed at his forehead again.

'Are you all right?'

'Just a bit of a headache.'

From the clipped way he spoke, she thought it was perhaps more than just a bit of a headache, but she accepted it.

'Why are you in Paris anyway? Is Corran here?'

He lifted his glass, and she watched his hand tremble. He finished his whisky and signalled for the waiter to bring another. 'I'm staying with Gus, an old rugby teammate. My commander at the hospital decided I needed a rest.'

'Have you been ill?'

'Ill? No.' But what sadness there was in his tone. The shadows below his eyes were so dark they looked like bruises and she could see various places where he had cut himself shaving. He didn't look at all well. The waiter appeared with his drink and as he took it, Rob leant over and lifted something from the chair beside him. 'I came here to bring you this.'

He pushed a battered brown leather writing case across the table. Stella glanced a question his way but received no reply. She took the case, undid the ties and looked inside without initially removing anything. She saw at once what it contained and looked across at Rob.

'How?'

'I was in Thurso last week,' he said. 'Corran wanted you to have it.' His tone was flat. There was something she didn't understand here but she pushed it aside for now. Instead she drew out the first piece of paper and laid it on the table between them. The gaudy hotel lights shone down on a sketch of her mother sitting in her favourite chair, her head turned to gaze out of the window. All at once the clean, northern air was in this grand Paris hotel. She gently traced her fingers over the familiar lines his pencil had drawn. As she did so she could see Jack leaning forward from the sofa, eyes flicking between his mother and the page, biting his lip in concentration as his hand moved swiftly. She could feel the heat glowing from the fire, and hear the creak of wind wrapping itself around the austere house. Her heart thudding, she slid the picture back into the writing case.

'I'll look at them upstairs.'

Rob nodded. 'Of course.' He finished his drink and handed her a card. 'This is where I'm staying if you want me. I'd be glad to see you.'

Hardly aware of what she was doing, she picked up the

card along with the writing case and left him without another glance. The bundle of sketches seemed to burn in her hands as she climbed the stairs. Up in her room, she opened the writing case and took out the drawings, one after another after another, laying them all across Lily's bed until the covers could no longer be seen. For a while she gazed at the vast collage they presented: a world, a life laid out on a grand scale. She was so glad there was no one else here – just Stella and Jack. As he had wanted it at the end.

There were drawings of home, drawings from Edinburgh, drawings of people she knew, drawings of people she didn't know. Some she remembered seeing before, as they emerged on the page, or when he pinned them to his wall. Others were new to her. Every one of them was to her mind exquisite, though he always found plenty to criticise in his own work. At some point there came a soft knocking on the door – Freddie perhaps, or one of her friends, wondering why she had not come down to dinner – but she ignored it. Here with Jack was the only place she wanted to be.

And then she heard the keening sound again, but this time it came from her own broken heart.

# Chapter Twenty-Seven

## Paris

On Saturday morning, Stella stepped out onto her balcony into another enticing Paris day. She leant over the iron balustrade, looking down on the corner below where a newspaper vendor was already crying out about *le jour de la paix*. She had stood here in the icy chill of her first morning at the Majestic, unsure what lay ahead of her. Now the sun was shining and today the German treaty would be signed. If only Lily were here to share the end as she had shared the beginning.

Breakfast was a sketchy but radiant affair, with everyone dressed in their finest daywear and far too excited to eat. Fierce negotiations took place amid bacon and eggs, as those lucky enough to have a ticket for the Hall of Mirrors were offered all manner of bribes and rewards to hand it over. There were rumours of tickets changing hands for exorbitant amounts. Stella joined the crowd of female typists and clerks waiting outside the hotel for the charabancs that would transport them to Versailles, where they would witness the historic occasion from the terrace. As they waited, they watched car after car arrive to collect Important People and whisk them off to the palace. Then their open motor coach drew up with its Union Jack fluttering. Stella climbed up and squeezed onto a bench beside Anne-Marie.

'Where's Mabel?'

'Who knows? She'll have found someone to take her in one of the cars, I imagine! No common charabanc for her.'

It was like a childhood Sunday school picnic. Packed together like sardines, they chattered, laughed and sang their way through Paris, sensationalism mingling with anticipation.

'Do you think the Germans will really sign?' one girl asked. 'I heard they've chosen two nobodies who are under orders to shoot themselves.'

'More likely they will shoot Lloyd George and Clemenceau.'

'That's absurd.'

'I wouldn't be so sure. Did you hear about their Scapa Flow stunt? If they're capable of sinking their own ships and making fools of the British Navy, they're capable of anything.'

The news of the scuttling of the German fleet in the chilly waters of her northern homeland, close to the site of so many childhood picnics, had been almost impossible for Stella to comprehend. The girl was right. If the Germans could pull off something like that, what else might they be planning? The shiver that ran through her had nothing to do with the heat of the day, which began to soar once more.

A few onlookers clapped as their convoy passed by, but it was not until they reached the residential area nearest the Palace of Versailles that they encountered real crowds. 'This must be how the King feels!' Stella laughed, setting her fears aside as they waved to the cheering masses. And then they drove into the avenue with the magnificent palace ahead of them, and every woman in the coach fell silent as they passed between assembled lines of motionless mounted French cavalry officers, their steel helmets shining in the sunlight and the fluttering red and white pennants on their lances providing the only hint of movement. There was something both splendid and sombre about them; for the French, today was about far more than the end of four years of war.

Within the vast courtyard the military precision of the troops was somewhat marred by a constant stream of cars disgorging civilians, journalists and dignitaries. The women clambered down and Stella looked about her. They were high above the town of Versailles with a view stretching back towards Paris. An unusually flustered Miss Bingham directed them round to the terrace behind the palace. She had a ticket for the Hall of Mirrors and so could not accompany them, instead rattling out instructions as though they were about to engage in battle. The courtyard was crowded, and when someone caught her arm Stella thought at first that it was an accident.

'Stella.'

She turned. There was Mabel, elegant in lilac, with a stunningly fashionable cloche hat on her head. She held out her hand and waved two tickets, a look of triumph on her face.

'It's fine, I have a ticket,' Stella said, clutching her pass.

'For the gardens. These are tickets for the Hall of Mirrors. Come on, before the best seats are gone.'

Stella stared at her. 'Where on earth did you get those? We can't possibly.'

'An American journalist friend owed me a favour. They're for the press end of the gallery. Of course we can! After all, we typed the bloody thing. Do you know' – Mabel had already taken hold of Stella's elbow and was steering her through the crowds towards the palace entrance – 'the French and Americans have allocated some tickets to private soldiers and NCOs. It's only the British who have kept them all for stuffy generals from London. This is an opportunity – I'd say it's our duty to take it!'

*Well, if you look at it that way!*

'Just look confident,' Mabel advised in an undertone as they reached the foot of a grand staircase and showed their tickets to a security officer. Stella held her breath but he only gave them a cursory glance. Even as her feet carried her up the marble stairs between ranks of the Republican Guard with swords drawn, the enormity of what she was about to witness was almost too much to take in. They entered an anteroom, walking on the softest carpet, and followed the crowd into the Hall of Mirrors itself.

Not even the Palais Garnier was a patch on this opulent gallery. Little wonder the French had had a revolution, she thought, when their leaders had indulged in such extravagance, such profligacy. Germany had used this very space to establish the German Empire in 1871, inflicting deep wounds upon the French people. Today the humiliation would be returned a hundredfold. You might say events had come full circle . . . but a circle has no end. And there must be an end. There must.

The huge hall was flanked by a Peace Room at one end

and a War Room at the other. They made their way between chairs to the end nearest the War Room, where members of the press were assembled. Huge windows lined one wall and overlooked the grand terrace with its fountains. Anne-Marie and the others would be out there among the crowds, no doubt wondering where she had gone. Sunlight poured in through those windows, reflecting on the wall of mirrors opposite and flooding the vast room with dancing light. Every remaining inch of wall and ceiling was decorated with intricate mouldings and heroic paintings. As they took their seats among the tightly packed press corps, Stella wished she had her shorthand notebook to make her look less of a fraud. On her right was a young man with an artist's pad before him, sketching the scene. Stella watched and couldn't help but think of Jack's drawings, which were still spread across Lily's bed. The artist felt her eyes upon him and looked round with a grin. 'Grand day,' he said and she felt a rush of pleasure at his familiar accent.

'Oh, you're Scottish! Where are you from? I'm from Thurso.'

'Dingwall,' he said. 'I work for the *London News*, though. Are you a lady journalist?'

'You could say that.' She wasn't sure it was wise to confess her ineligibility to sit among the press and hurried to change the subject. 'Your drawing is marvellous. My brother was an artist.' *Was.*

Liquid sympathy gleamed in the man's blue eyes but all he said was, 'Today is a day for all our brothers, don't you think?', before bending his head over his work once more with just the slightest tremor. And there it was again, that almost imperceptible connection. This man too had surely lost a brother, a childhood playmate alongside whom he should have grown old.

*There are so many of us,* she thought, *walking around, doing our ordinary work, eating and drinking and sleeping, and all the while struggling to contain the unruly monster of grief. He is another one.*

There was nothing to do for a long time but sit and watch as the room filled up. The members of the press were mostly there already, tightly packed and scribbling. One man constantly fiddled with an enormous camera on a tall stand. Mabel strolled over and spoke to him for a while, then came back to Stella.

'He's going to film the whole session,' she said. 'Isn't that exciting? It's never been done before.'

At the opposite end of the long hall was an equivalent section laid out for the various diplomats, military personnel and delegation members who had managed to acquire tickets. These too filled up rapidly, and multilingual conversation and smothered laughter filled the room. Stella noticed a line of French servicemen in the front row. Each one was disfigured by terrible injuries, and she guessed they had been positioned where the German representatives could not overlook them.

The central section was laid out in a horseshoe shape for the signatories from each nation, with the top table awaiting the arrival of the Big Four: Clemenceau, Woodrow Wilson, Lloyd George, and the Italian foreign minister, Sonnino, who would sign the treaty on behalf of his nation given the dramatic resignation of Prime Minister Orlando a few days earlier.

Another nation still in chaos.

Stella's gaze moved past these seats to a small, richly

decorated table on a raised dais. Here the completed treaty awaited the signature of the German representatives. Would they come? What would they do?

As she looked around, she saw many people she knew from the Majestic and felt her cheeks begin to burn. Every one of them knew perfectly well that she and Mabel had no right to be in the press seats. Why on earth had she allowed herself to be persuaded to take that ticket? When Miss Bingham entered the room, Stella tried to make herself as small as possible behind the man in front. How dreadfully embarrassing it would be to be called out and ejected in front of all these people, like a naughty schoolgirl! It might even be reported in the newspapers. What would her mother say? But then to her astonishment the fearless Mabel raised a languid hand in a greeting to their chaperone. Miss Bingham's eyebrows rose upwards towards her hat and Stella held her breath, until her face relaxed and she smiled and returned the wave.

Remarkable.

Now it was the turn of the signatories to arrive. Stella recognised most of them either from the hotel or from those interminable sessions at the Quai d'Orsay. Here was Jan Smuts stalking into the room and yes, there behind him was Freddie. They exchanged a few words then Smuts joined the signatories in the central area while Freddie moved towards the other end of the room to take up his seat. She had not spoken to him since they parted, dripping wet, in the foyer of the Majestic, and then of course she had failed to join him for dinner. She watched him address a laughing remark to the man on his left and felt a fleeting sadness for what might have been. With so few men left, would anyone else ever look at her, kiss her, as Freddie had done?

Clemenceau was the first of the grandees to enter the room. Stella watched as he approached the French soldiers in the front row and spoke to each one individually. From there he took his seat beneath the painted scroll that proudly declared *Le Roi gouverne par lui-même*, beaming to right and left as he did so. Soon all the leaders were in place. A row of five empty chairs was a stark reminder that the Chinese delegation felt so betrayed by the Western Allies that they refused to even be present. Woodrow Wilson and Lloyd George were among the last to arrive, and Stella thought just how weary the British prime minister looked. Those dances in the early hopeful days in the Majestic seemed a long time ago now.

The ushers called for silence.

All eyes turned towards the door. The Republican Guards stationed there raised their swords in unison. Sunlight caught the deadly shining blades and rebounded silently around the grand hall.

'*Faites entrer les Allemands,*' Clemenceau said, with just a slight tremble in his voice. So much of his life had led up to this moment. The room was completely silent now, and Stella watched the door, her mouth dry. Every rumour, every fear, returned, and she awaited the retort of the pistol.

Soldiers from the different Allied nations entered first, forming a military guard. Behind them came two men in civilian dress. Dr Müller and Dr Bell. They did not march in proudly but nor did they stoop, bowed by the weight of their nation's shame. Instead, they walked with slow, measured steps, eyes fixed ahead of them, avoiding the gaze of the assembled crowd. As she watched them, Stella felt a ripple quiver round the room, dispelling simple excitement and replacing it with something far more highly charged. Had the regime that sent its own battleships to the bottom of the North Sea really commanded these ordinary yet dignified men not to leave the room alive? They would soon know.

Clemenceau spoke first while the two Germans stood, faces blank. Stella watched them and tried to think of Jack, tried to think of a fitting retribution for all the suffering of the past five years – but instead it was Alex who came to her mind. Alex, the much older brother she had barely seen since she was a child. *Today is a day for all our brothers, don't you think?* Alex, still alive and still in danger.

*There has to be an end to this.*

The two Germans walked to the small table and, in a room packed with people, everyone was still. A breath of air came in through the open window, tugging at the curtains, shifting papers.

Dr Müller and Dr Bell took out their own fountain pens and leant over to sign the treaty they must despise. In the complete silence, Stella heard the scratch of nib on paper.

No shots. No drama.

It was done.

There was a movement in the corner as a messenger slipped from the room. Almost immediately a tremendous crash of guns sounded from outside, and was quickly followed by a cacophony of car horns. Cheering rose from the terrace, but inside the room the strange hush continued. The Germans walked to their seats. They showed no emotion, yet a deep sadness clung to their every movement. Beside Stella, the young artist sketched rapidly, capturing the moment of victory for readers back home in Great Britain.

Delegate after delegate rose to his feet and queued to add his name to the treaty. As time went on, a growing swell of chatter replaced the respectful silence, and some people even began to move about, seeking signatures for their programmes. Mabel, typically, had got to her feet as soon as she could and was across the room in deep conversation with an important-looking army officer. Still the Germans sat, stiff-backed and silent as relief spread throughout the room. The treaty had been signed and no disaster had taken place. The war with Germany really was over at last.

When the final signature had been added, Clemenceau pronounced the session closed to a room that barely heard him. The Germans were escorted from the Hall of Mirrors to return home to angry protests and a country in turmoil. As they left, there was a sense that the awkward party guest had gone and the celebrations really could begin. Even those with strong misgivings about the treaty, like Smuts, were smiling. The leaders departed and the crowd began to clear. Many journalists pushed their way out quickly to get to the terrace, and Mabel and Stella joined the throng. The fountains played in celebration, and the crowds here were vast and boisterous. Stella looked around to find her friends, and saw Lloyd George right in front of her. The crowd rushed towards him and he staggered, almost ending up with an undignified splash into the fountain. Somewhere a band played and the cheering and waving were completely unrestrained.

'I saw you in there.' It was Freddie. 'How in the world did you wangle that?'

'Mabel. She knew someone. She always knows someone.'

Freddie shook his head. 'Hellish, wasn't it? Such a ridiculous, bitter French performance. Still, at least it's over. For now.' Someone called his name. He looked round, signalled and then turned back to her. 'I must go. My car is leaving. Goodbye, Stella.'

'Goodbye, Freddie.'

She watched him go but there was no time to think about it. The other typists swarmed around her, demanding to know how on earth she and Mabel had got into the hall and what they had seen. She was swept along to the waiting charabanc in a rush of jubilation and chatter. They clambered in and made their way slowly along the avenue towards central Paris, through throngs of people who crowded around them, waving and cheering.

*Vive la France! Vive l'Angleterre!*

# Chapter Twenty-Eight

## Paris

The singing grew more uproarious, reverberating off the walls of the smoky bar amid spinning shards of light. The raucous crowd was in no mood to listen to the jazz band but instead made its own entertainment, lustily drinking to peace. Most of them were men: young men whose predictable futures had been ripped from them five years ago. Tonight they didn't give a damn.

Rob shared their elation that the treaty had at last been signed and the danger of renewed war averted, but the discordant sounds threatened to split open his skull from the inside. He shook his head when Gus ordered more champagne.

'I'm out of here. I'll make my own way back.'

He got to his feet and Gus tried to do the same but fell back down, absolutely steaming.

'C'mon, pal. Another one.'

'Not tonight. I'll see you in the morning.'

'For the rugger.' He might be pissed but he hadn't forgotten. 'We've tickets for the final, aye.'

Rob gave a quick nod, pulled on his jacket and made his way across the sweaty, smoky dance floor and up the steps into the Paris night above. The air was fresher but the pavement was almost as packed as the bar had been. It must be what – eleven o'clock – and still it seemed the entire population of Paris was on the streets, celebrating the signing of the treaty. A couple of dark-skinned doughboys came swinging towards him, arms around each other, and staggered into him, nearly knocking him over.

'Sorry, sir, so sorry, sir.'

There was an undertone of fear there. He knew how easily an imagined slight could lead to a charge for a black American soldier, and brushed off their apologies with a laugh. Then they were gone and he stood watching the crowds. On leaving Gus he had fully intended to return to their magnificent billet just off the Champs-Élysées, but here in the night air with gramophone music pouring from apartment windows and revellers dancing all around him, his tiredness lessened. Every café was open and yellow light flooded into the streets. He had sunk a fair amount of champagne himself this evening, but the fresh air seemed to have eased his headache slightly though no doubt he would suffer twice as badly tomorrow. Tomorrow. A frisson of fear. Gus was elated to have obtained tickets for the Inter-Allied Games rugby final between France and the USA at the Stade de Colombes. Other than kickabout matches behind the lines, it would be the first rugby match he had watched since before the war. He wasn't quite sure he could bring himself to do it.

The crowd moved and Rob found himself moving with it, not conscious of purpose but unable to stand still. He came to the river, where he paused and leant on the wall as a barge passed by, its lights reflecting on the black waters of the Seine. He listened to the gentle wash and thought of another river, the brown Somme, poisoned with the foul waste of a decaying landscape, its depths jammed with the drowned corpses of a thousand desperate men. He forced his thoughts instead to remember standing at Erskine with the River Clyde sliding quietly by far below. There at least men who had come through with breath in their broken bodies could fashion a future.

A throbbing sound caught his attention and he looked up to see a plane above him. No need to take cover. Within a few short months, aviation had changed from being a necessary part of the war effort to a symbol of adventure and hope. The newspapers were full of flight fever, and earlier that month Alcock and Whitten Brown had won the *Daily Mail*'s £10,000 reward for achieving the first non-stop Atlantic flight. He followed the progress of this plane above the bright streets of Paris until it disappeared behind the monstrous iron structure of the Eiffel Tower. He and Gus had gone up the tower a couple of days ago and taken in the spectacular views of Paris while the proud French attendant bombarded them with facts about this, the tallest man-made structure in the world. The signing of the treaty still hung in the balance then, and Rob found himself wondering about the progress of man, who could build a structure like this or a machine to fly all the way across the Atlantic, but seemed incapable of negotiating a fair and lasting peace.

But the treaty had finally been signed. He turned away from the river and skirted the Palais de Trocadéro, where revellers danced in the fountains. He was no longer sure where he was, but on this side of the river all roads led to the Place de l'Étoile and the Arc de Triomphe. He could find his way back to the Champs-Élysées from there. He set off along a broad boulevard and only realised after a while that this was avenue Kléber, location of the Hôtel Majestic.

He should turn right, cut through and find the apartment. But if he kept going he would come to Stella's hotel. He had meant to check on her, concerned by the bruised look on her white face as she silently pulled Jack's first drawing from the writing case. That was why he had left her his address.

Stella: Corran's little sister.

Corran, who had stood looking out to sea and told him with such certainty that she couldn't marry him. He had packed his own reactions away with his warmest pullover and jumped on the first train south, unable to remain in the place that had seen the last wreckage of his pre-war life sink beneath the waves.

He couldn't possibly call on Stella at this time of night, but somehow his feet carried him towards the Hôtel Majestic anyway. As he approached, the crowd thickened and he realised that the entire British delegation had spilt out of the hotel and was dancing on the street. People whirled all around and yet he saw her almost at once. She spun from the arms of one man to another, her shining dark bob swinging across her face. Not plastered with the yellow mud of death but full of life and laughter. She paused for breath, brushed her hair aside and saw him. She spread her arms wide in welcome.

'Rob!'

He took a step towards her through the cigarette smoke and the breathless, champagne-fuelled laughter of soldiers, delegates and typists alike. She caught his hand and pulled him towards what looked like some form of barn dance in the middle of the boulevard.

'Come and dance!'

'You dance. I'll watch,' he said. 'I've walked a long way on far too much champagne.'

'It's fine. I'm a bit lightheaded too. Actually, do you know, what I need is some coffee. Let's go inside and find some.'

He followed her into the grand foyer, which was deserted save for a few night porters and a couple having an intense and tearful conversation in one corner.

'Of course. I forgot it must be midnight, or even later.' She looked around. 'I have some cocoa in my room. If we could get hot water—' She walked over to the reception desk and spoke to someone, then returned to him. 'That's fine. They're going to send up some hot water. Come on. We'll have to take the stairs at this time of night.'

This was unexpected. 'Are you sure?'

'It's not a problem – you're more or less my brother. Come on.'

*Shit. She still thinks I'm going to marry Corran.* Rob opened his mouth and then closed it again. He couldn't exactly explain standing here. He followed her to the foot of the stairs and then found all his energy was required to haul himself up six flights. They came out into a deserted corridor. Despite her protestations that it was fine, Stella looked cautiously in both directions before hurrying him along and unlocking her door.

'I've been so lucky,' she said as she shrugged off her wrap. 'I shared this room with my friend Lily. She was ill – nearly died of flu – and had to leave, but they never put anyone else into our room. I've had this place to myself since March. I have my own bathroom and my own little balcony. It's rather swish.' She walked towards the floor-length shutters and pulled them open, about to step out onto the balcony. Rob had closed the door behind him and stood with his back to it. She turned back to him. 'Come on. The views are wonderful.'

She might not look much like Corran, but her gestures and her voice had blown in on the same northern breeze.

'There's something I need to tell you first.'

She was framed in the open shutters, the darkness of the Paris street behind her, the light in the room picking up the silver thread through her deep blue dress.

'Corran and I are to go our separate ways.'

*What a bloody stupid way to put it.*

She didn't move. One hand on each shutter. 'Oh,' was all she said.

'So you see, I won't be your brother-in-law after all. Perhaps—' He found his throat was dry. 'Perhaps I should leave.'

She stood very still. A knock sounded at the door. Rob stepped behind it and Stella hurried forward. She took the silver pot of hot water with a word of thanks, then closed the door firmly. Placing the pot on the bedside table, she turned back towards Rob and the sympathy in her eyes nearly undid him.

'Come and look at the view.'

They stood together high on the balcony looking down on the revellers in the street far below.

'What happened with Corran?'

'I visited her in Thurso. She took me to Orkney – we

watched the ships go down. That's when she told me she can't marry me.' He swallowed. 'She has chosen her job instead.'

What a humiliating admission. He had told Gus, of course, in an evening of whisky and cigars, but Stella was different. She was Corran's sister.

She was Corran's sister, and it was scrambling his head.

'She always was pretty single-minded about her work,' Stella said quietly. 'I'm sorry, though. That must be difficult after all you've been through.'

A loud whoop drifted up from the street below. The throbbing intensified in his head. 'Any chance of that cocoa?'

'Yes, of course, I'm sorry.' She turned back to the room. 'Just a minute.'

He followed her and watched as she spooned cocoa into two tumblers. 'I should have asked for cups.'

'This looks good.' He took the tumbler and sat down on the room's one chair. Stella perched on her bed. For the first time he registered that the other bed was spread with what must be the collection of drawings he had given her two days earlier. 'May I have a look?'

'Go ahead.' But she pulled her legs up onto the bed and hugged them tight.

He laid down his cup and moved across. A montage of overlapping images lay before him, some pencil or charcoal, some coloured. As he took in the exuberant style, a memory whispered, and he knew it would be there almost before he saw it.

There it was, just a corner sticking out below another drawing. Stella had laid the images of people and places she knew on top, relegating others that held less meaning for her. But it was there. Heart racing, he reached out and eased the sketch free. It was creased and crumpled where it had passed from hand to hand; it was smeared with mud and even blood. But the figures drawn by a talented dead boy were alive with movement, and every signature shouted the name of someone Rob loved.

He lowered himself to his knees on the hotel carpet, and smelt the mud and the grass of a distant Inverleith playing field. He held the precious sketch and took in a deep, ragged breath. It was the sound of an infant preparing to howl.

Stella was immediately beside him, her hands on his shoulders, her voice alarmed as she asked him what was wrong. There was no way he could speak. And then she gently raised him upwards and guided him to sit on her bed, easing the sketch from his fingers. He felt the solid warmth of her beside him. His head was in his hands and the tremor that usually ran through his fingers had convulsed his whole body. Her arm cradled him but she said nothing, just held him as he wept, his head against her chest.

He could hear his own gasping sobs, could feel the tears and snot on his face, and there was nothing he could do to stop them. He had cried at the front, they all had, but he hadn't cried in front of a woman since he was a child. Yet this grief was far more powerful than any sense of shame, and there was nothing but reassurance in the tender touch that gently stroked his hair. That movement reached inside him, some deep, long-forgotten physical memory from the time before his own childhood became comfortless, and very slowly it calmed him. Eventually he drew aside.

'Sorry,' he said shakily, and stood up. 'A minute.' He walked unsteadily to the bathroom and closed the door behind him. His face in the mirror was blotchy and his eyes were swollen. He splashed cold water on his face.

He had never expected to see that picture again.

It contained everything.

When he returned to the room, Stella had cleared the remaining pictures away and was curled on her own bed. She still held the tattered sketch. 'Tell me.'

Only just in control of himself, he wasn't quite ready to look at it again. He sat down on the opposite bed and clasped his shaking hands firmly.

'You know I played rugby for Scotland?'

She nodded.

'This was the final match we played before the war. The Calcutta Cup, March 1914. Scotland against England – the auld enemy.' There was no humour in his laugh. 'Enemy! The words we used. These chaps were our dear friends.' He took a deep breath. 'Corran and Jack came to watch. Jack did that sketch during the match, and then afterwards we passed it around and got all the lads to sign it. Jack was thrilled.'

She sat very still, and he watched a tear slide down her face. Then she stood up and crossed the room, sitting down close to him. 'Please tell me who they are,' she said.

Steeling himself, he looked at the drawing in her hand. The figures were outlines really, full of life and movement, but indistinguishable from one another with one or two exceptions. He pointed. 'That'll be our winger, George Will, scoring the try there. The Flying Scot. And here.' He pointed to a signature. 'That's Will's English chum from Cambridge, Cyril Lowe. They had a bet before the game that neither would let the other score. They scored five tries between them that day.' He paused. 'They both became pilots. Lowe came through. Will didn't.'

'Is that your signature there?'

He nodded. 'And this one beside it, that's Puss Milroy. Gus and I knew him from school. He was our captain that day – the finest Scottish captain save one. He was killed on the Somme, but his mother still sits at home in Morningside waiting for him to return. She keeps the lights on for him always.' He had to pause to steady his voice. 'The English captain was Ronnie Poulton. He played splendidly in that match. I heard he was shot through the head by a sniper.' He scanned the scrawled signatures. 'I think this is him, poor bugger.'

'And the others?' Stella persisted gently.

One by one, he let his finger trace the signatures and spoke aloud the travesty, the horror, the waste. Willie Wallace, Young and Huggan. Freddie Turner, full of promise. English lads like Bungy Watson and Mud Dingle, glorying in their victory that day. Talented boys, some not long out of school, bursting with pride to play for their country, their hearts full of notions of teamwork and sportsmanship, discipline and courage. Boys who still thought the future belonged to them. By the end, he felt as though everything inside him had been hollowed out.

'More than *half* of us, Stella. More than half of the boys who played in that final match are dead. How can that be? And as for the rest of us—'

'The man you're staying with was a teammate, wasn't he?'

Rob nodded, laying down the sketch. 'Gus wants us to play again. I'm sure that's why he's got tickets for the match tomorrow, to persuade me. He says it's the right thing to do for all the ones who didn't come through. But I don't think I can.'

'Why not? I can see what Gus means.'

He reached out, grasped the air, trying to grasp the thing that had tormented him for so long. 'I think – I can't quite escape the sense that rugby led them to their deaths. Do you remember what it was like that summer? All the fervour and excitement, the sense of heading off on a big adventure. The whole rugby community urged us to go, to do our duty, to carry our good Christian rugby values onto the battlefield and play the game.'

'That wasn't just rugby. It was everywhere.'

'True, but I think it was magnified in sport, and certainly in rugby. It was a way of thinking that came naturally to us, whether we were facing the enemy on the rugby pitch or the battlefield. Exactly the same words. Manliness, duty, honour, glory. That inspired us in 1914, but after everything that's happened since, how can we ever believe in those values again?' He looked up at her. 'There was one man who stood out,' he said, and even as he spoke the buzzing intensified in his head. 'John MacCallum. Scotland's greatest ever captain, and hardest forward. John refused to be taken in by the lies. He stood out, and they locked him up for it.'

'I didn't know.'

Suddenly unable to remain still, Rob got to his feet and began pacing around the room.

'I was frightened all the time at the front, Stella,' he said.

'But as time went on, the greatest fear wasn't fear of death or injury or of what injuries I might have to deal with in others. The greatest, most secret fear was that we might have to admit that this slaughter, this dreadful crime we were committing against the world, was all to appease the pride of a few vain men. They locked John up to keep him quiet, but it goes round and round my head, and I don't believe it's ever going to stop. If John was right, what does that say about the rest of us? If we had listened to men like him, could it have been stopped? *Should* it have been stopped?' He paused in his pacing and looked across the room at her. 'But what does that mean for Jack, or all these dear boys? Even to think that way feels like a betrayal of their sacrifice.' He broke off. 'Sacrifice: that's just another of those words we use to make ourselves feel better. The truth is, they were *sacrificed*. Oh, Stella, I believed the hell of the battlefield was the worst darkness I could ever encounter, but *this*' – he tapped his head – 'this is more terrible by far.'

Stella was completely still. No easy words of reassurance came. No words at all. There was a shadow, though, across her face, a tautness. Silent, she got to her feet and crossed the room, opening a drawer. Still that tightness in her movements, as if she could barely allow them. He watched as she carried something: rubbish, a little heap of screwed-up pieces of paper. She tipped it onto her bed and looked up at him, still without a word. Her desolate expression made something tighten in his chest.

She smoothed out the first ball of paper. It was another sketch in the same style, but these figures were no sportsmen and this was no game. Horror and fascination mingled as he leant over, and saw before him a scene through which he had staggered in reality and through which he still walked in his dreams. Barbed wire, with a man entangled in it, his mouth open in an agonised scream while the ground exploded behind him. Another figure in the foreground, his chest open and crawling with rats as his guts spilt out.

'There are more.'

Mutilated corpses. The hellish depths of a shell hole. A detailed drawing of a foot, blackened and swollen and rotting. A horse, its eyes bulging and frantic with terror as it disappeared into the mud. These drawings were grotesque. The stuff, quite literally, of nightmares. And the final one: a soldier sitting huddled into himself, his eyes staring blankly, utterly bleak. He felt the tears sting his eyes once more.

'Did Jack send these to you? But how would he ever get them past the censor?'

She shook her head. 'He came to see me.' She had climbed back up onto the bed, pulling her legs up beneath her, and wrapped her arms around herself. Rob glanced down at that final drawing. She was sitting in exactly the same posture as the haunted soldier in the picture. Her voice was small and strained.

'No one knew. Not Corran, not Mother. No one.'

Somewhere in the corridor outside there were running footsteps and a burst of laughter. A door slammed. The peace treaty revellers were returning, intoxicated by their wild celebrations, but here in this room Rob sensed that the foul layers of the past five years were slowly and painfully being stripped back.

'Tell me.' Passing her own invitation back to her.

'It was the autumn of 1917. I was at university in Edinburgh and Jack wired from London. We hadn't seen him for nearly two years.' She looked up. 'No one knows this. You mustn't say.'

'I won't.'

'He told me where he was staying and not to tell anyone. That was all. So of course I got straight on a train and went to London. He was—' She stopped and covered her eyes. Rob reached out and laid a hand on her arm.

'I can guess.'

She shook her head. 'He was in a dreadful state. Physically, yes – oh Rob, he had always been my strong golden brother and he was like an old man. He smelt dreadful too, and I hated myself for minding. But he wouldn't speak to me. He'd taken a gloomy room in an awful boarding house and he wouldn't come out and walk or anything, he just sat in the room and drank. Sometimes he huddled on the floor and made this awful keening noise, like nothing I'd ever heard before. I was so frightened. I tried speaking to him, I tried things we'd shared in the past but it didn't seem to get through to him. But he wanted me there. Whenever I went out to get us something to eat or drink, he was at the window watching for me coming back, like a puppy or a child.'

Rob had spent years controlling his own horror by helping others to deal with theirs. It was an easy role to slip back into. 'It will have meant the world for him to have you there,' he said. 'There was such a chasm between what the men were going through and the world back home that they – we – often found leave very hard. But I can promise you that he held on to those

354

days with you when he went back to the front. I've seen it time and again.'

'I understood that. Jack and I – it was always the two of us against the world. When I travelled down, I hoped to persuade him to let me send for our mother, but once I saw him I understood why he couldn't. It wouldn't have been good for either of them, although she must never know I saw him before he died and she didn't. But at least she didn't see him broken. Anyway, one day when I was out buying some food, I passed an art supplies shop and on a whim I went in and bought a sketchpad and a box of drawing pencils. I thought it might help him. I didn't expect—' She began to cry. 'He spent a whole day drawing *these*. He just sat there at this grimy table and drew one after another after another, tossing them out across the floor. Sometimes he screwed them up before he'd even finished and threw them across the room.'

'And you kept them.'

She nodded. 'I gathered them all up. I hadn't understood until then. Once I'd seen his pictures I knew. And I've known ever since. It makes a difference.'

'It does.' Rob was remembering their visit to the battlefield, and Stella's hunger to see everything, to know everything. That made sense now. He had tried to protect the sisters from the worst of the horror, but Stella had superimposed Jack's tortured sketches onto the scarred landscape around her.

'He left the next day and he was killed four weeks later. He wanted to die.' She leant back and stared up at the ceiling. 'I miss him every single day and the images of what they forced my beautiful, creative artist brother to go through will haunt me for the rest of my life. But I'm still glad I know.' She sat up. 'I buried his pencils below his cross in Duisans.' She gave a shaky laugh. 'Was it the Vikings who used to bury people with objects they might need in the afterlife?'

They were quiet for a long time. It was very late and the noises in the corridor had faded away. Stella lay curled in on herself, her eyes closed, and her breathing gradually became even. He sat on the opposite bed amid the sketches and watched her. He knew he should slip away, but he couldn't bear to leave this room in which truth had been spoken and grief had been shared. She wore only a flimsy blue dress, which had ridden up, exposing her thighs. She would be cold. Rob stood up quietly and tidied away the remaining pictures, then pulled the bedspread from the spare bed and laid it gently over her. She stirred but didn't wake. What a burden she had shouldered alone through the wasteland of her family's grief. Stella had been a teenager when he had known her in Thurso and he had continued to think of her that way through the years that followed: Corran's little sister. But the woman who had shared her pain this evening, and who had so gently helped him to reveal his, was no child. Her fierce desire to understand her brother's torment – and by extension his own – set her apart from many of those who had lived out the years of war at home.

But she was Corran's sister, and just a week ago he had asked Corran to marry him.

Rob eyed the empty bed, but although he was exhausted, sleep was far away. Instead he pulled a cigarette from his pocket and eased the shutters open quietly, stepping out onto the balcony. The street far below was deserted now. It felt as if a lifetime had passed since he had stood on that headland with Corran and listened as she gave her reasons for not marrying him. And yes, damned right he thought she was selfish. It was all very well for a woman who had stayed comfortably at home to say she loved her work too much to give it up. The men who walked slowly into raking machine-gun fire on the Somme didn't have the luxury of choice.

But Corran knew nothing of that. In one evening with Stella, fuelled by grief and champagne, he had shared far more of himself than he had ever done with Corran. As he looked down on the street below, he could see that his proposal to Corran had been a desperate attempt to cling to his last fragment of life before the war. His own world had been reshaped by these terrible years but it hadn't really crossed his mind that Corran's world might have changed shape too. He breathed out smoke into the Paris night. The life he had known before the war was completely gone. His teammates were gone. His dreams of marriage were gone. And – as the light glowing from his cigarette wavered in his hands – his career as a surgeon was surely gone too.

He dropped the end of the cigarette over the balcony and leant over. Hands gripping the iron balustrade, he rose up on his toes and moved his weight into his upper body. It would be easy, so easy. Lean over. Just go. Bring an end to it. He would be far from the first. They said Dave Howie, the big forward, was delirious when he blew his brains out in Cairo. Maybe he was. Dave was a farmer with the Fife soil beneath his fingernails: what horrors had he endured in Gallipoli? The result was the same: another teammate gone, the person he was meant to be cruelly unravelled by this war.

She wore no shoes and so he did not hear her until she was right behind him. 'Be careful, Rob.'

There it was again: that voice with its echo of her sister but a tenderness that was all her own. He turned. She was watching him with eyes that seemed to see right into his soul. All that he had told her and all that she had told him lay almost tangible between them. She reached out a hand. 'Come back inside.'

He took her hand in his and followed her inside. She closed the shutters. She was standing very close to him. She reached up and touched his face. So gentle. He closed his eyes and breathed in her scent. He felt her lips on his mouth, brief but firm. Even as he responded, she moved away.

'You should go. Before it gets light.'

He didn't want to go, to step back out into the Paris streets and back into his despair, but he must. 'Yes.'

'Make sure no one's watching and then go quickly down the stairs.' She paused. 'I hope you can enjoy the match tomorrow.'

He could barely remember what she meant. Today. Tomorrow. The treaty. The games. Nothing was real except this room, this honesty and this woman.

She held out the precious sketch of his last rugby match. 'Keep it. It's yours.'

He took it, unable to speak, and tucked it into his jacket pocket. A nod of his head, and he slipped from the room. The long corridor was deserted. It must be about three in the morning now. There would be night staff about, but surely no one else. He had no care for himself but knew that Stella's reputation and her job were both at risk. He passed a short corridor opening out of his long one and from the corner of his eye he caught a flash of white, a gasp and the sound of running feet. More night-time adventurers. He turned towards the stairs and stopped.

Leaning against the wall, for all the world as if he was waiting for him, was Freddie Shepherd.

Rob gave him a quick nod and made to pass but Freddie moved to block his way. He smelt of beer.

'Not so fast.'

'What the hell do you want?'

'A moment of your time.' Freddie held out a packet of cigarettes. 'Want one?'

Rob wanted nothing other than to get home to Gus's flat and lay his aching head on the pillow.

'It's late. Tomorrow perhaps.'

'Tomorrow I leave for London,' Freddie said. 'It would be better all round if I could do that without calling on Miss Bingham first.'

It was lightly said, but the meaning was clear enough. Rob sighed and took the outstretched cigarette. They descended a few stairs to a landing. 'What's this about?' Rob asked.

The staircase was dimly lit, and Freddie's face was half in shadow, lending a strange ghostliness to his easy good looks.

'As you know, I've had the privilege of becoming acquainted with Miss Stella Rutherford.' He put his own cigarette to his mouth. 'Well enough acquainted to be surprised that you should spend the night in her room.'

'I hardly see that's any affair of yours.'

'Perhaps not. But others would think differently. Your fiancée, for example.'

Rob crushed the cigarette in his fist. He had no intention of listening to this.

'You're misinformed,' he said shortly and made to go, but Freddie's arm shot out. Rob looked down at the hand clasping his jacket sleeve and saw the missing fingers. A lesser mutilation than those he treated in the Princess Louise, but a loss just the same. What exactly was the relationship between Stella and this man? Freddie let go of his arm and took a step back.

'Perhaps I am, but Stella has ambitions to stay on in Paris and even to work for the League of Nations. I doubt that will be possible if the authorities learn how the two of you spent this evening.'

Rob stared at him. 'Are you trying to threaten me? That's absurd. You've picked the wrong man, I'm afraid.'

'Have I?' Freddie spoke smoothly. 'I could make life very difficult for Stella. All I'm looking for is a small amount to help me on my journey.'

'You must be cracked.' Rob pushed past him and started to descend the stairs. To his irritation, he heard Freddie following behind.

'I don't think you understand me. Stella might be embarrassed by revelations about your night in her room, but she would be destroyed if I let it be known that she passed me information about the peace process.'

Rob stopped and turned. 'You're lying. Stella wouldn't do that.'

Freddie smiled. 'Oh, not willingly. I'm quite happy to admit that. But you don't really think I took her out because of her dazzling beauty or her sparkling wit, do you? There were people here willing to pay good money for information that might make the conference run more smoothly. I made it my business to find out. Stella and her friends were happy to welcome me into their typing room where there were all sorts of confidential documents lying about, never mind her chatter about her work in the evenings. She made things very easy for me.' He paused. 'And I could make things very difficult for her.'

Rob gripped the banister, struggling to process the words he was hearing. The pain in his head made him want to vomit and his legs were weak. He hadn't slept for almost twenty-four hours, and the emotional outpouring of this evening had left him defenceless. He knew he should just walk away, but his head was spinning and it seemed simplest to take out his wallet. The man was leaving Paris tomorrow and he would never see him again. Besides, if what he said were true, it really could mean trouble for Stella. He pulled out a handful of notes. 'Take this and get the hell out of here.'

Freddie took the notes, smiled and pocketed them. 'Wise choice, my friend,' he said. 'Good doing business with you.' He put his fingers to his lips. 'Your fiancée will never know. Keeping it in the family, eh?' He turned and ran back up the stairs two at a time. Rob rubbed his forehead and continued down. God, he needed to sleep.

# Chapter Twenty-Nine

## Paris

The next day was Sunday and, on a whim, Stella decided to go to church. She hadn't often been to a service in Paris, as their work continued seven days a week. When her day off coincided with a Sunday, she preferred to sleep in. But today there would be no work and her mind whirled with the implications of those unexpected hours spent with Rob last night. Perhaps if she went to church and sat in contemplation, she would find peace to make sense of it all.

Pulling on her hat, she walked through the hotel foyer. How quickly yesterday's festivities had been replaced by the melancholy of the morning after. The end-of-term party was well and truly over. At breakfast, the dining room was strangely empty. Many residents of the Majestic were leaving for good while others planned to take a long-overdue holiday. Some of those travelling to London had secured places on Lloyd George's special train, which would depart that morning. Rumour was that President Wilson had left Paris last night, so desperate was he to escape Europe. The foyer was crowded with trunks and suitcases, and car after car rolled up at the entrance to carry away the more important residents of the Majestic.

Stella picked her way around the luggage and out onto avenue Kléber. Their work in Paris was far from done, but it would be a very different conference now that the limelight had shifted with the signing of the German treaty. Long hours of negotiation still stretched ahead to settle the destinies of many parts of the world from Arabia to the Balkans. As she walked briskly through the Paris morning towards St Michael's Church, which lay a good half hour's walk away, it was not the turbulent affairs of the world that filled her mind, however, but her own equally uncertain situation. Last night she had invited Rob up to her room as her brother-in-law. She had ushered him out before dawn in the shocked realisation that she loved him. What's more, she had seen something in his eyes that made her think he might love her too.

But how could that be?

What about Corran?

And what about Rob himself, that damaged, grief-stricken, trembling wreck of a man gazing over the balcony to the street below, his shoulders slumped with despair. Was he in any fit state to know what he wanted, or was he just reeling from her sister's rejection?

And then there was the fact that if Miss Bingham got to hear about last night, she would be sent home immediately, her job and her reputation in tatters.

There were problems everywhere she turned, yet she hurried down the Champs-Élysées, conscious of a warmth spreading through her that she had not felt for many years. The horror of the last time she had seen Jack – the horror she had been unable to share with anyone – she had told Rob. That changed everything.

She passed the British Embassy and reached the ornate Gothic church improbably squeezed into the narrow rue d'Aguesseau. On her rare visits she had not been impressed by the chaplain, Stanley Blunt, but she craved space and stillness. A middle-aged woman in a floral dress stood in the entrance with a boy of about eleven at her side. There was no way past.

'Good morning. I'm Mrs Blunt and this is my son Anthony. I don't believe we have seen you before?'

'I haven't been very often,' stammered Stella, taken aback by the uncompromising welcome. *Blunt by name . . .*

'With the delegation?'

'That's right.'

'And the treaty has been signed! What a triumph. Well done, my dear, well done. We are all immeasurably grateful to you and your colleagues for finally securing a righteous peace and bringing those Germans to heel once and for all.'

Stella swallowed, a vision of the two German signatories, dignified despite their humiliation, before her eyes. She tried to step around the chaplain's wife but the woman wasn't finished with her yet. She drew closer.

'I do hope you aren't disappointed this morning after taking the trouble to come along to give thanks for our triumph. We have a guest preacher today. It can be hard to say no, you understand. Stanley always wants to be *gracious.* Personally I think he could have a bit more backbone. This Sunday of all

Sundays, when we bring our praises to Almighty God for the signing of the treaty, Stanley should *not* have given way. Still.' She gave a tight little smile. 'It's only a sermon. And Stanley prays the most beautiful prayers.'

Stella escaped at last and slid into a pew beside a typist she recognised from the Majestic.

'Mrs Blunt get you, did she?' the typist asked with sympathy. 'She always does that to new people. Just be careful or she'll ask you to listen to her beloved Anthony recite. There's a precocious child if ever I saw one.'

Stella smiled her thanks. The first part of the service ran along predictable lines and she was happy to let her mind wander, gazing at the high soaring ceiling and framing a letter to Corran in her head. *I've something to tell you about Rob* . . . It was her companion who brought her back to the present moment.

'Now we'll hear something,' she whispered.

Stella looked up. A thin, tired-looking vicar with prominent ears had mounted the pulpit steps. This must be the guest preacher Mrs Blunt had mentioned so disparagingly.

'Who is he?' she asked. Her companion turned to her in surprise.

'I thought that was why you had come! It's Reverend Studdert Kennedy – Woodbine Willie, you know. He's quite marvellous.'

Woodbine Willie! Stella had heard of him. An English vicar, he'd been a padre through the war. Many padres were mocked but Woodbine Willie earned the respect of everyone he encountered. His nickname came from the vast number of cigarettes he handed out to the men. The most famous story about him told that he had been part of a working party repairing barbed wire on no-man's-land. The soldier beside him asked who he was.

'The church,' came his answer. When the soldier asked what the blazes the church was doing out there, he replied, 'Its job.' Throughout the war he was celebrated for his inspirational preaching, and since the armistice he had published his own poetry. 'Poet, prophet and priest,' her neighbour whispered.

A few pews in front, Stella could see Mrs Blunt sitting very upright, Anthony by her side, as Woodbine Willie leant over the edge of the pulpit and said, 'There are no words filthy and foul enough to describe war.'

He was not particularly distinctive to look at and his voice was hoarse, yet there was something in the depths of his dark eyes and the honesty in his tone that compelled her to listen. He recalled urging young men from his parish to enlist in 1914, and Stella thought again of Rob's words the night before. *Do you remember what it was like that summer?* Woodbine Willie, it seemed, shared similar regrets.

'Battles were just the movements on the chess board of the world to me. I was as fatuously innocent as most young men of my generation. I carried all my interesting facts into my first battle, and there they came to life, they roared and thundered, they dripped with blood, they cursed, mocked, blasphemed and cried like a child for mercy. That's when I discovered that war is only glorious when you buy it in the *Daily Mail* and enjoy it at the breakfast table. It goes splendidly with bacon and eggs.'

There was a ripple around the church. Unease, appreciation,

or both?

'And now?' he asked. 'After all, we trusted that God would bring us out into a new world. But it is no new world that we find ourselves in, but an old world grown older, a world of selfishness grown more selfish, of greed that has grown more greedy, and of folly that knows no limit to its foolishness. There has come upon us a great disillusionment. We thought that the great peace conference was travailing to the birth of peace, and it has brought forth an abortive pandemonium.'

Stella leant forward. This was certainly not the message of triumphant victory that Mrs Blunt had hoped for, but by God, it found its echo in her own heart. She suspected the people at home didn't realise it yet, but they soon would. There was peace, of sorts, but there was not justice. Was it the best they could hope for?

The preacher clearly thought not, but the new Jerusalem to which he called them would be reached not by war – which must never be allowed to happen again – but through love. He spoke of social justice, of discarding old platitudes and seeking truth, of taking Christ out of the churches and into the factories. Stella looked around the congregation and decided they were fairly evenly divided between those who hung on to his every word and those who were appalled by his socialism and pacifism. And yet they could say little because this man was a war hero, whose convictions were shaped by years spent on the front line alongside his men rather than observing from the safety of home.

His words were uncompromising, but his message was laced through with a gritty kind of hope. The devastating cost of mechanised war in the twentieth century was so obscene that this must be a turning point: it could never happen again. Stella thought of the fledgling League of Nations. President Wilson had been widely mocked for not standing by his principles, and it was rumoured that his own American government might not back his league, but perhaps his idealism would yet bear fruit. Self-determination might be an important counter to centuries of imperialism, but it was not enough. All she had seen at the conference told her that nationalism itself was a cause of strife. Perhaps the League of Nations would encourage big and small countries alike to work together for peace and justice.

A tiny drop of hope wrung from four years of suffering.

The service came to an end. Stella slipped out and hurried round the corner, anxious to avoid another encounter with Mrs Blunt. She would walk back through the Jardins des Champs-Élysées. The air was warm and the gardens were busy with families enjoying a Sunday stroll. She thought about Rob, who would be at the rugby match with Gus this afternoon. How would he get on? Would it help him? Perhaps he would come to the hotel this evening and tell her about it, and she could tell him about Woodbine Willie. But would he come? For the first time it dawned on her that she had ushered him from the room in the early hours without a word about when they would meet again. She didn't even know when he intended to leave Paris.

By the time she arrived back at the hotel, her mind was in turmoil once more.

# Chapter Thirty

## Paris

Somehow, despite everything that had happened in the last twenty-four hours, Rob and Gus had made it to the Stade de Colombes for the Inter-Allied rugby final. At midday, this had seemed pretty unlikely. After a few hours' restless sleep, Rob had awoken to find Gus ushering a dishevelled young French girl from the apartment. Both men felt rough and had blurred recollections of the evening before, but Gus was determined not to let his precious tickets go to waste. And so they had found their way to the north-west of the city and joined the expectant French crowd who noisily awaited the victory of their heroes over the upstart Americans.

Rob thrust his hands in his pockets, fists clenched, as the two teams came onto the pitch. So familiar and yet so unsettling. The Americans ran out first, strong and fit in their USA vests. He looked closely at the French players as they emerged and didn't recognise any of them. He had only once played against the French, on the notorious occasion in 1913 when rioting broke out and the referee had to be carried to safety. The Scottish rugby authorities had refused to allow them to play France in 1914 in protest at the scenes the year before, little knowing that rugby would soon be annihilated by war.

Roland Gordon had scored two tries in that 1913 match. When Gus spoke, Rob was remembering Roland's guts unravelling in an Amiens CCS. 'Sorry, what did you say?'

'I said one or two of the French boys look familiar, but no one I really know. Don't think many of the mad bastards we played against came through.'

The match kicked off. The USA was not a rugby nation, but in this match as in most sports across the games, their prime physical fitness far outshone their rivals'. The war had not taken the same toll. During the first half they came at the French team with force, making up for their lack of prowess with sheer commitment. The French players made mistake after mistake, each greeted by exaggerated groans from their supporters. But gradually they seemed to remember how to handle a rugby ball and how to link up with their teammates. 'Scrum half's nippy,' said Rob.

'Struxiano. He plays for Toulouse,' Gus said. 'He's a bloody good player. Pretty sure he was capped before the war.'

Eventually, French skill won out against American enthusiasm and Struxiano, who scored all their points, was hoisted on jubilant shoulders. 'Come on,' said Gus. 'Let's go and introduce ourselves.' He hurried down towards the pitch. Rob followed slowly. He had surprised himself by being drawn into the action, with whole spells of time where he thought about nothing other than the progress of the ball down the pitch. A brief release from torment. He remembered Archie, the young patient who'd urged him to play again. How he would have enjoyed this. If rugby ever started up again in Scotland, he would take the lad along to watch.

He caught up with Gus, who was already deep in conversation with the French scrum half. A small man with dark hair and moustache, one eye had swollen and closed up but he grinned with delight as he shook Rob's hand. '*Vous êtes Écossais!*'

'Well played today.'

'Thank you. It is good to play again.' He spat. 'I have not played against *les Écossais*.'

'We both played against the French in '13.'

'Ah, *le riot*! I was in the crowd.' He laughed. 'I promise it was not I who assaulted the referee! I was at that time very anxious to play for my country, and my dream came true a few weeks later. That day I watched your scrum half, Milroy. Player *magnifique*. He was gracious enough to speak with me after the match.'

Rob and Gus looked at each other. 'He's gone. The Somme,' Rob said.

The sharp physical pain of speaking four short words.

'Ah so. And many of our players from that day, they are gone too. The damned Boche.' He spat again. 'I will go now and dress, and you will wait here for me. Then I will take you into Paris and show you the best places. We will drink to their memories, your friends and mine. *Allez les Bleus*.'

# Chapter Thirty-One

## Glasgow

Corran's book slid from her knee as the train slowed, waking her from fitful sleep. She peered through the grimy window at blackened Glasgow tenement walls and glanced at her watch. Another few minutes. She shifted position. She had travelled by train to and from Thurso regularly since her teens and the journey was as spartan and gruelling as ever. She would never, ever come to enjoy it.

Her mouth was dry – she hated dozing off during the day – and so she opened her handbag to find a boiled sweet to suck. She would get a cup of tea at the station. As she fished in the bag, she saw Stella's letter and pulled it out again. She had already read it several times, so her eyes skimmed over the account of the peace treaty celebrations and rested on the paragraphs at the end.

> *Rob brought me Jack's drawings – thank you. Did you keep any for yourself? If not, you must take a look and choose some. There's a lovely one of Mother, which I*

*thought she might like to have.*

*Rob also told me that it's over between the two of you. I'm sorry it's not worked out, but I know how much you enjoy your work at the university. Rob and I have become closer while he's here in Paris. I hope you don't mind.*

*Rob and I have become closer.* What did she mean, exactly? *I hope you don't mind.*

The train pulled into Queen Street station, and the others in the compartment stood up. Corran pushed the letter back into her bag and hauled her suitcase down from the luggage rack.

*Rob and I have become closer.*

She stepped down into the noise and bustle of the railway station. She always took a moment to adjust from the rhythmical movement of the train to the solid unforgiving platform beneath her feet. Immediately she was surrounded by ragged boys offering to carry her suitcase but she shook her head. She would put it into left luggage for the couple of hours until her journey south. After doing this, encumbered now only by her handbag, she made for the ladies' waiting room to visit the lavatory and to sort her hair and powder her nose. The bleary face that looked back at her reminded her of that first morning in the fairy cottage in the woods. How quickly her time in Dieppe had come to feel like another life! *I know how much you enjoy your work at the university,* Stella had written. And it was true. She had always loved the atmosphere of hushed reading rooms, the smell of ink and books, the company of others who understood the thrill of discovery and the glories of ancient literature. She loved to immerse herself in learning and to share that knowledge with others. If she had given that up for a life of domesticity, she would have resented it for ever.

But sometimes, as she looked around the daughters of the wealthy whose only interest in classics was to scrape through the exam required of every first-year student, she felt herself drawn back to a damp and mouldy tent or a draughty hut. She remembered teaching the conventions of letter-writing or the absolute basics of French and German to eager, uneducated Tommies, and thought she had never been so happy and fulfilled. France had unexpectedly left her wanting more.

She reached the entrance to the tearoom. A waitress in a frilled white apron showed her to a table and asked for her order.

'I'll wait for my friend.'

She glanced at her watch. Ten minutes late. Fifteen minutes late. She ordered tea and a scone, aware that the gap to her next train was shrinking. Then, just as she spread watery jam on a dry scone, a shadow fell over the table. She looked up. It was a shock to see him in ordinary clothes, his red hair longer than it had been in France, the vivid scar still slicing his face in two.

He gasped out breathless apologies as he took his seat. 'I'm sorry, Corran. My meeting ran on.'

It really was the strangest feeling. For several months she, Arthur and the rest of the team had worked so closely together, sharing meals, lesson plans and discussions long into the night, but then the scheme had been disbanded and they had dispersed. She watched him place his order with the waitress and felt a rush of pleasure. The last few weeks had been unbearably grim, as she sorted out her dead brother's possessions and prepared to empty the home she loved. Into her bleak loneliness came Arthur's letter: he would be in Glasgow for a few days . . . could they meet? She decided there and then to close up the house for another few months and return to Oxford, diverting to Glasgow on the way.

The waitress brought Arthur a bacon roll. He looked sadly at the meagre strip of meat before saying, 'Tell me about yourself while I eat this. What have you been doing?'

She told him about her mother leaving Thurso; about the decision to give up the house; about seeing the German fleet go down at Scapa Flow. She didn't mention Rob. He watched her as he listened and she remembered that about him, the way his green eyes focused so intently, as if your words were the only thing that mattered.

'And you?' she asked. 'Are you here to see your sister?'

'I'm staying with Cath,' he agreed, removing a handkerchief from his pocket to wipe some grease from his chin. 'Not that she has the space but she wouldn't let me go anywhere else.'

She remembered the day she had found him alone in the darkened sitting room in Dieppe, so distressed by reports of the George Square riots. 'How is she?'

'Cath and her family have it hard, but not as hard as some. She takes in mending to earn some money – there are no factory jobs now that the men are back – and two of her boys are working. Young Arthur is a smart lad. He's with Yarrow but he works at the Princess Louise Hospital, learning how to make artificial limbs.'

A frisson ran through Corran and she set her teacup down

carefully, but Arthur didn't notice. His vivid eyes looked beyond her into the middle distance. 'This country is in a far worse state than even I imagined,' he said. 'That's why I came to Glasgow this week. Cath and Allan have introduced me to some people they know.'

'What kind of people?'

'Those who want to do something about it. There's a powerful socialist movement here in Glasgow. We've been betrayed, Corran, and I can't sit back any longer and watch people suffer. If you could see some of the families in Manchester, it would break your heart. The school I work in is right in the middle of one of the poorest districts, and you would find it hard to comprehend how little these children have. And two thirds of them have – or had – fathers who went off to fight for their country, believing the government's lies about a better society.'

She caught the scent of Luneray woodsmoke. 'What will you do?'

He lifted his head and looked at her directly. 'I've been asked to stand as a Labour MP at the next election. I'm considering it.'

'Here in Glasgow?'

'That's still up for discussion, but there are strong socialist networks between Manchester and Glasgow and some good people to advise me here.'

Corran pictured him holding his audience spellbound in a damp, sweaty tent. 'What about teaching?'

'I can help individual families through the school, but this way I can make a difference on a far bigger scale. I've been speaking at socialist rallies and union events for some time now so it makes sense.' He finished his tea. 'I might not get elected, of course, but Lloyd George and the Liberals are finished. That travesty of a peace treaty is surely the end for them, and their "land fit for heroes" is a sick joke.'

'What does Mary think?'

He hadn't yet mentioned his wife.

'She wants me to leave the school I'm in just now – she says I smell of the slums when I come in from work. At the moment I think she quite likes the idea of having an MP for a husband. Whether the reality would measure up is a different matter.'

'Well, I wish you all the luck in the world.'

'Thank you.'

They sat in silence for a while, then Corran said, 'Rob asked me to marry him.'

She saw him glance at her left hand, and then his green gaze met hers. He waited.

'I'm fond of him, but it wouldn't have been right. I've worked too hard for my career to give it all up.' She tried to laugh. 'It's spinsterhood, eccentricity and cats for me from now on!'

'That can't have an easy decision.'

'It wasn't, but I'd known for a long time. Since we were in France and probably before. The hardest thing was telling Rob. He's been through so much already.' She paused. 'He's in Paris now. I think he might have taken up with my sister.'

She saw his eyes widen. 'Do you mind?'

She opened her mouth to deny it and then stopped. 'I do, rather,' she admitted. 'I suppose that makes me sound even more selfish than ever? Of course, I want him to move on. He seems to have moved on rather *quickly*, that's all. And to my sister!'

Arthur said nothing but he reached out and covered her hand on the table with his own. The unexpected gesture of kindness moved her. It was so good to have someone to share her pain. The last few weeks had shown her how stark and solitary the life she had chosen would be. She let her fingers intertwine with his.

'You said something once about this war making a lot of bad marriages. I was determined not to be another one.'

There was sadness in his eyes. 'Good for you. I admire you, Corran. I always have done, ever since the day I came to meet Mr Rutherford on the platform in Dieppe!'

They both laughed and the mood lightened but their hands remained interlocked.

'I have a train to catch,' she said eventually.

'And I have another appointment this afternoon.'

Yet neither of them moved. Here in the station tearoom, the moment was as dreamlike as those evenings in a hidden chalet. She couldn't bring herself to pull away, to wake up, and it seemed he felt the same way. His fingers were firm and warm and *now*.

It was the waitress who unwittingly brought reality back to their table. 'Shall I bring the bill, sir?' Their hands separated and there was only the busy tearoom and the relentless ticking of the station clock. They settled the bill and gathered their possessions. He accompanied her to left luggage and then to her platform. They stopped. He touched his hat.

'Write to me.'

'I will.' She paused. 'When you take up your seat at Westminster – which I am convinced you will – will you come and see me in Oxford?'

He nodded, his expression sober. 'Thank you for your confidence. This is something I must do.'

'And there's no better man to do it.'

Still they stood, neither one of them wanting to leave, and she couldn't remember afterwards which of them moved first, but suddenly she was in his arms, holding tight, and they were kissing in full view, heedless of the travellers rushing past them onto the train. Arthur pulled away first.

'My God, Corran, I am so sorry.'

'Well, I'm not.'

'But I can't—'

'No more can I.'

A conductor had begun slamming carriage doors. Arthur helped her on with her luggage. She stood in the doorway. 'I'll write.'

'Yes.'

The train eased away. Corran waited in the corridor, heart pounding. She should surely feel guilt, because Arthur was a married man, and regret, because their relationship had no future. But instead, she was aware of a profound sense of warmth and joy spreading through her.

*Love, and desire, and loving converse, that steals the wits even of the wise.*

She knew now what Homer meant.

# Chapter Thirty-Two

## Paris

Paris had one last grand show for a watching world: the victory parade on the hugely symbolic 14th July. As they walked each day between the Majestic and the Astoria, Stella and the others watched preparations taking place. The Champs-Élysées was strung with flags and coloured lights from the Arc de Triomphe down to the Place de la Concorde. Many hotels, shops and private houses joined in, competing for the most extravagant decoration, and even the Astoria had put on a fairly good show.

Halfway down the Champs-Élysées, at the *rond-point*, all the cannons and guns that had been on show throughout the city were gathered together into one enormous pile. Grandstands were erected along the pavements one day, and then dismantled a few days later.

'There was an outcry about the grandstands in the French newspapers,' Anne-Marie said. 'They are built for important spectators but block the view for ordinary people! In Paris that's unacceptable. The organisers have been made to take them down again.'

'I can't imagine that ever happening in London. Only VIPs matter there.'

On the evening before the parade there was to be a vigil at the Arc de Triomphe, where a monument to the dead soldiers had been erected. After dinner they came back out into the street and joined the crowds making for the Place de l'Étoile.

'We might not see much this evening so I haven't asked Lily to join us,' Hugh said. Lily and her family had returned to Paris, and Hugh now walked about with a permanent glow of happiness, which managed to be both endearing and irritating at the same time. 'She will come to the Astoria tomorrow.'

They eventually managed to squeeze through the crowds. In front of them, the Arc de Triomphe was in darkness with the Monument to the Dead lit up underneath. Flames burnt from two huge bowls on either side. Despite the crowds, there was near silence. One black-robed widow after another approached the monument and knelt in prayer. Wounded soldiers too were wheeled along, openly weeping, while many in the hushed crowd saluted them. Stella hugged herself tightly and thought of Jack.

It was a moving and solemn acknowledgement of the devastation this war had wrought across France and beyond, but tomorrow would be all about victory and they would have an early start. She turned to make her way back to the hotel but found she was hemmed in so tightly she could scarcely move. As she apologised to one person after another and tried to make her way through, a voice said in her ear, 'Rather magnificent, isn't it?'

Stella found she was standing right up against the actress

Poppy Wyndham, so close together that even in the dim light she could see tears on Poppy's cheeks. The actress laid a hand on her arm.

'I'm glad to see you again, Stella. I may call you Stella?'

Startled that she had remembered her name, Stella stammered, 'Of course.'

'And my real name is Elsie.' She adjusted her soft, silky wrap and looked towards the monument once more. 'It's very moving,' she said.

Stella glanced round. Her friends were gone, but she didn't like to follow, not when Poppy/Elsie had stopped her like that.

'Is your husband here?' she asked.

'No, Dennis is in London. But I had to come when I heard the dreadful news about Jean – Jean Navarre, you know.'

Stella didn't know.

'Jean is a pilot – a flying ace. He took me up sometimes. Terribly daring, and tremendous fun to be with. He was killed on Thursday.'

'Oh, I'm so sorry.'

'Jean and his friends were outraged that the authorities expected them to march along the road in this procession tomorrow, for all the world as if they were foot soldiers. After everything those boys have done! It was a great secret, but Jean intended to fly his plane right through the Arc de Triomphe. Only something went dreadfully wrong in practice, and now he's dead. After all he survived during the war.'

'I'm sorry,' Stella said again. What an awful story – and what extraordinary circles Poppy moved in. But she was an actress, after all. As if to emphasise this, the woman lifted her head, brushed her tears away and smiled. Stella remembered her making a similar gesture before, as though wiping the real woman from sight and replacing her with the film star. She slipped her arm tightly around Stella's waist as they watched the vigil, but rather than a gesture of companionship, Stella had the strangest feeling that the actress was hanging on to her for dear life.

Eventually Poppy relaxed her grip. 'I'm sorry, I've interrupted your evening. I must let you go. It was just so comforting, to find myself with someone from home at such a moment.'

Stella nearly laughed. 'From home' – somehow she doubted there was much similarity between her home and Poppy's, for all they were both Scots! But politely she said, 'It's no trouble and you haven't interrupted my evening. I'll go back to the Majestic. We have an early start tomorrow as we are to watch the victory parade from the Astoria. We should have a tremendous view.'

'That's sounds such fun,' said Poppy, as if she really meant it.

'You could join us if you like. We're allowed guests.'

Even as she said the words, Stella regretted them. The shabby grandeur of the Astoria with its lingering smell was so familiar to them that they barely noticed it but unpleasant to newcomers. And she looked forward to Lily being there so much, but if there was a famous actress in their midst, their conversation would become stilted and awkward. But as Stella wondered how to retract her invitation, Poppy shook her head.

'You are very kind but I won't intrude. I should return to

my hotel, and you to yours. Farewell, Stella. I feel sure we shall meet again. Here, take this. Contact me any time.' Poppy pressed a card into her hand as she pulled her into an embrace, and then slipped off into the crowd. She was soon out of sight. Stella waited, her eyes lifted to the blazing flames. She felt drawn to the other woman, just as she had in the nightclub, but she was struck too by the deep sadness in her tone. Every one of them carried sadness after the past five years, and Poppy had come here to mourn a friend, but Stella felt there had been something else in the film star's tone.

She was like a shipwreck survivor adrift on a stormy sea.

Stella looked down at the crumpled calling card in her hand. A London address. She couldn't imagine any circumstances in which she would use it, but Poppy's words – *I feel sure we shall meet again* – echoed in her head. *I hope so.*

Breakfast was served early the next morning. Stella glanced across the dining room at the table of military commanders who had been invited to the Majestic for the occasion. There was Sir Douglas Haig himself, bedecked in medals and tucking a napkin under his chin to protect his military finery from dripping egg yolk. There was little time to linger and watch, however, as they were to be in their places in the Astoria by 7.30 a.m. Even at this hour, the streets were thronged with people trying to get the best possible vantage point. Some had been there all night while others, finding the pavements already crowded, climbed trees and lampposts to see over the tops of heads. Stella paused near the Astoria, her attention caught by two French soldiers who were helping to shunt a couple of nuns up into a tree. A small crowd watched critically, providing advice and comments, and then cheered when the nuns settled onto a broad branch and gave them a thumbs up. Today was truly going to be an extraordinary day!

She joined the others in a room high up in the Astoria and embraced Lily tightly. 'You really do look well.'

'The air in Biarritz was marvellous. It was exactly what I needed. But oh, I have missed you. I've missed out on all the work and all the fun too.'

'The work has *not* been fun,' said Hugh with emphasis. 'But here we are, and there's peace – of sorts. Let's go out onto the balcony, girls. We couldn't have a better position if we'd searched all Paris.' He strode onto the balcony, stretching wide his arms as if he were personally responsible for arranging their viewpoint. Lily grimaced at Stella behind his back and she choked back a laugh. Oh, how very good it was to have Lily here, even for a day.

Hugh was right, though; their position was perfect. Their balcony overlooked the top of the Champs-Élysées with a fine view of the arc, through which the victorious armies would process. The crowds below were thickening all the time, watched over by French soldiers in blue and the Republican guard in scarlet. As each of the dignitaries appeared the cheering grew louder, and when a tiny girl wearing Alsatian traditional costume presented Clemenceau with a bouquet of flowers in the name of Alsace, the crowd was beside itself.

'And now the procession begins,' Stella said, as the first figures passed through the arc. These were no military generals but wounded soldiers: some blind and led by their nurses, others wheeled in chairs like those she had watched last night. The crowd on the streets below saluted.

'Every French military procession begins with veterans from Les Invalides,' said Anne-Marie. 'It's important we remember who paid the real cost of this war.' Then she gestured towards the arc. 'But here come Foch and Joffre.'

The French military leaders came forward on horseback and the band struck up 'La Marseillaise', which was picked up by voices all along the Champs-Élysées. As the sound swelled, Stella felt the hairs on the back of her neck stand up on end. A French soldier stood on top of the monument waving a huge tricolour, and half a dozen planes circled in the sky above. She looked up at them and thought of Poppy, her passion for flying and her grief for the pilot who had crashed. Surely he hadn't really intended to fly his plane right through the arc?

'When I was a little girl visiting my grandparents in Paris,' said Anne-Marie, as they watched the military procession continue down below, 'I remember playing on the chains that surrounded the Arc de Triomphe. My grandmother told me that no French person would ever walk through the arc since the German armies marched through it in 1870, dishonouring our nation. Today people of many different nations will march through – but not the Germans. They are gone, and all of France is ours once more.'

Anne-Marie didn't often speak as a Frenchwoman, but it was hardly surprising that her emotions were roused on this day when French triumph was ubiquitous. It was not only the French, however. American troops, Senegalese troops, Indian troops, each greeted with enormous cheers. When the kilted

Seaforth Highlanders from home marched by with their bagpipes and drums, Stella leant over the balcony as far as she safely could, joining in the excited shrieks of the crowds and searching for any faces she might recognise.

'These are men from my home,' she kept saying. 'These are men from Caithness and from the Highlands. My people.'

Lily gave her a curious glance. 'I didn't think you were so fond of Caithness,' she said. 'You couldn't wait to get away.'

Stella looked down on the kilted soldiers marching smartly down the broad Paris avenue. Those very men had staggered with weary, laden steps along muddy tracks that were blasted by shelling and littered with the corpses of men and horses. Now the north called them home, and she could hear the echo of that call in her own heart. As the crowd cheered, she thought again of Poppy wiping away her tears and fixing a smile of celebration to her face.

Today they would all do the same.

After the horses, after the foot soldiers, there came tanks, each with a flag waving proudly from the turret. The sight of those sinister machines of death made Stella shiver, for all the day was warm. *Dear God, let what we've done be enough to stop this ever happening again.*

The procession took all morning, and would be followed in the evening by fireworks, music and dancing in the streets. Hugh and Lily headed off to meet Lily's parents for lunch.

'I'll come and find you afterwards,' Lily said. 'There's so much I want to know! Let's take tea up to our room and we can talk properly.'

\* \* \*

Curled up on her old bed, Lily probed Stella for four months' worth of Hôtel Majestic gossip. Stella was happy to oblige, and to listen to Lily's stories of glamorous Biarritz and her happiness with Hugh.

'I loved him from the first, you know,' she said. 'I just didn't realise it. But Mummy and Daddy like him, and Daddy's going to get him a post in the Home Office, so we should be married before the end of the year.' She twirled the diamond ring on her left hand. 'What about you, Stella? Still seeing Freddie?'

Freddie! She had hardly thought of him these last couple of weeks. As far as she knew he was either in London or on a ship back to South Africa. She shook her head.

'Someone else then? There *is*! I can see it in your face. Come on, Stella, tell me. Who is he?'

Stella hesitated. There wasn't really much to tell – and yet a burden of doubt and confusion had weighed her down for more than a week. Why had Rob not made contact again? There was no one else she could speak to.

'It's Rob.'

'Who is Rob?'

'You know – he was going to marry Corran.'

'Goodness, Stella! Are you in love with your sister's fiancé?'

'No – no! I would never do that. Corran broke it off. She said she can't marry him because she won't give up her work.'

'What an extraordinary idea. Rather self-centred too. But when did you see him? I thought you hadn't been home on leave.'

'I haven't. He's here – at least, he was here. I haven't heard from him in ages. I've no idea if he's even still in Paris. And I thought—' She stopped. What *did* she think? 'We had an evening here,' she said slowly. 'I told him some things about Jack, things I hadn't talked about with anyone. And he spoke about people he lost too. It seemed – we were close. I thought he would come round again the next day, but I haven't heard from him since. I'm scared he's gone back to Scotland without saying goodbye.'

'Would that matter to you?'

'Yes, it would.'

'Then we have to find out if he's still here. No – listen to me, Stella. When I was so ill with flu, most of the time I didn't know what was going on, but I remember one night I was awake in the dark and I could hardly breathe. I was convinced I was about to die – and all I could think was how Hugh would never know that I loved him. I was so busy flirting with everyone and enjoying myself, and I thought I had all the time in the world to settle down. You would think the last five years would have taught us differently! If you want to find out whether Rob is still in Paris and if he cares for you then that's what we're going to do. Do you know where he lives?'

Stella nodded. Lily got to her feet.

'Where are you going?'

'For a walk. And you are coming with me. Let's go.'


The streets were quieter now. Many of the fine folks of Paris had retired to rest ahead of the evening celebrations, while street cleaners busily removed the manure left behind by the horses. Ragged family groups and beggars had reappeared in doorways and Stella wondered what had happened to them this morning. Had they still been there, unseen, as the mighty war machine swept down the boulevard, or had they been cleared away like the horse manure, pushed off into alleyways on the margins? It was little more than a passing thought, however, as she spent most of the journey from the Majestic to Rob's apartment arguing with Lily.

'We can't just turn up.'

'Why not? We'll ask him to watch the fireworks with us this evening. At least you'll know if he's still in Paris.'

'It's a waste of time. He's left.'

Lily didn't reply, just marched on. Stella sighed and followed. When they reached the apartment block, they found the door at street level standing open.

'Come on,' Lily said and led the way up the stairs to the first floor.

The dark-haired man who opened the door looked at the two women curiously. 'Rob's not in, I'm afraid,' he said. 'I don't know when he'll be back but do come in and wait.'

It was all the answer Stella needed. If Rob was still in Paris but hadn't come to see her, he must regret their evening together. She opened her mouth to decline but Lily was already over the threshold.

'My name's Alexander Angus,' the man said as he led them into a grand drawing room with three tall windows overlooking the street below. 'Generally known as Gus. Have a seat and I'll bring some drinks. Tea? Or lemonade?'

Lily replied, but Stella barely heard her. Lying on a low table was Jack's sketch of that last rugby match. She walked over to it. Somehow seeing Jack's pencil strokes, so important to Rob, helped to calm her.

'Jack did this,' she said to Lily.

Gus had almost left the room but he stopped. 'You're Stella?'

'Yes.'

'I'm pleased to meet you. Your brother was a gifted artist. I'm very sorry for your loss.'

She nodded, not trusting herself to speak. Gus left the room and returned with a jug of lemonade. Lily and Gus discussed the morning's procession as they sipped their drinks, but still Rob did not return. Eventually Lily glanced at her watch.

'I'm afraid we'll have to go,' she said. 'I promised my parents I'd be back at our hotel in plenty of time to have dinner before the celebrations this evening.'

'I'll tell Rob you called,' Gus said, getting to his feet and showing them out. 'I can't think where he's got to. He'll be sorry he missed you.'

Lily and Stella parted on the Champs-Élysées, and Stella walked back towards avenue Kléber and the Majestic. What an utter fool she had been, and how humiliating. Like a lovesick schoolgirl. How Rob and Gus would laugh when he came home. He clearly still cared for Corran, and had just transferred those feelings to her amid the shock and emotion of seeing the sketch. She must endure this evening's celebrations playing gooseberry alongside Hugh and Lily, and tomorrow it would be a relief to get back to some real work. And she would speak to Miss Bingham about leave: she would never have made such a fool of herself if she hadn't been overtired.

She walked up to reception and collected her key. As she turned away, she heard her own name and looked round. There, sitting on a chair at the side of the foyer, was Rob.

Time seemed to slow as she walked towards him. 'Hello.'

He stood up. 'Hello.'

'Have you been here long?'

'All afternoon. I didn't want to miss you so I decided to sit here until you came back.'

All afternoon! A bubble of hysteria rose within her at the preposterous notion of them each waiting in the other's accommodation, but the doubts of the last few days persisted. What did he want? Where had he been? She waited. He cleared his throat.

'Do you have plans for this evening? That is – I wondered if we might have dinner together before watching the celebrations.'

'I thought you must have left Paris.'

'I know. I'm sorry. I had a minor – problem – to sort out. But it's sorted now. I'll tell you later. If you'll join me, that is.'

He rubbed his forehead in that now familiar gesture. His grey eyes were hesitant, and his hands still trembled. She felt the burden of uncertainty slip from her shoulders and smiled.

'I would love to.'

'And now I need to tell you something.'

They had enjoyed their meal on the terrace outside the Café de Flore, the café in which she and Lily had watched the American poet months earlier, and now made their way back to the Seine. The Eiffel Tower was lit up magnificently ahead of them, but they crossed towards the Place de la Concorde, where crowds would gather for the celebrations. She had asked about his 'minor problem' during the meal, but he had refused to answer. Now the moment had come.

'Go on.'

They paused on their way over the bridge. 'The evening we spent together.'

'Evening' sounded better than 'night'. Her chest tightened. Was he going to say it had all been a terrible mistake?

'Yes?'

'After I left you, I met someone. He had been waiting for me. Freddie Shepherd.'

Whatever she had been expecting, she hadn't been expecting that. '*Freddie*? In the hotel?'

Rob nodded. 'Just along the corridor at the top of the stairs.'

Somewhere nearby a firework exploded. Rob flinched at the sound. Stella glanced at him then tried to gather her scattered thoughts. 'What on earth did Freddie want with you?'

'Money.'

There was another loud bang just as he spoke and Stella thought she had maybe misheard. 'Sorry, I don't think I heard you correctly.'

'Oh, you did.' Rob's tone was grim. 'And fool that I was, I gave it to him.'

'But – why on earth would you give Freddie money? You don't even know him.' She looked at Rob's profile, his gaunt cheeks, the dark shadows under his eyes, and a glimmer of understanding came to her. 'Does this have something to do with me?'

Rob sighed and leant on the stone balustrade overlooking the water. The crowds surged past them towards the Place de la Concorde, crying out in delight as light exploded above their heads. Without looking at her, he said, 'Shepherd threatened to have you dismissed. He said he would tell your Miss Bingham that I had spent the night in your room. I laughed at him, but then he made more serious allegations. He said you had passed him confidential information about the peace talks.'

She stared at him, scarcely able to grasp what he was saying. 'You can't possibly think I would do that.'

'I don't, Stella, of course I don't. He claimed you had done it unwittingly. Chatter over dinner . . . papers lying around in your typing room . . . that kind of thing.'

She took a step back. 'And you believed him.'

'I don't think so – not really. I wasn't thinking straight. I was tired and confused and he came at me, saying he would get you dismissed unless I gave him money. I knew I had a good pile of notes in my wallet, so I gave some to him. I thought that would be the end of it.'

'You utter fool!'

He looked a little offended at that. 'Look, I know it's never a good idea to give in to these people, but it was only to protect you.'

'Protect me!' She laughed, but nothing was remotely funny. Instead, she felt every bit of the evening's pleasure disintegrate within her, burnt up by a white-hot anger. 'If that's your kind of protection, you can keep it.' She spun round and walked quickly away.

'Stella!' She could hear him running after her. 'Stella, wait, please wait.' The crowds were packed and people turned to look. At the far side of the bridge, he caught hold of her arm. 'Stella, stop! You're right. I was a fool.'

She pulled herself free and turned to face him. 'How could you ever think that of me?' She hated the tears in her eyes, but more than anything, she hated the feeling of a dream blown to pieces almost before it had begun. Again.

'I didn't, I swear I didn't. I just didn't want him to make trouble for you.'

His hands were outstretched, pleading. Around them in the Place de la Concorde, soldiers and civilians danced as the band played, and floodlights lit up the fountains. Stella balled her fists in frustration.

'Do you really think I didn't know what Freddie was up to? Do you think we didn't all know? We laughed about him after he'd been in our typing room, pretending to be so casual as he asked us what we were working on. But he was good fun to be with and he knew all the best places for an evening in Paris. It was all under control.'

Rob stared at her, his face white. 'You knew what he wanted all along, and still spent time with him?'

'Not all along, perhaps,' she admitted. 'Early on I was swept away by him a little. But we worked him out soon enough. It just didn't do to take him too seriously. That was your mistake, Rob.' The anger was abating, replaced by searing pain. 'I can't believe you thought so little of me.'

'Believe me, it was never that. But I'm sorry.'

They walked around the edge of the crowd towards the Jardin des Tuileries, open and strung with lightbulbs for the celebrations. Stella thought back to the emotional wreck that Rob had been that evening. She could scarcely believe he had imagined she might betray details of her work, but she could accept that he hadn't been thinking clearly. As for the rest, he had made the mistake most men make, of underestimating the women around him. Perhaps now he would learn.

'What happened?' she asked. 'I take it he came back for more?'

'Not exactly.' They sat down on a bench overlooking the gaping crater in the rose garden where a shell had landed months earlier. 'He cabled from London to say his funds were low and he was sure I could oblige, or some such rot. That's when I realised he thought he was onto a good thing. It took a bit of organising but I went to London and confronted him. I demanded evidence, and of course he had none. So I told him I had taken legal advice and he would be charged as a spy if I heard from him again. He laughed then. Told me not to take myself so seriously, and wished us luck.' Rob shook his head. 'Rum fellow.'

He *had* left Paris – that was why he hadn't been in touch. It was almost funny. While she had been worrying that he was avoiding her, he was actually off on some misguided crusade to protect her honour. Her thoughts moved to Freddie, the cause of all this turmoil.

'I don't think Freddie's a bad man,' she said. 'He just tries his luck. He has his own demons, and he idolises Jan Smuts.

It probably started as an attempt to gain favour with him, though I'm sure Smuts knew nothing about it.' She looked to her left. Rob looked so bereft that the need to touch him was overpowering. She placed her hand on his leg. He turned towards her and tentatively took her hand in his own. Another huge explosion of fireworks sounded behind them, and once again Rob flinched. 'Can we move?' he asked.

As they walked, their hands remained clasped. They skirted the crowds and made their way up the Champs-Élysées, passing the great heap of German guns, and Stella thought how tentative the peace still felt, despite the celebrations.

'I'll be glad when today is over and we can get on with the work once more,' she said. 'This peace was won at such a cost. We simply mustn't take it for granted.'

'What will you do next?'

'I might go home for a while. We're all due some leave, and I surprised myself today by feeling homesick when I heard the bagpipes. But then I'll come back. There are still the Austrian and Hungarian treaties, and I'll apply for a move to the League of Nations once it's up and running. Some of the girls are going with the commission to Danzig, to work on the borders there. Would you believe they've been issued with special screens to attach to their hats in case the Huns spit on them?' She shook her head. 'The only prospect I can see of avoiding further war is if countries come together and work for peace, rather than pushing their own interests. I want to be more than just a typist, as well. That's more likely with the League of Nations, I think.' She paused. 'What about you?'

'I'll go back to Erskine. There's good work to be done there – although I don't know how much use I will be with my shaky hands.'

His words were edged with fear. She stopped walking, and he stopped too. 'Give it time,' she said. 'You will recover, but it's bound to take time.'

He nodded, and then reached out and put his hands on her shoulders. 'I messed up about Shepherd,' he said. 'I can't tell you how sorry I am. Do you forgive me?'

Forgiveness. A big word on a day like this.

'Of course I do,' she said, and in turn her own hand reached up, her fingers on his neck. As she looked into his grey eyes, she saw every emotion that had been there on that evening in her hotel room, and something more amid it all. A light, a spark. A smile. She could still feel the tremor in the hands that held her as they came together. Shouts and music drifted towards them as they stood in the pool of light cast by a glowing streetlamp and kissed and kissed.

When they finally broke away, Stella asked, 'What about Corran?'

'Corran won't mind. She realised long before I did that we were clinging on to something from the past. That was my mistake.'

Stella was far less sure, but as she looked into his steady grey eyes she decided that Corran was a problem for another day. Just then a group of young French officers came running down the pavement towards them, chasing one another with shouts of laughter, and Rob and Stella had to move quickly out of the way.

'I think I've had enough of the crowds,' Stella said. 'Do you want to come back to the Majestic? I still have a room to myself.'

Rob looked at her. 'Are you sure?'

'I'm quite sure.'

He slipped his arm around her waist and they walked slowly towards the grand hotel that had been her home for so many months. Pressed against him, Stella felt the tension ease from her body. For the very first time she could almost believe that this happiness was real.

A scrap of a dream of a future.

# AFTER
## *The First Rugby Match*

# 1st January 1920

Parc des Princes, Paris

Rob was sweating, and it was only partly the effect of the many Hogmanay drinks he had downed the night before. The changing room was sparse and cold, but his hands were clammy and he hugged his arms tightly round his chest. He could feel his heart thudding beneath his ribs. It was absurd, but this feeling of sick, fearful anticipation reminded him of nothing so much as the long, heavy moments waiting to launch an attack.

They sat on hard wooden benches, fifteen men, eyes not quite meeting. Some he knew well from before the war; others were new, brought in to fill the yawning gaps in the team sheet. Charlie Usher was there, his long legs jiggling incessantly with the need to get underway. He was meant to be on honeymoon, but had interrupted his holiday to join his teammates. His wife understood, he assured them all as they drank away the old year. Wouldn't have married her otherwise.

And Gus, captaining Scotland for the first time – but the significance of this match went far beyond any personal honour for any of them. Gus stared at the wall, his lips moving silently.

You might have thought he was praying, but Rob knew he would be planning his final words to the boys, his captain's message. What do you say to prepare your team for the first match in six years? What do you say to the boy who knows that he's earned his first start because the legend he replaces was blown to bits on the Somme? Or to someone like himself, one of the lucky ones who 'came through', but with a damaged body and other, deeper wounds that will never heal?

Still screaming at the outrage that is the loss of all those dear men.

The wooden door creaked open and they all looked up, glad of a change of atmosphere, something to break the tension. It was two of the men in suits.

'Shirts, lads,' one of them said and opened up his bag, going round and handing out shirts to the few boys who still sat shivering in their shorts and vests.

Jock Wemyss, the big strong prop forward who had been left half-blind by the war, stuck out a hand.

'What about me?'

The suit barely glanced at him. 'You don't need a jersey.'

'Why not? Aren't I playing?'

'You got yours in 1914,' he said, continuing round the circle. 'You should have brought it with you.'

Jock laughed. 'You're not serious, man. There's been a war since then.'

'And what does that have to do with it? Do you think the Scottish Union can afford to buy you a new shirt each match because you're too careless to bring it with you?'

A ripple of laughter ran round the room, as Jock stared at

him in disbelief through his one remaining eye.

'I'm telling you, I don't have a shirt,' he said. 'I swapped it with one of the Irish boys after my first cap in 1914.'

'Not my problem, son,' the suit said, and left the room to howls of mockery, as all the fear and emotion found release in Jock's outrage. The prop looked round his teammates.

'It will be his bloody problem when I play in my vest! Tight-fisted bastard.'

Gus stood up. 'I'll have a word,' he said and left the room.

'The Frogs'll think you can't see to find your own wardrobe, you blind eejit,' said Charlie, helpless with laughter.

Gus returned. 'Sorry, pal, he says he doesn't have a spare.'

Jock spread his hairy arms. 'What will I do?'

'What you said. Play in your vest.'

The prop stared at him for a minute and then laughed. 'Fuck me, we all did worse at the front. I'm not letting you boys down, nor the ones that went before, for the sake of a shirt. Bloody misers.'

Now that the tension had eased, the banter started to spark back and forth across the changing room.

'I'd say a shirt is the least of Jock's problems,' said someone. 'How will he manage a lineout with one eye?'

'No worse than you, pal; sure you can see straight after last night?'

'What bastard thought it was a good idea to hold Scotland's first match in six years on Ne'er Day anyway?'

Jock winked at them with his good eye.

'It just so happens I had a friendly drink with Lubin- Lebrère – that big strong forward of theirs. Would you believe he's lost

404

the opposite eye to me. So when our blind sides are adjacent we've made ourselves a wee arrangement to keep contact with our elbows, so we each know where the other is. Should work a treat.'

All Jock's patter had lifted the atmosphere, but now it was time to head out onto the pitch and Rob's stomach churned as they rose to their feet. Gus urged them into a circle, arms around shoulders, tight and complete. Earlier they had avoided catching one another's eye; now Rob looked into each face in turn and saw reflected back at him the same fear, the same grief, the same determination – and yes, the same pride. Whatever words Gus had been preparing were discarded.

'Let's go, boys,' he said quietly.

*Harder, boys,* MacCallum would say.

Gus might have gone for understated leadership, but there was nothing understated about Charlie. As Jock Wemyss squeezed into a shirt that the officials had finally managed to rustle up from somewhere, Charlie strapped his kilt around his waist over his shorts and picked up his bagpipes.

'God, I have waited a long time to do this.'

'Well, wait a bit longer till we're out on the field or we'll be deaf as well as blind!'

Charlie led the way, playing 'Scotland the Brave', and the team followed on. The sound of the bagpipes was soon drowned out by the enormous roar that greeted them from the French crowd. The French team was already out, jumping up and down on the soft muddy ground to keep warm in the persistent drizzle. Rob watched as Jock Wemyss and Lubin-Lebrère, the big one-eyed French forward, slapped one another on the back.

And there was Struxiano, the wee scrum half who had shown Gus and himself such a good time in the Paris nightclubs back in the summer. Then Charlie handed over his bagpipes to an official and stripped off his kilt once more. Rob took as deep a breath as he could and wondered if his lungs would possibly hold out for eighty minutes of running about in a swamp.

It was time for the rugby to begin once more.

Stella tucked her gloved hands inside her coat, trying to keep warm. It was a beast of a day in Paris but she wouldn't have missed Rob's first match for the world. Through long evenings of discovering one another and through long letters written between Paris and Erskine, they knew they belonged together. She still felt awkward around Corran, but her sister was immersed in her work and had professed herself pleased for Stella and Rob. The real test had come last week when Rob joined them all in Aberdeen for a couple of days just after Christmas, but the presence of Alex, home on leave at last, did much to alleviate any tension. In an unguarded moment on the station platform, as Alex and Corran came to see them off, Stella caught a glimpse of longing in her sister's expression and wondered, but Corran was looking beyond Rob into the distance. They boarded the train, Rob squeezing her hand, and Stella shrugged off her doubts. Corran had made her choice.

Stella had shared in Rob's struggle over the decision to start training again. He eventually agreed in order to rebuild some strength in his weakened body. But then came the invitation to play in this, the first match of the revived Five Nations Championship, poignantly taking place just a stone's throw from the wasted battlefields where many of his teammates lay. All his old horrors returned – the way John MacCallum continued to be cold-shouldered by the rugby community; the role sport had played in urging young men to their deaths; the simple, devastating absence of so many of his friends.

And yet, here he was, ready to pick up an oval ball and run once more.

'Kick-off!'

She looked to her left and smiled. Young Archie leant forward, heedless of the incessant rain, his face radiant. It had been a bit of a devil to get him here safely through the crowds: he was good on his 'Erskine legs' but she had seen by his pallor that the jostling caused him pain. But he and Rob were both determined to get him to Paris for this first match, and Stella suspected it was because Archie had played some kind of role in persuading Rob to rejoin the team. Rob would meet them afterwards to escort Archie back to the hotel, where to the boy's ecstatic delight he had a room alongside the Scotland players. Stella would leave them to it, returning to her lodgings, which were far less glamorous than the Majestic had been, but within easy reach of the British Embassy, which was now her workplace.

She turned her attention to the action. She had watched enough rugby to recognise that today's match was not much of a spectacle. Perhaps it was inevitable. It wasn't just the awful weather; it wasn't even the fact that individual players were out of practice and had never played together before. No, in walking down the tunnel onto this pitch, she sensed that these thirty men were walking right out of hell into a new life. They could be forgiven for taking some time to adjust.

By half time there was still no score. Stella and Archie agreed that Struxiano was by far the best man on the French team, and that neither Rob nor Gus had played too badly.

'They're nothing like as good as they were before the war,' Archie said critically. 'But I suppose that's to be expected. Scotland should get the win in the end.'

Stella looked at him. He was soaking wet and shivering, and it surely wouldn't be good for the boy to get a chill.

'Are you sure you want to stay for the second half?' she asked. 'It's not much of a match and you don't want to get pneumonia.'

He gave her a quick scornful glance. 'As if I would leave, after all these years. And besides, no real fan ever leaves the sports ground before the final whistle.'

Exactly what Jack would have said. For the hundredth time today she thought of his now immortal sketch of the last time Scotland had played a rugby match. She could think of Jack now without that overwhelming sense of panic, and knew that was something to do with having brought those awful drawings out of the darkness into the light. But oh, how she missed him. Today and every day, how she missed him.

Thoughts of Jack brought thoughts of Alex, who had strolled in three days before Christmas, the familiar stranger. Corran and Alison seized him and held him close but Stella hung back, unexpectedly blindsided by his similarity to Jack. Here before her was the weathered and worldly-wise man that Jack would never become. Then Alex looked at her over his mother's shoulder, and saw in her womanhood the years he had lost.

'My God. Stella.'

They all spent those few days over Christmas tentatively unwrapping old customs and trying them for size against this new version of family. There was still a long way to go.

The second half of the match struggled on towards its grim conclusion but the crowd refused to be downcast. 'La Marseillaise' rang out around the ground, and Stella remembered hearing the same spine-tingling refrain during the victory march down the Champs-Élysées. That day had been filled with summer sunshine, glory, pride and military might. Today there was no sunshine, there was a great deal of mud and there were thirty exhausted men. The final whistle: one goal to Scotland and none to France. The crowd swarmed around the referee, not in protest this time but in gratitude, and hoisted him shoulder high. The very fact the match had taken place at all was a cause for celebration for French and Scots alike.

She watched as Rob hugged a French competitor, and her heart burnt with love. She knew what it had cost him to drag himself out of the dugout and onto the rugby field after everything he had endured. Here on the rugby pitch, and not on the battlefield, there was space for a very different sort of glory and pride.

Together, Stella and Archie made their careful way down the steps. Rob stood on the touchline waiting for them. His face was streaked with mud and perhaps tears, but his grey eyes shone.

Today was a victory for hope.

# Acknowledgements

This work of fiction owes a great debt to some real people who do not appear in it: three of my great-aunts from Thurso. Mildred and Julia Keith trained at Hoster's before working as typists at the Paris Peace Conference, and their sister Christina served with the army's education scheme in Dieppe. Corran and Stella's characters and stories are entirely made up, but I would never have been able to create them without drawing on the experiences of Auntie Tiny, Auntie Mil and Auntie Jul. Mildred's letters to her mother from the Hôtel Majestic in Paris were particularly helpful.

Remembering also Willie West, my husband's great-uncle. We have visited his grave in Duisans Cemetery and have some early photos of when it was marked by a cross, before the CWG headstone was erected. Willie's grave is the model for Jack's grave.

As for Rob's story, in March 2020 I attended what turned out to be the last rugby match at Murrayfield before a long break, as the Covid pandemic changed all our lives. In the programme for that match between Scotland and France was a short article commemorating the equivalent match that had taken place in Paris a hundred years earlier on 1st January 1920, and which had been the first Five Nations match after the war. I was already working on the peace conference story, and now Rob's story came into focus too. The more I explored the lives of the men who played for Scotland before and after the war, the more drawn in I became. What would it have felt like if they had been the stars of 2020? What role did rugby play in encouraging them to their deaths? What's the relationship between sporting pride and war? I then read about John MacCallum, forgotten rugby hero and conscientious objector, and wanted his choice and consequent experience to be honoured and remembered too.

Many useful books have helped me with research, but here are a few I turned to again and again. For the peace conference: Margaret MacMillan, *Paris 1919: Six Months That Changed the World* (2001) and Harold Nicolson, *Peacemaking, 1919* (1933). For the experience of a surgeon in the war: Richard Dennis (ed.), *Medicine and Duty: The First World War Diary of Harold Dearden* (2014). For the Erskine Hospital: John Calder, *The Vanishing Willows: The Story of Erskine Hospital* (1982). For rugby: David Barnes and Peter Burns, *Behind the Thistle: Playing Rugby for Scotland* (2010) and Stephen Cooper, *After the Final Whistle: The First Rugby World Cup and the First World War* (2015). For the army education scheme in Dieppe: Flora Johnston (ed.), *War Classics: The Remarkable Memoir of Scottish Scholar Christina Keith on the Western Front* (2014). The words spoken by Studdert Kennedy in his imaginary sermon are taken from a number of his writings: *The Hardest Part* (1918), *Lies* (1919) and *Food for the Fed-Up* (1921).

Thank you to Jenny Brown, my agent, for believing in this story, and to all at Allison & Busby, Susie Dunlop, Lesley Crooks, Daniel Scott, Christina Griffiths and Fiona Paterson.

To my first readers and writing friends, Susan, Clare, Jim and David, thank you so much for all the support.

Thank you too to James Robertson for his consistent encouragement, which has helped me believe in my writing.

Thank you as always to David, Elizabeth and Alastair, for everything.

Finally, a special mention to Sandy Morrison, my brother who is rarely seen without sketchbook in hand. His is the style in which Jack sketches.

FLORA JOHNSTON worked for over twenty years in museums and heritage interpretation, including at the National Museums of Scotland, which has greatly influenced the historical fiction she now writes. Her debut novel, *What You Call Free*, was published by Ringwood Publishing. She studied at the University of St Andrews and lives in Edinburgh.

*florajohnston.com*
*@florajowriter*